MASSACHUSETTS, CALIFORNIA, TIMBUKTU

BY STEPHANIE ROSENFELD

Massachusetts, California, Timbuktu
What About the Love Part?

MASSACHUSETTS, CALIFORNIA, TIMBUKTU

Stephanie Rosenfeld

Ballantine Books • New York

A Ballantine Book
Published by The Random House Ballantine Publishing Group

Copyright © 2003 by Stephanie Rosenfeld

Massachusetts, California, Timbuktu is a work of fiction. Names, places, and incidents
are either a product of the author's imagination or are used fictitiously.

A section of this novel appeared in somewhat different form in *The Massachusetts
Review* in 1999.

www.ballantinebooks.com

Library of Congress Cataloging-in-Publication Data is available from the publisher
upon request.

ISBN 0-345-44825-1

Text design by C. Linda Dingler

Manufactured in the United States of America

First Edition: May 2003

10 9 8 7 6 5 4 3 2 1

ACKNOWLEDGMENTS

Many thanks to Callie and Luciano, for being flexible, patient, and generous, as always. Thanks to the members of my writing group, Betsy Burton, Ann Cannon, Margot Kadesch, Dorothee Kocks, Michelle Totland, and Stephen Trimble, for offering support, insight, and expertise, not to mention fortitude in the face of having to read large amounts of stuff, over and over again. Thanks also to readers Kathy Ashton, Julie Howell, and Karen Manazer, who were generous enough to help me for no good reason except that I asked. And a big thank you to my excellent agent, Wendy Sherman, and to Nancy Miller, my editor, whose enthusiasm for the book propelled me through the hard parts.

CONTENTS

The Year of the Cat   1

Mom Before   10

Sun Shining on Orange Juice   23

Wrecked   31

Dead Squirrel   45

Leaving   49

Irish Twins   56

Aka God   81

A Grand Adventure   100

Marie   111

John Henry   122

Heart-to-Heart   128

Massachusetts Boys   134

Day on the Town   138

Positive Aspects of the Pioneer Experience   150

Lake of the Shadow Valley   166

The World's Smallest Horse   173

Owner of All the Sadness   198

1-800-HELP   213

The November Fairy   228

Decision Making and Personal Responsibility   252

Missed Connections   263

Thanksgiving   277

Rearranger of the Sky   293

The Sad Princess Smiles   317

The Loris   330

Snow   346

Electric Person   366

Massachusetts, California, Timbuktu   378

MASSACHUSETTS, CALIFORNIA, TIMBUKTU

THE YEAR OF THE CAT

It wasn't really the year of the cat—that was just a stupid song on *All Oldies All the Time* Mom liked to go around singing, even though she didn't know any of the words except for that one line.

"The year of the *cat*!" she'd blurt out in a half-talking, half-singing voice, and you'd wait for her to connect it to something—a thought or a reason or another piece of the song—but she'd just go back to what she was doing. She got Rona doing it, too, and sometimes the two of them would sing it to each other a hundred times a day, wiggling their eyebrows and hunching their shoulders, like two aliens telling each other a fascinating fact in the language of their planet.

Mom had gotten Rona a cat; that was why she'd originally started saying, "The year of the *cat*!" Every time the cat walked by, she'd bend down and look it in the eye and say it. Sometimes she'd make a claw in the air with her hand, and the cat would flinch and jump sideways. I felt sorry for the cat, because I could tell it was losing its mind, but Mom, of course, didn't seem to notice.

Mom's noticing was weird: Mom noticed everything, actually. She just noticed things in kind of an abnormal way.

"Did you see that woman's checkbook?" she might say in the grocery store. "It was made of very fine leather. She probably got it in Europe. She's probably *from* Europe—her facial structure was very aristocratic."

"Did you notice Kristoffer Billings lit his cigarette with House of Tibet matches? I wonder if he's interested in Eastern culture and religion. His clothes smell like incense—I'll bet he's a very spiritual person."

As far as noticing things about me, Mom was going through a phase I particularly didn't like. It reminded me of when your teacher comes around to admire your art project and she picks it up totally up-side down and says, "How *fascinating*—look, everybody!"

"Oh, look!" Mom said to me one day in the bathroom, right in front of Rona. I was trying to give myself a French braid after my shower. "A hair!" She tickled me in the armpit. "Congratulations, Justine!"

"Is something the matter, Justine?" she'd ask if I came home from school down in the dumps. "Did something happen?"

Sometimes I wanted to answer her, but then before I could think of what the real answer was, she'd say, "Is it a *boy*?" She had started to ask me that all the time; she'd study my face and give me a weird, slanty smile I hated, and I started to think I knew how that cat felt: I wished I could jump onto the mantel and arch my back and look down on her from far away, too.

The cat was supposed to be a present to butter us up about moving—that was one of those things I figured out later, like a missing puzzle piece you find in a dusty corner behind the door a long time after you've given up without finishing and put the puzzle away.

"Don't you just love cats?" Mom asked one day, standing at the kitchen sink. She was doing dishes, looking out the window at the sky; I was reading a magazine, not about cats; and Rona was coloring, not a picture of cats. I looked all around the room, I checked the yard through the window, but I couldn't figure out where that thought had come from.

My new idea was that if I could figure out where an idea came from before it popped out of Mom's mouth like a magician's paper flower, I would be able to cut down on my stress. I personally didn't care about stress, but when Mom came home from parent-teacher conferences last time, she walked in the door and said, "Fifth-graders aren't supposed to have stress, Justine!" and burst into tears.

There's a long list of things that make Mom cry, and I try to keep them from happening. I actually used to have a page in my notebook for writing them down, but I quit making it when it started to get too weird to read: when besides the normal things like the toilet backed up again, or they called to say they were turning off the electricity, there were things like she lost the ticket stub from some hippie concert twenty years ago where she met the guy she should have married but never saw again, or the color of the dryer lint made her remember a sweater she once had when she was an exchange student in Belgium, back when she thought she would become an archaeologist when she grew up, but now she was only someone who worked in a deli and sometimes did catering and couldn't even say one sentence in Flemish anymore.

I didn't know what to do about stress, though. I stole a booklet from the health center when we went for Rona's skin corrosion, but the suggestions were idiotic: Sit down when you eat your meals; stop and smell the roses; enroll in a yoga class. The only thing I could think of was to try to smile more, which didn't work, because then Mom would say, "What are *you* smiling about?" and jiggle her eyebrows and look at me as if we were about to have a big, juicy mother-daughter moment.

"Don't you just love cats?" she said again. She'd finished the dishes, and she wasn't looking out the window anymore; she had turned around and was looking at me and Rona like someone was supposed to answer her. Then she said, "Do you remember Marie and Bill? Remember the pictures Marie sent, of their kids, and their farm in Massachusetts? Justine? Remember?"

I tried not to answer questions with the names of people or places in them, because they always led to other questions that I *really* didn't want to answer.

"Remember the time we visited Arizona?" she might say—something that sounded like a perfectly normal question. "The sun, the mountains, wasn't it beautiful there, Justine? You liked Arizona, didn't you?"

Then if I said, "Yeah, I guess," she'd say, "So, would you like to move to Arizona?"

Or, "I met someone named Kristoffer with a K today. Isn't that an interesting way to spell it?" She'd just keep asking till I answered.

"Yeah, I guess."

"That's what I thought, too! Well, would you like to meet him?"

Rona didn't understand the trick yet, though.

"Oh!" she was saying. "I love cats!"

"If you had a cat," Mom asked her, "would you be a happy little girl?"

The cat came in a Ryder box. I should have figured it out right then, but I didn't.

Mom came home from work one afternoon, a few days after she'd brought up the cat question, carrying the cardboard box, and when I saw the look on her face, I knew what was in it.

"Ta-da!" she sang, and she handed the box to Rona.

"*Oh!*" breathed Rona. Rona gave me the box so she could reach inside and take out the cat.

"I don't want that," Mom said when I tried to hand her the box. "Take it outside."

"His name's going to be Blackie," Rona said when I came back in.

"You can't just name everything after the color it is," I told her. We had already had two fish named Greenie and Whitey and a snake named Tanny.

"Justine," Mom said to me, "is something the matter?"

"I don't want a cat," I told her.

"Can it be mine?" Rona asked Mom.

"Yes, it can, sweetheart," Mom answered, putting her hand on Rona's head and smiling down at her.

"Who's going to take care of it?" I wanted to know. I had had to take care of the fish and the snake all by myself, and they'd all died, one by one, even though I hadn't done anything wrong.

"I will!" said Rona.

"Well, what about when she doesn't?"

"Then I will," Mom said in a tone of voice like the answer was obvious, and like it wasn't very important anyway. Then she gave that cat a look as if it were lucky to have ended up in a life with us.

"Today is the *first* day of the *rest* of your life," she told it, which was a deep thought she liked to say sometimes. And which, I have to admit, I liked a lot until I realized it was only a deep thought if you didn't say it all the time.

Mom never actually said the words, "We're moving." One day I came home from school and there were all these Ryder boxes in the living room.

"What are these for?" I asked.

"Just to put a few things into," Mom said. When I asked why, she said, "Oh, just in case." When I asked, "Just in case of what?" she pretended to lose her train of thought.

One night about a week later, we were sitting in front of the TV watching women's gymnastics, which was a show I didn't like. It wasn't women, first of all, it was girls, and it bothered me that they kept calling them the wrong thing: "These women work so hard"; "You couldn't find a more dedicated group of women." If the camera went up close, though, you could see they were little freakazoids, with big heads and tiny bodies. They looked like seven-year-olds with little breasts and makeup, and they'd say things like how hard it was, but also kind of fun, to be living in their own apartment with a chaperone, in a different city from their parents, and about how they didn't have any friends or do any normal kid things because they worked fifteen hours a day on gymnastics.

"What incredible drive that would take," Mom said, then she said, "Speaking of drives," and she sat up and muted the sound on the TV. She put her arm around Rona and her other arm around me. "Remember when I was telling you about Massachusetts? About what a neat place it is? And how much you liked it there?" Rona was nodding her head; she was such a sucker.

"And Justine, do you remember Marie, my good friend who knew you when you were just a baby?" I was one year old and Rona wasn't born the time we visited.

"No," I answered.

"Oh, sure you do!" she said.

On TV, the girl I liked best was on the balance beam. The reason

I liked her was that she was bigger than the others. And even though she was totally coordinated, there was something a little bit awkward about her, too, like maybe her hands and feet were slightly too big for the rest of her, so that it almost looked like a real person might be about to climb out of her strange girl-woman body, like a baby dinosaur out of an egg.

"Well," said Mom, "Marie invited us to Massachusetts. We're going to go stay with them for a while—with Marie and Bill and their kids, who you're *really* going to like!"

"Goody!" piped Rona.

I wished they'd both be quiet. They were wrecking my concentration. The girl on the beam was getting ready to do something—you could tell by the way her ribs were getting huge, she was breathing in so much air. She looked like she was waiting for something—for the exact right moment, maybe, that she knew was about to fly by like a bird, and when it did, she was going to catch it.

Anyway, what did it mean, that Marie had invited us to Massachusetts?

On the television, the girl suddenly launched into a front flip, the kind with no hands—the kind where, if you mess up, you come down right on the top of your head and either die or have to spend the rest of your life in a wheelchair—and I was so mad at myself: I closed my eyes. I did it every time. When I'd open them a split second later, there she would be, standing with her arms outstretched, and once again I had missed the part I wanted to see.

"Remember Danny Martone?" Mom said. A commercial for Sara Lee coffee cake had come on. Maybe Mom and Danny Martone had once had coffee cake together. Rona had her thumb in her mouth, watching with fascination as the coffee cake got its creamy white glaze poured on.

"You met him at a Germs concert," Mom said to me. "When you were about three. He was in town with his band, and they came to our house to spend the night, remember? He lives in Connecticut now—Hartford, I think. That's right next to Massachusetts."

When she said that, something weird happened. The split second before she said "Massachusetts," I knew what was going to happen: Two days after we got to Marie and Bill's, Mom would suddenly get a burst of energy; she'd start calling 411, writing down numbers, getting out maps. Then we'd go to the library; and the day after that we would go to Hartford, which would suddenly be, according to Mom, a very interesting, historical place we had always wanted to see.

Every once in a while, Mom would wake us up early on a Saturday morning and say, "Get out of bed, sleepyheads, we're going to the library." When we got there, she would haul a big pile of phone books and tourist books and state history books to a table and start trying to choose a place for us to live. Sometimes she'd just pick up one of the phone books and read the name of the place off the front: "Boulder! I always liked Boulder!" or, "Ann Arbor—doesn't that sound like a wonderful place?" Or sometimes we'd start with the name of a person, someone Mom had once known a long time ago and just started to wonder, Whatever happened to So-and-So?, and we'd look up his name in every book to see if we could figure out what city he was living in.

The part I didn't like was when Mom would start asking me questions.

"Which of these sounds like the kind of street Andy Loomis would live on: Silver Birch Drive, 107th Avenue, or Front?" When I didn't answer, after a minute she would start answering herself: "Silver Birch sounds like a suburb. He doesn't strike me as the suburban type. And it looks on the map like 107th Avenue is right in the middle of downtown. Let's try Front."

The reason I didn't like to answer Mom's questions was this weird feeling I'd suddenly get sometimes: What if I did ever actually happen to know the answer to her question, and I answered it wrong on purpose and ruined her life?

Say for some reason I actually knew what street the guy lived on. Say his name was John Smith and he lived in Los Angeles. There would be so many of them, Mom couldn't possibly call them all. Actually, she probably could, but just say she wouldn't. And for no reason except that I was feeling selfish, I decided I didn't want to help Mom find John Smith. I didn't want to hear his name, for one thing, a hundred times a day, attached to the things in my life I was perfectly happy with: "Oh, I wonder if John Smith likes Mexican food! We could bring him here to Mi Casita someday!"; "Oh, I'll bet John Smith *loves* putt-putt golf! Wouldn't it be fun to play putt-putt golf with John Smith?"; "Oh, look, a schnauzer! I just *know* John Smith loves animals."

And I didn't want Mom to have a John Smith face, which was the way she'd look, after a while, whenever anybody, including herself, would mention him.

And so what if, if Mom guessed right, I just said, "Oh, don't try that one, that sounds like a street where only happily married people would live, not John Smith." And then it turned out John Smith was the only person in the world who could solve the big problem of Mom's life and make her happy. It would be my fault that her life was ruined.

It made me feel so bad, even thinking about it, that when Mom asked me those questions, I would pretend to be cryogenically frozen. I would imagine being some other kid, from another time, all frozen—frozen eardrums, frozen mouth, a frozen brain—waiting to wake up somewhere else.

"Danny Martone was always such a *kind* person," Mom was saying. The show had come back on, and a different girl was on the balance beam. I didn't like her as much as *my* girl, but the crowd had cheered especially loud when she came on to do her routine. She was standing with her arms stretched upward, with a look on her face like she had no worries in the world.

"Don't you remember how *kind* he was?" Mom said. I didn't answer her. I wasn't going to miss it this time; I was going to keep my eyes open for the scary part.

"I'll never forget," Mom said, "how, the time he visited us, when he did his laundry, he took ours out of the dryer and *folded* it, instead of just dumping it in a pile on top."

I did it—I couldn't believe it: the girl sprang backwards into the air, and I kept my eyes open. But the weirdest thing happened. Instead of seeing what I expected to see—the girl tumbling gracefully through the air with all her muscles tight—I was seeing things rushing by:

lights, and upside-down Coke signs, ceiling beams, and the blurs of people's faces. I don't know how it happened, but suddenly I could see out of the girl's eyes. But the weird thing is, I can't tell you if the feeling was good or bad, chicken or brave. You didn't get to think about that while you were twisting around like a cat thrown out a window, searching the air for the place your feet needed to be.

MOM BEFORE

Rona thinks she invented Mom. I try to remember if I thought that too when I was her age—if I felt like my being born was the burst of energy that started the universe. I don't think so.

I actually remember being born, but no one believes me.

It was dusk, and I was being carried down a woods path through a tunnel of trees by someone I couldn't see. And there was Mom, coming toward me, wearing a red-and-white sundress. She looked different from the way she does now: her face didn't have any lines in it, and her smile was big and happy and a hundred percent real. Her hair was long, tucked behind her ears, and so light it was almost white, as if she'd been spending every minute in the sun. Then whoever was holding me gave me to Mom, and she carried me off into my life, and my next memories were from a different time, two or three years later.

"I don't think that ever really happened, honey," Mom told me. She said I was born in the regular way, and Grandma Bobbie told me the same thing.

Well, maybe a stranger didn't actually hand me to Mom in a tunnel of trees, but still, I know Mom's life didn't start with me—that the tunnel of trees was just a piece of time I slipped into, the time between when Mom was the way she was before I knew her and the way she is now.

When I was Rona's age, there was no Rona; there was just me and Mom—and, for a while, there was no Dale, either—and Mom was different. Mom the way she is now is just Regular Mom to Rona, but I can remember Mom Before. Mom Before swam in the ocean, and smiled, and had friends over to barbecue and play music and sing, and talked to Aunt Bridget every day on the phone, and when there wasn't money, she made rice and beans, which was my favorite dinner anyway, or took us over to Grandma Bobbie's, before Grandma started hating Dale and calling him the Jesus freak. Mom Before was sometimes okay for a whole day at a time, even if I forgot to worry about her.

For a while, a few years ago, I was on a crusade to try to find out everything about what Mom was like before I was born. It was ridiculous—I was like one of those characters in a cartoon, tiptoeing around to the sound of little violin plucks with a huge magnifying glass and a hat with two brims.

"We're doing a project on family history for school," I told Aunt Bridget. "I'm doing 'This Is Your Life, Colleen Hanley,' for Mom's birthday," I told Grandma Bobbie, to try to get her to tell me stories. I'd seen the show *This Is Your Life* with Mom a few times on cable, and I thought it was the greatest—the idea that your life was like a road, with people standing in different spots alongside it, like pieces of the landscape—mountains or buildings or thousand-year-old trees—just waiting there for the day you'd come back and say, "Tell me the story of my life."

I used to ask Mom all the time for stories about when she was a little girl, but she'd just say, "I can't remember."

"It was boring," she'd say. "Nothing happened." But I thought it was weird that she didn't want to have a life story. Or that she didn't want the story of her life to be about real things, things that had actually happened to her or were happening now; that she just wanted it to be about the imaginary future—places she hadn't been yet, things she hadn't done, and people she barely knew.

"But what were you like *before*?" I asked her once.

"Before what?" she said.

I almost said, "Before you had me and Rona," but that wasn't exactly what I meant. Besides, I didn't like the idea of us coming along like some big catastrophe that changed everything.

"Before you were the way you are now."

"And how is that?" she asked.

I didn't have an answer to that, either. I could tell her the things she did. I could tell her what it was like to listen to the things she said all day long. Like, if you made a mistake and asked for peanut butter in your lunch instead of tuna fish, it would turn into, "Oh, God, I forgot to buy peanut butter. I was so tired from work, I couldn't think straight when I was at the store. If only I had some skills to get a decent job. Why have I always been such a failure at everything I've ever done?" Or if you snuggled close when you were sitting on the couch watching TV, so that she was looking down on your head, she might suddenly wail, "*Why* didn't we wash your hair this morning? What kind of a person lets her children walk around with dirty hair? You'd be better off being raised by chimpanzees. God, Dale is right—I am a terrible, terrible mother."

But I didn't know how to explain any of that in a way that wouldn't make her feel bad, and also make her start saying exactly those kinds of things, so I just said, "I don't know. Sad or something?"

Sometimes I thought I could see Mom's face adding a layer to itself inside, like a tree growing a ring—just a tiny, quiet look that was there for a split second, then gone.

"I'm not sad, Justine!" she said, and she smiled at me and put her hand on the back of my neck.

"Well, I don't know," I said, then I just said, "Before you had Rona and me, I guess." I couldn't explain to her the feeling I had, that maybe she had lost something and didn't know it. Or maybe not lost something but *left* it—like when you forget your purse under the table in a restaurant.

"Oh," she said, and she gave my neck a little squeeze. "Before I had you and Rona? Well, I wasn't really *me*, then, was I?" and her saying it gave me a feeling like someone had just dumped a hundred pounds of wet sand in my lap.

One day, though, when I was about four or five, I found a book in her old bedroom at Grandma Bobbie's. At the time, I didn't even know what it was—I probably just thought it was a book about a lot of happy, smiling people. That might sound like a story to you, if you were four or five.

I loved that book so much. For a while, every time we went to Grandma Bobbie's, I'd go to Mom's old room and get it out first thing. On the first pages were rows and rows of little square pictures of smiling people's heads, and they all looked the same, except some were boys and some were girls. After that came pages of people dancing, singing, acting in plays, playing instruments, playing sports. The one I liked best, though, the one I'd turn to and stare at for a really long time, was a picture of four boys in striped sweaters, each with a girl in a matching sweater sitting on his shoulders.

The girls were smiling and clapping and yelling, and their faces were all turned the same way, watching something you couldn't see, that you wished you could see, because whatever it was, the girls seemed so happy and excited to be seeing it.

The way I figured out one of those smiling girls was Mom was that one day I was practicing my writing. I used to make Mom write the names of everyone in my family, then I'd copy them: Justine Victoria Hanley, Rona Margaret Hanley, Colleen Frances MacNeil Hanley, Bridget Marie MacNeil, and Barbara Louise MacNeil—Grandma Bobbie. She'd write down Dale's name, too, but I only copied it once and never did again, because for one thing, it was boring—I hated capital Ds, and he had no middle name, just plain old Dale Hanley—and for another, it made an ugly sound in my head, a sharp, angry bark, that reminded me of him.

One day we were over at Grandma's, and I had been practicing the names all morning. Grandma Bobbie asked me if I'd like to go outside and play, but I said, "No, thank you."

After my finger had gotten a stained dent on the side and I couldn't write anymore, I lay down on my stomach on Mom's old bed to look at the book of smiling people. Suddenly, I noticed something. There, on one of the pages with all the heads, was something I could read: Colleen MacNeil.

I brought the book in to Mom.

"Look," I said, pointing at the words. "It says your name."

"Hmm," said Mom. She leaned over to look. "Yes, it does, doesn't it?" she said after a few seconds. Then she pointed to the second girl over in the row of faces and said, "And there I am." We stayed there for a minute with our faces together, looking at the picture, then she said, "Want to see another one?" and she turned the pages to another picture, of a bunch of girls and boys, standing packed together in two rows. After a minute, I found her, the same smiling girl as in the other picture.

"The Beachcomber Club," she said. I didn't know Mom had gone beachcombing with anyone besides me. Then she said, "There's one more. But it's a secret. You have to promise not to tell anyone," and she turned the pages right to the picture I liked so much. It was like stepping outside into the sun—it took my eyes a minute to adjust from real Mom, beside me, to the bright, smiling, super-happy-looking one in the picture. But then I could see it really was her, on top of the tallest boy's shoulders. All the girls were pretty, but she was the prettiest one. Her smile was so big, it couldn't be any bigger and still be a smile.

"You didn't know I was a cheerleader, did you?" she asked.

"What's a cheerleader?" I said, which made her laugh.

"Oh, honey," she said, shaking her head, "hope you never find out." Then she told me: It's the kids at school everyone likes the best—the happiest, most cheerful, most popular ones—and everyone votes on you to stand in front of the whole school yelling and singing and doing flips and, if you're a girl, getting lifted up in the air—and I remember being confused: Why didn't she want me to know about that?

"Does Dale know you were one?" I asked her. In my five-year-old brain, it felt like a really important question. I was surprised to see her face change, to hear the weird sound in her voice.

"Why do you ask that?" Mom said.

I wasn't exactly sure why I wanted Dale to know: there was a Mom Before him, too—someone happy and smiling, sitting in the air on top of another boy's shoulders, not even imagining there was such a thing as Dale in the world.

There's another thing about Mom Before that Rona doesn't remember: She had had friends, and in the days before Dale, they still used to come over to our house. Sometimes they all came over at once, and that was the best. I loved the way the air around my head felt—swirly and full of excitement—when they all talked and laughed at the same time, and I loved the colors of them, too: shiny blond hair and tan skin and bright turquoise and green and red and pink and orange clothes. They would sit in the backyard in bikinis and flowered sarongs and thin golden necklaces, and once, I remember, they drank bright blue drinks and laughed so much, and stayed so long, it felt like the best day of my life.

Mom doesn't remember. She just says, "Honey, are you sure you didn't dream it?"

I was probably about three years old. I remember I was wearing a dress the color of raspberries, and green-and-white sandals, and I had my own blue drink, in a real glass. We were in the backyard of the house she says I don't remember, but I do.

"That huge house," I told her. "With the big orange flowers that grew in the back."

But she said, "That was just an apartment, Justine. It was so tiny there wasn't even a bedroom for you, don't you remember?"

I don't know why Mom wants to pretend that day never happened.

"Honey," she says, "I just don't think it happened that way." And if I say, "Okay, then what *did* happen that day? Who *were* all those people?" she says, you guessed it: "I don't know."

They sat in lawn chairs, the long, low-to-the-ground kind that leave stripes on the backs of your legs, that they'd pulled into a big circle in the backyard. I remember I went around the circle all day, climbing onto one person's lap and clinking glasses, then climbing down and going over to the next person, who would be smiling, waiting for me, holding out her arms.

"One of them was named Donna, I think," I told Mom.

"Hmh," she said. "Diana?"

"And one was Jessie." I remember it was a name that sounded like mine.

"I never had a friend named Jessie," Mom said.

The one I loved most, though, was Kim.

"Kim was there?" said Mom. "Well, I'll have to ask her if she remembers, next time I talk to her. Though, gosh, I don't even know where she's living now."

When it was Mom's turn for me that day, I'd climb up onto her lap and clink my glass with hers, and she'd give me a kiss and put her hand in my hair, then after a minute I'd get down and go on to the next person, and I remember how good that felt—sliding down off Mom's lap and scampering away, knowing she would come around again in a little bit, the way a tree in the yard stays in the same place even when you're running crazy circles around it, trying to make yourself so dizzy that you fall down laughing.

On one of my trips around the yard, though, Mom was gone. Kim, the one who was my favorite, came up behind me, where I stood looking at Mom's empty chair.

"Come on, J," she said, "come over by me," and she swooped me up and took me over to her long chair.

At first I liked it, because everyone was paying me extra attention, asking, "What's your favorite color, Justine?" "What's your favorite animal?" "How high can you count to?" "Do you know any songs?"

But after a while, the air started to get cool and the colors of everything started to change, like somebody was slowly turning down the brightness. Kim kept getting up and going into the house and coming back without Mom. She'd sit down again and smile at me, but she wasn't laughing anymore, and soon no one else was, either. The blue drinks had turned into puddles of cloudy water in the bottoms of the glasses.

After a while someone said, "Let's go get something to eat."

"Okay," somebody answered, then another voice asked, "But what about Justine?" and I'll always remember that—the sound of my name, and then the silence, like I was a question no one knew the answer to.

"You guys go ahead," Kim said.

"You're not coming?" someone asked, and Kim sounded mad when she answered, "No, I'll stay with Justine." Then someone said, "Where's Colleen, anyway? What's her problem?" and I started to cry.

"It's okay, sweetie," Kim said, then she said, *God,* to whoever had said that, "never have any kids, okay?" and she carried me through the yard and into the kitchen, where Mom stood with Dale, who at the time was just some guy I'd never seen before.

Mom says it wasn't Dale. But if, as she claims, she doesn't remember the whole day, how can she remember for sure it wasn't him? Anyway, it was.

"Colleen," said Kim. Mom had a weird expression on her face. You couldn't see any trace of the smile from the backyard. She was standing close to the guy, and I didn't like it.

"Is it okay if I take Justine for a walk down to the beach?" Kim asked her. "Maybe we'll find the ice-cream truck on the way." It was a nice thing she was saying, but a strange look went from Kim to Mom and from Mom back to Kim. I didn't know then what I was seeing, and maybe they didn't, either. But now I do: I was seeing something starting to end.

That's why I'll always feel a little bit bad that we *did* find the ice-cream truck—that I walked around on a night like that, a night when nobody knew, yet, that there would never be another one like it, with Good Humor Toasted Almond, an amazing kind of ice cream I'd never had before, dripping down my arm.

After the ice cream, Kim and I watched the sun go down over the ocean, then we walked back home. When we got there, Mom wasn't even there anymore, so Kim put me to bed. She lay down with me and sang me a song I wish I could remember now.

When I woke up the next morning, Kim was gone, and when I got up and went to find Mom, there was the guy Mom says wasn't Dale, asleep in her bed next to her, and after that he was always around, and eventually he moved in.

For a while I thought that if I just thought the right thoughts, or said or did the right things, maybe I could make that perfect day happen again.

"When is Kim and everybody coming over again?" I would ask Mom, but she would just say, "I don't know, sweetie."

"Remember the blue drinks?" I said, so many times, I guess, that she finally asked me to stop. One day I even spent almost the whole morning in the backyard by myself, dragging out all the lawn chairs and arranging them in a circle. I remember standing and looking at them, and thinking that now maybe the friends would show up any minute and we'd get to have that day over again.

We never did, though. Every once in a while, one or two of them would come over, but it wasn't the same. They'd sit at the kitchen table, or on the porch, but their voices didn't sound the same as they had that day—like a flock of birds flittering through the air. I couldn't see the smiles and looks that had connected them like a shimmery spiderweb. Dale would be watching TV in the living room, or working on the car in the driveway, coming in the door every few minutes to get something he needed, or stepping out of the bathroom at the end of the hall with a towel around his waist, and the talk was just mostly boring stuff—"How've you been?" "How's your job? How's your sister?" and, "Oh, hi, Dale, how are you?" and the answers were always: Fine, Fine, Fine, Fine.

Kim came, too, every once in a while. She always brought me something, just like before: postcards with animal pictures, a carved bamboo animal from Chinatown, a bead necklace.

Dale especially liked it when Kim came over. As soon as Mom opened the door, she'd call, "Kim's here!" to Dale, wherever he was, and I could see Kim's body stiffen and her face close like a door.

"Hey, Kimbo!" Dale would say, and he'd come into the kitchen and settle down in a chair. I wondered why I was the only one who could see that she hated him.

Then Mom would start talking: "Kim, Dale's brother is visiting next week from Vancouver; Dale wrote the greatest new song; Dale's band is playing two weeks from now in Pasadena," and sometimes an hour would go by like that, and you could see Kim's smile getting smaller and smaller until she'd stand up and say, "Well, I should go, I guess."

More and more, though, when Kim came over, she'd say, "Let's go for a walk," as soon as Mom opened the door. I'd go along, and I'd try to walk in front or behind, so I could listen to the sounds of their voices. It was getting harder and harder not to hear what they were saying, though.

"If he makes you so unhappy, why don't you ask him to move out?" Kim asked Mom one day. Mom didn't answer.

"It can't be good for Justine, to be seeing this sort of thing," Kim said, and I remember I looked around, because I didn't know what she was talking about.

"Don't go!" Mom would always say when it was time for Kim to leave. They'd stand in the driveway for a minute more, and Mom would say how they didn't spend enough time together and had to plan to do it more. Then, almost every time, Kim would say, "How are you *really*, Colleen?" and Mom would answer, "What do you mean?"

Once, though, Mom looked at me first, with an expression on her face that was right exactly in between laughing and crying, and then she leaned to whisper something to Kim. Kim looked at her with really wide eyes and an expression I'd never seen before except on Grandma Bobbie.

"You've got to be joking," she said.

Mom stared back at Kim for a minute, then she took a deep breath and started shaking her head.

"Well, *Colleen*," said Kim, "I'm sorry not to be totally elated for you, but after everything you've told me, this is a little disturbing."

I don't know why it took me about three years to figure out what happened that day: Mom told Kim that she was going to have Rona. Because the very next day, she told me, "We're going to have another baby, isn't that exciting?" And I *was* excited, for one second, before she added, "You and I and Dale are going to have a baby!", because when she first said it, I thought she just meant the two of us were going to have one, which seemed like a perfect idea.

Kim came over just one more time after that—to see Rona, the week after she was born. Of course, Rona doesn't remember, and I never told her about the way Kim held her and smiled at her and touched her practically invisible hair and said, "Oh, isn't she cunning; Colleen, she looks just like you!" She lifted Rona so that Rona's ugly little red face was resting on her shoulder, and I swear Rona gave me a dirty look, like, Ha ha, when Kim kissed her on the head.

Every once in a while, I'd get out the things Kim had given me and look at them again. I'd touch each one, turn it around in my hand to make sure I remembered everything about it, then I'd put it back. I kept the presents in a box in my bottom dresser drawer, hidden, like a secret; I can't remember why.

I also don't remember when the secret went from being a good one to something bad, something I didn't want anyone to know about, because telling it made me feel so ashamed—I used to have a grown-up friend, who loved me and brought me presents and sang me special songs and smelled like perfume when she bent over my bed to give me a kiss good night, but I don't anymore.

Not that I had anyone to tell. Even after Rona was big enough to really hate sometimes, I never told her about Kim and me. I knew it would make her feel bad, even though first of all she would pretend not to believe me and say she didn't care anyway, and second she would go straight to Mom, and then Mom would probably start talking about what a bad friend she was and end up crying.

After a while, I started to feel bad that I'd never told Rona the story of the day Kim held her and said how wonderful and perfect she was. But I still didn't. I told her other stories instead: Once upon a time, I'd always begin, Mom had a friend named Kim who had bright blond hair and used to come over to see me every day at five o'clock.

"Justine!" she'd cry, coming through the door, and every day she had a big box with wrapping paper on it.

"What was in the box?" Rona would ask, every time. I never even had to make up another story if I didn't want to—just change the present. After a while, though, Rona started getting smarter.

"Where is it?" she would ask a little suspiciously, about the present—the life-size stuffed tiger, the princess dress with real jewels sewn onto it, the twin Labrador retriever puppies. She went to Mom.

"Tell me the story about Kim," she said.

When Mom said, "What story?" Rona said, "About when she came over every day at five o'clock with a special present for Justine."

Mom looked at me funny. "That never happened, sweetheart," she told Rona.

Mom never even apologized to me for taking Kim away. She doesn't even know I still think about Kim, that I'm not like her—a human eraser.

Most of the things from my box, I ended up giving away to Rona, though I never told her where I got them. I pretended they were presents from me, which I guess in a way they were, and I gave them to her when I thought she needed them—when Dale yelled at her, or *Rugrats* didn't come on when it was supposed to, or Mom was acting weird and forgot for a few days in a row to read Rona a story at bedtime—and I thought about Kim when I did. I would imagine, when I gave the presents to Rona, Kim still being our friend, still remembering me and loving me, and I imagined the new things she would give me, too. Picturing the presents, flowing from Kim to me to Rona, made me think of something I liked: the fountain Grandma sometimes took us to, at the park near her house. The fountain was made of steps, with water falling down them, and I loved the sound the water made, tinkling and high-pitched, as it fell; and the way the sunlight looked, shining on the water's smooth, buttery surface; and the way the coins, that stupid people threw in, thinking they were going to get some good luck for twenty-five cents, looked, gleaming on the bottom; and I always ended with a picture of Rona and me, sitting on the warm concrete at the edge of the steps, alone but not scared or lonely, opening our presents.

The Story of Zebulina Walker *Justine Hanley, Room 12*

I remember being born. I remember bursting from a dark, quiet place into bright light, the blur of an upside-down face above me; two arms of someone I couldn't see, lifting me into the air and holding me there for a long moment.

"It's not possible," Mother told me gently, long ago, when I told her. "No one can remember being born."

Then how do I remember this: I was born knowing everything. We all are. Inside of us, from the very moment the man and woman get together, is planted the tiny little seed of everything you need to know to be a human being. Only, in the flash of being born, that knowledge disappears completely—it evaporates into the air of what's going to be your life and waits there, invisible, for you to gather it up again over the days and months and years. That's your job in life: to remember what you forgot. To turn into yourself.

I made the mistake of telling Thaddeus once. "Hush, wife!" he scolded me. "Pray to be forgiven. The Lord's plan would never make as little sense as that!"

Then why do I remember it so clearly—the moment of forgetting? Understanding flapping away like a flock of magpies, leaving me dangling in the air, blank and newborn, being lowered into my mother's arms?

SUN SHINING ON ORANGE JUICE

You'd think Mom would want to take a little break from men after Dale left—maybe hang out with me and Rona at the beach, or at home, let the days unfold like a long, sort of boring, but good story—just a time to walk around in our underwear, eat dinner anytime we wanted, keep the world's longest game of Monopoly lying out on the floor, and not worry about the days getting chopped into little pieces of shouting and doors slamming and things breaking and people getting called fuckin bitches. But it turned out almost the opposite.

It sort of started to seem like, to Mom, Dale was a missing part, and our life couldn't run till we replaced him. Did you ever go shopping at the junkyard? Dale took me once, and that's what Mom's crusade had started to remind me of: wandering around, looking inside each of the crushed, rusty wrecks, as if we were going to find just what we needed in there.

I was working on my own ideas about love, though I thought you probably had to actually fall in love to be able to *really* get it, and I wasn't planning that anytime soon. But love was such a big part of our life, the reason for basically everything we did, everywhere we went, everyone we got to know, after Dale left, that I thought I ought to at least make an effort—like, if you go to a foreign country, you try to learn a little of the language, at least enough to be able to ask for a drink of water or something to eat, to say please, thank you, and I need help.

Mom was always telling me what love was, but I didn't think any of her theories sounded right. For one thing, she said something different every time.

"Love is a deep, spiritual connection of tranquillity and mindfulness," she said when she met a guy with a weird name I'd never heard of before, who wore little slippers everywhere and brought his own straw mat for sleepovers.

"Love is realizing you don't have the power to change anything but yourself," she told me when she was getting ready for her date with the guy David, who'd just graduated from rehab.

"Love is meeting each other on a healthy, physical level and never forgetting to *play*!" she said when she went on three dates with Justin, the guy who sold us Rona's bike.

"What did you *play*?" asked Rona after each of Mom's three dates with Justin. Rona didn't exactly *get* dates.

The first time they went windsurfing. "It was so exhilarating," Mom said, "I can't even describe it. You just feel so *alive*." The second time they went biking, and Mom said, "You find this incredible energy source, deep inside yourself, that you didn't even know you had," and the next day she went out and bought a pair of weird shorts and a Hacky Sack for Rona. The third time, though, she just said, "We didn't play anything. We had a talk about how much he likes and respects me, but we won't be seeing much of Justin anymore," and she went in her room and closed the door.

I knew love wasn't any of the things Mom said it was after she came home from a date with someone new. My best idea so far was one that came to me when I was reading a magazine article for my archaeology report in the fourth grade. Maybe the answer to the question What is love? was buried, like the missing bone of a dinosaur skeleton, deep down underneath the big pile of your life—everything that had ever happened to you, or ever would, everything you knew and didn't know, all the different ways you felt. And the meaning of life was to dig it up, so you could finally put the whole thing together and see how it made sense.

The only problem with my theory was that it seemed like a flaw of nature. Nature is supposed to be organized according to such a magnificent plan, but if that's true, then why would love be at the bottom of the pile? Why wouldn't you just be born knowing what it was and how to do it?

The way we usually got a boyfriend was that Mom would meet someone somewhere for about one second—at the Laundromat, or the library, or Sharp's Deli, where she worked—and she'd get him to write down his address, then we would send him an application.

Mom was always saying she wasn't good at anything, but she had once almost gotten a degree in graphic arts; and she was really good at making stuff at Kinko's. She had a black leather portfolio with handles, and when she opened it, all sorts of things would come fluttering out: words cut out of newspapers and magazines, pictures, wrappers, ribbons, dried flowers, ticket stubs, money from foreign countries, and once—I couldn't believe it—a thin, lacy bra.

"Come on," she'd say to me and Rona sometimes, even if it was really late at night; and we'd drive across town to Kinko's. "You can help," she'd tell us, to make it sound like fun. When we got there, she'd dump everything out and start arranging things on the glass. But if Rona or I put anything into the picture, she'd tilt her head and say, "Oh. Hmm," and then take it out when we weren't looking, and after a while, we just went to our own counter and made paper-clip necklaces or painted our nails with Wite-Out or copied our hands and faces to keep from being bored.

There was one thing I liked about Kinko's, though, and that was Mom's tiny words.

Mom didn't know that I saw her sometimes, late at night, writing in her red book. But if I woke up and saw the living room light on, I would make myself get up and tiptoe down the hall, even though I hated to get out of bed and lose my dream, the same way Grandma Bobbie would get up at four in the morning sometimes to drive to a faraway marsh just to see one little bird that was never there in the day.

Mom would be lying on her stomach on the living room floor, in the middle of our big red-and-blue braided rug, with a tippy glass of red wine by her hand, her red book open in front of her, and I loved the way she looked as she wrote: so calm and still, sometimes smiling to herself, pausing now and then to look down at the words she'd written as if she loved them.

At Kinko's, she'd take her red book out of her purse, open it to one of the pages, and lay it facedown on the glass and make a copy. Then she'd copy the copy, reducing every time, till the words were exactly as small as they could get and still be big enough to read. I just loved that, and I don't know why—why the smaller they got, the more perfect they got, and the moment just before their meaning was about to disappear was the most perfect one of all.

Each application we sent was a little different, but they were all the same. They looked like imaginary worlds to me, with the familiar things in the landscape—the ticket stubs, the pieces of maps and seed packets and pictures and words—arranged a little differently each time; and in every one, peeking out from a different spot, were Rona and me, small and smiling, like hobbits or talking rabbits or some other creatures that didn't really exist.

The picture Mom liked to use best was one of me and Rona dressed up in our Easter dresses, hugging opposite sides of a tree trunk in the backyard, smiling, like, This is the most wonderful Easter ever, when really it was November and about forty degrees out the day Mom made us put on the dresses and go stand outside for four hours while she took the pictures; and it always made me mad to see.

There was another one, though, that made me even madder. It was one of those ones that come in a strip from a little booth you put money into, and it was of the three of us—Mom, me, and Rona.

It wasn't that I didn't like the pictures. I was five when we made them, and I remember everything about that day, even what I had for breakfast. When the pictures came sliding out of the little slot on the outside of the machine, I loved them so much that I made Mom take me to a store right there in the mall and buy me a red plastic wallet just so I could have a place to carry the strip around in.

The reason I remember what I had for breakfast was that I'd woken up at Grandma Bobbie's house, even though I had gone to sleep in my own bed. I used to love going over to Grandma Bobbie's, back before she started making Mom cry every time, asking questions

Mom couldn't think of any answers to, like "When are you going to wake up and smell the coffee?"; "Why don't you stand up on your own two feet?"; and "Do you think God gave you a perfectly good life to waste on that creep?"

Grandma Bobbie had a red-and-white checked tablecloth with tiny roosters on it, and the sun shone down in a diamond shape on top of my plate of poached eggs and on my glass of orange juice. In case you never noticed, sun shining on orange juice is beautiful. Every time Grandma got out the juice, Mom would say the same thing: "That glass is too big for Justine." I loved when she said it, because then Grandma Bobbie would say, "No it's not, Colleen. Justine is a big girl." At home I was only allowed to use a little glass, even before Dale broke all the big ones. The little ones only bounced when he threw them. It was like when he moved in he made himself King of the Glasses, along with everything else. And if a glass of juice or milk went over, he would start to yell, "Oh, For Cryin Out Loud!" which was an expression I had never heard before, and which I didn't like at all, because every time he yelled it, Mom ended up crying.

Something that nobody but me knows is, sometimes, at Grandma's, I used to spill my glass of orange juice on purpose. When no one was looking, I would just nudge the bottom of the glass till it tipped over, because I loved the way Grandma Bobbie would turn around and say, "Oops!" in her normal voice when she saw what had happened, and come right over with her sponge, move everything out of the way, and lift me up, too, to keep the juice from dripping down onto my legs.

"We'll have to try again, won't we?" she'd say, and she'd pour another big glass full of juice.

That's one of the reasons I loved the picture strip—because it was part of a day that started out like that. I was wearing my puffy pink bathrobe that was the same as Grandma Bobbie's, only smaller. She had made them both on her sewing machine. Mom was sitting in the living room holding Rona, who was just a blobby little baby at the time, and I felt so happy, looking at Grandma Bobbie's puffy pink quilted back across the kitchen, that I took my finger and gently lifted one edge of the bottom of my tall glass.

"Oops, Justine," said Grandma when she heard the clink of the glass and turned and saw the puddle of juice, "we'll have to try again, won't we?"; and I remember I felt sort of smiley and excited all day, because of the sneaky secret between me and Grandma: A glass of orange juice had spilled and gotten cleaned up, and nothing bad had happened, and Mom never even knew about it.

Rona was being good that day, too, just making gurgling sounds like a cartoon fish and not making Mom cry and ask a million times, "*Oh*, what is it you *want*?" And when Mom said, "I think we'll go to the mall," since we couldn't go home, in case Dale was still on a rampage, Grandma gave Mom some money and said, "Have a good time. Buy yourselves something on me." It felt like Mom and Rona and I were a normal family that day, with a normal life—just the three of us, wandering around the mall—and not what it usually felt like: like our life was a confused movie village with a monster walking down Main Street. At the very end of the day, on our way out of the mall, we saw the picture booth, and Mom got all excited.

I probably looked at those pictures a thousand times: Mom laughing, her head tilting a different way in each one; Rona looking the way babies look in pictures, her eyes wide and flat like someone colored them in with a black crayon; and me, half-in and half-out of each one, laughing as I fell off Mom's lap. I kept the strip in the red wallet in a box in my dresser drawer.

But one day, not too long ago, at Kinko's—I couldn't believe it— Mom pulled that picture out of her portfolio. "I found this," she said. "I can't even remember taking these. Aren't they great?"

I was so mad, standing there watching her move the picture strip this way and that, trying to figure out where it looked best.

"Look," she showed me when she finally had the page the way she wanted it. "Do you like it?" There we were, in between a poem in writing so small that you'd need a magnifying glass to read it and a flower seed packet whose colored edge was growing over my face.

I didn't like it. First of all, the picture was mine, and she stole it from me. And second, I thought it was like lying, to send someone a picture of a family that didn't even exist anymore. What if whoever it was for came over and expected to find what was in the picture? Because I wasn't five anymore, and Rona wasn't just a blank-faced baby—she had turned into someone who could say, "Shut-up,

poop-face," and liked to flush toys down the toilet on purpose—
and it had been a long time since Mom had smiled four times in
a row.

___ *Flour*
___ *Sugar*
___ *Salt*
___ *Baking soda*
___ *Yeast*
___ *Lard*
___ *Rice*
___ *Cornmeal*
___ *Molasses*
___ *Beef jerky*
___ *Pork jerky*
___ *Other kinds of jerky?*
___ *Horse food*
___ *Oxen food*
___ *Soap*
___ *Candles*
___ *Diapers*
___ *Seeds*
___ *Blankets*
___ *Clothing*
___ *Pots and pans*
___ *Spoons, forks, knives, etc.*
___ *Matches*

"What are you doing?" asked Thaddeus.
"Nothing," I said, closing my book.
"Silly little goose," he said. "Making your lists again?"
"No."
"You needn't worry," he said. "I have everything taken care of."

* * *

    __ *Flower seeds*
    __ *Fruit tree cuttings*
    __ *Photographs of Mother*
    __ *Children's baby teeth and hair locks*
    __ *Grandmother Walker's carved oak chest*
    __ *Locket with picture of best friend Tabitha Narcissa Peepwhistle in it*
    __ *Rubbing from poor brother Edgar's gravestone*
    __ *Peeled-off piece of bedroom wallpaper*
    __ *Favorite china cup with pictures of kittens on it*

Thaddeus keeps his list in his head. "It's better that way," he says. "There's less chance of losing it."

I disagree. In fact, the thought gives me the williams. It's frightening having your head be in charge of everything. All the facts of everybody's life crowded into your brain like fireflies in a jar, being carried in a child's small hands, getting heavier and slipperier and harder to hold, the harder she thinks about not dropping it.

WRECKED

The Ryder boxes sat in our living room all winter and all spring. At first, Mom would just put things in them now and then: "We won't need these till we get to New England," she said, packing up the sweaters and rain boots. Or sometimes she'd get a burst of energy and she'd jump out of bed and start putting in anything she saw, not even bothering with the categories she'd written in Magic Marker on the tops of the boxes.

After a while, though, things started to come out of the boxes: all of Mom's sundresses and sarongs, because the weather was getting hot again; her silver sandals, to go with an outfit she was wearing to a party at Fake-Aunt Paula's; her cannoli tubes, because she'd met a guy who was half Italian in Sharp's Deli. And when we had to have a garage sale to make money for the phone bill, Mom pulled a bunch of our so-called precious possessions out of the boxes for that.

It gave me a stomachache to see the big brown boxes sitting in the living room like furniture, stuff flowing in and out of them, but every time I asked Mom, "Well, are we moving or not?" she found a different way not to answer me.

"The trees in Massachusetts are probably starting to bud just about now," she'd say. "I can't wait to see Marie." Or, "Hmm, that reminds me—I need to look into reserving a truck."

One morning, though, I woke up at Grandma Bobbie's and lay in bed listening to Grandma and Mom talk. Usually, when Mom talked about her life, she would say things like "I really should . . ." and "If he only would . . ." and "Well, we always could . . . ," and her sentences sounded like questions, even though they weren't. That morning, though, her voice sounded different—hard and sharp, like jagged pieces of metal.

"I'm going to do this," she said to Grandma Bobbie. "I've thought a lot about it." And when Grandma didn't answer right away, "It's not like anyone gives a shit anyway."

"You know that's not true," said Grandma.

"You'll miss the girls," Mom said, and Grandma sighed.

"Yes, I will," she said, "but that's not the point. This doesn't seem like any way to solve your problems."

There was another silence, then Mom said, "I need a thousand dollars."

I told Mom later, at the beach, that I was sorry, but she just said, "Don't be sorry, Justine—we've had some good times here, but the next part of our life is going to be a great adventure." What I meant was, I was sorry because it was my fault we had to leave. She didn't say, "It's not your fault," though; she just stared out at the ocean.

That morning, Grandma Bobbie had come in my room after their conversation and sat on my bed and put her hand on my hair.

"Good morning, merry sunshine," she said. I didn't mind it when Grandma was corny. Then she rolled me over onto my stomach and lifted my pajama top to look at the place where Dale had punched me in the back so hard that I had to go to the hospital for an ultrasound on my kidney. "That bastard," she said.

Maybe it was true that Dale was a bastard—a lot of people called him that. I hadn't always hated him, exactly, though. At first, Dale hadn't seemed that bad. He knew how to boil hot dogs and steal your nose, and most little kids liked those things, though I always just pretended, because, one, I'd never liked hot dogs like a normal kid, and two, even when I was really little, I didn't think that little piece of thumb that grown-ups would show you, stuck between their two fingers, looked like a nose at all.

Also, he liked Jiffy Pop, Cream of Wheat, and American cheese, all things I did, too, and once when Mom left him in charge of us, we had all three of those things for dinner, and it was almost a good night. Except he couldn't unwrap the cheese without breaking it, which made him really mad; it made him yell at the cheese and call it a motherfuckin bastard.

After a certain point, though, Dale wasn't very much fun anymore. It was like he had turned into some weird kind of force field: every time he got near Mom, she would start to cry. Like, we would be sitting there eating our breakfast, and Mom would be standing at the sink doing the dishes and not even know he had come back into the room, but suddenly tears would start falling down her face. Sometimes, back in those days, I used to picture Mom as a soft, gray cloud, smudgy around the edges, spreading out toward the corners of the room, full of warm, salty rain. And if Rona and I moved around like ghosts all day and didn't fight, if it was a day nothing bad happened, like a diaper accident, or the car not starting, or not having enough money at the grocery store, the cloud could float around all day and not break.

But all Dale had to do was shut the front door sometimes; then it was like an invisible spike went straight through the grayness and the insides of it washed over us like a flood.

"For Cryin Out Loud!" he would yell, just seeing us sometimes. He was always yelling after he got saved—which, incidentally, in my opinion was a stupid thing to call it because it didn't seem like he got saved at all, it seemed like he got wrecked.

Dale's getting saved was the thing that made him not have a name anymore, according to Rona. That was my theory, anyway.

Before Dale got so-called saved, he used to yell, "Jesus Fuckin Christ!" and, "God Dammit All!" all the time, but after he got saved, everyone had to stop saying "God" and "Jesus" except in the religious way, which none of us ever did anyway. One Saturday when Mom didn't get out of bed, and I had set up Rona's easel and paints in the kitchen to keep her from bothering Mom, Dale walked in, looked around at the mess, and yelled so loudly that my paintbrush went flying out of my hand, *"Cheese and freakin crackers!"*—which sounded so idiotic, even to Rona, who was only about three at the time, that she started giggling. Dale walked over and cracked her in the face. That was the last day Rona ever called Dale Daddy. She didn't even call him Dale, like I did, she just stopped calling him anything and would put her chin down on her chest whenever he came near her.

Mom said I was supposed to feel like Dale was my real dad, but I didn't. At least I don't think I did. I didn't know what having a real dad felt like, though I *did* sort of have an imaginary one. Well, he wasn't actually imaginary, since he was based on a real-life person—my real dad, whom I had only met one time, before I was even old enough to remember. His name was Timothy Walker; that part was real. Grandma Bobbie told me, and Mom got really mad at her when she did.

"Colleen," Grandma said, "you'd've had to tell her sooner or later."

"That's not true," said Mom. She wanted him completely out of our story, but that only worked until I found out where babies came from. Grandma told me because I was confused—at first I thought it was Dale who gave Mom the seed. When I said that to Grandma Bobbie, she got a weird look on her face and called, "Colleen, could you come in here?

"I think there's something you need to tell this child," she said, and she told Mom what I'd asked her.

"What did you tell her?" Mom said.

"I didn't tell her anything," Grandma said. Mom looked at me a long time, probably deciding whether or not to lie to me.

My father's name was Timothy Walker, Mom finally told me. I tried to get her to tell me more facts, like where he lived and how old he was, but she just said, "Oh, Justine," to every question I asked.

"What was he like?" I asked her two different times.

"A real shmuck," she said the first time, and, "A complete dooshbag," the second. I couldn't find either one of those things in the dictionary, but I was pretty sure by the way she said them that they weren't good things.

Whatever they were, they didn't match the picture I had gotten in my head the minute Mom said the name "Timothy Walker." He was tall and thin, with long legs, and he had straight brown hair and a face you could draw using only straight lines.

"Did I ever see him?" I asked Mom, and I saw Grandma Bobbie give her a weird look like she better not give the wrong answer.

"You saw him once," Mom said finally. "When you were a week old, he came to see you for the first and last time." I waited for her to tell me more, but she didn't. While I was waiting, I pictured Timothy Walker walking through the hospital room door, smiling, with a big bouquet of flowers and balloons.

"Justine," Grandma said, bunching her eyebrows at Mom, "he was very, very young."

"Oh, come on, Mother," Mom said. "He wasn't any younger than I was."

"That's not what I meant," said Grandma Bobbie in an irritated voice.

"Well, what *did* you mean, then?" Mom said.

Grandma Bobbie was shaking her head, and Mom was zipping the zippers on Rona's diaper bag in a way that meant we were leaving.

"Will you tell me about that day?" I asked.

"What day?" said Mom.

"When he came to see me at the hospital."

Mom was about to say no, I could tell, but just then Grandma Bobbie said, "I'll go see if Rona's awake."

When she left the room, Mom sat back down and said, "Oh, baby." Then she said, "First of all, it wasn't the hospital."

For a minute it sounded like she was speaking Chinese: my brain couldn't understand what she had just said. My picture, even though I'd just barely made it up, already felt like a memory to me: Timothy Walker coming to the door of the room where Mom sat up in bed, smiling, holding me in a little pink blanket. He had a huge bouquet of flowers, and he was smiling, too, because he had a new daughter—me.

"I was at home," Mom said. "You'd been born a whole week. We stayed at the hospital three days, but he never came to see us. Then I took you home to the apartment we lived in, which you don't remember. Timothy and I got it just a couple weeks before you were born, but he never moved in."

"Yes, I do," I almost blurted out to Mom, because the minute she said it, I *did* remember the apartment. It was small and sunny, and had big plants everywhere, and a living room at the end of a long hallway, with a maroon couch where Mom and Timothy sat holding me and making silly noises in my baby face the day he came to visit.

"And do you know what he said to me when he finally did show up, after I'd been home in our empty apartment with you, alone, for four days?"

"No," I answered.

"He said he just couldn't *picture* himself as someone with a family."

"What?" I asked, even though I had heard her.

"He said he needed time to think. He said he needed *space* to decide what to do."

"Well, what did you tell him?" I asked.

"When you're older, Justine," Mom said, "you'll understand why the answer to that question is: It doesn't matter.

"And that's the story of Timothy Walker," she said. "That's the story of your father's involvement in the life of the Hanleys. Except for a check he sent once, for fifty dollars. He never came back."

"MacNeils," I said.

"What?"

"We were MacNeils back then," I reminded Mom. She shook her head.

"Isn't Dale better than a father who you only saw one day of your life?" Mom asked, but the way she said it surprised me. She sounded like she knew it was a question sort of like Which would you rather do, empty out the cat box or clean the toilet bowl? and she let the conversation end without my having to answer her.

After Dale moved out, he still liked to see us every once in a while. He had a *right* to see Rona, he said, and Mom agreed, but only if I went along, too. Because Dale had no clue about Rona, even though he was her father and had lived with her for three and a half years. He said things like "Shut it" if she started to cry, or he would pull out a candy bar and eat the whole thing without offering us a bite and then ask, "What's her problem?" when she whined. So every time Dale called to say he wanted to do something with Rona, I went along and "helped," which basically meant I did everything, and he just sat there and every once in a while poked her in the side and said, "Ya havin a good time, princess?" or told her "For Cryin Out Loud" to stop doing something or other.

The day he called to say he'd gotten free passes to Disneyland from someone he had played a gig for, and wanted to take us the next day even though it was a school day, Mom just happened to be in the middle of a catering job, so even though she mentioned all the time what a shithead Dale was for leaving us with no money, taking the car, turning into a raving nut case, and using up all the best years of her life, she said to him on the phone, "Oh, I guess that would be okay. As long as you don't let go of Rona's hand for one minute, and make sure the girls get some good food to eat."

Those would be my jobs, along with taking Rona to the bathroom, telling Dale when it was time for her to eat again, changing the subject if she was about to cry, and not letting her lose Billy Jane, her corroded sock doll she insisted on taking everywhere.

When Dale came to get us at eight A.M., Mom was already crying. Usually she didn't cry before her coffee, she just lay in bed and stared at the ceiling if it was going to be a bad day. But that day she was already up; in fact, she'd been up all night, and the night before, too, working on the catering job.

Catering was a weird job. The way it worked was someone would call Mom and ask if, like in three or four months, Mom would make them some food for a party.

"Oh. Hmm. I think I could do that. Sure," she would say. Then the minute she hung up the phone she would moan, "*Why* did I say I would *do* that?" For two or three months, she would mention every now and then how she didn't want to do the job, because it was going to be so much work, and how she wasn't even going to make any money. Meanwhile, the person would call every once in a while to check in, and Mom would go, "Oh. Okay. . . . Okay. . . . Okay. . . . Oh, no, no, no, no, no—no problem." As soon as she hung up, though, she would say, "She just asked for fresh flowers at all the tables! She wants me to add passion fruit sauce *and* a chocolate truffle to all the desserts! I'm not even going to break even on this job!"

After she had told everyone about the job coming up—about how much work it was going to be and how much money she wasn't going to make and how she was probably going to screw it up anyway—she would get out the Martha Stewart books and look at all the pictures of the things she really *should* make but probably wouldn't. Then about a week before the party, she'd start talking about how now there *really* wasn't any time, and she didn't have any money to buy the things she needed—the pea pods and crabmeat and lamb's ear lettuce and tenderloin and flowers and gold wire ribbon to tie around the flower stalks and platters and candles and candied violets and real gold dust for decorating the dessert—because she had already spent the deposit. She didn't have any idea how she was going to do any of it, and she was going to ruin the person's party, or their wedding, and possibly even their entire life.

The day she planned to start would go by. So would the next. She wouldn't actually start cooking till the day before the party, and sometimes not even then. She'd take the day off work at Sharp's Deli, which she couldn't afford to do, so she could get everything done, but when we came home from school she'd be sitting in the same spot as when we left, talking on the phone to someone, saying how she had this huge job to do and no time to do it. Or else she'd just be sitting there, with the Martha Stewart books open next to her, staring out the window.

Sometime in the middle of the night, I'd wake up to the sound of the Cuisinart. In the morning the kitchen would look like a hurricane went through, and Mom would be standing at the counter, working and crying, which was what she was doing the day Dale walked in the door to pick us up for Disneyland.

"Oh, for cryin out loud, Colleen," Dale said in a disgusted voice.

"Jesus Christ, don't start with me," Mom answered.

For a second, when I thought about it later, I tried to convince myself maybe it was that—Mom's mentioning Jesus in that way—that had planted the seed of everything that went wrong that day. Maybe it wasn't what I said next: "Why don't you just leave her alone?"

When I told Dale to leave Mom alone, he looked at me like a cartoon man about to have his body twist into a corkscrew and shoot to the moon. Watching him, and hoping to get that feeling I liked, of zooming away from my body and up into a corner of the ceiling, I was thinking about how weird grown-ups were. Except for Grandma Bobbie and Kim, there seemed to be something really wrong with most of them. Sometimes, listening to Dale yell and Mom talk like she was an alien who just *couldn't* figure out the puzzle of human life, I wished there were something you could be besides a grown-up when you grew up, and it gave me a horrible feeling, like thinking about where you go after you die.

I spent the whole day trying to erase what I'd said, but Dale's moods were like when you throw up in the car and the smell doesn't go away for a really long time, no matter how many of those little pine trees you hang from the mirror. Before we even went on the first ride, I had a stomachache and Rona was acting weird. It had been a month or so since we saw Dale, and at first she acted like she'd forgotten who he was.

"How's my girl?" he asked Rona after he had gotten finished yelling at Mom and telling her she was never going to get her life together, and that the problem she was having that day, as she stood at the counter crying and trying to roll 250 tiny chipotle–cream cheese balls to stuff inside 250 hollowed-out pea pods, was *"Typical! Just typical!"*

"It's *fucking* Martha Stewart's fault!" Mom wailed.

"Watch it!" Dale said.

"Fucky Martha Stewart," said Rona, which of course made Dale turn to her and say, *"Hey!"* so loud she jumped, though, surprisingly, she didn't cry.

"Doody," she said a little while later, when we had finally gotten out of the house and were sitting in the backseat of Dale's, formerly our, car, waiting for him to finish up the last little bit of yelling at Mom.

"Shhh," I told her. Dale was nearly to the car, and the windows were open. Mom was standing in the doorway trying to wipe tears off her face with chipotle–cream cheese hands, saying, "You know, you are really something; I should just take out a restraining order. You girls have a good time. Justine, make sure Rona eats something besides junk today—and you too, okay?"

But just as Dale was opening the door, Rona said it again: "Doody."

"Doo-dee-doo-dee-doo," I sang, and I tickled her to get her to laugh, so it would sound like we were just playing baby games, because I had a suspicion, and it turned out I was right: after she said it about twenty times, I figured out it was her new name for Dale. Not that I cared what she called him—it was just another thing for me to worry about for the day not to turn into a disaster.

Because if Dale figured it out, I didn't think he would be pleased. If Dale figured it out, he might start yelling his head off, or he might do something worse. He might go into his philosophy of life again, which he liked to tell us every time he got us away from Mom— something about Satan hiding behind every door, either in disguise, like an old woman in a fairy tale, or, somehow, according to Dale, morphed into Mom. And even though Satan was trying his hardest to wreck our life, as if Dale and Mom needed any help doing that, there was something that would save us, and that was the Family. Which Dale apparently was the king of and, according to him, consisted of me, Dale, Rona, and Dale's mother, who was an evil old lady who unfortunately for Rona was her grandma but not mine. When we saw her, which we had to do more now, since Dale had moved back into her house, Dale made me call her "Grandma Evelyn," but I made sure everything possible to cross on my body was crossed when I said it.

I didn't know how the Family was supposed to save us from Satan. Dale had a special prayer to go with the talk. Dale tried to load on the prayers when Mom wasn't around; her not wanting him to pray was another sign that she was the devil or the devil was her, whichever it was.

"Please, Dale," she'd say, "this is so confusing for them; could we just not?" Or, if she didn't care if they got in a fight or not, "Oh, another McPrayer, great. Hold the crap, please."

If Dale heard Rona calling him "Doody," he'd probably stop the car and say a prayer at us right there on the side of the highway, on the way to Disneyland, with all the cars and trucks roaring by. So I spent the whole drive, and wore my voice to the bone, singing stupid songs to Rona, and telling her stories, and pretending to play goofy games with her face—holding her lips shut with my fingers when I thought she was going to say something.

We didn't last too long at Disneyland. Rona wet her pants on Mr. Toad's Wild Ride, because Dale bought her a large Coke, even though I told him Rona never got to have large Cokes.

"That's crap," he said. "Whose rule is that? Colleen's?"

Then, after we had stood in line for an hour, Rona said, "I have to go to the bathroom."

"Tough noogies," Dale said.

"Can you hold it?" I whispered to her. She nodded her head yes, with her thumb in her mouth. But she had the weirdest look on her face.

In the middle of the ride, Dale jumped halfway out of his seat and screamed, *"For cryin out loud!"* Rona didn't even look at him. The ride was on the part where you go through hell, and it was actually pretty scary, with all these devils popping out all around you, but Rona had no expression on her face. She was just staring straight ahead. My stomach felt like a little sack of throw-up catapulting toward my throat.

"What the *frig* did you do that for?" he yelled as soon as we were off the ride. Rona didn't say one thing; she kept her thumb in her mouth and looked at him.

"What the *frig* is the matter with you?!" he said. "What the *frig* is the matter with her?" he asked me. "What do we do now?"

I didn't know. I hadn't packed Rona any extra pants because it had been a couple of years since she'd had an accident. I didn't know whether we should let Rona walk around in wet shorts or if they had any for sale in one of the shops, and if we did buy her some, whether we should we take her underpants off and carry them around wet all day or just throw them in the garbage, or whether we should just go home, even though I knew Dale would be furious about wasting the free passes.

"Well, I don't know what the hell to do," Dale kept saying in a disgusted voice, and every time he did, Rona took her thumb out of her mouth and said, "Doody," then popped it back in when he turned to look at her.

A woman with a little boy and a little girl came and sat down at a table right by where we were standing. The woman had a big bag, and she started taking out juice boxes and Goldfish crackers, and when the boy tried to take some goldfish out of the girl's pile, the mother said calmly, "Please leave your sister alone," and he did. For a minute I thought of going over to her and asking her if she knew what I should do, but I didn't know if that was a good idea or a bad idea, and before I could decide, suddenly my stomachache, which had been going away and coming back all day, blared like a loud horn inside me, and before I could say or do anything, I threw up right onto Dale's feet in his stupid fisherman's sandals.

"For cryin out loud!" he screamed, and this time Rona started to cry.

No one said anything the whole way home. Mom and I practiced small talk sometimes, and we had different things you could say to different categories of people, but there was no category for someone furious at you, whose feet you had just thrown up on, who you kind of hated anyway. When we got to Dale's house, Grandma Evelyn was out front, bending over to pull something out of the garden, and she looked exactly like one of those painted wooden polka-dotted yard butts, only not funny at all.

"Well, hello, Rona," she said, coming to the car and opening Rona's door.

"And Justine," she added, making a face. She didn't like me much; I didn't know why, and I didn't care. "What's that smell?" she said as she leaned into the car to help Rona out.

"Doody," Rona said.

"What?" Grandma Evelyn barked.

"Justine," said Dale, "what do you say to your grandmother?"

"I don't have any idea who you're talking about," was what I wanted to say, but instead I answered, "Pee and vomit."

"Who's in charge of teaching this young lady manners?" Grandma Evelyn asked.

"Colleen," said Dale, and Grandma Evelyn sighed like someone in a play.

When we got inside I told Grandma Evelyn I would give Rona a bath, but she said, "*I'll* do it." Dale went straight to the back room to watch television, so I just went in the kitchen to wait. There was nothing to do in Dale and Grandma Evelyn's house except watch TV, read *TV Guide* or the Bible, or look at the pictures of Dale on the walls.

I didn't think anyone could hear me, so I went to the fridge and opened it up to look around. I opened the freezer and saw some Popsicles, and I took one out and unwrapped it. Right then Dale came in.

"Did you bless that?" he said. The Popsicle was already on its way to my mouth, and I let it go there.

"Did you *bless* that?" he said. "In this house, you thank the Lord for every blessing you receive, *period, the end.*"

Something weird was happening inside me. Maybe because I had already thrown up and didn't have anything left in there, but suddenly, things didn't feel complicated, like they usually did. I had an emptied-out feeling, which was surprisingly kind of nice, like a house when you've packed everything up and you're ready to move. You walk in one last time to look around, to see if you've left anything; you go stand in your empty room to check to see if there are any weird feelings hanging around in there—good memories, or happiness, or the mixed-up feeling of wanting to leave but also wanting to stay—but nope. Things seem simple, even if it's only for just that one minute: the decision is made, even if you don't exactly remember making it.

"No," I said to him, and I bit right through the green ice. He looked at me like he couldn't believe it. "I don't bless Popsicles," I said. "*Period, the end.* If you ask me, it's a pretty freakin stupid thing to do."

I knew he was going to do it. So why didn't I stop it from happening? Maybe I could have jumped out of the way. As I turned, and his fist hit me in the back so hard that the air turned colors, I could feel something inside me that I never felt before. I had no idea what it was, but it was burning red, with a coal black center, and it was right in the middle of my chest, but it wasn't my heart. It was something else, drawing his anger like a magnet—Dale told me sometimes that I had evil inside me, but I don't think it was that. Because whatever it was felt like a good thing—a broken part, maybe, that I never even knew I had, that had suddenly started working again. Maybe the furious look in Dale's eyes stripped the rust and corrosion right off of it. Whatever it was, I could feel it drawing his anger out of the atmosphere, away from everyone else and toward me, clamping onto the angry ball of him like one of those huge car magnets picks up the rusty, crumpled square that used to be a car and swings it around toward the junk pile and lets go.

DEAD SQUIRREL

I wondered if we were going to leave California without saying good-bye to Grandpa Victor. The last time we'd seen Grandpa had been a couple of years before—the week Dale left, actually. When Dale left, he took our car and tore the lid off the washing machine; and for three days, Mom pretended it was going to be so much fun and such great exercise for us to go everywhere on our bikes. But on the fourth day, when she tried to tie a huge bag of dirty laundry onto the child seat and her bike tipped over when she was trying to get on, she said, "*Fuck* this *fucking shit!*" and the next day we took a taxi for thirty-five dollars to Grandpa Victor's house to get the rusty Ford Fiesta he told Mom he was lending her against his better judgment.

We hardly ever saw Grandpa Victor, and I didn't know why, but I didn't care too much. He had weird breath and a voice like he was always about to yell at you, and he never gave us any presents, not even on our birthdays. When he saw me, he'd just look at me, probably because he didn't remember my name. Sometimes he called me Jessica, and other times nothing at all, and he acted like Rona was just some weird thing growing off the end of Mom's arm.

Even though Grandpa Victor had lived with Mom and Aunt Bridget and Grandma Bobbie till Mom was seventeen years old, she hardly ever talked about Grandpa Victor, except when it had been a really long time since she'd paid the bills and people were calling to say they were going to shut things off. "I am *not* going to ask him for help," she'd say; then she'd call him and start to cry and hang up when he told her no.

Grandma Bobbie hardly ever talked about Grandpa Victor, either, though I didn't think she hated him. He just seemed like something that had once been around and then wasn't anymore, like a disappointing Christmas toy you shoved in the closet and after a while didn't even remember you'd ever had.

"Why did you marry Grandpa?" I asked Grandma Bobbie once, and I'll never forget what she said: "Because he asked me."

"Was he a good man?" I asked, but all she said was, "No, not particularly."

One time, Grandpa and I were alone together. I don't know why—usually if Mom didn't have a baby-sitter, she just took us with her. "They love grown-up activities," she would tell anyone who looked like they thought it was weird to see kids standing in line all day to get a driver's license, or at a poetry reading of some guy she'd just met, which actually made standing in line at the driver's license place seem like it had been a pretty fun day.

Maybe it was an experiment, to let Grandpa and me get to know each other better. I was pretty little at the time, but not too little to know it was a weird day. After Mom left, Grandpa Victor set out some dry cereal in a bowl for me, like I was a dog, then he went outside and spent the whole day under the car. For a while I wandered around in the house, but it was small, and there wasn't anything to look at, except for one thing I didn't like looking at but couldn't stop looking at, which was a lamp made out of a dead squirrel. The squirrel was stuffed, and it had its eyes open. It was standing straight up, attached to a pole that held up the lightbulb and the lampshade.

After a while I went outside and looked at Grandpa's legs for a while and listened to him. Well, he wasn't really talking. He didn't know I was there. Sometimes one of his legs or feet moved a little, then in the middle of the silence he'd suddenly clear his throat with a kind of *h-r-r-r-h-rrr* noise that made me jump, or he'd say something like "You *motherfucking cock*sucking son of a *bitch!*" and then be quiet again. After a while, I went back in the house and sat by my bowl of cereal, and that was the story of the one day I spent with my grandfather.

Every once in a while after that, I would wonder what it meant, that Grandpa had that dead squirrel lamp. Maybe there was a story behind it, like he had caught the squirrel himself. Or maybe an ancestor had handed it down to him. Or maybe Grandpa had just seen it in a shop somewhere and said, I *have* to have that. But what would that mean about a person? And what would it mean about you—to be related to a weird old man who kept a dead squirrel in his house? For a long time, I made the squirrel question into a big mystery, then I sort of forgot about it, which was fine, I guess, because in the end, it turned out not to matter very much anyway: we were going to move, and we were probably never going to see the lamp again, or Grandpa Victor, either.

Thaddeus came home with two head of oxen today. So I guess we are really going.

"I'm going to teach you to drive," he said. "Get your bonnet and meet me at the wagon."

"I know how to drive," I told him. My mother taught me. It was a great moment, holding the reins of the carriage all by myself for the first time.

"It's different with oxen and a prairie schooner!" Thaddeus said. "Oxen are bigger; you have to cut your turns a little wider or they'll bump into each other and get tangled up and tip the wagon!"

"Well, how different can it be?"

"This is important, Zebulina!" he said. "Can't you see?! We are undertaking a very important journey!"

Men are strange creatures, I sometimes think. They either take up the whole world, breathe up all the air—their voices trample through your brain like a stampede of demented ponies; or they disappear completely, even when you try your hardest to keep a picture of them in your mind, like my dear friend Tabitha Narcissa Peepwhistle's husband, Nathaniel, who never says a word and spends all his time making horseshoes in a little house behind their house; like kind Uncle Stephen, who sits at the dinner table at Christmas once a year, smiling at his potatoes. Like Father.

"Like this!" Thaddeus cried, cracking the whip and shaking the reins like maracas. The oxen started up and I fell into my seat. "Like this! This is the way to do it! I'm showing you how!"

It's not all that hard. Late tonight, after he went to sleep, I crept out of bed and went to the barn and attached the oxen to the wagon, praying he wouldn't wake. I spoke to them in a low voice, and we headed down the lane.

I drove all the way to town. I made left turns, I made right turns, I went over bumps and around ditches. We turned into the church parking lot, and I made big circles and small circles and spirals and figure eights.

"Okay," I said, not exactly sure who I was talking to. The moon was moving across the sky, and I knew I should get back. "I'm ready," I lied. "Tch-tch," I said to the oxen, and we headed for home.

LEAVING

The day before we left, Dale came over and parked his, formerly our, car in back of the Ryder truck and said to Mom, "I will not let you do this." He had brought Grandma Evelyn with him, and when they got out of the car, it was like one of those scary, old-fashioned movies—they both moved slowly toward Mom as if they were going to catch her in a net and take her somewhere to dissect her brain.

"We want you to pray with us," said Dale.

The truck was half-full—Mom's friends Jimmy and Chris had come over at seven in the morning to help load it, but at ten o'clock Mom had stopped, with an armful of poster tubes, on the ramp leading into the back of the truck, stared at the pile inside, and said, "Oh my God, oh my God, oh my God." Then she said, "Why don't we take a break for a while," to Jimmy and Chris, and went in the house to sit, curled in a ball, in the spot where her bed used to be.

She'd come out of the house when Dale drove up.

"You can't take my children," he was saying. I waited for Mom to remind him that I wasn't his child.

"Can't you see Satan at work here?" Grandma Evelyn said. "He wants the children." She was such a phony; of course she was only interested in Rona. "Come here, Rona," she said. Rona was standing behind Mom's legs, sucking her thumb.

"Rona Margaret!" said Grandma Evelyn.

"Evelyn," said Mom, *"please."*

"Come here, dear," Grandma Evelyn said, and she undid the snap of her purse so Rona would think she had something good in there—one of those round metal things full of tiny candies she would give out one of sometimes, or a piece of gum. Poor Rona walked right over. As soon as she was close, Grandma Evelyn grabbed her like a hostage.

"Oh, for God's sake!" Mom said. "Dale!"

Dale had dropped to his knees in the driveway, and he was wailing and stretching his clasped hands up to Jesus like a freakin idiot.

"Hey, Colleen." That was Jimmy. He and Chris had finished their lunch and their cigarettes. "You want us to get the rest of this stuff in the truck or what?"

I was waiting for Mom to tell them to unload the truck and take everything back in the house. What I was thinking—and I wanted to say it in a loud voice, to everyone, except I didn't feel like getting punched again—was that this whole day seemed like excellent proof God didn't exist. Because if he did, why would he have put grown-ups in charge of life?

"I won't give you any money," Dale said to Mom.

"I know you won't," Mom replied. Her eyes were flat and dry as stones. "I don't need your money. We'll be fine."

I was hoping Mom would say more about money besides that we'd be fine—like how much we had, how much it was going to take to get to Massachusetts, where we would get more when we ran out. I'd collected all the money I could find—forty-three dollars from Rona's and my room, a twenty that Grandma had given me, three thirty-five in change that I'd found lying around in cracks and jars and pockets, some Italian coins Grandma had given me after her trip there last year, and a receipt for fifty dollars of credit at the Gap I found in an old purse of Mom's, but I was still worried.

Mom's system of money was different from other people's, and sometimes it confused me. It seemed like it should be simple: money was about math, and math was about facts. But Mom had a way of taking facts and mushing them into kind of a paste of feelings, turning them into something that made her cry or stare at the wall and say she never should have been born.

An electric bill, for example, was a fact. So was money, and the two things were related: you got the money, and you paid the electric bill with it. At least, that's what I would do if I were a grown-up.

But when Mom got the electric bill, first she would set the envelope on the hall table and look at it like it was a tarantula every time she walked by. After a few days, she'd pick it up and put it someplace where she couldn't see it. Then one night, when she was going through all the papers she'd put where she wouldn't have to see them, she'd run into it again. "I don't have the money to pay this!" she'd wail, and she'd start to cry, and on the weekend we'd have another garage sale.

Once Grandpa Victor called Mom "fluff-brain" right in front of us, but I knew she wasn't stupid. She had gone to West Mar High School, and two different colleges, and she had almost gotten a degree in graphic arts. What I thought was, you had to have a good imagination to get Mom. And maybe that was the key to understanding her money system—you had to try to figure out the special way things made sense inside her brain.

For example, Fake-Aunt Paula sent Mom a card for her birthday. When Mom opened it, a fifty floated out. Mom stared for a second, then she said, "Oh, my gosh. Why did she do this? She didn't have to do this!"

I knew why Fake-Aunt Paula had sent the fifty—because when she'd called the week before, Mom had said to her, "Oh, I'm sure we'll be okay. We always are. It's just that right now, I don't even have the money to pay the electric bill and I don't have any food in the house for the kids."

The electric bill had been sitting on the hall table, under the phone bill, for a long time—since before this guy, Eric, a guitar player Mom had known a long time ago and hadn't talked to in ten years, called to say his new band had some shows near us and could they stay at our house.

The day after they called, Mom went out and bought a huge turkey, since Eric had told her how sad it was that the band had missed Thanksgiving, being on the road. She also bought steaks for the grill; Gardenburgers and portobello mushrooms in case any of them were vegetarians; five different flavors of ice cream so there'd be something for everyone; four different kinds of beer; whiskey, because a band always had to have whiskey; champagne, because it had been so long since she'd seen them; seltzer, soda, juice, and nonalcoholic beer in case any of them were on the wagon; seven tiny boxes of Godiva chocolates so we could pretend we were a hotel and put them on their pillows the first night; and a can of paint to paint the hallway so it would look nice for our guests.

That—if you looked at things the way most people would look at them—was what happened to the electric bill money. But maybe in Mom's mind, things looked different. Maybe she had the money broken into separate categories. Maybe the electric bill, milk, bologna, and bread money was different money. Maybe it was the *next* money we were going to get, after we spent all the money we had on the band.

Dale had gotten off his knees, and he was standing in front of Mom. "I don't know why you're doing this," he said.

"You don't know why I'm doing this," Mom repeated.

As I watched them, I had the sudden feeling that I had slipped into a crack in life, a place that was right in between everything: our old house was empty now, and there was no new one yet; maybe we would see Dale again, maybe not. Mom might be right about there being enough money, or maybe she wasn't; maybe we would get to Massachusetts without anything bad happening. Mom looked small to me suddenly, standing next to the truck; and three thousand miles, which I knew was the distance we had to drive, seemed like such a huge space to head off into the middle of.

"Well, anyway, you can't stop me," she said. It was a weird thing to say, because we all knew that wasn't true: Dale could let the air out of the truck tires; he could come over in the middle of the night, break down the door, and steal the money and the credit cards; he could take Rona and me hostage.

The next morning, though, Dale didn't show up at all. Grandma Bobbie was the only one who came to say good-bye. It was early, about six o'clock, and she just stood there crying and saying, "I am *not* going to cry."

"I'm going to miss you!" she said to Rona and me, taking our faces in her hands. "I'm going to worry about you! I'm going to miss seeing how big you get every week, and hearing about everything you learn in school." To Mom she said, "I'll miss you, honey. Please, please try to . . ." But then she just looked at Mom and gave her a hug that lasted a long time.

I wished she had finished what she was going to say. Whatever it was, I would remember it, even if it was something I didn't understand. I would probably write it down, actually, in case it was something important, like the key to happiness or the thing that was going to make our new life work out okay.

Or maybe it was nothing. Maybe all Grandma was going to say was, "Please, please try to remember to moisturize your skin every day," or, "Write to me a lot." Because, of course, I knew: Life doesn't work that way—the truth about things never just comes waltzing out of someone's mouth through a smile-shaped opening. I gave up on listening for Grandma's advice, and I let her kiss me good-bye again and got in the truck next to Rona.

"Say good-bye to the ocean," Mom said a little while later, when we turned onto Alameda. I looked toward it; the sun was just coming up, and the water wasn't sparkling yet; it was just lying there, like something breathing softly in its sleep.

"Bye, ocean," said Rona gaily.

"Where's the map?" I said.

"My God," Mom was saying, "I can't believe they let people like me drive these things!" I could see the ocean, stretching out alongside of us, into the distance. We were supposed to be headed for the desert.

"We need to go to Highway 15," I said. Grandma had ordered a bunch of AAA books and maps for our trip and given them to Mom, but Mom had just thrown them on top of one of the boxes in the living room. I'd opened them up and looked at them, though. I'd gotten out my notebook, actually, and written down the names of all the roads, in order, that led to Massachusetts.

"Where's the map?" I asked Mom again. I'd put the Western United States one on top of the last pile of stuff that was supposed to come with us in the front seat, and now it wasn't there.

"The ocean looks just beautiful today," she said.

"This isn't the right way," I said to Mom.

Just then, as if it felt exactly the way I did, the cat, whom it had taken us about an hour to catch that morning and was now in a carrier under Rona's feet, started to make the weirdest noise. I could tell, watching it that morning as it slunk from room to room, with Rona following it, trying to grab it, and Mom chirping to it, "*Time* to go to *Massachusetts!*" that it couldn't believe its life.

The sound it was making was like nothing I had ever heard before. It was like the hugest sadness and fear in the world blurting out of the cat's mouth; it was like a black hole—as if the fear and sadness had its own gravity so huge that it sucked a hole out of the universe, became a place so real, it didn't even exist, in a weird way.

"Wowee," said Mom.

"What's wrong with it?" asked Rona, worried.

"You better be quiet," Mom joked to the cat, "or we'll stop and let you out."

"No!" Rona said.

"You never know"—Mom winked toward the carrying case—"we might get awfully hungry on our way to Massachusetts."

"Mom!" Rona screeched.

"We need to go back," I said. "We need to get the map."

"Oh, honey," said Mom. "Just let it go." She smiled reassuringly at me. "We'll be fine," she said, and she kept on heading in the wrong direction.

"Shouldn't we get a map?" I asked Thaddeus again today. I've asked him a bunch of times—all he has is a piece of paper with words printed on it: "Jobs in California! Big sale on farmland! Come one come all!"

"Hush!" he said finally. "It's not for you to worry about. I got directions from a man."

"Well, I'd still like to have a map," I told him. I like maps. "Maybe I'll drive to Amherst tomorrow and see if I can find one."

"There's no time for that!" he said. "Don't you have candles and soap to make? Don't you have apples to dry?"

But I like a map—I like seeing all the roads and how they connect, where the towns are, and the number of miles from one to another; I like the tiny pictures of landmarks. Landmarks that tell you where you are, like furniture, when you wake up in the dark, confused: the bedside table you can reach with your outstretched arm, the rocking chair right next to the door; the mirror halfway down the hallway; the bump in the carpet just outside your mother's door when you were little and went looking for her in the night.

"I'd just feel so much better with a map," I said.

"I'll draw you a freakin map!" he said. He pulled a pencil out of his pocket, tore my ladies' book out of my hands, jabbed the pencil lead into its cover, and drew a straight line, scarring the paper, all the way from one end to the other.

"Massachusetts," he said, stabbing the lead at one end of the line. "California," he named the other. "All right?" he said. "We just follow the ruts. We have faith in God. Do you have a problem with that?"

IRISH TWINS

The cat lasted till Utah, where we almost stayed, too, even though we almost didn't stop at all. The plan was, we were going to stop and visit Aunt Bridget, who lived there now and who we hadn't seen in a really long time, except for a few minutes two years ago at Easter, when she came to visit Grandma Bobbie.

Mom didn't call Aunt Bridget till the night before we left, though. "We'll be there Tuesday sometime in the afternoon," she said. But as soon as we saw the sign that said "Leaving Nevada, Welcome to Utah," Mom started talking to herself.

"We don't have to stop if we don't really want to. What would you like to do, Justine? I could always say you girls just wanted to go on and get settled before school starts. Rona, what do *you* think?"

The last time we'd seen Aunt Bridget, the day we went over to Grandma's on Easter, she and Mom had hugged each other and sat down at the kitchen table with big iced teas and started gabbing. I went to the living room, which was just around the open doorway. I had a book, but I didn't open it.

A few times that I can remember, Mom and Aunt Bridget had a conversation where nothing went wrong, but that was when I was pretty little. Sometimes, back then, lying in my bed at night, listening to them, I couldn't tell their voices apart. They sounded like one person to me—someone asking herself questions in a soft voice and answering them, making herself laugh, someone who was her own best friend. Once, when Rona was still a baby and she was in bed with me, sleeping with her soft, bald head right up against my cheek, I fell asleep listening to Mom and Aunt Bridget talking softly in the other room, and I dreamed that Rona's breath on my neck was a hot wind and I was walking through the desert. Only it wasn't the scary kind of desert, with snakes and scorpions and the bones of things that had died lying around—it was a beautiful one, like the postcard on our refrigerator: the sand was light orange; the sky was bright blue; tall cactuses with red and yellow flowers as big as babies' heads blooming out of them grew in clumps in front of the sky. I always hoped I'd have that dream again—whenever Mom and Aunt Bridget talked at night, I'd close my eyes and try, but I never did.

The day Aunt Bridget and Mom sat down with the iced teas at Grandma's, their conversation only lasted about one minute. Aunt Bridget asked Mom how she was.

"Good," Mom said. "I quit my job."

"You did?" asked Aunt Bridget. "Why?"

"Because Dale wanted me to."

"What kind of a reason is that?" Aunt Bridget said. "Colleen, that's ridiculous."

Suddenly Mom was in the living room doorway.

"Get your sister," she said to me. "We're going."

"Oh, for God's sake," said Bridget.

Grandma Bobbie came in, too. "Now, Colleen; now, Bridget," she said.

"I just can't say anything to you, can I?" Mom snapped at Aunt Bridget as she headed for the door.

"Sure you can. You can say anything you want," Aunt Bridget answered. "Just don't expect me to say, 'Oh, that's nice, Colleen,' when you tell me you're handing your life over on a silver platter to some out-of-control, abusive nut job."

The ride home was completely silent, except for when Rona pulled her thumb out of her mouth and said, "Outer control abusive nut job." Mom swerved the car over to the side of the road, slammed on the brakes, then she turned around and said, "Don't you *ever* say that again, do you hear me?"

"Okay," I answered, even though I hadn't been the one to say it, and she screeched back onto the road again.

* * *

Mom changed and unchanged her mind about whether we were going to stop all the way to Salt Lake City, while I looked out the window at the desert, which it seemed like we had been driving through forever. It wasn't like the desert in my dream. There was nothing in it but fences and dirt, and some dusty-looking clumps of plants, and the far-off brown mountains, and, about once every twenty miles, one lonely, twisted tree.

"I'm hungry," Rona whined. It was really hot inside the truck, because every time we turned on the air conditioner, the red temperature needle started to go up, so we couldn't use it. Mom was humming to the radio.

"Can't we at least stop and get something to drink?" I asked. It was a stupid question; there was nothing, as far as the eye could see. Mom pretended not to hear. Then suddenly she said, "It's just like being pioneers! Traveling across the country all day with no food or water."

That was before we studied the pioneers at my new school, so I didn't answer her like I would now: There were a few things wrong with that idea. One, the pioneers weren't stupid. They didn't just get in some crappy wagon and set off across the country with their kids and animals and no food or water or plan, like, Oh, we'll see what happens. Look! Billy Bragg just *happens* to be playing in Fresno on the second; we might as well go that way instead. And actually, don't we know someone in Reno?—since we're almost up there anyway, why don't we swing by and see if we can take him to lunch, even if it does add eight hundred miles to our trip, overheat the truck engine, and max out the credit card?

The pioneers would prepare for up to a year, collecting tools and clothes, preserving food, saving money, choosing what to bring and what to leave, saying good-bye to their friends and families. And if they *did* run out of food and water on the trail, they wouldn't act like it was some fun adventure. Another thing Mom got wrong was—duh— we were going the wrong way. West to east—if we were pioneers, we'd be traveling backwards.

Finally, we saw tall mountains and the pollution of a city in the distance.

"There it is!" Mom said, then she said, "Oh God, I don't know." When we saw the exit Aunt Bridget told us to take, Mom almost drove the truck off the road, going, "Should we? We should. Maybe we shouldn't," and turning the steering wheel every time she changed her mind.

Finally I said, "Take the exit," not because I cared so much whether or not we stopped, but because, looking at Rona beside me— her eyes huge and her cheeks all hollow from sucking her thumb so hard—and listening to the trucks zooming past us in the other lane, feeling our truck going left, right, left, right, I suddenly felt sorry for her, and for me, too, picturing us dying in a big wreck right there underneath a picture of a huge chicken potpie on a billboard for Marie Callender's.

Mom looked at me for a split second, then we were on the exit. "Okay," she sighed, as if I'd just told her to jump out of an airplane, "if you really want to." I took the directions from the window visor and unfolded them. "Does anyone want to stop for lunch?" Mom asked. "A soda? Anyone need to go to the bathroom? Maybe we should try to find a flower shop. We really shouldn't arrive empty-handed."

"Who's that?" said Rona when Aunt Bridget came to the door. Aunt Bridget had red hair now. She stood in the doorway looking like she didn't know if she wanted to come out, which Mom didn't see, because she was trying to park the truck. A minute later, though, when she looked over and saw Aunt Bridget, Mom got the same look on her face.

The cat was the first one out of the truck. It clawed its way off Rona's lap and out her half-open door and ran into the bushes.

"Oh, no!" screamed Rona.

"Oh, honey!" Mom said. "I *told* you not to let it out of its case!"

"But we were stopped!" Rona wailed.

"*Shitfuckdamnhellpissandcorruption*," Mom said under her breath. I knew it wasn't a good time to point out to Mom that it had been her extremely bad idea to get the cat in the first place. I had been trying to imagine, on the trip, what the cat was thinking about its life: it had come to our house in a box, gotten dragged around by Rona whenever she could catch it, which wasn't very often, because after about the second day, the cat would trot away fast whenever it saw any of us coming. Sometimes it got cat food, if Mom remembered to buy a can, but usually it got something else: old cream cheese balls—"A little mold won't hurt a cat!" according to Mom—or eggs, which it didn't like, or Cambozola cheese, which it liked a lot, though Mom almost killed Rona when she came out of her room and saw the cat's face in the wrapper; and one night, probably the low point of its life, Mom had made it "kitty pesto" out of the end of a package of Chee-tos that she threw in the food processor with some oil. Then it had gotten shoved in a cage and stuck on the floor of a hot, rumbling truck with Rona's feet on top of it. And since it didn't understand human talk, it didn't get the so-called benefit of hearing Mom talk nonstop about how great all our lives were going to be when we got to Massachusetts.

Rona ran right past Aunt Bridget, yelling, "Cat! Cat!" She'd changed its name so many times, she didn't know what to call it.

"Justine!" Aunt Bridget said. She hugged me first. Then she said, "Colleen!" and for a second neither one of them moved. When they hugged each other, something weird happened: with their faces close together like that, the two of them squeezed into such a small space, you could see how much alike they looked, and just for a second, Mom looked completely different to me than she always did. She looked like someone who suddenly made sense, who wasn't so mysteriously different from every other human being in the world. Then she stepped back, and she just looked the same as she always did.

Across the street, I noticed, a little girl stood watching us from behind a metal fence. When I came back from taking the cooler to the house, she had come out from behind the fence, and she was sitting on the sidewalk with her feet in the gutter.

"There's Merilee," said Aunt Bridget. I wasn't sure what she was talking about, because I had never heard of that name before. "Hi, Merilee!" Aunt Bridget called. The girl jumped up and ran over to us.

"Oh!" Mom said, beaming at her and then at me. "A friend for you two!" Which sounded like another one of her bad ideas—Mom had already told Aunt Bridget on the phone we were only staying overnight or till Thursday at the latest.

"Hi," Merilee said. She looked closer to Rona's age than to mine.

She could be Rona's friend—Rona didn't remember things very long after they were gone.

"What's that girl doing?" Merilee asked, looking over at Rona, who was kneeling at the edge of the bushes.

"That's Rona," I told her. "She lost her cat."

"No, she didn't," Mom smiled at Merilee. "It's just stretching its legs."

Rona noticed Merilee and came running over. "Who's that?" she asked me, staring at Merilee.

"I'm Merilee Monson," Merilee said. "I don't have a middle name because when I grow up and get married then I will."

Merilee was just like a little grown-up, I could see as soon as she started talking. Grown-ups love to talk to people they've just met about anything that comes into their heads. We sat down on the dry, crackly grass, and Merilee told us about her school, her teacher from last year, her best friend, a TV show she had watched the night before, her brothers and sisters. There were seven of them not including her, and their names all started with M—that part was actually sort of interesting, though it seemed like they had run out of normal ones by the end, because the youngest ones were named Misty, Marimba, and McDoogle, or at least that's what it sounded like when she listed them all, really fast, like a person saying the Pledge of Allegiance. Her dog was named Moroni, after the golden angel that stood on top of the Mormon church.

"When the world ends, we're all going to get sucked up into his horn and taken to the Celestial Kingdom," she said.

"I don't want to," said Rona, twisting a piece of her hair.

"Are you Mormon?" Merilee asked. Rona looked at me.

"No," I told her. Mom had told us about Mormons on the way to Utah. It was a religion that couldn't drink coffee, Coke, or beer or smoke cigarettes; their mascot was the bee; and the men talked to God and then told the people who God wanted them to vote for, and not to be gay, and things like that.

"Then you don't get to anyway," said Merilee. "You have to go live with Satan on the moon." Rona stuck her thumb in her mouth.

"We get our own planet," Merilee said. "With everyone who's ever been in our family. We get to live there forever. "

I wondered if Merilee had made that up or if everyone in her religion believed it, even the grown-ups. I didn't feel like telling her: I had had the idea of planets a long time ago. I can't remember when I started to imagine that every man we met was like a planet Mom had discovered and was trying to take us to live. What was different from the Mormon planets, though, was that the boyfriends didn't live on the planets—they *were* the planets. Which meant that when we got there, we were still alone. We'd wander around, trying to think of something to do, somewhere to go, but they were boring places, mostly—stupid and small: you could walk around them in a week and be back where you started. Except for Dale—the Dale planet was big; it was the place where Rona was born, and we had actually spent almost four whole years, but that didn't stop us from falling right off the face of our life there, as if there were no gravity at all, as if Dale were just a big blob of dirt nothing could stick to.

Merilee was still smiling, thinking about her planet. Across the street, Merilee's mother stuck her head out the door. Merilee jumped up. "Bye!" she said. "I've got to go do chores! But I'll come over tomorrow after I get back from getting baptized for the dead!"

"I don't want the world to end," Rona said as soon as Merilee was gone. She sounded like she was getting ready to cry.

"Don't listen to her, she's a freak," I said, but Rona said, "She is not," and sat there staring, with her thumb in her mouth, at the front door of Merilee's house.

The next afternoon, we were still in Utah.

"How long are we staying?" I asked Mom.

"I don't know," Mom answered. "How long would you like to stay?" Then she said, "Why don't you come help me get a few things out of the back of the truck."

So far, we had been in Utah twenty-seven hours and Mom and Aunt Bridget hadn't had a fight yet. They'd even talked about Dale and nothing bad had happened. The night before, their voices had floated down the stairs to our room in the basement.

"You were right about Dale," Mom said to Aunt Bridget.

"Well, it's not like I wanted to be right, you know," Aunt Bridget said. Then she said, "You're a strong woman, Colleen. You don't need him to get by," and Mom had said very softly, "I know."

You know the way it feels when you're lying in bed at night and suddenly you can feel yourself sliding across the line from awake to asleep? Especially if someone's talking or reading to you—you can hear their voice, soft and steady like dripping water, and you can see their words sometimes, in beautiful, clear pictures, and your brain suddenly understands things, for one second, that you never understood before.

That's how I felt when Aunt Bridget said, "You're a strong woman, Colleen." *Strong*, I heard as I slipped over into dream thoughts, and suddenly everything was *strong*—the smell of the air, the color of the designs I could see inside my closed eyes; it was the name of the taste inside my mouth and the feel of my skin where the sheet was touching it. Even the silence, when Mom and Aunt Bridget's talking stopped, sounded strong.

When I went upstairs the next day, though, Mom was still just Mom, and even though I tried, I couldn't remember the half-dreaming feeling.

When I was awake, *strong* confused me. You heard people—Aunt Bridget, Grandma, Mom, Oprah—talk about strong women a lot: "So-and-so is such a *strong* woman," they'd say about someone whose husband had gotten a new girlfriend, or who had gone to college when she was Grandma's age, or had her stomach stapled and lost two hundred pounds.

The day Dale broke everything that still worked and said he was leaving and never coming back, Mom yelled, "Fine! I am a strong woman!"

"I will get through this!" she yelled as we listened to the car screeching backwards out of the driveway; then she went into her room to cry. Or if a song about strong women came on the radio, she'd throw her arms straight up in the air and shake her body and yell along.

I didn't get it. It seemed like, according to everybody, all you had to do to be a strong woman was to stay alive—not die every single time something bad happened to you—and that seemed bogus. It was like your teacher giving the whole class As and then saying everyone was smart. If no one was weak, if you weren't allowed to say the word or even think it, then strong didn't really mean all that much, did it?

It made me nervous, thinking about everyone being strong. Because what if you didn't turn out to be? Would there still be a category of human life for you?

"Do you know what you'd like for lunch, honey?" Mom asked me. She was standing in the doorway holding our giant suitcase she'd gotten out of the back of the truck, the one that had the stuff in it she'd said we wouldn't need till we got to Massachusetts. It had taken both Jimmy and Chris to lift the suitcase in, but she'd lugged it all the way up the walk by herself. She was standing there holding the suitcase in front of her with her wrists bent, as if she were lifting iron weights.

"So are we leaving tomorrow?" I asked.

"What's your hurry, Justine?" she said.

The next day Mom said, "Bridget, maybe you and Mark could show us around Utah this weekend."

Mark was Aunt Bridget's boyfriend. The day we got to Utah, Mark had pulled his car into the driveway around six o'clock and come over to where we were sitting on the porch. He had a bunch of clothes from the dry cleaner's in his arms.

"You must be Colleen and Justine and Rona," he said to us, and he smiled. "Welcome to Utah."

"I picked up your cleaning," he said to Aunt Bridget.

I watched Mom's face. Her eyes were glittery like a bird's, and I knew what she was doing: she was noticing every single thing about him—the color of his hair and eyes and skin, how tall he was, what he was wearing, the size of his hands, the shape of his face, the structure of his facial bones, the length of his eyelashes, whether he had any moles, scars, or birthmarks, the fabric his shirt was made of, the style of shoes he had on, the name of the jeans he was wearing.

After Mark had said hello to me and Rona, he said to Aunt Bridget, "Why don't you give me a call when everyone's all settled in?" Then he gave her a kiss on the cheek and left.

"He seems like a great guy," Mom said as soon as Mark's car door shut.

"Yep, he is," Aunt Bridget nodded.

Later, when Mom and Aunt Bridget were cleaning up the kitchen after dinner, I heard Mom ask, "So what's the deal with Mark?"

"Deal?" said Aunt Bridget.

"Well, you know," Mom said. "Are you two serious?"

"Yeah, pretty serious," Aunt Bridget said. "We've been seeing each other almost a year and a half." Her voice was so normal, it was weird. When Mom talked about men, her voice got funny, looping in and out and around and around and all over the place, like a flock of birds that had gotten lost on their way to South America.

"Will he come back tonight?" Mom asked.

"Probably not," said Aunt Bridget.

"Oh!" Mom's voice was worried. "I hope we didn't scare him away!"

"Oh, no," said Aunt Bridget. "We both have to work early tomorrow anyway."

There was a long silence from Mom, then she said, "Huh . . . ," as if Aunt Bridget had said something too complicated for her to figure out.

Mark came over for dinner on Friday night and stayed for a sleepover. I liked him, so far. There didn't seem to be anything wrong with him. I was getting a pretty good sense about how to tell losers. Maybe I was developing *intuition*, which according to Grandma Bobbie is the stuff you just sort of *know* and don't know how you know, because no one ever taught it to you. It was something you just *got* at a certain age, she said, which made it sound sort of like your period, but in your brain. Loser ID felt like a form of intuition to me. Unless it was just a quality I was born with, like good eyesight, and being good at math, in which case I'd probably gotten it from Timothy Walker.

There were a few ways to meet losers that I knew of. Guys who were invited to be an odd or an end at Fake-Aunt Paula's holiday parties for people who didn't have anywhere else to go—which we went to if Mom was mad at Grandma Bobbie—were usually losers. Fake-Aunt Paula always made them sit next to Mom. Usually they were artists, poets, or musicians, and they would tell Mom all about themselves all night long: how they were going through a phase of eating

healthy, getting rid of material possessions, and they were very interested in the idea of communal living, which I heard Aunt Bridget tell
Mom once just meant they didn't have any money to take Mom out to
restaurants, they were selling everything they owned to pay their rent,
and they lived with a lot of roommates.

Church was a good place to meet losers, too, I learned after Dale
got so-called saved. Every Wednesday his new "friends" would come
over and follow Dale down into the basement like he was God Jr. to
play guitars and sing stupid churchy songs all night, and the men reminded me of those zombies from old movies, with spirals painted on
their eyeballs, and the ladies had weird hair and smiled at you like they
wanted to eat you.

Another way to meet losers—I almost forgot—was if you liked
someone, to go out with one of their friends instead. That was the way
we met Dale, I figured out, from hearing Mom and Aunt Bridget having a fight a long time ago. Mom liked the guitar player, but the bass
player was the only one who didn't have a girlfriend.

" 'The Great Salt Lake was once part of a vast, ancient lake that
covered the entire Salt Lake Valley,' " Mom read from the map as
Aunt Bridget drove through downtown on Saturday morning. "Isn't
that interesting, girls?"

Mom was sitting in the front with Aunt Bridget, and Mark, Rona,
and I were in the back. When we were getting in the car, Mark had
said, "You get in the front, Colleen."

"Oh, no, no, no, no, no, no, no, no," Mom said. "You two should
sit together!"

But Aunt Bridget had said, "Just get in, Colleen," and Mark
climbed into the back with me and Rona before Mom could stop him.
As we drove, Mom kept turning her head to talk to Mark, except she
was trying to talk to Aunt Bridget at the same time, so everything she
said came out weird.

"Bridget, do you guys like living here? Mark?" Her head was facing Bridget, but her body was turned almost backwards in the seat.

"Oh, my!" she said, peering out the window. "Look, girls, there's
the famous Mormon temple!" It wasn't as fancy as I thought it would
be: just a big gray building you almost didn't see, standing behind a

skyscraper. There, on the top, was the golden angel Merilee's dog was named after. He wasn't what I was expecting, either. When I saw his skinny little horn—the one that all the Mormons were supposedly going to get sucked into at the end of the world—all I could picture was a huge long line, like at the supermarket at dinnertime, everyone in it getting crankier and crankier as they watched the people in front of them trying to climb into the little thing, and the fat ones having to get squeezed and tucked and shoved inside, before finally disappearing with a big sucking *pop!*

"Are we in hell?" Rona asked when we got near the lake. Aunt Bridget's air conditioner was broken; the car windows were down, and a hot wind was blowing in. The grown-ups all laughed, so Rona acted like she'd made a joke on purpose, but I guessed she was still thinking about what Merilee had said. It did look a little like the moon outside the car—there were no craters, obviously, but the ground was a weird colorless color, a place where nothing grew, and the air was so hot you could barely breathe it.

"Mark," Mom was saying, "do you need more legroom?" though she was already jammed up as close to the dashboard as she could go in the tiny front seat. "Would anyone like a soda from the cooler? Mark?"

Out my window, I could see that the lake, which had been far away in the distance for a long time, was now right alongside of us. But Aunt Bridget just kept driving. I wondered if it was going to start looking like a normal lake soon. The water just looked like miles and miles of mirror-colored flatness, and I didn't see any beach, though Mom had said at least fifty times that morning how exciting it was that we were going to the beach.

Suddenly, though, Aunt Bridget said, "Finally!" and pulled off the road into a parking lot.

"Wow!" Mom said, opening her door. "That is *really something!*" We all piled out, and I went to the edge of the parking lot to see what they were talking about.

The beach was huge, and grayish white, and perfectly flat, and when you stepped on it you found out it wasn't made of sand, but a kind of hard mud with a white crust on it.

"It smells bad here," said Rona.

"Look, girls! Brine flies!" Mom said, pointing to a big black cloud of bugs coming toward us. "I just read about them. They're a vital part of the lake's ecology."

"What's wrong with this lake?" I asked.

"Justine," she answered, "please don't be negative." I hadn't said it to be negative—there really was something wrong with the lake, and after a few minutes I figured out what it was: The water didn't get deep like at a regular lake. There were people walking all over the lake—not just close to shore, but everywhere. The water was like a big, wide prairie, and there were people trudging around in it, like, two miles away, still trying to get to the spot where it was deep enough to dive in.

It was making me feel sort of worried, actually. I was wondering if people ever got lost, wandering so far out in the ankle-deep water that when they finally remembered to look up, they couldn't see the shore, or their car, or their kids, or their tiny towels laid down on the crusty mud anymore—just water all around them and the dry, brown mountains, which were the exact color of the ugliest crayon in the Crayola box, raw umber, in the far distance.

"Well, I'm going in," Mom said when we had walked down the flat, hard mud to the water. "Is anyone going to get in with me?" No one said anything.

"Race you to the other side," she said, for a joke. "Oh, come on. Nobody?" Then she said, "Well, I for one am going to bob like a cork! Did you know that the Great Salt Lake is four to five times more salty than the ocean? That makes your body lots more buoyant than in regular water—they say you can't sink even if you try."

I had to admit, that sounded pretty interesting. Floating was something I'd never been able to do. I wasn't afraid of lots of the things other kids were afraid of—snakes, bees, rapists, kidnappers, tornadoes, earthquakes—but there were a few things that gave me the creeps, and floating was one of them. I'd been afraid of floating ever since the first time Mom tried to teach me, in the ocean. Every time, she'd hold her hand under my back and say, "I won't drop you, I promise," but every time, she lied. She'd drop her hand away and I'd sink right under; then, when I came up choking and panicking, she'd say, "Oh, Justine, you're just being stubborn. You're not giving it a real try."

So I was thinking that day that maybe if Mom and I walked all the way out to where the water in that stupid lake was deep enough to float, about four or five hours from shore, finally I'd be able to do it, and she'd be happy, and we'd have a nice time, bobbing side by side like corks. And anyway, there was no way I was going to let Mom take off across the lake alone. I took off my flip-flops and followed her into the water.

"Wait!" yelled Rona, and she splashed into the lake, but as soon as she did, she got a horrible look on her face and started to scream.

"What is it? What is it?" the grown-ups all cried. She lifted her foot out of the water and pointed, sobbing, to a little red dot the size of a pinprick.

"Oh, poor baby, the salt can really sting if you have a cut or a sore," Aunt Bridget explained. Rona had climbed up Mom's body and was clinging to her like a baby monkey. Aunt Bridget reached out her arms.

"Come on, sweetie," she said, then she said to Mom, "You guys go ahead. We'll stay here and play in the sand." Mark looked like he didn't know what to do. I saw Aunt Bridget tip her head in our direction, and Mark nodded and stepped our way, like an intelligent, obedient dog.

"Mark," Mom said as soon as we started walking, "where exactly outside of Chicago did you grow up? Do you have any siblings?"

I'd decided I definitely liked Mark a lot. I liked the way his voice sounded when he talked to Mom—quiet and slow and always ending with a question, like someone stepping out of the way, and not the way men usually sounded to me: like they had a wheelbarrow full of bricks they had to push somewhere in a hurry.

"Can you tell me exactly what you do in your job, Mark?" Mom was saying as we walked and walked. "It sounded fascinating, the little you mentioned. Where did you go to college? And tell me: How did you ever end up here in Utah?"

I hoped we didn't die of heatstroke before we made it to the floating place. I was having a bad feeling, trudging along behind Mom and

Mark. I couldn't exactly describe the feeling, but it had started in the car; and it was the same one I got when I looked at the little picture on the blow-dryer tag, the one trying to tell you, using only pictures, not to drop the blow-dryer in the bathtub.

I'd started thinking about mirages. About the way, when you saw them far away in the distance, they looked like water. That made me wonder: If a mirage on the sand looked like water, would a mirage on the water look like sand? For one second, that seemed like such a beautiful thought to me, two true things shining back and forth at each other like someone playing a game with mirrors, until I realized how stupid it was. It was like something a kid Rona's age would think.

"I'm so glad Bridget found you," Mom said. "You seem so good for her."

I wished she would stop talking.

"In fact," she said, "I hope you don't mind my saying this, but I think maybe she found the world's one perfect guy."

Even if I hadn't been watching Mark's face, so that I could see the way his eyes sort of came to a screeching halt inside his head, like Roadrunner at the edge of a cliff, I knew it was an embarrassing thing to say to someone.

Watching Mom, smiling and gazing at Mark, I could see exactly what was going to happen—the idea of Mark was going to blink on in-side Mom's brain, like a star being born in the universe, and it would need a whole story, like a constellation, to go along with it. And that story, of course, would be our story, changing once again. And since Mark already had a girlfriend, who happened to be Mom's sister, I didn't think it would turn out to be such a great one, either.

Unless maybe there was something I didn't get. Maybe, I thought, as I watched Mom standing in the desert in sparkly water up to her shins, the sky bright blue around her blond head, the dull brown shape of the far-off mountains meeting the blue like a jigsaw puzzle, and Mark right there next to her like another piece of the puzzle, there was some other way of looking at things, besides trying to see how they made sense, that I didn't know about. Maybe there was some reason, bigger than my brain could handle, that I was here, in Utah, standing in the middle of a lake in the middle of a desert, watching my mom look at my aunt's boyfriend as if he were the answer to our dreams. I waited for understanding to start to glow like a sunrise around me, but nothing happened; and after a few seconds Mark said, "You know, I think I can feel myself getting a little sunburned, maybe we better get going."

The trip back from the lake didn't go very well, though I was the only one besides Mom who knew it. We'd finally given up on the floating idea; walking back, Mom had been smiling and laughing, talking to Mark nonstop. Her mood, as we trudged back toward the shore, was getting better and better, like a balloon getting blown up too far. By the time we got to the car, I was almost jumping out of my skin. Because I knew that with Mom, happiness had an opposite that went with it, something that was always there underneath, though you wished it weren't, like the ugly olive green side of the reversible poncho Grandma brought me from Mexico.

When we got in the car, Mom leaned her head back against the seat and smiled. "Thank you, Bridget and Mark," she said, "for showing me this magnificent place."

"The salt flats are so *fascinating*!" she said as we headed back onto the highway. "The desert is so *alive*. Oh, look! Is that a *tumbleweed*? How *wonderful*!"

"Look at the Mormons!" she said as we drove back through town. "They're all so blond and healthy looking! Look at the big wide streets! Look at the mountains!"

I could tell by the look of Mom's smiling, laughing face that the unhappiness had already started, even if she couldn't feel it yet—that as soon as the other grown-ups had gone to do something else, and it was just us, in our room in the basement, and Mom thought Rona and I were asleep, she'd pick up the remote control and surf to all the weird channels and just sit there staring at the lady with the ab machine or the zircon diamond earrings, letting tears fall out of her eyes.

Aunt Bridget was driving, and Mom was in the front seat, and Mark was in the back with Rona and me, just like on the way out. Mom kept turning around to ask Mark if he was sure he was comfortable, and telling him how nice he was to entertain us when he must be so busy, and what a great state he had chosen to live in.

Suddenly Aunt Bridget turned to Mom and said, "Colleen, why

don't you just hop in the backseat with him; I wouldn't want you to get a kink in your neck."

If it were a fairy tale, all the clocks would stop and Mom's face would turn to stone.

But Mark was smiling. "Yeah, come on," he said, and patted the seat. "You come, too, Bridget, there's room for everyone. Justine, you can climb up front and drive, can't you?" Rona giggled.

Mom wasn't smiling, though.

"I'm sorry, Bridget," she said.

"I'm just teasing," said Aunt Bridget. "Everybody flirts with Mark. I ought to be used to it by now. It's no big deal."

"Rona's been flirting with me all day," Mark said, and Rona giggled.

"Oh," Mom said, shaking her head over and over again.

As soon as we got out of the car at Aunt Bridget's, Mom said, "You know, all that sun seems to have given me a headache. Just leave all the unpacking for me to do later, Bridget, okay?" and she headed into the house and down the stairs.

"What's the matter with her?" Aunt Bridget asked me.

"I don't know," I answered, which was half-true. I *did* know, I just didn't know how to explain it. But then I realized, Aunt Bridget must know, too. After all, she had known Mom her whole life. They had been babies together, Irish twins, Grandma Bobbie said. I looked at her, trying to figure out if I was right, but I couldn't tell.

"Well," she said, "why don't you take her down some Advil?" and she got me some pills and a glass of water.

"Maybe I'll invite someone over tonight," she said, and she sounded like she was talking to herself, but she also looked at me, like she wanted to know what I thought of that.

"Who?" asked Mark.

"Greg," she said.

"Really?" Mark said, and he made sort of a face: pulled up one corner of his mouth and raised his eyebrows.

"Sometimes her headaches last a pretty long time," I said.

"What's wrong with Greg?" Aunt Bridget asked Mark.

"Nothing, I guess," he answered. He stood up and laid his hand on Aunt Bridget's shoulder.

"Sometimes they go away fast." That came out of my mouth without my knowing it was going to. I looked at Aunt Bridget and wished she could tell what I was thinking: I just wanted her to know what to do.

When I got downstairs, Mom was already in her bed under the covers.

"Here," I said, holding out the pills to her. She didn't even raise her head.

"You know, Justine, I really think they have true love," she said. "It's so wonderful."

"I have Advil," I said. I didn't know what I was supposed to say. Aunt Bridget and Mark hadn't kissed or anything in front of us. They hadn't said anything particularly lovey-dovey. In cartoons, the girl character's eyelashes would suddenly get really long and her eyes would start blinking fast, and the boy's heart would start to beat so hard you could see the outline of it jumping out of his chest, but I had no idea what true love looked like in real life.

Mom lifted her head. She looked like someone struggling to say her dying words. But she just took the Advil out of my hand and reached for the glass of water. On the other side of the bed, Rona had made a nest out of blankets.

"Come in here, Justine," Rona said, and even though it was still daytime, I got in next to her and lay there while she channel-surfed, as she called it, which meant she held the remote control and clicked through all the channels as fast as she could move her thumb. At first I said, "Hey!" every time she would go by something I wanted to see, then we both started to laugh because of the way it sounded—the TV switching channels every half a second and my voice going, "Hey! Hey! Hey! Hey!" like Grandma Bobbie's record of Russian folk songs.

After a while, our laughing made Mom sort of stick her head up and say, "You two goofballs—here, give it to me."

"No!" Rona said, but I pried the remote out of her hands and gave it to Mom, and after clicking a little bit, she found Judge Wapner, which made Rona and me laugh even more because it was our favorite kind of case—a lady whose hairdresser had burned off her hair. Even Mom smiled.

By the commercial, though, her smile had faded.

"You know the thing about true love, Justine?" she said. I pretended not to hear her.

"Mom, go to QVC," Rona said. She loved QVC, and we didn't know why. Mom switched the channel. They were selling stuff to fill driveway cracks with, and Rona stuck her thumb in her mouth and opened her eyes wide to watch it. "Can we get that?" she said.

"The thing is," Mom said, but then she looked at Rona and said, "What do you want that for? We don't even have a driveway, let alone a crack.

"The thing is . . . ," she started again, then she wailed, "Oh, God, I can't even remember the thing!" She looked at me, and suddenly—maybe it was the long day in the hot sun—I felt so tired, I wanted to lay my head down, too. Miraculously, though, she gave a little laugh.

"Shhhhhhh!" said Rona, turning to look at us with her eyebrows in an angry V, which made Mom laugh more, and I laughed, too.

"Knock knock," called Aunt Bridget. She'd come down the stairs and was standing in the doorway. "How's your headache, Colleen?"

"Oh," said Mom, "it's a little better. I'm going to just take it easy, though. Maybe I'll start packing. I guess we really ought to be getting back on the road."

"Huh," said Aunt Bridget. "Well, you know you're welcome to stay here as long as you like. Oh, I invited our friend Greg over for dinner. You can join us if you want, but don't feel like you have to."

I wondered if Aunt Bridget meant it, that we were welcome to stay. I wondered if she meant that she *wanted* us to stay. But all she said was, "Well, do what you want. I came down to see if anyone wants to go to the grocery store with me," and she smiled and headed back up the stairs.

"Justine," Aunt Bridget said when we were in the car on the way to the store. She clicked on the radio. She listened to the song for one second, then she clicked it off again.

"Your mom," she said. I waited, but two or three neighborhoods went by before she said anything else.

She looked over at me for a minute. People had started to do that to me, I'd noticed—hesitate, as if they were trying to remember how to speak in the language in between kid and grown-up, not remembering that there wasn't one.

"Jesus," Aunt Bridget finally said, "she just drives me crazy.

"I'm sorry," she said. "I know it's not fair to say that to you." Then she said, "There was a time, really long ago, when she and I were best friends. Can you believe it?"

"No," I answered. As I said it, though, a picture flashed by, so fast I didn't have time to look at it, really—I saw Mom and Bridget my age, or a little older than me, lying on top of their twin beds, listening to the radio and painting their fingernails and talking. Then the picture was gone, and all I could see was Mom's grown-up face, looking like she had never been a kid or a teenager, like she had never had a friend.

"Well, what happened?" I asked.

"I don't know," Aunt Bridget said, shaking her head. Then she said, "Aliens stole her brain." I felt bad for smiling.

"Did she ever tell you about the time we ran away from home?" Aunt Bridget asked.

"You did?" I said. "How old were you?"

I was picturing them little, like Rona and Merilee, making peanut-butter sandwiches and tying bandannas to the ends of sticks, but Aunt Bridget said, "We were teenagers. We threw a bunch of stuff in our backpacks and set off for Mexico. We hitchhiked all the way to San Ysidro before we turned around."

She thought for a minute, then she said, "You know the thing that bugs me the most? That Colleen doesn't even remember it.

"How can that be true?" she asked, but the way she said it, I knew she was talking to herself and not me. "She remembers the hitchhiking part; and that we slept on a golf course in La Jolla; and that we snuck into a bar and met these guys we thought were about sixty, but were probably really only about thirty; and that we let them take us out on their boat in the ocean, in the middle of the night—we're probably lucky to be alive, I might add. But the part about being so mad at your grandfather, and stealing all the money we could find in the house, and deciding we were going to get jobs and live in Baja—she doesn't remember any of that."

"Why were you so mad at Grandpa?"

"Actually," Aunt Bridget said, "Colleen was the one who was mad."

"What did he do?" I asked.

"It's kind of hard to explain," she said. Then she said, "No, maybe I should say it's hard to *understand*. He was just really awful to her, a lot of the time." She thought for a minute, then she shook her head. "It was like he always had to have an enemy, and for some reason, he picked her."

That seemed weird to me. Mom could be annoying sometimes, I knew, but she was also the Nicest Lady in the World. She would clean your entire house, or baby-sit your kids for free, or bring you home-made soup and a carton of your favorite cigarettes if she heard you were sick. She could drive you completely out of your mind most of the time, but how could you choose her for your enemy? Thinking about it gave me the same bad feeling I had gotten one time when I walked into the kitchen at Fake-Aunt Paula's New Year's Eve party and heard Mom's name: "Colleen Hanley?" And then Paula's mean sister, Nora, held up her fingers in a vampire-repelling cross and said, "Arrgh, get away from me, victim from hell," and everybody laughed, before they noticed I'd come in the room.

"Did Grandpa hate you, too?" I asked Aunt Bridget. Her answer wasn't what I expected.

"No," she said. "Or at least he left me alone. He scared me, so I always just did what he wanted. I never talked back. But Colleen *always* did. She wasn't afraid of him at all."

I guess I was looking at her like I didn't believe her, because she said, "I know—weird, huh?

"Colleen wasn't always like she is now, you know," Aunt Bridget said. "She used to have strong opinions about things and she'd just tell them to you. She used to know exactly what she wanted to do." I pictured Mom in a superhero suit—dashing into a phone booth the way she was now and bursting out of it with a strong opinion, a definite plan.

"She used to be smart, too," Aunt Bridget added. "Before she talked herself into believing she's not."

"Tell me some of the things she used to do," I said.

"Mmm," Aunt Bridget said, then she said, "Okay. But you can't tell her I told you. Though I'm sure if you do, she'll just say she doesn't remember. One day Colleen and I went to a picnic at the beach. A party. There was a keg there."

"What's a keg?" I asked.

"A big thing of beer," she answered.

"Oh, yeah," I said, as if I had just forgotten.

"Anyway, it was a typical party—we hung around on the beach, made a fire, laughed a lot, drank some beer. When we got home, Grandpa was waiting up for us, and he made us sit down at the kitchen table and talk to him. He wanted to see if we'd been drinking.

"We both had, but Colleen was the one he kept looking at. So she got all fidgety, and when she reached across the table to straighten the napkin holder, she knocked the salt shaker over. Grandpa grabbed her by the wrist and looked right in her face and said, 'You're drunk. Everything about you disgusts me. Get out of my sight.'

"And this is the way Colleen was: She didn't cry, she didn't get mad or stomp out or apologize or say, 'You're right, I'm a terrible person, I should never have been born.' She didn't say anything. She just got up and calmly left the table, while I sat there for another half an hour listening to Grandpa tell me how irresponsible Colleen was, how she never did anything right, and how she was wrecking the whole entire family.

"When I finally went up to our room, she looked at me and said, 'Stay awake, Bridie, because after that motherfucker goes to sleep we are blowing this shit-hole,' and about an hour later, when Grandma and Grandpa had turned out their light, she made me sneak downstairs with her and out of the house."

"She made you?"

Aunt Bridget smiled. "No. Whatever Colleen did, she made it seem like a good idea, and like it was really fun. You *wanted* to do it."

"Where did you go?"

"The beach, of course. On the way out she grabbed the keys to Grandpa's Cadillac. And even though she didn't even have her learner's permit, and she'd never even practiced driving before, somehow she knew how to do it. I mean, she drove really slowly, right down the middle of the road, but still. She wasn't even scared.

"We went and got all our friends," Aunt Bridget said, "Lizzie and Barbara and Tammy and Valerie and Kim. We threw rocks at their windows to wake them up. By that time, it was about one in the morning. So, we're headed for the beach, and suddenly Colleen stops the car in the middle of the road and says, 'Okay, everybody get naked.' "

I could not believe my ears.

"She wouldn't go until everyone took off every single piece of their clothing, and then she took all the clothes and put them in the trunk." Aunt Bridget saw my horrified look. "We thought it was hilarious. We thought we were so cool."

"So what happened?" I asked.

"Well," said Aunt Bridget, "I hate to have led you all this way and have to tell you this, but nothing happened. We drove through town, past all the stores and restaurants, which were closed, of course, and past the houses of everyone we knew, who were all asleep; then we drove down to the beach and went in the water, and after a while, we got cold, so Colleen got the clothes out of the trunk and we got dressed and went home."

"You didn't get caught?" I asked.

"Nope," said Aunt Bridget.

"Or crash the car or anything?"

She shook her head.

"What if Mom had lost the keys on the beach? That would've been awful!"

Aunt Bridget's smile looked far away. "You know," she said, "even though not much happened, it was perfect. It was a small piece of my life that was just perfect. And I bet if you talked to any of those other girls, they'd remember it that way, too.

"And Justine," she said, "sometimes I get so mad at her now. Because that's the part Colleen doesn't remember, along with everything else: You don't always have to be having some big adventure, or some big love affair, or some big goddamn trauma, for your life to be good. You could just be driving around with your sister.

"The part that makes me maddest," Aunt Bridget said, "is that *she* took *my* good memories and now just pretends they never happened. Is *that* fair?"

I held my breath, waiting, I guess, for Aunt Bridget to tell me the rest of the story, the part I really wanted to know. When had Mom changed from that girl who drove around naked in the Cadillac in the middle of the night, laughing with her friends? And why? What had happened?

But when Aunt Bridget looked over at me, I could see that the story was over. We had pulled into the grocery store parking lot. "What do you and Rona like for a barbecue?" she asked, but I didn't answer her, because I was suddenly mad, too. At her, for doing what grown-ups always did to me—refusing to tell me what I wanted to know—and at Mom, too. Because it wasn't fair: that person Aunt Bridget was talking about sounded like someone I really would have liked to know.

When we got back from the store, Mom's headache was gone, apparently. She was in the kitchen with the Comet, the Formula 409, the Windex, and the bleach, and she had cleaned everything: washed the dishes, scrubbed the counters, washed the floor, and probably other things, too, that it wouldn't occur to the normal human brain to clean, like the time she unscrewed all the drawer and cabinet knobs and soaked them in vinegar because she said just the thought of all the gunk she couldn't see underneath them was driving her crazy.

"What are you doing?" Aunt Bridget said.

"Oh, I just cleaned up a little," Mom replied. "I didn't feel right, just lying around when you had company coming over. What's his name? Gregory? Gosh—maybe I ought to make something, too. Do you have any idea what he likes? Hummus, maybe? Oh, but some people can't take all that garlic. You don't have any grape leaves lying around, by any chance, do you?"

I wasn't quite sure what had happened, but looking at Aunt Bridget's expression, I could see that whatever feelings she'd had in the car, about her big sister, Colleen, and the memory of the perfect moment, were gone. And suddenly I wanted to tell them both how mad they were making me right then, not just changing from how they had been with each other twenty years ago, but from how they had been an hour ago, and a minute ago, too. In five minutes, they'd probably be different again. Stop it, I wanted to tell them. *Grow up.*

But that made me even madder, because then I felt confused.

Because maybe what I really wanted to say was, Can't you be more like kids?

I pray to the Lord to grant me strength of body and spirit so that we may safely reach the conclusion of our journey. Well, it's a little soon to be thinking about the conclusion of our journey, since we've only been on the road one day. Only 224 days left to go.

Thaddeus is filled with a great energy. It blows across the landscape of our life like a big wind.

"Why are you crying, wife?" he asked as we turned the bend and clopped away from the town where I'd spent my whole life. There was my mother, waving and getting smaller and smaller. There was my dear friend Tabitha Narcissa Peepwhistle, jumping up and down. Her mouth was moving, but I couldn't hear her voice anymore. There was the cemetery, and poor brother Edgar's gravestone, just disappearing behind a tree.

"A bit of dirt got in my eye," I told him.

"I'll pray for it to come out," he said, and he did: "Oh merciful Lord," etcetera, etcetera. He was up early this morning, blessing everything: the children, so that they will make the journey safely; the horses and oxen, to remain strong and healthy; the food, to nourish our bodies; the seed wheat and corn, so that every kernel will grow when we plant it in our new home; the wagon; the wagon wheels; the horse's shoes—I mean, it got a little ridiculous.

We didn't hear a peep out of Amethyst today. That girl is a complete mystery to me.

AKA GOD

Greg was kind of like if you took the head from one boyfriend, the arms from another, the body from a third, etcetera—he seemed like someone we had seen before, but not necessarily all at once. It didn't even matter which parts went where: if you really could create mix-and-match boyfriends, you could put together five or six different ones out of the guys we'd met, and they would all, basically, be Greg.

"This is Greg Winowski, everyone," said Aunt Bridget.

"It's so great to meet you, Gregory," said Mom. "Girls, what do you say to Gregory?" She looked at me like I was supposed to think of something besides "Hello."

"Hi," I said.

"Pthhht," said Rona, which of course sent Mom into a conniption. While Mom was apologizing to Greg, I took Rona into the kitchen and made us peanut-butter-and-jelly sandwiches for dinner, then we went downstairs to our room in the basement.

I lay in bed later, after Rona had fallen asleep, listening to Mom and Greg talking upstairs. Mark and Aunt Bridget had gone to bed, and Mom and Greg were alone, and they were listing all their favorite bands: "The Drongos! I thought I was the only person in the world who remembered them!"; "I have *all* the Violent Femmes albums!"; "Oh, and what about X?"

"The girls really have a good appreciation of music," I heard Mom tell Greg. "They were exposed to so much when they were little, having a musician for a father," which I guess meant the stuff we heard when it was Dale's band's turn to practice at our house. I remember the sound of it reminded me of someone taking everything in the house and throwing it down the stairs for about five hours.

"I try to take them to hear everything I can," she said, and I was glad I was downstairs and not up there having to nod my head and smile, like it wasn't the worst when Mom made us go to concerts with her. By the time we got there, it would already be a couple of hours past our bedtime, and Rona would be crying, which always seemed to puzzle Mom, or so she'd say to whoever we were with: "I don't understand it; she loves the Flesheaters," and then she'd stick these huge, uncomfortable earplugs in our ears and we'd have to sit there at a tiny table crammed full of people with thirty glasses of beer on the table and not move.

It's weird, though, how nice it is to lie in bed and listen to the sound of your mom's voice, rising and falling, rising and falling, just staying in one place and not skittering around like a gerbil on drugs, even if she was talking to a loser and telling lies. I fell asleep with Mom's voice saying, "I *love* the Dream Syndicate," sliding down into the black part of my brain.

When I woke up the next morning, Mom was already up, arranging some little rocks and a feather on the shelf near her bed. She'd filled a juice bottle with water and stuck a black-eyed Susan in it. As soon as she saw my eyes were open, she said, "Good morning, Justine! Did you have a good time last night?"

"Are we leaving today?" I asked. She looked surprised. "You said we were staying five days at the most," I reminded her.

"Did I?"

"You said school starts in Massachusetts on August twenty-ninth," I told her.

"Does it?" she said.

Greg came over again that night and the next three nights after that. Unbelievably, they were still thinking of bands they could talk about and listing every concert they'd ever been to.

Every day I asked, first thing, "When are we going to leave?" and every day Mom said something different, with a big smile on her face: "Well, good morning to you, too!"; "Why? What's your hurry?"; "It's either Aunt Bridget's basement or Marie and Bill's basement—wouldn't you like to stay here a while and see what happens?"

On the eighth day we'd been in Utah, when we came up for breakfast, Mom said, "Orange or grapefruit juice, girls?" I already had a stomachache; it had turned on like a staticky radio station the minute I saw Mom's smile that morning.

"Orange," said Rona.

"Grapefruit," I said.

"How would you like it if we stayed in Utah a while, instead of going straight to Massachusetts?" said Mom.

"What do you mean, a while?" I said.

"Like, just, *a while*," Mom said. "You know."

"How long?" I asked.

"We'll have to see," said Mom.

"Like, stay here till after school starts?" I asked.

"Maybe," said Mom.

"Yes or no?" I said.

"You know, Justine," Mom said, "I really think you'd be a happier person if you learned to go with the flow a little more." "Go with the flow" was a stupid, hippie way of saying, "Do what other people want you to do," and I usually did do that, because living in Mom's life, you had no choice, though she was always trying to make it sound like you did.

"Besides," Mom said, "maybe if we stay, the cat will come back."

As soon as she heard the word *cat*, Rona jumped up from the table.

"That's a stupid reason," I said. Everybody but Rona knew the cat wasn't coming back. We had seen it, crouching deep in the bushes, giving us a look like there was no way in hell.

"Justine," Mom said, "that is really cruel."

"I'm finished with my breakfast, Mom," Rona said, and she headed for the door.

"Besides," Mom said as if she hadn't just been mad at me, "Utah is really starting to grow on me, what about you?"

I followed Rona to the door, so I wouldn't have to listen to Mom anymore, who was listing all the supposedly wonderful things about Utah she had been noticing, like the nice wide streets made it easy to make U-turns; and the Mormons might be a little weird, but they had such a strong sense of community; and there were whole restaurants just for scones.

"What should we do today?" Mom was asking herself.

"Leave," I said on my way out the door. Mom gave me the hairy eyeball.

"Maybe I'll unpack the sewing machine from the truck and make Bridget some new place mats," she said.

I sat down on the porch to watch Rona. She was lying on her stomach on the sidewalk, hanging her head in front of the sewer hole that went under the street.

"Hello!" she called like she was talking on the phone. "Cat? Kitty?"

After a minute I got up and went over to the other end of the sewer hole, across the street, and lay down on my stomach, too, but I couldn't see anything in there, just blackness.

"Cat," I said, "cat." I sounded like a baby saying a new word, only I was talking to a hole in the ground. When I raised my head a minute later, I saw that Merilee had come over. Rona had gotten up from the ground, and she and Merilee were sitting on the curb in front of the gutter like little swamis, with their legs crossed and their arms folded and their chins on their chests.

"We're praying," Merilee said when she saw me looking at her.

Rona nodded. "We gave it a new name," she said. "Lehi!" she called.

"Lehi!" Rona and Merilee called together.

"My mom said I could ask you over for dinner today," said Merilee.

I ignored her. I didn't want to be rude, but that was the last thing I wanted to do. I already felt like I had had enough of Utah for one day, even though I'd just woken up. But Rona said, "Goody!" and they ran inside to ask Mom if it was okay.

Merilee's house was different from any house I'd ever been in. They had two of everything—two stoves, two refrigerators, and two dishwashers—and there were signs and pictures about God and Jesus everywhere—Bless This, Bless That—and also a picture of those creepy praying hands you see, just floating in the sky in white sleeves, not attached to anything. Also, the walls in every room had pictures of Merilee's family hung on them, including these big ones of everybody standing together dressed up in Christmas outfits, and in each one you could see the mom's hair was weirder and the dad was bigger and there was another baby.

Dinner was different than at our house, too, with the eight brothers and sisters including Merilee and both a mom and a dad at the table. At five P.M. Mrs. Monson brought out the food and poured everybody huge glasses of milk. Just as I was about to pick mine up to take a drink, though, I noticed everyone had their heads down like something bad had happened. Then Mrs. Monson sat down and put her head down, too, and Mr. Monson started saying a prayer, "Thank you, Heavenly Father, for the bounty we are about to receive," that sounded a lot like Dale's prayers to me—just an excuse, basically, to let everyone know what a special buddy of God's he was.

As soon as everybody said, "Amen," Merilee picked up her glass of milk and took a big drink, so I did, too, and got a horrible shock: it was the powdered kind. But Merilee and her brothers and sisters were all drinking their milk as if nothing was wrong with it, and I knew I was going to have to, too. I tried to say my own prayer silently, though I couldn't really remember how it was supposed to go: In the name of Jesus Christ, don't let me throw up, thank you, love, Justine Hanley, amen, but there was nothing I could do about Rona, who was sitting across the table from me and said to Mrs. Monson, "My milk tastes weird, can I have a different glass?"

The second worst thing about dinner was the so-called salad Mrs. Monson tricked me into taking. "Would you like some salad, Justine?" she asked sweetly, and when I said, "Yes, please," she dumped a huge spoonful of yellow Jell-O with all this weird stuff hanging in it—nuts and peas and those little red things that come out of the insides of olives—on my plate.

As soon as everybody had food, Mr. Monson said to me, "What does your father do?" He just assumed everyone had a father, I guess.

"He's a Jesus freak," Rona said before I could think of what to answer. "But he left."

No one said anything, then Merilee's mother asked, "And where do you live again?" as if she knew but had just forgotten. I was starting to be a little suspicious of her; she seemed sort of tricky.

"Nowhere," Rona answered. "In the basement. Sometimes in the truck."

"We're moving to Massachusetts," I said.

"To a Pilgrim village," added Rona.

"Oh, how darling," said Mrs. Monson. "And does your mother have a job?"

"No," I said. "Yes. Well, sort of. I don't know." Mrs. Monson looked at me weirdly.

"Yes, she does, Justine!" Rona said.

"What does she do?" asked Mrs. Monson.

"Sometimes she cooks people dinner in a maid suit," Rona said.

"She's a freelancer," I interrupted. That's what Mom said she was going to do when we got to Massachusetts. I loved that word: I pictured someone riding around on an armored horse, stabbing a long, shining needle into anything that got in the way.

"And how long will you be staying here in Salt Lake?" Mr. Monson asked. They wouldn't stop, and all the honest answers to their questions were things like "I really don't know," "Maybe, maybe not," and "Search me," which I knew sounded kind of rude. But I was starting to get a little mad. I didn't like the way it felt like they were trying to unravel a big mystery, get me to tell them just the kind of story they liked to hear, one that would make a lot of sense to them, like "Once upon a time there was a jolly fat man and a jolly fat woman, and they had two of every appliance, and eight children, each one with a name beginning with M, and they lived in the same wonderful house all their life and prayed to God every time they had any little problem."

I was still thinking about it as I lay in my bed that night, getting madder and madder. What I should have told them, I thought as I lay there, was: Maybe there are *other* kinds of stories, too.

I played a game at a birthday party once where everybody got a paper bag, and inside each one, the birthday girl's mother had put a bunch of different objects—say, like a can opener, a baby sock, a pomegranate, and a dollar bill—but you weren't supposed to look at them till it was your turn. You sat in a big circle, and when it came to you, you had to dump your objects out on the floor in front of you and make up a story, right then and there, with all of those things in it.

Maybe that was the other kind of story, I wanted to say to Mr. and Mrs. Monson. I actually wanted to call and wake them up, I was so mad. Maybe not everyone got to choose their own objects. Maybe sometimes you didn't know till the moment you shook all the weird stuff out of your bag how it was all going to make sense. And maybe, I wanted to tell them, too, if you happened to get God in your bag, it made things a whole lot easier. Then you could just say, "God commanded, 'Take the can opener and jam it into the baby sock. Oh, and cut the pomegranate in half, and put the dollar bill in your pocket; it is my will, and one day you will understand.' "

After a while, I got sick of thinking about it all, and I just wanted to go to sleep, but there was all this weird stuff I couldn't get out of my brain. Not just the powdered milk, and the Jell-O salad, and the big pictures of everybody in their red Christmas sweaters and green hair bows and bow ties. Dinner at Merilee's had been really queer, but in a strange way, I wanted to go back. There was something in her house that I wanted to be able to see more clearly, even though it wasn't something you could see at all. It was something invisible, like darkness or air, but real—and it felt like a mystery to me. Which I liked the idea of, because in our life there weren't very many mysteries, just things that didn't make sense.

Actually, it wasn't that hard to figure out. What they had in there—the so-called mystery—was the thing they called Heavenly Father, aka God.

Maybe it was the same thing I'd felt at the lake, I suddenly thought—the jumble of sky, the heat, the miles and miles of water, Mom smiling in that shining way at Mark, the way I'd suddenly seen everything coming together like a big puzzle—maybe that was God, too.

Maybe all of it—Mark, Aunt Bridget, the lake, Merilee, Greg— was God telling me: I was supposed to stay in Utah. I was supposed to join the Mormons, pray, eat yellow Jell-O, drink powdered milk, and start figuring out who was going to live on my planet. And suddenly, all the stupid stuff that had ever happened in our life made a kind of crystal-clear, perfect sense, because of the way it had all been leading up to that moment.

It was so brilliant, it made so much sense; that was the second to last thought I had in the moment before I fell asleep. Upstairs, Mom was saying to Greg, "Oh! Oingo-Boingo!" Her voice bounced around in the air and bumped into my last thought as I tipped over the edge into sleep: Duh. What a crock. I knew none of it was true.

When we had been in Utah for nine days, I said to Mom, "Aren't we supposed to turn in the truck?" It was one of the things she had had a stress attack about when we were leaving—"We have ten days to drive this thing across the country; do you think we can make it? Don't let me forget to turn the truck back in, Justine."

I had a page in my notebook for things she told me not to let her forget, and I had written that one down in black ink. Black was for things that could actually be done, but Mom had to do them, like turn in the truck, deposit money in the bank, pick up Rona in the car from kindergarten. Blue was for things it might be easier to do myself, in case reminding Mom made her cover her eyes with her hands and moan, "God, why can't I get my shit together?" and start to cry—like water the plants in the garden, take something out of the freezer for dinner, put the laundry in the dryer so the clothes didn't mildew and have to get thrown away like they did the one time Mom asked Dale to do the laundry. Red was for things no one could really do, but I wrote them down anyway. Red ink was for things like when Mom sat down on the stairs the day Dale left for good and said, "God, Justine! Please remind me never to sacrifice my self-esteem to such an abusive jerk again!"

All Mom said when I asked about the truck was, "Don't worry about it, honey; we've still got plenty of time." Then she called down the hall to Aunt Bridget, who was getting ready to go to work, "Do you have shelf paper, Bridget? I need a project to do today."

"Um, no, I don't think so," Aunt Bridget called back. Mom didn't hear what I heard Aunt Bridget say next, in a low voice, to Mark: "Shelf paper? Oh, my fucking Lord, what am I going to do?"

"I *like* Gregory," Mom said at breakfast after Aunt Bridget and Mark had left for their jobs. Not that anyone had been talking about Greg. Rona and Merilee were outside playing Lost Tribe of Israel. They'd asked me to play, but I didn't want to. I felt like sticking around Mom. Not because we were having a great time or anything, or because I wanted to get involved in whatever project she was going to think up. I just had a weird, worried feeling, maybe the same feeling cows and horses get before an earthquake. Mom was kneeling in front of the cleaning supply cabinet, waiting for one of the products to give her an inspiration, and I felt like I just didn't want to leave her alone.

She was waiting for me to say something about Greg, I didn't know what. I hated the little square patch of beard on his chin, that he probably thought made him look like some cool sixties guy. His voice sounded like Kermit the Frog's.

"Do *you* like Gregory?" she asked.

"Greg," I said.

"Excuse me?"

"Aunt Bridget and Mark call him Greg," I said.

Mom tilted her head to look at me. "Well," she said, "I like to call people by their given names unless they ask me otherwise."

"Did he tell you it was his given name?" I asked.

"What?"

"You don't actually *know* his given name is Gregory. Maybe it's just Greg."

"Justine," Mom said, "*why* are you being so difficult?"

"Because I want to leave," I said. She sighed.

"So, *do* you like him?" she asked again after a few seconds had gone by.

I was thinking about Mrs. Monson, Merilee's mother. I had come home from dinner that day thinking I was so glad she wasn't my mother. And I still was. Except—this is why I was thinking about her, I guess—if she *were* my mother, somehow I knew she wouldn't be asking me a question like Mom had just asked me. She'd be teaching me to mix up a big batch of powdered milk, or driving me to wherever you go to get baptized for the dead, or telling me to go find the baby, who had gotten lost again somewhere in the house. And suddenly I got scared, thinking I didn't even know which thing was more normal. It felt like being in the tiny room in the funhouse where all the walls and the ceiling and the floor tilt, and suddenly all you want to do is find one normal thing, one little piece of the room that's the angle of real life, so you can keep from freaking out.

"You know," Mom was saying, "you could *try* to like Gregory. He's very kind and interesting. He knows more about the music industry than anyone we've ever met."

"We don't even really know him," I said to Mom.

"Justine!" she said. "That's not a very nice thing to say!"

"And we're supposed to turn in the truck tomorrow."

"Thank you, Justine," Mom said icily. "But I'm on top of it."

I didn't know what happened to you if you owed a truck and didn't turn it in. Maybe Aunt Bridget knew; I was kind of anxious for her to get home so I could ask her, even though it was morning and she'd just left. I had some other questions to ask her, too. Maybe, I thought, after our talk in the car, when she had said swear words in front of me and told me secrets about Mom, it would be okay just to ask: What exactly had she meant when she said, "Stay as long as you like"? Had she meant stay till the end of the summer, like houseguests? Or for the school year and be sort of roommates? Or did she mean stay forever and let's be a family? Also, why had she introduced Mom to Greg? I just wanted to know if there was some sort of reason or plan, some way it made sense that I couldn't see. And if not, maybe she could help me come up with a plan to get Mom to leave.

Greg came over that afternoon before I could talk to Aunt Bridget. Rona and Merilee and I were downstairs watching *The Love Connection*, which Merilee had never seen before. Rona and I loved *The Love Connection*. She liked the bad dates, where the man and woman ended up calling each other names and yelling at the host, Chuck Woolery; and I liked the good ones, where both people agreed with everything the other one said and nodded their heads up and down like crazy when Chuck asked if they'd like to go out again.

I was distracted, though, and after a few minutes I left to find out what was causing all the thumping I could hear coming from upstairs.

"Oh, hi, honey," Mom said when she saw me, as if she hadn't been telling me all day long what a mean, cruel, *negative* person I was. "Can you get this door for me?" She was carrying a box labeled "Colleen Misc." through the front door. Greg followed with three more: "Bathroom," "Kitchen," and "Girls."

"What are you doing?" I asked.

"Unloading the truck," she said, smiling at me like the most polite lady in the world. "We need to return it. Would you like to help?"

I worried all day about what would happen when Mark came over and saw that Mom and Greg had piled all our stuff in the place where his car usually went. It was Aunt Bridget, though, who didn't look too happy when she came up the porch steps at the end of the day.

"What's going on?" she said.

Greg had finally left just a few minutes before.

"Come here," he'd said to Mom when he was leaving, in a weird voice that made my ears prick up, because there was something about it that reminded me of Dale on a pre-rampage. Greg was smiling, though. As Mom stepped closer to him, he put out his arm like he was going to hug her, but instead he grabbed her around the neck with his bent elbow and pulled her down the porch stairs. Then he backed her up against the side of the house, between some bushes, and leaned his body into hers. He looked over at me for a second and then looked away, as if I were made of air. I was trying to figure out how I was going to know if I needed to call 911, but Mom started giggling.

"Gregory!" she said. "What—"

But he shut her up by smashing his face into hers and giving her one of those gross kisses like he was yelling into her mouth. It lasted a long time. Then he sprang away from her, went to his car, and drove off so fast that his tires chirped. Mom just stood there smiling to herself; and when she turned and saw me watching her, she smiled at me, too, like that kiss was some sort of secret between us now. I smiled back, a totally fake smile, so she wouldn't be able to tell what I was thinking: how great it would be if there was such an invention as Wite-Out for your brain, that you could slap on the minute you saw something you wanted to forget right away.

"What's going on?" Aunt Bridget said again. "What's with all that stuff in the garage?" Mom was still recovering from the kiss with Greg; she was standing on the porch in a weird position—her arms crossed as far around her body as she could get them, as if she were trying to keep herself from flying apart.

"We emptied out the truck," Mom said.

"Why?" asked Aunt Bridget.

"Well," said Mom, "I thought we'd stay for a while. I have to take the truck back, or else they'll charge it to my credit card." Aunt Bridget raised her eyebrows.

"Just until we find a place of our own," Mom said. "All that stuff will be out of the garage in a few days, I swear."

"Find a place of your own?" Aunt Bridget repeated, then she said, right to Mom's face, "Don't give me that *look*, Colleen." Aunt Bridget was the only person I'd ever heard talk to Mom that way, and maybe that was why we only saw her once every two years.

"What look?" Mom said.

"Your Miss Universe smile. Give me a fucking break." I looked over at Rona and Merilee, who were sitting on the grass. I knew Merilee wasn't allowed to say swears, and she probably wasn't allowed to hear them, either.

"Go inside, you guys," I said to Rona, which, I realized as soon as I said it, was the same as saying, "Make sure you stay right here." So I said, "There's the cat."

"Where?" cried Rona.

"It ran into Merilee's yard."

"Let's go find that fucking thing!" Merilee cried.

"That fucker!" said Rona, agreeing, and they ran off.

"Why are you so angry?" Mom was saying to Aunt Bridget. Aunt Bridget didn't answer. Then she said, sounding suddenly like *she* was the one who was angry, "Anyway, what do you care where I live?"

"I don't," said Aunt Bridget, and I wondered if those words felt the same to Mom as they did to me: like someone had wung a little pebble right into my skin. "But what about *making a plan*?"

I waited to hear what Mom's answer would be. Hopefully something with a date in it, and a place—the name of a city, a street, or a school would be great.

"What about Justine and Rona?" Aunt Bridget asked angrily.

"What *about* them?" Mom shot back. "This is our life, and we're living it—how's that for a plan? And anyway, where are you with your concern the other fifty-one weeks of the year?

"Let me ask you something, Bridget," Mom continued. "Why

did you introduce me to Gregory, anyway? Was that just to amuse yourself?"

"Oh, my God in heaven," Aunt Bridget said. "Tell me you're not staying because of Greg."

Mom just looked at Aunt Bridget. She looked like Rona did sometimes, when Rona did something embarrassing like hiccup or trip—she'd look around to see if anyone had noticed; then, if you had, she'd say, "I *meant* to do that," and do it again, really fakey, to try and convince you.

"No," Mom said in her Strong Woman voice. "I am *not* staying because of Gregory." Aunt Bridget and I both waited, then, to hear the reason we were staying, but it was like Strong Woman had left the room, and after a minute Mom said, "I'm going to go and put in some laundry, now, if that's okay," and she left, too.

The next afternoon, Mom said, "You know, maybe I'll apply for some jobs." Aunt Bridget, who was standing at the refrigerator, looked like when you put someone on pause on the VCR—like her mouth was trying to open but couldn't, quite.

Later, Mom said the same thing to Greg when they were sitting on the porch steps after dinner.

"Why?" Greg said. He still came over almost every night, but something was different, I didn't know what. Maybe they had listed every band that ever existed and they didn't have anything left to talk about.

"Because I need money," Mom said in a super-cheery voice. "Help me brainstorm!"

"I got lucky!" Mom said when she came in the door at the end of the very next day. She pulled something out of her purse—a tag that said, "You'll Find It at Fred Meyer!" with her name printed underneath it.

"Who's Fred Meyer?" I asked.

"It's a store!" she said. "I'm going to be a greeter! Doesn't that sound like the perfect job for me?"

Every day for the six days she worked there, she came home crying. The greeter's job wasn't really just to stand there and say hello and good-bye to people, Mom found out the first day—she was supposed to be watching to see if anyone tried to steal anything.

"So many people try to steal things," she said. "It makes me so sad." The first day, she got in trouble for not noticing on purpose that an old man put a can of beer down his pants.

"He was so *old*," she said. "I didn't want him to get arrested."

The second day, she caught a kid stealing a hat, and she just asked him to go put it back instead of taking him to the office like she was supposed to. The third, fourth, and fifth days, she ended up buying everyone the things they were trying to steal. She bought one woman a lipstick and a pair of jelly shoes, and another woman a votive candle holder, and believe it or not the same old guy came in again and was about to put another beer down his pants, so she bought him a whole six-pack.

The sixth day, she came home, sat down on the couch, and started crying. "I can't do this anymore," she said. "We've got to get out of here. Why does everything I try to do turn out so badly?"

It was also the sixth day Greg hadn't shown up. I wasn't quite sure what had happened to him, but it was something that had happened before: just as Mom was discovering how perfect the new boyfriend was, and getting more perfect every day—more kind and wonderful and fascinating and intelligent and sensitive and amazing, like a ball thrown in the air, going up, up, up, up, toward the one moment where the whole thing would be exactly the way she had always dreamed it would be—his interest in her was already starting on its way down.

I had gotten pretty good at telling the signs of when a guy would be leaving soon: it was mostly weird little things that no one else saw, like if he leaned back instead of forward when Mom talked; or if he didn't say her name anymore, just called her "you"; or if his Adam's apple bobbed almost invisibly every time Mom laughed. With Greg, I first noticed it, actually, the day they unloaded the truck, the day of the yucky kiss. Mom was talking about where she might put our *furniture*, in the *future*, and I noticed that whenever she said either of those words, Greg looked like a cat when you pull a tiny tuft of its hair in a place it can't see.

"Maybe I'll find a nice two-bedroom apartment we can afford," she said to him. "Maybe I'll find a little house. There've got to be some decent affordable rentals around here, don't you think?"

"Do you remember a band called Floy Boy and the Hoys?" Greg said, and Mom got a weird look on her face, but she didn't say out loud what I knew she wanted to say: "Gregory, that was a non sequitur."

He just stopped calling. One day he told Mom he was getting tickets for the most incredible concert that had ever come to Utah— "Gregstock," Aunt Bridget said after Mom had mentioned it about two hundred times—and then she didn't hear anything from him until a week later, when she called him to find out what the deal was.

"Well?" Aunt Bridget asked after Mom hung up the phone.

Mom didn't answer right away. Then she said, "He said he just had a lot of personal shit."

"Yeah, no kidding," Aunt Bridget said, which made Mom run down into the basement. Surprisingly, though, she came up a minute later.

"I'm sure he had some really good reason," she said to Aunt Bridget.

"Like what?" Aunt Bridget asked.

"Maybe he had a family emergency," Mom said. "Oh, I hope not!" Aunt Bridget rolled her eyes. "Maybe it's money trouble," Mom said.

"I just want to kill him," Aunt Bridget said. "He's been a real shit-head to you."

Mom's eyes filled with tears, and she headed for the stairs again. When she came back up she said, "I really hope Gregory gets through whatever difficult thing he's going through."

"I cannot understand why you're being so generous to him, Colleen," Aunt Bridget said.

"He's a kind person," Mom said. "He just doesn't know what he wants. I hope you guys will keep an eye on him for me—be a friend to him."

"He is not a *kind person*," Aunt Bridget said. "He's a narcissistic asshole, and I'm sure he won't have the balls to come around here for a long, long time."

Mom ran down to the basement so many times that day, it was like the time we saw the football team working out at the university stadium. Each time, though, she'd come right back up to say something else about Greg. Then Bridget would call him a few more names, and even though Mom would say, "I can*not* say one thing to you!" and stomp back down again, I started to think maybe there was something she liked about talking to Aunt Bridget that way. Maybe, finally, the two of them were figuring out how to act around each other. Which would be ironic, of course, since Mom had told us we were leaving in two or three days.

It wasn't very hard to leave Utah. Well, I was going to miss Aunt Bridget, and Mark, too, a little bit, I thought as I watched the grownups loading the new truck. It was a weird day—everybody trying to act like all the stuff that had happened in the past few weeks hadn't happened at all. Aunt Bridget and Mom were smiling and chattering away, saying, "I'll call you a lot," and, "You'll have to come visit," things that weren't true.

After we had rolled the back of the truck closed, though, and locked it, and put all the stuff we needed in the cab, Mom and Aunt Bridget sat down to drink glasses of iced tea on the porch, and suddenly they were quiet.

"I'm sorry, Colleen," Aunt Bridget said after a little while.

"Oh, Bridget," Mom said.

I wished I could tell them both what I thought: that, watching them together those few weeks, I'd decided that even though they fought sometimes, Mom needed someone like Aunt Bridget in her life, someone who was like a friend and also a glass of cold water in the face at the same time, and I knew she was never going to find it with any guy, no matter how many she tried.

Rona didn't want to leave, because of the cat. She still thought it was going to trot up any minute and say, "Just kidding," and climb into the truck. Merilee promised to set food out for it every day and to take care of it if it ever came out of the bushes. Also, Merilee and Rona were best friends now.

"Bye, you freak," Rona said to Merilee as she got in the truck, and she touched Merilee on the cheek with her wet thumb. As soon as we were on the highway, though, she snuggled into Mom as though we had never even stopped in the first place.

"Whew! Utah! What an adventure!" Mom said. She just couldn't let any silence go by; she couldn't leave any space for the thoughts about what had just happened to us to wander around in. "No harm done, I suppose. At least we didn't put down any roots. Right?"

I found out something I didn't know, right then: You didn't even have to make a friend to grow a root. Or have a school, or a pet, or a favorite restaurant. Nothing really even had to happen to you. Maybe the roots just wanted to start growing the minute you stopped somewhere. Then, whatever you could see from where you stood would start to look familiar and halfway good—like our basement room at Aunt Bridget's. I had kind of gotten to like the coolness down there and the sound the water made when someone flushed the toilet and it came rushing down through the pipes. It reminded you there were people above you. And the smell of a certain tree in the yard, that dropped a layer of bright green powder on the ground; and, even though I didn't want to be best friends with her, Merilee, standing across the street watching our every move. There was even, amazingly, something I would miss about Greg—though it wasn't him, actually, that I was picturing; it was the little square of beard hair—something that showed up in the same place every night, at least for a little while, and sat next to Mom while she talked and laughed, and kept her from going anywhere.

"Right?" Mom said again.

Well, maybe half a root, I thought, and I pictured myself as a tree, my feet as the places roots would grow from. I lifted one foot, like someone walking through mud; there was a little tug and the root pulled free, and that was that.

Driving out of town, I kept having the feeling that we had left something behind. Besides the cat, though, I couldn't think of what. I had packed the stuff from our room really carefully. I had put myself in charge of that, because Mom was so distracted, trying to act like she had everything under control and trying to make up a story about Greg at the same time, which, come to think of it, might have been her way of saying good-bye.

I went down to our room about ten times, to make sure we weren't forgetting anything. I was glad I did, because the last time, I found one of Rona's Little People in the crack between the mattress and the wall. It was just a little purple plastic peg with a face that she liked to hold in her fist while she sucked her thumb and fell asleep, but still, I had this feeling: I didn't want to leave anything, not a box or a book or a sock or even a hair clip, along the way on this trip. It's not that I cared so much about that stuff. But there were just certain times it seemed important to keep everything together, your life all gathered up around you like a blanket, and not start losing little pieces of yourself along the road.

—⁓⁓—

Well, we are really on our way. The children bounce up and down beside me on the wagon seat, chattering away like hyperactive bluejays. Thaddeus rides ahead on Jake. Amethyst lies in the back of the wagon. She went back there to lie down before we were even a mile out of Hadley and hasn't been up since. I can't figure out what her ailment is. There doesn't seem to be anything physically wrong with her: her color is fine, her appetite strong, she has no fever.

I'm not exactly sure how we ended up with Amethyst, to tell you the truth. I hardly even know her, except for seeing her around town now and then. But there she was, standing in front of our house the afternoon before we were to leave.

"I'm ready!" she said. She had a small knapsack in one hand and a sandwich in the other; and she was wearing a filmy party frock and a pair of cloth slippers.

"For?" I said.

"For the grand adventure!" she said.

"I'm sorry. I don't know what you're talking about," I told her.

"Here," she said, and she took a folded piece of paper out of her pocket. She smiled sweetly and handed it to Thaddeus.

Thaddeus held the paper away from me while he read. The girl stood watching him, smiling and wiggling her eyebrows up and down.

Finally he looked up. He studied Amethyst for a minute. Then he said, "It's from Reverend Mallethammer. He says we must take her."

"*Now, wait a minute . . . ,*" I said.

"*He says God commands it,*" said Thaddeus.

"*Oh, for crying out loud!*" I said.

"*Zebulina!*" said Thaddeus. "*You are very wicked.*" He didn't notice Amethyst's tiny, triumphant smile. "*Go pack some more provisions,*" he told me.

A GRAND ADVENTURE

We'd been driving about an hour and a half when Mom said, "So, Danny Martone?" as if we'd been right in the middle of a conversation about him. And maybe the way she saw things, we were; maybe on the map inside her brain, where she was always rearranging things, a straight line ran from the last time she had talked about him, nine months ago when we sat in front of the television watching gymnastics, to right now, and all the stuff that had happened in between had just fallen out of her memory like rain from a big storm and soaked away into the ground.

I didn't answer her. I was looking at the landscape: the tan-colored hills with nothing on them—no trees or bushes or grass, no houses or animals—just barbed-wire fence running alongside the road as far as you could see; the huge, blank sky; the dull, far-off line of the horizon. "Fort Bridger," said a big, ugly billboard with a picture of a cartoon Wild West guy on it. "Steaks Ribs Chops," the billboard said, "Gas Sundries Gifts."

"Maybe we should stop and buy a gift for Danny," Mom said.

"Justine," she said when I didn't answer her, "is something the matter with you?"

Nothing was the matter with me, I'd just decided I didn't want to say one word about Danny Martone or answer any question having to do with him. I looked out the window and tried to zone out. I tried to let myself get hypnotized by the rhythm of the brown hills going by on both sides of my eyes and the straight, gray road in the middle, plodding into the horizon.

Everyone thinks the horizon is so inspirational. You hear about it all the time, in poems and stories, television shows and songs and radio commercials; it was the name of the all-natural grocery store at home I always prayed Mom wouldn't go to. Even our school's valedictorian, Heather Philpot, talked about the horizon in her speech at the end of the year: Always keep your eye on the horizon, she said, very originally. Never lose sight of it.

Not that you could. It didn't seem to me like the horizon was a very easy thing to lose, like an earring or a hair clip. It was pretty much always just right there, exactly in the place you'd look if you *had* actually managed to lose it, a line at the end of what you could see, the hinge that attached the sky to the world like a lid.

According to Heather, you should always keep checking for that stupid line. Why? If you spent all your time looking into the distance, wouldn't you miss what was actually happening around you? Even if it was just stupid stuff, you should probably pay attention anyway, in case there was a problem you had to fix, for one thing, but also, how did you know there was going to be anything better happening at the horizon? It would probably be just another ordinary place—like the place you already were—but farther away. The only thing for sure you could know about the horizon was that you'd be older when you got there. Except one of the main points of the horizon was that you never got there.

Watching the horizon seemed like a dumb, grown-up idea to me, and actually, when Heather said, "Indeed, an airplane pilot depends so much on the horizon that his plane is equipped with an artificial one," I knew that her father had written her speech for her, because a) she loved to tell everyone her dad was a pilot, and b) why would any kid care about something like that?

"So, Danny," Mom said, trying again.

I wondered if I was going to have to start a section for Danny in my notebook. I didn't want to. I was hoping to keep the boyfriend pages clean and blank for our new life and not waste any on false alarms or losers. I'd already ripped out the page for Greg, which had had hardly anything on it, and I'd enjoyed carefully picking every trace of him out of the spiral metal wire and letting the little flecks of paper flutter to the ground in Aunt Bridget's yard.

I didn't really have any facts about Danny, anyway—just the things that spurted out of Mom's mouth as we drove: His birthday was either February sixth, ninth, or twelfth; his favorite band used to be the Circle Jerks; and even though she had only known him for two years in Santa Cruz, it felt like a lot longer; and I didn't want to write any of those things down because I hated it when the pages turned out stupid. I liked my notebook to be a totally organized place, clean and neat, without any cross-outs.

Maybe I should start a Massachusetts page instead, I thought—a page about our new life. For a second, that seemed like a good idea. I reached into the space behind the seat and got my notebook out of my backpack and a purple pen I hadn't used yet. I'd been saving the pen for a good topic, one that deserved a cool color and wouldn't end up having to get ripped out in the end. I opened the book to a clean, new page, and I sat there thinking about the things Mom had told us about Massachusetts: it had lots of beautiful, old, deciduous trees and quaint, historical houses; people made their own maple syrup; you could skate on the ponds and jump in leaf piles and visit a place where people dressed up like Pilgrims and spun wool and churned butter and made candles; we would make all sorts of friends and go to a million parties, and all those things were going to put Mom in such a permanently good mood that our life was going to be great.

Usually when I opened my notebook, especially when Mom's voice was filling the air around my head like a mosquito attack, I could feel my insides settle down as soon as the words started flowing off my pen. Now, though, I just sat there with the pen on the starting line, not knowing what to write. I wondered who my best friend would be. I hoped I had one by Halloween, so I would have someone besides Rona to go trick-or-treating with. I wished I knew the name of my new school. Maybe it would be good this time. I hovered the pen over the paper, waiting for words to fall out, but nothing did. I turned my head toward the window so no one could see the tears building up.

"Well, I just *know* you're going to like Danny," Mom was saying. "Look!" she said, and she pointed into the brownness. "A jackrabbit! Did you see it?"

"No!" Rona wailed.

"This really is God's country." Mom sighed. "So vast and magical."

"Was it a magical rabbit?" Rona asked. I couldn't find the cap to my purple pen. I looked on the floor and felt under where I was sitting, but it was gone. Now I'd have to leave it off, and the pen would dry up, and even if I did ever manage to start the page, I wouldn't be able to finish it.

"What's the matter, Justine?" Mom said. "Do you have a bee in your bonnet?"

"Did you wet your pants?" Rona giggled.

I rolled down the window and let the pen go flying out.

"What was that?" asked Mom.

"Nothing," I said.

"I wonder if Danny's ever seen a giant rabbit like that," she said.

"Tell about the magic rabbit," said Rona. I tried closing my ears, the same way you hold your breath underwater, to keep sounds from coming in, but I couldn't, of course.

"Hmm," Mom said. "Okay. Once there was a magic rabbit, who lived in a vast land of rolling hills and cloudless skies, with a little girl named . . . Rona! . . . for a friend, in the realm of a good king called Danny."

"Sign this postcard," Mom said to me the next day at breakfast in Laramie, Wyoming. On the front of the card was a picture of a rabbit with horns on its head, and on the back Mom had written, "Hey Danny! Having grand adventures on our trip across the country. Brain flash for a band name: Jackalope Attack! It will be wonderful to see you again, Your Friends, Colleen, Justine, and Rona Hanley."

"No," I said.

"Why not?" Mom said, like she was so surprised.

"I don't want to." I was the one who was surprised then—usually I didn't say things like that to Mom, or like the next thing that came out of my mouth: "And do you think we could possibly talk about something else today besides Danny Martone?"

Mom looked at me in a shocked, hurt way, then she said, *"Fine,"* icily. "What would you like to talk about?" She stabbed at a piece of sausage and glared at me.

"I'm going out to the truck," I told her.

"Fine," she said again.

"Can I have your pancakes?" piped Rona, and before I could answer, "Be my guest," Mom had picked up my plate and screeched her knife across it, dumping everything onto Rona's plate.

"Hey!" said Rona.

Even though I was mad at Mom, before I was even out of the restaurant I realized it was a good question she'd asked me, and the answer was: If I could talk about anything with Mom, I had no idea what it would be. We used to have lots of things to talk about—all the different things I wondered about when I was little, like Do squirrels have bones in their tails? Can cats get hypnotized? and Which is Jesus, anyway—a man or a baby?

It had been a long time, though, since we had any topics of conversation that belonged to the two of us—that weren't just about the weird, discombobulated things that trampled through Mom's brain. I missed it, I realized as I walked through the parking lot toward the truck. And it seemed weird, too, that now that Mom was telling me to pick anything I wanted to talk about, my brain was blank. I tried to think of something to say to her when she came out of the restaurant. There were things I had been wondering about for a long time, things I'd wanted to ask Mom about and hadn't, questions like Not that I cared, but were we ever going to see Dale again? And why, actually, did grown-ups choose people to marry who yelled at them and called them names, scared them, and made them cry? Was there anything good about turning into a grown-up, besides being able to drive? Why didn't we believe in God? And if you didn't believe in God, what if you decided you wanted to? How did you get all the weird, disbelieving thoughts out of your head and the magical, impossible ones in?

But I couldn't picture talking to Mom about any of those things. It had been so long since we'd talked about anything important, it felt like we might need a whole new language, one that might not even have been invented yet, to speak in.

Rona came skipping out of the restaurant. Mom came behind her, frowning into her purse.

"I got a peppermint pattie," sang Rona.

"Well, Justine," Mom said in a very snotty voice as we climbed back into the truck, "did you think about what you'd like to talk about?" She started the engine and made it roar. "Choose a topic, any topic." She didn't have to be such a jerk.

Rona took the licked peppermint pattie out of her mouth and held it in front of my face. "Mmmm!" she said. I slapped her hand away, and the peppermint pattie went flying onto Mom's leg.

"Justine!" Rona screeched. "Mom!"

"Why do you have to be so rotten?" Mom said to me, throwing the peppermint pattie out the window and roaring out of the parking lot.

"Oh, no!" wailed Rona, and she started to cry. The truck tilted as Mom zoomed up the ramp to the freeway. I put on my Walkman. There was no tape in it, but I pretended there was. I turned up the volume and rocked out to the white, rushing sound of the road.

The trip just got more and more stupendous.

"It's such a *grand adventure*, driving across America like this, don't you think?" Mom kept asking, like something in her brain had gotten stuck, and she'd look over at us with a big, fake smile. Then she'd look back, and the smile would disappear and her face would crinkle as she watched the red needle of the temperature gauge going up and the white needle of the gas gauge going down.

The high point of our adventure was running out of money in Adel, Iowa, and spending two *fabulous* days there. Of course, Mom didn't actually *say* we were running out of money, but I started to figure it out from little things, like the way she stood there watching the numbers on the pump fly by when we stopped for gas, saying, "Shit, shit, shit, shit, shit, shit, shit," quietly to herself; and the way she frowned down at her purse every time she went to pay for something, as if it were the purse's fault she couldn't find what she needed in there. And I knew for sure when we stopped at a gift shop in Council Bluffs, Iowa, and Mom didn't buy anything for Danny. She didn't pick up one of the tiny little glasses with a map of Iowa on it, or a stuffed cow with suction cup feet, or one of the foam beer can holders that said "Hawkeye State," look at it lovingly, and say, "I'm so broke, I *really* shouldn't get this," and then carry it up to the cash register and buy it to go along with the bag of saltwater taffy from Utah, the cowboy-boot key chain from Wyoming, and the corncob refrigerator magnets from Nebraska.

"Do we need gas?" I asked Mom about two hours after Council Bluffs, when the needle started pointing toward the bottom.

"Worrywart!" she said, but she didn't stop watching the gauge. A few minutes later, when she saw the sign for Adel, she said, "This looks like a nice place to spend the night!" and veered onto the exit, even though it was only two o'clock.

As soon as we'd carried our suitcases into the room, Mom said, "Can you girls go outside and entertain yourselves for a while?"

"No," said Rona. It was about 112 degrees outside. Breathing the air was like trying to inhale wet cotton.

"Please?" Mom said.

"Why?" I asked.

"No reason," she said. "Now go!"

I found out the reason a few minutes later, though, when I came back inside for the truck keys so I could see if we could find any money for the soda machine in the seat cracks. Mom was on the telephone. "Oh, Marie," she was saying as I opened the door. "You don't know how much I appreciate it; I promise I—" She stopped talking, though, when she saw me and waited for me to go out again.

That night, after we had dinner in our room—peanut butter and bread we got at the Texaco store with the credit card—Mom said, "I guess we'll stay here one more day."

"*Why?*" Rona and I said at the same time.

Outside our window, a set of car tires rolled by. Our room was in the basement, and the Burger King drive-through went right past our heads. A lady's voice, sounding like her head was wrapped in a towel, said, "Can I help you?"

"Oh, just to rest for a bit," Mom said.

"Why do we need to rest?" asked Rona. She was still easy to trick, though, and Mom knew it.

"Maybe there's a mall around," Mom said. "We can get some of those fancy malted milk balls you like so much." She looked at me. "We'll have a good time, I promise," she said, and right then I realized something kind of unbelievable: Mom didn't know that she couldn't just look at me anymore as if I were five years old, and lie, and have me believe it.

"I don't want to go to the mall," I said.

"No onions on the cheeseburger!" a man was yelling into the drive-through speaker.

"Milk balls!" Rona whispered to me urgently.

"Well, we'll talk about that in the morning," Mom said, smiling a smile that looked like a picture of a smile. "Okay?"

"Thank you!" said the towel-head voice. The car tires rolled away, and a new set rolled up. "Can I help you?" the voice chirped, something it had already asked a hundred times that night, and I wished I had something I could go out and smash the speaker with.

In the morning, Mom set out the peanut butter and bread again, then she said, "I'll be right back," and left the room. When she came back, she said, "I got directions to the mall!"

"Why can't we just wait till we get to Massachusetts to go to the mall?" I said. I was starting to get a creeped-out feeling. If we stayed here one day, what if we stayed another? What if we met someone Mom decided she'd like to get to know a little better? What if we were driving to the mall and Mom said, "Oh! That looks like a nice road! Why don't we just see where it goes?" What if we couldn't figure out how to get more money, and Mom got a sadness attack and wouldn't get out of the motel bed?

In California, there had been Grandma, and I knew how to get me and Rona to her house on the bus. There was Empey's market, and I could walk there, and usually I could find thirty-three cents somewhere in the house for a box of macaroni and cheese. In Utah, there had been Aunt Bridget and Mark, so it hadn't felt like if things went really wrong, we might just disappear completely and never be heard from again. But if something bad happened to us in Iowa, I didn't know if I'd be able to figure out what to do.

"Oh, come on, Justine," Mom said. "Think of this as an opportunity. You might never be in"—she checked the plastic card on top of the bureau—"Adel, Iowa, again. You might have an interesting experience here."

"I don't want to have an interesting experience here," I said.

"Well, that is downright small-minded of you," she said. "How will you grow if you close yourself off to the different sights and sounds life has to offer?"

We drove a long way to the so-called mall.

"Where are we?" I asked when Mom slowed down and started looking for a place to park.

"I don't like this mall," Rona said, peering out at a dirty building with a big plastic sign on the front. "Checks Cashed—Payday Loans—Western Union—Money Orders," said the sign.

"Oh, no, sweetie, we're not there yet," Mom said. "I just have to run in here for a second. I have to mail a letter."

"As if," I said.

"Excuse me?" said Mom. I stared at her the way you do in a staring contest—I tried to make all my thoughts and feelings rise out of myself and let my empty body sit there holding up my eyes. She didn't look back at me, though.

When Mom came out again, she had a weird look on her face. "The mail isn't in yet," she said as she climbed into the truck. "We have to come back later."

"Hey!" said Rona, fifteen minutes later when we pulled back into the motel parking lot. "But, the mall!"

"Oh, honey," Mom said, "Justine's right. There's so much of this big country to see. Why should we go to a mall in Iowa?"

"I never said that," I said.

"But what about the milk balls?" Rona wailed, then she turned to me and said, "Stupid Justine!" and hit me.

The next morning, I did a bad thing. After we'd gone to the money store again, and Mom had come out smiling this time, and we were stopped at a gas station filling up the truck, I stole a map. Actually, it was a road atlas. It was $14.95, and there was no one inside the station, and I slid it up the front of my shirt. I know it was a terrible thing to do, and I'm not sure why I did, except that it had to do with a feeling I was having, the same one I got, once, when I drank a can of Jolt cola by accident—like everything, even the way my hair felt growing out of my head, might turn into an emergency any minute, and I needed to do something, even if I couldn't figure out what.

When I got in the truck, I snuck the atlas into my backpack. Then I sat there and held my breath for three hours, till we were out of Iowa. That night, I took my backpack in the bathroom and turned on the water so Mom and Rona would think I was taking a shower, but instead I sat on the lid of the toilet seat and opened the atlas to the map on the fourth page—the one that showed the whole U.S.A.

Then I got out a red marker, and I made a big red X through the state of Iowa, slowly, tilting the tip of the marker a little to make the line nice and thick. Which wasn't my original plan. My original plan, when I took the map, was just to *have* it, I guess—to be able to open it up and look at the line of the road we were on, the names of the cities we were passing, the number of miles from one place to another, to make sure Mom was going the right way. Not to do what I was doing now: making big red Xs through every state we'd been in so far. California, Nevada, Utah, Wyoming, Nebraska. And if everything went all right, tomorrow I'd get to make a big red X through Illinois, and the day after that Indiana, then Ohio, Pennsylvania, and New York; and the thought of that calmed me down, except that at the same time, I also got an awful feeling, wondering if this was what my whole life was going to be now: just waiting for each new, horrible little piece of it to go by.

—⟋⟋⟋—

We have made one hundred miles already. We are somewhere in the state of New York. The weather has been clear and the temperature mild, the scenery not much different from home. We pass many houses and towns; sometimes people come out and wave at us, ask where we're going, and wish us good luck. Sometimes they give us eggs and milk for the children.

So far I have done most of the driving. And the cooking and cleaning up and gathering firewood and caring for the children and animals. Thaddeus rides ahead "scouting" and talking to men he meets along the way, but by about four o'clock he says he is exhausted and goes to lie down next to Amethyst.

I am a little worried about the baby. She woke very fretful this morning and has not had a mouthful to eat all day. She was fine yesterday.

———— ∽ ————

Thaddeus is still under the weather. He spends at least half of every day lying down in the back of the wagon.

"Perhaps we should turn back," I said to him tonight after the children were asleep.

"Turn back?" he said.

"If your health doesn't improve. Maybe it's not sensible to continue. We could turn around now and be home in three weeks."

He looked at me as if I'd called him a dirty name.

"We will not turn back, Zebulina," he said. "You must pray to the Lord for more courage and faith."

Thaddeus says I have something wicked in me. The way he says it makes me picture an angry little animal thrashing and clawing around in there.

I don't love God enough, he says. Mostly he says it when I don't jump to do as he commands me. When we were loading the wagon: "Pray to God to help you see why you can't bring your grandmother's copper washtub, Zebulina!" he told me. "You're being blasphemous again," he said when I suggested that God couldn't possibly give two hoots about the tiny china cup I'd wrapped in stockings and put in the corner of my bag. I told him I didn't think God was going to strike me down over it.

"I just don't think God's such a bully as you do," I told him. I have to admit, sometimes I just enjoy giving him a conniption.

"Wife!" he gasped, then he dropped to his knees and started ranting gibberish. "You must ask for forgiveness! Right this minute! Now!" He grasped at the hem of my dress, but I moved out of the way.

Sometimes I think it's true, actually—about the thing inside of me. Whatever it is, though, I don't think it's evil. Stubborn, maybe. Maybe mad sometimes. Or frightened. Or maybe both of those two things together, like a red, screaming baby with a pain no one can figure out.

MARIE

Living at Marie's gave me the same stomachache as when I was little. When I was Rona's age, I used to sit up in bed every night at eleven o'clock and throw up. Mom would come in and gather my hair out of my face and say, "Poor sweetie." Then Dale would follow, yelling, "Can't you see she does it on purpose?" and, "Just let her lie in it, for chrissakes!" which would make Rona wake up and start to cry, and pretty soon everyone would be either crying or yelling except me. I would stand in the corner feeling all emptied out, thinking about how I was never going to let myself throw up again. But the next night I'd wake up to the same awful, familiar feeling of everything outside of me—the thick, dark air of the house, filled with Dale's voice and the smell of whatever we'd had for dinner that night—trying to rush in, and everything inside of me trying to get out at the same time.

At Marie's house, though, I didn't throw up. I would lie in the dark, my stomach hurting, and I would think of Cronus. He was the Greek god who swallowed his children, and when I was little I used to love that page in our big book of myths—Cronus stretching his mouth like a boa constrictor around a cloth-covered bundle. When the last baby, Zeus, was born, though, his wife tricked him by wrapping a stone in cloth instead. That's what I'd picture as I lay in my bed at Marie's: I'd imagine that the pain in my stomach was a big, round stone, so heavy that nothing from down in there could possibly come up, and it would make me feel weirdly better—usually I'd even fall back to sleep. Also, Rona had started to wet the bed, and I knew it would be the thing that made Mom lose it completely, having to gather up two sets of sheets and carry them past Marie to the laundry room in the morning.

"You know," Marie said to Mom the second time Rona did it, "you obviously have some serious control issues with that child."

Marie didn't like Rona very much. Which was weird, because according to Mom, Marie was her best friend in the entire world. And Rona, basically, was an attachment of Mom, so if you were going to be friends with Mom, you got Rona, too, whether you liked it or not.

The day we showed up, Rona hid behind Mom as we walked up the long stone path to the house. Marie and her kids, Cassidy and Cavanaugh, stood on the porch watching us. Marie held Emerson, the baby.

"Colleen!" Marie cried. She came down the steps and put an arm around Mom, then she pushed Mom away with one hand and reared her head back, so she could look up and down Mom's body. "You haven't changed one bit!" she said. Then she smiled a smile I didn't know I would later hate and said, laughing, "Well, maybe just a little.

"And Justine!" Marie cried, putting her hand on my shoulder, and she did the same thing to me—pushed me back to the end of her arm. "*Look* at you!" she said. She looked straight at my chest, not that there were any so-called points of interests there. Then she stared in my face and said to Mom, "I'm sorry, Colleen, but I am having a really hard time picturing you with a daughter this age."

I wondered what she meant, because there we were, standing right in front of her. But Mom smiled and said, "I know."

"I'm five and a half," said Rona, peeking out from behind Mom. Marie didn't even look down.

"You've never met Emerson!" Marie said to Mom, and she held the baby out toward Mom and shook it up and down at her. Emerson looked a little like the ex-president Richard Nixon.

"What's wrong with that baby's cheeks?" Rona asked Mom.

"Rona!" said Mom, and she laughed. "Nothing's wrong with Emerson's cheeks!"

Marie looked down at Rona then. "She's a *baby*," Marie said in a not-very-nice tone of voice. "Babies have chubby, pinchable cheeks. What's wrong with *your* cheeks?" Rona put her hands up to her face and scooted back behind Mom.

"Rona loves babies, don't you?" Mom said, twisting her head to try and see Rona.

"No," Rona answered. Marie got a look on her face that I didn't like at all. A second later, though, it disappeared.

The second time I saw that look was a few weeks later. It was the fourth day of school, and finally, that day, someone had talked to me at recess. It was a kid named Alex Brennan. Alex stood by the tetherball pole, giggling with his friends, then he walked up to me and said, *"Hubba, hubba."* Which I thought was so retarded that I told the next person I talked to after that, who happened to be Rona, on the way home from school. She thought it was hilarious, of course, and when we walked up to the house that day, and Marie turned to look at us from the flower garden where she was kneeling, Rona said, *"Hubba, hubba!"*

Marie turned her eyes toward Rona and said, "What did you say, you little snot drop?" She said it very slowly and dramatically, so that you could hear every letter as it came out of her mouth. Rona stuck her thumb in her mouth.

"Hello, you two!" Mom said, opening the screen door. "How was school?" Rona ran over and glued herself to Mom's leg.

"What's this?" said Mom. "What's wrong? Did something happen?" Rona didn't answer; she just stared from behind Mom's leg. "Did something happen, Justine?" I looked at Marie, who was holding up a flower she'd just dug out of the ground by its roots and frowning at it.

"No," I said, but I tried to let Mom know, by the sound of my voice, that that wasn't exactly true.

"Come on," Mom said to Rona. "Is it all right if I get them a snack, Marie?"

"Of course," Marie answered, like that was a stupid question. "Help yourself to anything you like. Just be sure to leave the organic teddy bear cookies for Cavanaugh and Cassidy." Cavanaugh and Cassidy didn't go to the same school we did. They went to a *wonderful* school, where, according to Marie, we should be going, too, but Mom hadn't applied for scholarships in time.

"Oh," said Mom. "Sure." As I followed her into the kitchen,

though, I thought I heard her say, in a voice so quiet I couldn't be sure I'd heard right: "I'll just go find some of those *poisonous supermarket* cookies for *my* children." But when I said, "What?" she turned and smiled and said, "Oh! Justine! I didn't know you were there!"

I don't remember my father.

"You must," my mother said whenever we spoke of it. "He was around till you were five years old. You called him Pretty Pa and rode on his shoulders. You baked jam twists for his birthday. He taught you how to skate and whistle and add numbers and write your name in Greek." He was the perfect father, she told me. It grieves my heart to think I can't remember that. Mostly, though, I don't think about fathers at all. When someone says the word father, *my brain gets a bright, white hole in it—sort of the opposite of a pit—filled with an emptiness so thick you'd suffocate if you fell into it; and I am careful to stay away from its edges.*

Even though Marie was supposedly Mom's best friend in the whole wide world, I'd never even heard of her until a couple of years ago. One night, when we were sitting on the living room floor folding laundry, Mom had said, "It's been so long since I saw Marie. I wonder what she's up to these days."

"Who's Marie?" I asked. Dale was sitting across the room, reading a magazine; when Mom said Marie's name, he made a scoffing sound through his nose and said, "That druggie punk-wannabe groupie bimbo from Santa Cruz? God, did I dislike that woman."

"Marie," Mom said to me, ignoring Dale, "is my very best friend in the whole wide world.

"Remember how I met Marie?" she asked Dale. He blew air through his nose again and turned the page of his magazine.

"It was when I worked at the newspaper in Santa Cruz," she told me. I knew that Dale and Mom had first met each other in Santa Cruz, when Mom was either going to college there or only sort of go-ing to college, living with a bunch of people who did. "I got sent to write a story on this band," Mom said. "The Deluded. Isn't that a fantastic name for a band? They were a great bunch of guys—*super* musicians." Dale snorted.

"I was supposed to interview them, but they were all so high, no one could talk to me. It was a totally lost cause. Then Marie showed up." Mom smiled to herself. "I still remember the first time I saw her. I looked up from my tape recorder, and there was this beautiful, pink-haired person with an amazing smile on her face, floating over. Marie was such a free spirit back then. She was the guitarist's girlfriend."

"That week she was," said Dale. Mom ignored him.

"She was the one who ended up giving me the interview," she said. "We had such a long, wonderful conversation. And from that moment on, we were best friends."

"You mean she liked having a love slave," Dale said.

"What's a love slave?" I asked, but Mom just said, "It's nothing. He's just jealous because I have a friend like that."

Now, Marie worked upstairs at her computer, thinking up things to sell to old people. "It's technologically very complicated," she said when Mom said her work sounded fascinating and asked her to tell us more about it. It didn't seem complicated to me. Basically she thought of things old people needed done around the house by remote control, like turning the lights on and off without having to go over to them, raising and lowering the blinds without having to stretch your arms, or working a chair that dumped you out all by itself. Then she commanded someone else to invent it.

"It is such important work you do," Mom told Marie. "Improving the quality of the lives of the elderly."

"*Seniors*," Marie corrected her. But I thought it sounded dangerous, and I wondered if Marie actually knew any old people—if she had ever seen someone like Grandma Bobbie, for example, trying to talk upside down into her cordless phone or standing with the garage door opener in her hand, punching the buttons and saying, "Oh, shoot! Oh, shoot!" as the door went up and down, up and down, one time practically cutting the cat in two.

Marie made thirty-five dollars an hour. I knew that because she mentioned it all the time. The first day we were there, Emerson pooped and Marie was about to carry her up to the bathroom to change her diaper when she changed her mind.

"Here," she said to Bill, and she handed Emerson to him. "It doesn't make sense for me to do this when I could be upstairs making thirty-five dollars an hour."

Bill was pretty nice, though you didn't notice him too much. He would wander in from his work, whatever it was, which he did in a little house out behind the real house. Whenever Marie saw him, she would tell him to fix something, or move something, or clean something up, or run out and buy something, or change Emerson's diaper. "Okay," he'd say, and he'd go do it, and then you wouldn't see him for a while.

He would smile and say, "Hello, ladies," whenever he saw me and Rona, and he'd tell Cavanaugh, who was an eight-year-old devil-boy, to leave us alone when he teased us. Sometimes he'd ask us a question, like how did we like our new school, or did we miss the weather in California. He was nice to Mom, too.

"Hey, Colleen," he'd say if he caught sight of her scurrying around, doing housework or working in the yard. "Come sit down. You're working too hard." Sometimes Mom would smile and sit down with him, and they'd start to talk about books, or music, or a movie one of them had seen.

I didn't know how, but Marie always knew when they were doing it.

"Oh," she'd say, coming out onto the porch or wherever they were. "You're sitting out here?"

"Join us!" Mom would say.

"Want me to get you a beer?" Bill would ask.

Then Marie would say something to Mom like "So, you want me to finish doing the bathrooms?" and Mom would jump out of her chair and say, "No! No! I'll do it! You sit down with Bill!" but Marie never did; she'd follow Mom inside, and Bill would shuffle off to his little house behind the house.

"Marie's kind of weird," I said to Mom one day when we were sneaking to the Store 24 for contraband. That's what Mom called it when we told Marie we were going for a nature walk but instead walked to the Store 24 for white doughnuts, red licorice, Bazooka gum, M&M's, and barbecue potato chips.

It was Sunday afternoon, and Mom and I were alone. Rona had fallen asleep. I hadn't wanted to leave her, because I was afraid of what would happen if she woke up and found herself alone with Marie, but I hadn't been able to figure out how to explain that to Mom, because Marie was right there when Mom said to me, "Oh, come on, lazy-bones. I need the company."

When I told Mom I thought Marie was weird, Mom practically had a conniption there on the side of the road.

"Don't say that, Justine!" she gasped. "Why do you *say* that?"

That morning, when Mom had come down to the kitchen, Marie took one look at her and said, "Nice getup."

"What?" Mom said.

"Surf's up," said Marie. Mom had on her favorite sundress. I hadn't seen it since before we left California. "How old are we now, Colleen?"

"You think this is a stupid outfit?" Mom said.

"I *love* this dress!" said Rona. She came over to Mom and wrapped her arms around Mom's legs and kissed the dress.

"Not for a fifteen-year-old!" Marie said, and she gave Mom a big smile. "But you always did like to play the onjanoo." I had no idea what that word meant, and I couldn't figure it out, either, by looking at the look on Mom's face, or find it in the dictionary later. Some kind of musical instrument was my only guess—something stupid that a kindergartner would play, like the triangle.

"I did?" said Mom, and she looked like she was trying to figure out, too, what Marie meant, but then she just said, "Well," and waited for a few moments to pass. "I could change, I guess. If my outfit's bothering you."

"God, Colleen," Marie said then. "Why do you always have to get so defensive? We used to talk this way all the time. You never used to have such a thin skin."

"Well, she's kind of mean sometimes," I said as we walked.

"Justine, don't say that!" Mom gasped. "Marie and Bill are such good friends to welcome us into their home, give us a car, lend us money, and feed us till we get settled. Marie is a very kind person!"

"She's bossy," I said.

"No, she's not," said Mom. "She just has some very definite opinions. That's a good thing. It's the mark of a strong woman."

"She does some weird things," I said lamely. I'd been trying to decide for two days whether to tell Mom what had happened on Thursday, when she was out buying a new sponge for Marie's mop. The little kids were playing with Play-Doh on the kitchen table when Marie came in and told them to put it away and wash their hands for lunch.

"No way, José," Rona said.

I was in the living room, reading, but I jumped up and went to the kitchen door just in time to see Marie put her face down close to Rona's, look into her eyes like one of those hypnotizing snakes, and say, "Eat shit and die, you little motherfucker." When she looked up and saw me, she just smiled and said, "Justine, will you please help the kids clean up and then set the table?"

"What are you talking about, Justine?" said Mom.

"I don't know," I said. "I just don't really see why you're friends with her."

"Why do you say that?"

"Well," I said. I was trying to think of something to say besides, "It doesn't seem like she likes you very much."

"You know," Mom said, "that first day Marie and I met, in Santa Cruz, we never even went to bed. We talked the whole day and all night. Marie had this wonderful honesty and vulnerability; she'd tell you anything."

Maybe that thing, I thought, had sort of turned itself inside out and become the thing she did now: just blurted out whatever she wanted without thinking about whether it would hurt anyone's feelings.

"We were basically inseparable from that moment. We had a great time, and we went some really incredible places and met a lot of amazing people.

"And," Mom said, "Marie and Tim, her boyfriend, had this *great* relationship. They were both so talented and so smart and so *attuned* to each other. It was really wonderful to be around." When Mom said that, I had a strange sensation, something barely even noticeable, as if twenty feet behind me someone had dropped a cinder block into a pile of sand. Ridiculously, I glanced back, but of course there was nothing there.

"Marie's a very generous, nurturing person, you know," Mom said.

"She doesn't like Rona very much," I said.

"What?" said Mom. For a split second, I thought I saw a shadow of a feeling, like a scared mouse, go running across her face. By the time she opened her mouth again, though, it was gone. "What are you talking about, Justine? Marie loves us, and she's helped me out of some really tight spots. She's like family to us. And you know what else? Right now, she's about the only thing we've got, so I don't want to hear you talking negatively about her again, do you understand?"

"Come on, now," she said when we were in the store. "No pouting. We're going to have a really nice life here. It just takes a little time for everybody to adjust." We got our stuff and paid for it, but when we got to the door she turned back and asked the counter guy, "Do you sell single cigarettes?"

"No," he said. She just stood there.

"Are you going to start smoking again?" I asked.

"No," she said. Then she turned back to the guy and said, "Oh, fuck it, just give me a pack of Marlboro's, please. And some matches." When we got out the door, she ripped open the pack, put a cigarette in her mouth, and lit it, and when she breathed in, she closed her eyes, the way Rona used to do when you'd bring her her bottle at nap time.

The children, young as they are, have been a great help on the journey so far. They gather firewood and pick berries and carry water and hold the baby while I drive. In the evening, Annabelle Amanda helps with the cooking, while Ezekiel Obadiah tends to the animals.

I wish I could say the same about Amethyst.

Mother tried to talk me out of bringing her. "The girl will be a burden," she said. "It'll be like having another child. And what will you do with her once you're out there? No one's ever going to marry her—let's face it, the girl's a few eggs short of a custard, if you know what I mean—and you know you're too softhearted to put her out on her own."

I'm beginning to fear Mother was right.

Today, Amethyst stuck her head out from the canvas, squinted, and said, "Where are we?"

"Ohio," I said.

"Oh," she said, "what a lovely place," and she climbed up next to me. Two minutes later, she said, "I can't possibly be expected to sit on this hard wagon seat all the way to California. The jostling upsets my stomach," and she went to lie down again. "Maybe you could bring me a little chamomile tea," she said as she disappeared through the canvas opening. "Oh, and I could go for a biscuit, if you've got one."

I should probably put her on the train back to Springfield right now, before it's too late. Except that in some strange way that I don't understand, it's already too late. I don't have any idea how it happened, but somehow I knew, the second she climbed onto the wagon in Hadley and the Jeppersons left without even looking back once, that she belonged to me.

—⁓—

Maybe I would understand Amethyst better if I knew more about her. Like her age, for example. She won't say, and the more you look at her, the harder it is to guess. Around twelve, the Jeppersons said. As if! Thirteen. Hardly. Fourteen? Maybe, but I doubt it.

Mr. and Mrs. Jepperson found her, one Saturday morning last summer, wandering the old highway between Amherst and South Hadley, smiling and singing to herself, dressed in a pair of cloth slippers and a heavy frock much too warm for the weather, carrying a hard-boiled egg and a piece of horehound candy.

"Slow the carriage," Mrs. Jepperson told Mr. Jepperson. "Are you all right, ma'am?" she called. "Do you need a ride?"

"Are you going to the ocean?" the stranger asked.

"The ocean?" asked Mrs. Jepperson, puzzled. "No . . ."

"Oh," said Amethyst, pleasantly. "Well, thank you anyway."

"Why, dear," said Mrs. Jepperson, "the ocean's eighty miles from here."

She said Amethyst just smiled and kept walking. Mrs. Jepperson worried all afternoon, though, and at four o'clock she made Mr. Jepperson take her back out to the road, where they found Amethyst sitting glumly on a rock in her tattered shoes. And though they brought her home to stay with them temporarily, she refused to tell them anything: where she was from; who her mother and father were; whether or not she had any brothers or sisters; or if she was just sort of a nut job, or what. Well, they didn't actually ask her that last one, but I would have.

JOHN HENRY

One good thing about moving, at least, was that when Mom told us we would be going to Massachusetts for a little visit and not coming back, I didn't think, Oh, how will I ever leave my beloved school?

My last teacher in California, for the fifth grade, was Mrs. Covelli, and something I noticed about halfway through the year was that you could actually spell the words *evil one* from the letters of her name, if you used her first name, Elaine.

I liked school in the first and second grades, when my teachers didn't really notice me, and I was good at the quote-unquote work, which was basically drawing pictures and learning stuff like your address, phone number, and the day's date, how to tie your shoes and cut with scissors, and why you shouldn't pull people's chairs out from under them when they went to sit down.

Third grade was when things started going downhill. The very first day of school, we had to take a test with questions on it like How many bathrooms are there in your house? Who exactly lives there? What did you have for breakfast this morning? and What time do you go to bed at night?, and the next week, the parents of the kids who gave wrong answers had to come in during school time and have a meeting with Ms. Weixler, the counselor.

Ms. Weixler gave me the creeps, the way she seemed to know everything about me, and not just the normal things, like "I see your birthday is January twenty-fifth, Justine. I see you have a little sister, Rona, and you live with your mother and stepfather on Laurel Road," but also things that weren't on the test.

"It can be upsetting when adults fight, can't it?" she said to me one day, and I wondered if somehow she had happened to be driving by our house the night before, just at the moment Dale ripped the TV antenna off the TV and threw it across the room at the lamp, which fell over and broke, and if she saw the big spark through the living room curtains that the lamp made when it fell.

"Children have to remember: When grown-ups fight, it has nothing to do with them," she said. That made me wonder if she was as smart as she thought she was. Or maybe she had just never seen certain things, like a grown man yelling at a little baby because it wouldn't stop crying, which made the mother cry, too, which made him yell even louder; or a kid getting a stomachache and throwing up in the middle of the night, and the fighting starting that way. It might not exactly be the kids' fault, but you were wrong if you said it didn't have anything to do with them.

The day after my first meeting with Ms. Weixler, everything was different. Suddenly my third-grade teacher, Mrs. Garff, started watching me with an eagle eye. Even if I just sat completely still at my desk all day, with my mouth in a straight line, Mrs. Garff would say, "Justine, you seem quiet today. Would you like to go see Ms. Weixler?"

I got to hate it when I could feel Mrs. Garff getting ready to ask me a question.

"For the family history unit, Justine, I see you've left out everyone on the paternal side of your family. Do you remember what 'paternal' means? Would you like to talk about that? If not with me, then with Ms. Weixler?"

"Justine, I notice you forgot your lunch two days in a row. Is there anything going on that you'd like to discuss with Ms. Weixler?"

"I notice you're drawing the sun black, Justine—what an interesting choice. Oh, by the way, have you seen Ms. Weixler this week?"

Then she'd send me down the hall, and I'd have to sit there and watch Ms. Weixler smile, thinking she was so brilliant, unraveling the fascinating mystery of me, when really there were simple explanations for everything: How was I supposed to know my paternal history when I didn't know my father?; I hadn't forgotten my lunch, I just didn't get it out of my backpack because I didn't feel like lying to people that I *liked* pickle relish sandwiches on miniature rice cakes left over from a party Mom catered probably before I was even born; and the sun was black because I was drawing an eclipse.

My new school was named Oak Grove Elementary, which made it sound like a nice place—when I heard the name, I pictured a cool, shaded building nestled under big trees, with light that came through the branches and in the windows and made playful, dancing shadows on the pages of your notebook as you wrote.

It was nothing like that, though. It was just a big tan box, standing on some bare grass next to a roadful of cars. I didn't lose hope right away, though. I hadn't met my teacher yet. I had a new binder that I really loved. Also, the school had sent a letter with a list in it of what the sixth-graders would learn, and some of it actually sounded pretty good: astronomy, geometry, world cultures, Shakespeare.

For about forty seconds, walking down the hallway toward my classroom by myself, I imagined the great year I was going to have. When I walked in the door, though, my stomach skidded. Even though the bell hadn't rung yet, everyone was already at their desks, smiling and laughing and shouting and throwing things, and I could see that I was the only one who didn't already know everybody else.

The teacher, Ms. Taylor, looked at me when I came in and said, "Now, who are *you*?" like I was someone who'd shown up at a birthday party without an invitation. So of course everybody stopped their talking to look at me, and when I said my name, it sounded wrong to me— weird and embarrassing—as if maybe somehow I had said, "Irma Hickenlooper," or something in jabberwocky by mistake. Since I'd registered so late, I wasn't on the regular list, so Ms. Taylor had to check the roll three times—chanting my name out loud—"Justine Hanley, Justine Hanley, Justine Hanley"—before she found me; then finally she looked up and smiled, as if I'd suddenly become visible, and said, "Justine Hanley. Hello and welcome," which for some reason made some of the boys start to laugh little high-pitched laughs and hit each other.

"Madison," Ms. Taylor said to a girl with shiny brown hair and a face like a magazine picture, "could you be in charge of showing Justine around today? Show her the lunchroom and the playground and the bathrooms and so on?" When she said "bathrooms," the boys all had a massive conniption.

"*Boys,*" Ms. Taylor said, and she tilted her head at them like she was mad, but you could see she also had a twinkle in her eye, like, You are so adorable.

Madison looked at me for a minute. I looked back, instead of at the floor, because I realized something right then: Bravery was the only thing that could help me even a little bit, though it probably wouldn't help much.

Finally Madison said, "Okay," and smiled at Ms. Taylor, and Ms. Taylor smiled at me, and I smiled at Madison. Every year, I hoped my teacher would be good, and I hated the feeling of that hope disappearing—sometimes it took a while, and sometimes it happened pretty fast, but this was a world's record. I was hoping halfheartedly that I was wrong, but I was pretty sure, from Ms. Taylor's mistake, that I wasn't—you don't ask the prettiest, most popular, beloved girl in the class to baby-sit a new kid.

I learned a lot on the first day of school: who was popular and who wasn't, who was smart and who wasn't, who was nice and who wasn't. The whole first day was just like a big popularity contest, run by Ms. Taylor, probably so she could figure out who her pets were going to be.

"First, let's get to know each other," she said. "I want you to split up into small groups." Of course, when she said that, everybody said, "Ooh, ooh," and rushed to the sides of their best friends, leaving me and a girl named Jane Brown and a boy named Bryce Boorman.

"Once you get into your groups," said Ms. Taylor, "I'll give you half an hour to come up with anything: a play or a poem or a rap song, for example, telling us who you are, some things that you like, and what your hopes for the sixth grade are."

Madison had gotten in a group with the prettiest girls, Lauren, Kara, and Kirsten, and when she looked over and saw me looking at her, she turned away. Then she came over and said sweetly, "Don't take this the wrong way, but I just, like, really want to be in a group with those guys cuz we're, like, best friends from last year and we have this idea that, like, would only really work with us four."

"That's okay," I told her, and I sat by myself until Ms. Taylor said why didn't I get in a group with Jane Brown and Bryce Boorman. So I went over and sat by them, but none of us said anything to each other.

When the half hour was up, everybody went, *"Aaaw!"* so Ms. Taylor said, "Okay, I'll tell you what—why don't we extend this project till the end of the week. I'll give you half an hour in class every day, and on Friday we'll have presentations."

Every day, all week, at both recesses and lunch, Lauren, Kara, Kirsten, and Madison would get out their boom box and practice their dance, and on Friday, even though everyone had basically seen the entire thing a thousand times already, we had to stay in for afternoon recess and watch it again.

What their dance had to do with who they were, what they liked, and what their hopes were for the sixth grade, I had no idea. Their song was a really mushy one; and they just danced around like they were in love with each other, though you could tell Ms. Taylor thought it was the most beautiful, creative thing she had ever seen. In one part, Lauren and Kara connected their hands in the air, like kindergartners doing "London Bridge," and watched with love as Kirsten and Madison, holding hands and gazing into each other's eyes, walked underneath. Of course, all the boys were cracking up and whispering "gay," which was, truthfully, what it looked like.

Our group didn't even do a presentation, but Ms. Taylor never noticed. The first couple of days we sat together and no one said anything, except when Bryce suggested we could make up a rap about NASCARs and Jane and I both said, "No thanks." The third day I went to the back of the room by myself and tried to write a poem, but the weirdest thing happened: It was like my imagination had evaporated. I just sat there trying not to panic, wondering if it was ever coming back—if it was just temporarily paralyzed, or in shock, maybe, from everything that had happened since we'd left California, or if it was permanently dead—if its heart had given out, like John Henry's, trying to do a job that was just too big for it, trying to hold on to the fading picture of our great life in Massachusetts.

—∿∿—

We crossed the Mississippi today. Remind me never to do that again. There was a huge wagon jam at the ferry. We waited the entire day. I made the poor children sit with their bottoms on the wagon seat for hours, after

Ezekiel almost got run over playing among the wagon wheels. They practically wept with boredom. Amethyst managed to rouse herself today. She emerged from the wagon in her ridiculous filmy frock. "Oh, my goodness!" she said. "There are gentlemen everywhere!" There were ladies, too, but she didn't mention them. "I think I'll stretch my legs a little," she said, and she jumped down and went strolling through the chaos with a ridiculous smile on her face.

No one really gave her the time of day. I can't explain why it hurt my heart, even though I thought she was acting like an absolute idiot, to see her weird, hopeful look, flickering on and then off again, like a candle with a defective wick.

HEART-TO-HEART

One Friday night, Marie told me I was going to get to be mother's helper for a day. Marie's regular baby-sitter, Cinnamon, who had gone to Hampshire College and reminded Marie of herself when she was younger, had to go to New York on Saturday, probably to shop for more black clothes.

"Your mom and Rona can have a day by themselves," Marie said. "It'll be just you and me and the kids. It'll be fun." She stood in the doorway of my room, staring at me for a minute, then she gave me a weird smile and said, "Justine, I have a feeling you and I are going to have a very *special* relationship," which gave me such a horrible feeling, I practically stopped breathing, because I could tell she hadn't seen Mom, who was standing in my closet, hanging up clothes.

But Mom just poked her head around and said, "Justine will love that—it'll be great experience."

"But where will you and Rona go?" I asked Mom.

"Oh, I don't know," Mom said. "Shopping, maybe?" Rona, who was sitting on the floor of my closet, tying my shoelaces in knots, clapped her hands. Marie looked at Mom and raised her eyebrows.

"Or, do you have a suggestion, Marie?" Mom asked.

"There's a wonderful science museum in Springfield," Marie said. "There's a tour of Emily Dickinson's house in Amherst. I think there's a farm technology exhibit at the Vocational High School in Northampton. Some of the cemeteries around the hilltowns are quite interesting."

"The mall is quite interesting," Rona said.

"You know," Marie said to Mom, "maybe you ought to teach your children that there's more to life than the mall." But she made her voice kind of high and light, like a balloon flitting away, so you couldn't tell if she was being rude or not.

I found out the next day what mother's helper meant: free slave. Marie had said, in my bedroom the night before, that she would pay me, but as soon as Mom left the kitchen after breakfast Saturday morning, Marie told me that, actually, I could do it for free that day, then next time, when I had experience, she would pay me. "I think that's fair," she said.

When I went upstairs to get dressed, Mom was lying on her bed. She didn't look ready for the science museum. She looked ready for a rest, even though she'd just woken up an hour ago.

"Could you go get your sister, please, and get her ready?" Mom said listlessly. On my way down the stairs, I passed Marie.

"Where's your mother?" she asked, but she didn't even wait for me to answer. She kept going, up the stairs and into Mom's room. I snuck back up to listen.

"What happened to the museum?" Marie asked.

"Oh," said Mom, "well, we haven't decided yet what we're going to do."

"It's an absolutely gorgeous day out," Marie said. "You don't want to waste it."

"No," agreed Mom.

"Would you like me to draw you a map to the cemeteries?"

"Oh, Marie," said Mom, "I know it's stupid, but cemeteries sort of give me the creeps."

Marie sighed. "You know, Colleen," she said, "I'll be up on the third floor working all day, but Bill's computer's free. It's pretty old, but it's certainly good enough for you. If you don't end up going anywhere, it might be a good day for you to start working on getting some computer skills. I can give you a tutorial to start with."

"Mm," said Mom. If Marie was such a good friend, why didn't she know what the sound in Mom's voice meant? It meant, "If you don't stop talking and go away, in twenty seconds I'm going to start to cry."

"You can't just waste an entire day," Marie said. That made me wonder how well she really knew Mom.

"Mm," Mom said again. Then she said, "That's so generous of you to offer to help me with my computer skills. I think maybe later this afternoon I *will* take you up on that. But is it okay if I do some laundry first?"

Marie sighed again.

"I'll do it all," said Mom. "If that's okay with you. Why don't you just put yours at the top of the basement stairs." There was a silence. "Or you know what? Why don't I go up and get it? Is it okay if I go into your bedroom?"

Marie came down from her office at about ten-thirty A.M. I had put Emerson in her crib for a nap, Cavanaugh was outside pushing trucks around in a pile of dirt, and Cassidy was watching her baby manatee video.

The day we got to Massachusetts, Rona had asked Mom what time *Rugrats* was on. Marie had answered cheerfully, "It's never on in this house!" Her children didn't watch television, Marie said. Rona had looked up at Mom with a terrible, shocked expression on her face.

"You can watch the baby manatees with Cassidy, though," Marie said. "Or suffer!" she added in a cherry candy–flavored voice when Rona stuck out her bottom lip.

Mom had seemed surprised for a second. But then she said to Rona, "You'll like the manatees, honey. They're like seals," and pretty soon Rona was sitting in front of the manatees with Cassidy, both of them staring with zombie eyes and sucking their thumbs.

"You see?" Marie said to Mom as they left the living room and went into the kitchen. "You just have to provide children the chance to choose quality, educational programs," and Mom nodded and said, "Yes, that looks like a great video," but maybe she was really thinking what I was: that from the look on Cassidy's and Rona's faces, baby manatees were basically just Rugrats with flippers.

"Oh!" said Marie, stretching, as she came in the living room. I was folding laundry, which Marie called "light housekeeping." After that, I was supposed to empty the dishwasher.

"It's time for a break!" Marie said. "Would you like to sit down and have some iced *chai* with me, Justine?"

I really didn't.

"Come in the kitchen," she commanded. She went to the fridge and got the *chai*. My heart sank. Marie got really mad if you wasted anything, even garbage. "What are you doing?" she'd say if you put something in the plastic garbage can that belonged in the stainless-steel compost bucket or vice versa. Then she would sigh and stick her arm down into the brown slime, give you a dirty look, and tell you the compost rules once again.

I knew what the compost bucket was made out of because Marie had mentioned it every day since September first, her birthday, the day she'd gotten it from Bill.

"A stainless-steel compost bucket! A stainless-steel compost bucket!" Marie started screaming when she saw it. "Just what I've wanted all my life!" Marie would still be talking about that compost bucket when she was an old lady with white hair, lying on her deathbed: "Yes, I remember when Bill bought me that bucket, the most joyous day of my life, on my thirty-seventh birthday, the year Colleen came to live in our house with no computer skills."

Marie brought the *chai* to the table and poured two huge glasses of it; then she sat down, and she looked at me until I sat down, too. I hated *chai* more than almost anything else in the world, although I felt that way about most of the things we had to eat in Marie's house.

"So, Justine," Marie said. "You and I have never really sat down and had ourselves a heart-to-heart."

What was it about grown-ups and heart-to-hearts? The idea grossed me out. It always made me think of mouth-to-mouth, which we learned in Baby-sitting Skills, with those dirty rubber dummies. Also, maybe it was weird, but I didn't really like thinking about hearts all that much. I didn't actually think real hearts were something you were supposed to picture. That's why valentine's hearts were invented. Real hearts aren't cute like you're supposed to think they are, for one thing. Mrs. Covelli made us look at a cow's heart in science, even though I forged a note that day, saying, "Justine may not look at a cow's heart. This is a despicable unit," and every time someone mentioned a heart-to-heart now, all I could think of was a couple of those raw-meaty-looking blobs lying next to each other, trying not to die while they had a conversation out in the germy air.

Marie was waiting for me to say something back to her. I was trying to figure out how to make my *chai* look like it was getting lower without actually drinking any of it.

I wondered what Marie thought she and I would have to talk about in a heart-to-heart, anyway—if she would want to know the usual things grown-ups wanted to know: Did I like any boys? Did I have any questions about sex? Was there *anything at all* I wanted to talk about? Also, I wondered, why did she think I'd want to have that kind of talk with her and not Mom? It was true that I didn't want to have one with Mom, but how did Marie know that?

"So," Marie said, leaning toward me, "how's it going for you here, Justine?" She was looking at me strangely, like you might look at something you felt really sorry for: a butterfly with a wing torn off or one of those kids you see in the newspaper, with a huge, bald head, holding up an empty bowl. "I mean, I know you've had it pretty hard," she said. "You've really had the deck stacked against you."

I wished I could close my eyes and vaporize.

"You've never really had a chance to *shine*, have you?" Marie said. When I didn't answer, she said, "We should really figure out a way to do something about that. Don't you think?"

I had no idea, really, what she was talking about. I was trying to picture myself shining, but all I could see was me, on a stage in a fluffy pink tutu, lighted up by a spotlight, flailing around.

"Well," Marie said when I didn't say anything, "this really isn't much of a conversation, is it?"

"May I please be excused?" I said, and I got up. "I have to unload the dishwasher."

"Oh," said Marie. I could see that I'd hurt her feelings, and I felt mad at myself for caring; then I felt mad for feeling mad; and for some strange reason, I laughed. Which was the wrong thing to do.

Marie could give the hairiest eyeball of anyone I'd ever seen. She sat there giving it to me the whole time I put away the dishes; it was so hairy that it had grown bangs, braids, and sideburns by the time I finished.

"Where are you going?" she asked when I turned to leave.

"Nowhere," I said, and I left the room and went up to check on Mom, who had collected the dirty laundry and put it in a basket and was looking like maybe she was getting ready to carry it to the basement sometime soon.

The baby's health does not improve. She has hardly eaten anything for a week, and today she is running a temperature. I am very worried.

She is a strange little thing. I thought I would know her a little better by now, but it's starting to feel like maybe she doesn't want me to. She doesn't smile, she barely moves, she turns her head when I try to feed her. And she looks at me so strangely sometimes. With such dark, accusing eyes, as if she knows something, but what? Is it something about me? She looks so afraid, so untrusting. She looks as though, if she had muscles, she'd jump out of my lap and run.

MASSACHUSETTS BOYS

Another thing I found out on the first day of school was that the boys in Massachusetts were different from the ones in California. In California they were idiots, too, but they just sort of did their own thing—obsessed over their Power Ranger toys, drew pictures of race cars in their notebooks, played their games at recess that were mostly about screaming at each other over the rules in their frantic, high-pitched voices.

The boys in Massachusetts didn't like girls or girl things any more than the boys in California did, but the difference was, they weren't happy to stay inside their own little world of TV characters and gross-out games and sports rules, either. They just wanted to ruin your life, for the fun of it. Whatever you were doing—talking to someone on the playground, sitting at your desk doing your math, raising your hand getting ready to answer a question—they wanted to get in the moment and wreck it, like those guys you see on the TV news sometimes, jumping up and down in the background, making peace signs, waving, and yelling, "Hi, Mom!" They wanted to make sure their voices, their faces, and their idiotic comments and gestures were a part of every moment you lived through, like they thought if they shut up for one second, they might disappear.

The thing that seemed to bother them most, actually, was if you were just sitting there quietly, thinking private thoughts. Then they wanted to get inside your brain and ruin that, too.

"Jus*ti-i-ine*," the boys in my class would say, walking by my desk, and there was nothing I could do to keep it from happening. Even though it was only my name, they could make it sound just as bad as the other rude things they liked to say to girls when teachers weren't around, like "Yo, bitch" and "Suck me," to name a few of their very original special favorites.

It was the kind of thing kids were supposed to talk to their parents about, I knew. And I actually did try a few times. But when I did, it was like my words were a big gust of wind and Mom was a little sailboat, zooming away in the wrong direction while I stood watching from the shore.

"The boys here are weird," I told her one day after school.

That day, Alex Brennan, who was sort of the leader of them all, and who all the girls unexplainably liked, did something so incredibly queer: He walked over to where I was standing by Ms. Taylor's desk, waiting for her to explain the math to me, and he dropped a pencil on the floor, on purpose, right by my feet. His friends, Noah, Jake, and Joey P., were watching him, trying not to giggle. Then he got down on the floor and started crawling around, pretending to get the pencil, but when he was down there, he looked up my dress. The boys started to laugh then, and finally Ms. Taylor looked up.

"Are you okay, Alex?" she asked when she saw him crawling around on the floor. Usually I wasn't a baby, but for some reason the sound of her voice saying, "Are you okay?" made tears come into my eyes, and even though, thankfully, I didn't cry, they kept coming back all day.

On the way home from school, I changed and unchanged my mind about whether or not to tell Mom. It was the kind of thing that might make her cry, and I'd pretty much decided not to, but a weird thing happened—as soon as I saw her, the thing about the boys being weird just blurted out of me.

"I bet you won't be saying that for long," Mom said. She was reading the newspaper.

"There's this one?" I tried again.

"Oh, yeah?" she said, and she lifted her eyebrows with a smile. "Who is he? Tell me all about him."

"It's this kid named Alex," I said.

"Is he nice?"

"No," I said.

"Not nice?" Mom said, but she wasn't even looking at me. It looked like she had found something interesting in the newspaper. I got up to leave, but as I did, Mom said, "Justine," in her serious voice. She looked up from the paper. "I know what you mean," she said. I had no idea what she was talking about. "That boy in school? It's hard at first, to figure out what you're feeling. And how to act.

"It's such an intriguing mystery, the way it all works."

It didn't feel like a mystery to me. Alex Brennan had gotten down on his hands and knees and looked up my dress in front of everyone, and the teacher hadn't said anything. Also, I knew exactly how I felt—I felt mad at myself. I wanted to scream and hit myself in the head with my fist a hundred times, even though I couldn't think of why.

We have crossed the Missouri and entered a beautiful valley. There is plenty of firewood and water and thick, sweet grass here for the animals to eat; the road is flat and smooth; and the weather is fine and pleasant. Yesterday we saw hundreds of fat rabbits. Watching them, I started thinking about how nice a rabbit stew would be for supper. So I got out Thaddeus's gun and tried to shoot one, but I missed.

"What's going on?" roared Thaddeus from the back of the wagon. He has not been out of his bed since Council Bluffs.

"I'm just trying to get dinner," I said.

"For crying out loud, Zebulina!" he bellowed. "You don't know how to shoot a gun."

"We haven't had fresh meat in a month," I said. "Maybe it's time I learned."

"That's ridiculous!" he said. "You shouldn't even be touching that thing. You might kill someone."

I think his words had the effect of reverse psychology, though—now I am filled with a burning desire to learn to shoot. It feels kind of dire, actually. Like today, when I sat on the front of the wagon under the bright blue sky with the cool breeze kissing my cheeks, and I remembered how my shot missed that rabbit by a mile and knocked me on my hindquarters, too, I was filled with a nervous stomachache-y feeling, and I felt sure that the only thing that would make it go away would be to learn to shoot Thaddeus's gun.

I don't know how to do it, though: it's kind of hard to practice in secret.

DAY ON THE TOWN

On Saturday morning, the weekend after our heart-to-heart, Marie came to the door of my room before I was even out of bed. I didn't see her standing there at first.

"Good morning, Justine," she said. My whole body jumped, as if an electrical shock had gone through it.

"Hi," I said, and I waited for her to go away.

"I thought today maybe you and I could do something together," Marie said. "Have a day on the town."

"Well, I'm probably going to do something with Mom," I said.

The night before, Mom had told us we might go out and look at some apartments. The idea of a little old-fashioned house, just for the three of us, was *on hold for now*, just like every other good thing that was supposedly going to happen to us in Massachusetts.

When Marie had seen Mom reading the little newspaper ads at the kitchen table, she'd said, "Colleen, do you really think it's a good idea to start looking for apartments now?"

"What do you mean?" Mom said, looking up from the paper.

"I mean, where are you going to get first and last months' rent and security deposit?" Marie said. "Let alone rent. Don't you think you ought to focus on a job search first? Even though it's crazy to think you can work in today's world without computer skills," she added.

"I have an interview on Monday," Mom said.

"With?"

"It's at the Vermont Country Store."

Marie snorted.

"What?" asked Mom. "Isn't that a good place?"

"Well, for starters," Marie said, "you'll note we're not in Vermont, which should be your first clue that that place is completely bogus."

Mom was silent for a minute. Then she said, "Well, I have pretty much experience in the retail food area, though. I ought to be able to get hired there. Maybe I'll go to that Bread and Circus supermarket, too. They must have a pretty big staff to make all that prepared stuff they sell."

Marie just shook her head.

"What?" said Mom. Marie kept shaking her head.

"Well, *somebody's* got to make all that high-priced fancy organic stuff people like you buy," Mom said. "Some poor, underachieving loser, for slave wages. It might as well be me."

"*What?*" breathed Marie.

"Marie," Mom said, "I know you're right, about the computer skills. But I just don't have them right now. And I have to get a job *somewhere*."

Marie sighed. She was still shaking her head.

"Well," Mom said, "what would you do if you were me?" Marie looked at Mom like Mom had just asked her to imagine being a protozoan, or a Neptunian, or a rock.

"What about the colleges?" said Marie.

"What would I do there?" Mom asked.

"I don't know," Marie said. "Something clerical?"

"Oh, I wouldn't be good at that," Mom said.

"You can't file?" Marie said. "You can't answer a telephone? You don't know how to work a copy machine? That's ridiculous."

"But you probably need computer skills," said Mom.

"Whatever you'd need for a job like that, I could teach you in one day."

I couldn't figure it out—it was like Mom had a black hole in her imagination. Whenever she heard about someone else's job, the first thing that came out of her mouth, automatically, was, "I could *never* do that." I knew it was true about some jobs: you couldn't be a doctor if you hadn't gone to medical school; you couldn't just walk in and get a job building skyscrapers if you didn't already know how to. But Mom had said it to our friend Kendra, who made clay pots and sold them, and I had learned how to make a clay pot in one day, at summer camp; she'd said it when we were watching a show about professional dog walkers; she'd even said it once when she was getting ready for a catering job, tying crepes up into little bundles with chives. Grandma Bobbie had come over to help.

"Here," Mom had said, and she'd showed Grandma how to tie a chive into a little bow.

"You could be like that lady on TV," Grandma had said. "That one who looks like a man—what's her name? You could show people how to make these things; you do such a nice job, honey."

"I could never do that," Mom had said, and I remember Grandma and I had looked at each other like, "What is she talking about?" since, obviously, the thing she said she could never do she was standing there doing.

Marie didn't get it, though. "The colleges have great benefits," she said.

"They'd never give one of those jobs to someone like me," Mom said.

"I'll take a look at your résumé if you like," said Marie.

"Oh, I'd be embarrassed for you to see my résumé," said Mom.

"Christ, Colleen," Marie finally said, but Mom just looked at her and said, "What?"

Marie was still standing in my doorway.

"But I thought we could go out to lunch and then go shopping," she said. I didn't think it would be a good idea to remind Marie that she didn't believe in shopping.

"I don't have any money," I told her.

"I'll buy you two things," she said. "Or fifty dollars, whichever comes first."

"Thanks," I said. "But I'll probably just do something with Mom."

There was something I didn't understand, and that was the way Marie could make you hate her and feel sorry for her at the same time. She looked at me as if I had stabbed her in the heart. As if I was supposed to feel like it was my fault that the only thing she didn't have in her perfect life was an eleven-and-a-half-year-old best friend. She turned slowly, without saying anything else, and walked out of my room. I tried to focus just on the hating her part, but I couldn't.

Maybe I should go on a campaign of being nice to Marie, I thought as I lay there in my bed. Maybe after she was done being weird to you for forty days and forty nights, you would start to see all the wonderful things there were to see about Marie, the ones Mom was always talking about. Maybe I should go out on the town with her today after all, though I really, really, *really* didn't want to.

I got out of bed and went to find her. She was down in the kitchen. She had Mom in a corner, and she was hissing at her like a mad cat: "Here I am bending over backwards to be nice to Justine and all she can do is insult me. What kind of children are you raising, anyway?!"

I changed my mind and snuck back to my room, but five minutes later Mom came in, wiping her eyes, and told me to get dressed because I was going out to lunch and shopping with Marie, no ifs, ands, or buts.

"Well!" said Marie, as if nothing bad had happened, as soon as we were inside her minivan. The day we got to Massachusetts, before we had even gone inside the house, she had pointed to it in the driveway and said to Mom, "Can you believe I drive a minivan? See my bumper sticker?" she'd laughed. On the back was a bumper sticker that said, "Minivans Are Tangible Evidence of Evil." "Would you *ever* have thought I'd be someone who'd drive a minivan?" she'd asked Mom.

"No!" Mom had replied, looking at the van and laughing.

Marie had given her a weird look, then said, as if she and Mom were suddenly in an argument, "Well, we needed something with more space. At least we didn't get one of those planet-raping sport utility vehicles."

"I just want you to know," Marie said before we were even out of the driveway, "I realize it must be strange for you, to have come all this way, and to have to adjust to a new house, and a new school, and make all new friends and everything. And I also want you to know: I'm here if you need anything. If there's something you don't feel comfortable talking to your mom about." I had a rude thought right then—it was so rude, for a second I wondered who had thought it: I wonder what Marie's going to buy me at the mall today?

The first place we went was to a restaurant, Santa Fe Grille. Grown-ups think kids like going out to lunch a lot more than they really do. Mom was fun to go out to lunch with, actually, because she would take you somewhere you wanted to go, like Taco Bell, and let you order whatever you wanted. Usually, though, with a grown-up, like Grandma, you went to a sitting-down place, the kind where your heart sinks as soon as the waiter comes to tell you the specials—crusted tuna with raisin sauce, cold eggplant soup with ten thousand hot chili peppers in it—and then you sat and sat and sat, waiting forever for the famous food to come.

"You are going to *love* this place!" Marie said as soon as we sat down. "They have the best grilled veggie salad."

The only thing worse than sitting next to someone in a car who you couldn't think of anything to say to was sitting across from them in a restaurant.

"So, Justine, what do you want to be when you grow up?" Marie asked after the waiter had taken the menus away and we had sat there in silence for a little while.

"I don't know," I answered truthfully. I had never, ever understood why it was so important to grown-ups that you be able to say what you wanted to be when you grew up, even if you were only five or six years old. The first thing, practically, that you learned when you got to kindergarten was how to answer that question—the teacher would get out those cards with pictures of workers on them and make you choose which one you were going to be, and if you didn't want to be a doctor, teacher, firefighter, or police officer, oh well. I politely didn't point out to Marie that I bet she had never, when she was a kid, said proudly, "When I grow up I want to sit at a computer all day selling automatic light-shutter-offers to old people."

"Well," she said, "whatever you do, computer skills are essential. And you know, actually, I could start teaching you some. Would you like that?"

"Maybe," I said.

Then she sighed and shook her head and said, "Your mother."

"We didn't have a computer till last year," I told her.

"That's no excuse," said Marie.

"She writes e-mails," I said. Mom wrote e-mails all night sometimes.

"That's not what I'm talking about," said Marie. Then she said, "You know, I feel like Colleen just really took a wrong turn somewhere." I didn't like the picture, of Mom behind the wheel of a car, squinting and smiling like Mr. Magoo, veering off the road where it curved.

"Maybe not really," I said to Marie.

"Well, how would you put it?" Marie said challengingly.

How *would* I put it? I didn't know. I had a picture, and maybe it didn't make any sense. I could see a place—huge and dark and empty, like a big field at night. It was a place you could wander around in; you could make all the turns you wanted—it didn't matter, because there was no way you could get lost. And there was Mom, standing out in the dark, alone, looking up at the stars. There was something weird about the picture, and it took me a minute to figure out what it was: There were no constellations. In real life that wouldn't be so weird, but in my picture, it was the most important thing. It was as if Mom had gone out into that field before any other human beings had looked up at the sky and given names to things—before a story existed about everything already. But I couldn't tell, from looking at my picture, whether that would feel like the loneliest or the greatest thing to her.

Anyway, I didn't feel like trying to tell any of that to Marie. She was still waiting for me to answer. I didn't think there was much chance of her understanding. Maybe Mom wasn't lost at all—maybe, really, she was standing right in the middle of everything, just temporarily a little overwhelmed by the idea of arranging the universe the way she wanted it.

"How *would* you put it?" Marie asked again in a mean voice that surprised me. Then she said, "I'm not saying these things to be mean, you know. I just think it's important for you to see that the way your mom does things isn't necessarily a good way. That you don't necessarily have to follow the example she's setting in your own life."

I wondered if Marie would let me get a miniskirt. Madison, Lauren, Kara, and Kirsten all had them, and even though I hated myself for thinking anything about those girls was cool, I did like their skirts, even if they weren't made of real leather like they thought they were. I wondered if there was an army-navy store where we were going, because I kind of liked those olive green pants people had.

Marie sighed. "The thing Colleen doesn't understand is that we just want her to be *happy*."

Grown-ups were so obsessed with everyone being happy. When I was little, Mom used to ask me every night when she put me to bed, "Are you a happy little girl?"

"Yes," I would always answer. It was the same thing Rona answered every night, when the ritual passed down to her. Though it had been a while, actually, since Mom had remembered to ask Rona the question.

"Yes," Rona would say with her thumb in her mouth.

"Good!" Mom would say, and nuzzle her head into Rona's. I liked when they did that, across the room from me; it made me feel calm and safe; and it was nice to know that the answer would be the same every night, even if Rona had had a world-class shit-fit a few hours earlier, or Dale had yelled at her, or the time Billy Jane's smile had come off in the wash and she'd cried so hard I thought maybe Mom should take her to the hospital.

I was glad Mom had stopped asking me that question, though. Because when you got older, it wasn't as easy to answer yes anymore. Even if you liked the feeling of lying there in the dark as much as you ever did, and nothing was wrong, exactly, you couldn't help thinking weird things, like Happy all the time? Happy compared to what? And what does happy really mean, anyway?

I once had a deep thought: that happy was just one of a bunch of different ways you could feel, and the problem with happiness was everyone had blown it all out of proportion, so that it had become like horses' ankles or ostrich wings—something that wasn't strong enough to hold up the weight it was expected to. But of course if you ever tried to explain something like that to a grown-up, they'd look at you like they were about to run and call the suicide hot line.

Marie was still talking to me. "For one thing," she was saying, "I really would love to find her a quality man." She looked at me. "What do you think?"

The waiter came to the table with the food.

"Oh, yum!" Marie said, and she picked up her fork.

My sandwich looked suspicious.

"I mean," she said, "why do you think she always chooses such abizmul losers?" I didn't know what abizmul meant, but if it was a kind of loser, I figured there was a good chance Mom had tried it. Still, it made me mad to hear.

Marie took a big bite of her Southwest Grilled Veggie Salad and looked at me, chewing. "You're not eating, Justine," she said. "Try your sandwich." She put her hand across the table and touched my arm. "Are you upset? I didn't mean to upset you."

I looked at my sandwich, but I didn't touch it.

"The fact is," Marie said, "I love your mom. I really do. But I just want to see her *make* something of herself, you know what I mean?"

My sandwich was supposed to be grilled cheese, but there was something white and stinky dripping out of it. I felt my stomach take a dive, and I couldn't tell if it was the sandwich or what Marie had just said.

Mom was so good at inventing other people—she spent her whole life, practically, making up other people's incredible lives: their perfect jobs, their wonderful boyfriends and girlfriends and husbands and wives, their fantastic personalities, all the amazing things they were busy doing or would be doing if they weren't already too busy doing even more stupendous things. But she was like the anti-inventor of herself. All she ever talked about was the things she *couldn't* do, and maybe nobody but me and Grandma and Rona would ever know about the things she *could* do, like stuff pea pods till doomsday, or clean a house in four dimensions, or baby-sit someone else's kids for a week for free and never even get mad at them once.

But none of those things counted for "making something of yourself," I knew. Making something of herself was the thing that Mom might never, ever do.

"Come on, Justine," Marie said, sopping up tomatillo-crema dressing with a sweet-potato chip, "eat some more of that so we can get going. We have worlds to conquer today!" She grinned as if we had just had a nice, calm, normal lunch. I noticed a woman from another table looking over at us, and I hated realizing that she probably thought Marie was my mother.

"What do you think you might be in the market for today?" Marie asked as we drove.

"I don't know," I said.

"Justine," she said after a minute, "are you normally this uncommunicative, or do you just not feel comfortable with me or what?" We were turning into the mall parking lot.

"I don't know," I said. She parked the minivan, but when I went to open my door, she clicked the lock shut with her automatic controls and turned to look at me.

"We're going to have a really great time," she said to me, and she sat there with her finger on the button until I said, "Yeah." I was thinking two things: how much I really wanted to go home and, also, how I might like a black ribbed turtleneck to go with my miniskirt, if Marie let me get one. And maybe some black, chunky-soled shoes. And a pair of flare-leg jeans. Mom had given me thirty dollars, and even though I had no idea where we got money anymore, and thought maybe I shouldn't take it, I had taken it anyway. Probably I won't spend it, I'd said to myself as I'd put it in my purse. Now, as I sat there looking out at the ugly mall building, I could picture myself, so clearly that it felt like having a memory in advance, coming out in three hours with my new stuff and all the money gone.

For someone with such a low opinion of shopping, Marie was pretty good at it. At every store we went to, she'd charge to the racks and start pulling things out, saying, "Here! Try this one on! Oh, and try this one!" Once I got in the dressing room, she kept coming back and throwing things over the door: "Look, I found another one, in red!" "Try this pair—I think the style would look great on you!" It wasn't like shopping with Mom, who would just wander around the store till I came out of the dressing room and then say, "That looks really cute on you!" no matter what I tried.

When I came out in a black ribbed turtleneck just like the one I'd been imagining and a perfect denim miniskirt, Marie said, "Hmm," and ran her eyes over my body. It was the exact same look I'd hated the first time she did it to me, but right then, I didn't mind it so much. It actually gave me almost a good feeling. Like being protected or something, which made no sense, since there was nothing scary in the store—just some other girls and moms and a bunch of salesgirls patrolling around. Finally Marie said, "You know, that's a nice turtleneck, but black isn't your color. It makes you look washed out. And that skirt isn't the right size. You need it smaller, actually, for the true mini effect." She had to be wrong about the turtleneck—I loved it so much. But she said, "I saw the same one in a sort of bottle green out there; I'll get it for you." And the second I put it on I saw she was right—it was perfect, and the tiny skirt, too.

I was having the weirdest feeling there in the dressing room, and a minute later, when I went back out to the store, it got even weirder. Watching Marie, as she stood at the counter telling the girl to please hold our items while we went and shopped around some more, I suddenly got the strangest urge to go and stand right next to her, maybe even put my hand in hers. I felt my face go red and my head get light and buzzy. I wanted to go home, but I also hoped Marie would say, "Let's shop some more."

I wondered what Mom was doing at home. Maybe looking at the apartment ads, waiting for me to come home so we could start shopping around for our new life. I was glad I was here and not there. That thought sauntered defiantly across my brain, like a bad kid.

"Lord & Taylor next?" said Marie.

When we got home everyone was gone, and I was glad. Even though I had had a good time shopping, I was dreading the thought of walking in with my bags, Mom asking to see what I'd gotten, and Marie watching, as if she owned me now, telling Mom how much fun we'd had.

I went to my room and laid out my new stuff. I didn't notice at first, but after a minute I realized I'd put them in the shape of a person—the turtleneck, and the skirt below it, and then, underneath that, I'd put the shoes, too—right on top of the bed. But the weird thing was the way I put them—I'd put them on their sides, both facing the same way, the way Rona drew people's feet.

I heard voices downstairs—"Hel-lo-o-o!" Mom calling, and Marie saying something back, then Rona's feet running up the stairs. Rona burst into the room.

"She's in here!" she yelled when she saw me, then I heard Mom starting up the stairs, and Marie, too.

"I have to tell you," Marie was saying, "she is *one* intrepid shopper. Are you *sure* she's your daughter?"

"Ha!" Mom said, then they burst through the door. I tried to gather up my new clothes, but Mom said, "No! Let me see!"

"Aren't these great?" Marie said.

"Yes!" said Mom. "They're great! They really are. Thank you, Marie. Thank you, thank you. Justine, did you say thank you? How much money do I owe you?" she asked Marie.

"Nothing," said Marie. "I told you I was buying some things for Justine. I want her to look nice, and feel good about herself."

"Oh," Mom said.

"I think that's important."

"I do, too," said Mom.

"I think Justine's life is tough enough without having to worry about looking like a geek," said Marie. She said it like she was making the funniest joke.

Mom just looked at her. "Well," she said. Her voice sounded like talking Barbie when her battery got low.

"You should see her in this skirt," Marie said. "Put it on, Justine!" She winked at me.

Mom nodded at me. "Put it on," she said. I gathered up the clothes and headed for the door.

"Don't be modest!" Marie said. "We're all girls here."

I took the clothes down the hall into the bathroom. I didn't put them on, though. I knelt by the toilet and threw up—one disgusting fake grilled-cheese sandwich and a pineapple-mango spritzer—and I wished I could throw up the picture I was having, too, of that imaginary person on the bed, invisible except for her skirt and her turtleneck, her feet pointing off into the sunset in her clunky new shoes.

The poor baby still does not improve. I rock her and sing to her, make her special potions to suck off my finger and poultices to put on her tiny chest. I mash anything mashable and try to spoon it into her, but she squishes her lips tightly shut. I wish I knew what was wrong with her. She was fine before we left home, but this journey certainly does not seem to agree with her.

POSITIVE ASPECTS OF THE PIONEER EXPERIENCE

It seemed like even though Ms. Taylor had been teaching the sixth grade for probably about a hundred years, she hadn't ever noticed what sixth-graders were like. She treated us like babies. She loved to give us drawing assignments, for example: Draw a picture of *A Midsummer Night's Dream*; draw a picture of the Massachusetts State seal; draw a picture of an American president's head. That way, no one had to think too much about anything. She didn't like reasons: she liked to know when things happened and where they happened, but not why they happened or how you felt about them; and if you tried to tell her, she'd mark you wrong.

At first, I was actually sort of excited for the pioneer unit, even though Ms. Taylor just stood up at the front of the class for thirty minutes every Tuesday and Thursday reciting facts to us: what number of people left every year; how many miles it was between this place and that place; how many pounds of food a team of oxen could eat in a month. But sometimes she would say something interesting by accident, like "In some places today, you can still see grave markers of people who died along the way"; and my brain would veer off the facts to something like What if you were a kid, and everyone in your whole family died except you?

Of course, when Ms. Taylor said, "Write a pioneer diary," none of the boys could just be an ordinary person—they all had to be in the Donner party, writing about some new dire circumstance every day, like having to eat their dog, or the mom boiling the family's shoes into soup. Ms. Taylor probably didn't even mark them off for getting the facts wrong. Like by the time it came down to eating your dog, you probably wouldn't be smiling, like in Alex's drawing of his diary character Donny Donner, who sat by a fire waving a dog drumstick in the air with a big grin on his face. She probably sat there at home reading Alex's diary and laughed and laughed. Just like she probably went home the day Alex Brennan looked up my dress and laughed, remembering it. Ms. Taylor probably had a laughing fit, picturing her little darling crouched on the floor pretending to pick up a pencil with his face turned upwards, right at my underpants, and Jake, Noah, and Joey P. watching him, little squirts of laughter coming out of their noses.

By the second week of the assignment, though, I wasn't excited anymore.

"One more thing," Ms. Taylor told us the day she gave the assignment. "I want your diaries to be written from a child's point of view." Then she told us we could use *Timothy and Tabitha Cross the Plains* as a guide, if we weren't sure what to do. *Timothy and Tabitha Cross the Plains* was a baby book she'd passed out about two pioneer children, a brother and sister, who just watched everything going on around them and said things like "Look! The mighty Mississippi!"; "The sky is big and blue"; "Our three yoke of oxen are very strong"; and "Mother pulled out the old black kettle and measured out a handful of flour."

I guess that's what Ms. Taylor thinks a child's point of view is supposed to be like—this thing happened, that thing happened, la-di-da, no reason, end of story.

What I think is that inside children there's actually an adult. Not a real adult, but sort of the seed of the one you're going to turn out to be. Which is why you can usually figure out the reasons for things, and what to do, if you think hard enough. However, I suppose Ms. Taylor thinks that's boring. I suppose she thinks it's more interesting to read about someone's head burning off from scarlet fever, or how their dog tasted surprisingly like Kentucky Fried Chicken, which wasn't even invented at the time, obviously.

On Friday, Ms. Taylor called me up to her desk and said, "Did you turn in your diary yesterday, Justine? I can't seem to find it."

"No," I said.

"Well, what's the problem?" she asked, and I wished I could tell her the truth: I didn't know what the problem was. I had never had a teacher before who made my imagination go completely white. I'd sat with a blank sheet of paper in front of me for an hour after school on Tuesday, trying to think of something to write. I'd looked at the pioneer books in the school library, where Ms. Taylor got all her lame ideas, but they just said the same things Ms. Taylor had already told us.

"I couldn't think of anything to write," I said.

"Well," she said to me as I stood next to her desk, "what are some ideas of ways you could start? Let's brainstorm." She stared at me, and I tried to look like there was something happening in my brain.

Everybody else's journal, pretty much, was starting at the Mississippi River. "I could start at the Mississippi River," I said.

"That's a great idea!" said Ms. Taylor. "Who will your characters be?"

I thought of Timothy and Tabitha. "A girl and her little brother and her parents?" I answered.

"Excellent," she said.

—∞—

We reached Fort Kearny today. Frankly, it's a little disappointing—mostly just a bunch of men hanging around, talking about their wagons: "I built this wagon out of the strongest wood in the history of the world"; "These metal tires are hurricane-, tornado-, and volcano-proof"; "Well, my skeleton is designed to cut down wind resistance by thirty-two percent."

Thaddeus got out and dragged himself around a little. I told him he should find a doctor, but he just harrumphed. "No need for that," he said. "I will be fine in a few days."

Amethyst, surprise, surprise, managed to pull herself out of bed, comb her hair, and take a stroll down the dusty street in front of the supply post.

"Fort Kearny is a lovely place," I heard her remark to a soldier. "I could see living here." I don't know why the sight of soldiers and storekeepers fills her with energy, when all day long, though I try to get her to come sit up front and look at the landscape and talk to me and the children, all she does

is lie on her bedroll, moaning and groaning. It's as if her own company makes her sick. Talking to us makes her tired. But strange men are a health elixir to her.

I bought some supplies—flour, beef, lard, coffee, salt, and bacon. Thaddeus doesn't know yet. According to his calculations, we are not supposed to be running low on anything, and I didn't feel like arguing with him. He was already collapsed in the back of the wagon after his long walk down the block, and I just went ahead and did it. Probably he'll yell at me and start criticizing me to his pal, God, when he wakes up and finds out.

The next Wednesday, Ms. Taylor called me up to her desk again. "What seems to be the problem, Justine?" she said. When I didn't answer, she said, "You know, if you need help with the homework, we can work these things out. But you have to tell me. I can't just guess what's wrong." Some of the eagle-eared girls heard that and looked over.

"Okay," I said, hoping that was enough of an answer.

"Maybe you need a study buddy," she said. Lauren and Kara, who were sitting about one foot from Ms. Taylor's desk, cracked up when she said that.

"Shh, class," said Ms. Taylor. "Continue quietly reading the chapter." To me, she said, "Sometimes it helps to have someone you can share ideas with—you know, who can help you brainstorm, or quiz you, who you can call at night if there's a problem you can't do. A study buddy!" She smiled at me. "Now," she said, looking out at the room. "Who are you special friends with?"

I had never hated a grown-up as much as I hated Ms. Taylor at that moment. Lauren and Kara were watching and listening to see what I would say, their mouths contorted from trying not to laugh.

"Who do you play with the most?" Ms. Taylor asked.

"P-p-h-p-p-h-p-h-h!" went Lauren, and Kara started to shake silently.

I had to do something to stop Ms. Taylor, so I looked out over the room and picked the person farthest away from Ms. Taylor's desk, with the least chance of hearing. I turned my body so that Lauren and Kara couldn't see my mouth move, and I whispered, "Jane Brown."

Ms. Taylor looked surprised. Maybe she thought Jane Brown was a loser just like everybody else did. But she said, "Oh! Okay!" Then she said, in a voice like a megaphone, *"Jane! Jane! Could you come to my desk, please?"* Everybody stopped what they were doing.

"Oooh," whispered Joey P. "Justine and Jane! Lez be friends!"

Jane Brown came over and stood next to me, but she didn't look at me. One thing I'd noticed about Jane Brown was that she could make the blankest face of anybody I'd ever seen. She could make her mouth perfectly straight. It was kind of amazing, really—she could make you forget you were looking at an actual face, made out of flesh and bones and skin, with feelings underneath, and make you think you were looking at a drawing on a piece of paper, a stick figure's head.

"Jane," Ms. Taylor said, "Justine would like you to be her study buddy."

Jane blinked once.

"Would you like to do that?" Ms. Taylor went on. "You give her your phone number, and she'll give you hers, and maybe you could get together and go over the notes from the unit so far, and talk about ideas for your journals?" Jane blinked again. Apparently Ms. Taylor had decided that meant yes.

"Good!" she said. "Okay, you two can go sit down. Write down your phone numbers for each other. And Justine, I'll see your journal on Thursday?"

After Ms. Taylor told us to go sit down, Jane Brown went to her desk at the back of the room, and I went to mine at the front. I tore a piece of paper out of my binder and wrote my phone number on it, and I looked back to see if she had done the same thing, but I couldn't tell. She was sitting at her desk with the straight line across her face. I folded up the piece of paper and decided to give it to her at recess. But when the bell rang, Jane Brown just walked past my desk without saying anything. On the playground, she stood near the kickball game, and I knew what she was doing: she was pretending she was thinking about joining the game any minute, so that no one would wonder why she wasn't playing with anyone, but really she was just waiting for recess to be over. I was standing near the four-square game. The piece of paper with my phone number on it was folded up and hidden in my palm, and I kept picturing myself going over to Jane Brown and handing her the paper; but when I stopped picturing it, I was still standing in the same spot. When we came back to the classroom, I looked on the top of my desk, and inside of it, too, in case Jane had left a piece of paper there, but she hadn't.

I started a fake journal when I got home from school that day, while Rona and I watched *General Hospital*. It was about a girl named Hecate Lorelei Watson, and I let Rona make up all the stories in it: Hecate Lorelei and her little brother fight about who gets to sit on the horse, Hecate Lorelei almost loses her rag doll in the river. I put in dates and places and facts from the chapter in our book: "May 15, 1851, Independence, Missouri—We loaded our 48-square-foot wagon with food, tools, and furniture. Tomorrow we will be on our way." "May 30, 1851, Platte River Valley—The grass is very green here. We have come 300 miles." "June 1, 1851—We reached Fort Kearny, Gateway to the Great Plains. Maybe we will see a buffalo." Ms. Taylor liked it if you showed everything going in a straight line and all in the right order—nothing like real life.

On Wednesday, Ms. Taylor handed back my diary. "Excellent start!" she'd written on the top, and my heart sighed with boredom, thinking now I'd have to think of more things to write about Hecate Lorelei. Hecate Lorelei gathers flowers. Hecate Lorelei sees an Indian. Maybe Rona would have more ideas.

———⋙———

Last night I dreamt of a man choking on a felt beret. When I woke up, Thaddeus was hacking and twisting on his bedroll. He hardly gets up at all anymore, except to answer the call of nature. He just lies in the back of the wagon and calls to me: "Wife! Zebulina! Wife!" Sometimes I pretend not to hear him, but it makes no difference.

"Drive faster!" he calls.

"Yes, Thaddeus," I say, but I don't urge the oxen on.

"Don't drive so fast!" he yells.

"Yes, Thaddeus," I answer.

"Bang a left at Council Bluffs," he calls from his fevered fog.

"Yes, darling." Council Bluffs was a month back.

"Make sure you don't take the wrong turn and head for Santa Fe!" As if I'm a freakin idiot.

"Wife!" he called this afternoon. "I would like a little chamomile tea!"

"You mean," I said in a low voice, "you want me to stop the wagon, unpack the teakettle, gather wood, start a fire, fetch water, and make you a cup of tea right now?"

"What?" he called.

"Nothing!" I called back. I kept driving.

"Wife!" he called.

I think his voice is getting weaker.

In the gym on Monday, they had an assembly on sexual harassment, which is what crawling around on the floor looking up people's dresses is, but it was stupid. It was the same as the "changing bodies" talk we'd had the week before—the boys sat on one side and made sick jokes and cracked up every time Ms. Weintraub said a dirty word, and the girls sat on the other and giggled and got made a total fool of. It was like Ms. Weintraub just stood up there telling all your secrets— how you're going to get your period any day, and now your body's this gross thing you have to be careful not to let anyone touch in a bad way or make jokes about or date-rape; and she looked right at the girls the whole time she was giving her speech, her eyes saying the opposite of what she was saying in words: that whatever bad thing happened to you was your own fault, for changing from your perfectly good body to a new, grotesque one that caused trouble for everybody.

One minute after the sexual harassment assembly was over, Kevin, Alex, Noah, and Joey P. walked by me, and Joey picked up two spots on his shirt with his fingers and made little tents out of them. "Any *recent developments*, Justine?" he asked, which I don't have anyway, and they all laughed.

Sometimes I try to picture what it is they think they see when they walk by me and say, "Jus-ti-i-i-ine." But I can't. It isn't even a real person they've invented; it's just their sick idea of something called "girl," which according to them is made up of breasts and secret places you have to get down on the floor to see and untrue stories about things that would never happen. Like when I heard Noah say to Alex, "I bet you could get second base off of Justine."

I had no idea what he was talking about, but of course I didn't ask. And it actually sounded less rude than some of the other things they said, so I sort of forgot about it for a while. But a few days later, I heard Lauren and Madison giggling about the same subject, and I realized: It wasn't about baseball. Whatever it was was something that could happen inside a closet at a party. "Kara and Noah went to first base!" Lauren whispered to Madison, and she smiled, and I pictured two happy people running side by side, holding hands and laughing. But when the boys talked about it, it was different. It sounded more like a contest the boys were in that somehow involved the girls, but I couldn't tell who was against who, exactly, or even where the girls were, actually. Because when Alex said to Noah, loud enough for everyone around him to hear, that his brother in the eighth grade had gone out with a girl and gotten all the way to third, I got a totally different picture, one without any people in it even. All I could see were the bases—those dusty white bags—lying in the dirt with footprints all over them.

I was horrified when I found out what they were really talking about.

"What's second base?" I asked Mom one day when I got home from school. Noah had said it again: "Justine goes to second base," he'd whispered to Joey P., just loud enough for me to hear when I walked past his desk, and Joey had gone, "Ew. Gross."

"Second base?" Mom asked. "Like in baseball?"

"Like when people say, 'So-and-so and so-and-so went to second base.' "

"Aa-a-a-h!" Mom said, like Confucius. Then she said, "Why do you ask?"

"Some girls were talking about it at school," I told Mom.

"It's about making out," Mom said. "Kissing and stuff." I wished I had the magic power to make life go in reverse.

"Oh," I said, "okay," and I started going through my binder, like I was ready to start my homework, but Mom was making girl-talk eyebrows at me.

"First base is kissing," she said. "You really haven't ever heard this? And second base is, well, it's a little more than that. It's like, well, if you were kissing, and . . . um . . ."

The back door opened and closed, and we could hear Marie rustling in with grocery bags. "Marie," Mom called, "how would you describe second base?"

"Second base?" Marie called back. "Like when someone feels your tits?" She came around the corner and looked surprised to see me.

"Oh, do we have to put it like that?" Mom said. "I was thinking something a little more romantic. Let's say second base is when—"

"What is this, Colleen? Child abuse?" said Marie.

"What?" said Mom. Marie just stood there glaring at Mom.

"Justine asked me about the bases," Mom told her.

"Can I go upstairs?" I said.

"You don't have to go anywhere," Mom said. "Since when did it get to be not all right to talk about sexuality in front of you?" she asked Marie.

"In front of me?" said Marie. She was standing near me now, and it was weird: I was having the feeling, like a hallucination, of being under a big, tall, shady tree. "In front of me is fine. But is this really appropriate to be talking about in front of a child?"

"What child?" said Mom, and I felt weird, as if I had just flashed off, like a picture in a slide show, only someone had forgotten to put in the next slide, so all there was was a square of bright, blinding whiteness.

"*What child?*" repeated Marie. "Oh, that is so perfect, Colleen. That is so, so perfect."

"Justine is not a child," Mom said. Her voice was almost angry. "Justine is a young woman, and I, as her mother, am allowed to speak frankly with her on any subject I choose."

"Justine's in sixth grade," Marie said, "and she'll find out about this stuff soon enough without you pushing her into it."

"Pushing her into it?" said Mom. "If the kids at school are talking about these things, then Justine needs to know them, too. And instead of giving her the message that sex is nasty, I'd like her to know that it can be a respectful, enjoyable—"

"Fine!" said Marie, and I was glad she'd said it and stopped Mom from finishing her sentence. Marie leaned down close to me, and just for a minute, I pretended that Marie was my mother. I imagined her saying sternly, "I forbid you to think about breasts and bases and re-productive tracks and sexual harassment till you're much older. Now run along and play Candy Land with the kids." Instead she hissed, "The base system." A piece of spit went in my eye. "Kissing, feeling, fingering, fucking—first, second, third, home run. A *respectful, enjoyable* sport for everyone."

I felt like I'd been slapped on the head from four different direc-tions. I wanted to disinfect my brain. I wanted to erase what she'd just said immediately, but I knew the words were like some hideous de-formed monster baby that could never get unborn and were going to live in my brain forever.

Alex Brennan's obsession with the Donner party had spread all over the class. Every Tuesday morning before the bell rang, the boys would read their journals aloud to each other, making sure everyone heard. Listen to this one, they'd say: Today I roasted my sister's eye-ball on a stick. Yesterday my mother ground the dog's toenails into flour. I'm so hungry, it feels exactly like a rat's gnawing a hole through my stomach.

Madison, Kara, Kirsten, and Lauren would congregate around them, going, "Ew!" "Gross! Sick!", then they'd quiet down so they wouldn't miss a word.

Also, everybody except me and Jane Brown played Donner party at every recess. The boys would run around in one part of the play-ground, trying to stab each other, shoot each other, and choke each other to death over anything edible; and the girls would huddle in a corner and giggle and moan, pretending to be hungry, pretending to be cooking things in big pots, yelling things over at the boys' camp like "Oh, no, poor cousin Edward is dead; well, at least we'll get to have a *wienie* roast tonight!" and everybody of course would go into convulsions.

One Tuesday morning, Ms. Taylor said, "Class, it has come to my attention that many of your journals are becoming, how shall I say, rather morbid and depressing. Now, I don't want to put a damper on your creativity. But I just think you could put your imaginative im-pulses to a better, more constructive use. Besides," she said, winking at

Alex and his crew, "think of me, grading these things all weekend. Think of how depressed I get, reading all these horrible, sad stories. Besides feeling like I'm going to toss my cookies."

"*Wha-ha-ha!*" went all the boys.

Ms. Taylor looked their way lovingly. "So I'd like you to focus a little bit more on the positive aspects of the pioneer experience." The boys groaned. "I'm sorry," said Ms. Taylor. "But I know you can do it. So remember: Nothing heavy. Nothing depressing. Let's keep things upbeat, okay?" I got a picture of upbeat pioneers bopping along the trail, snapping their fingers like people in a musical, getting ready to burst into a song. "Let's move away from the Donners. Don't make me sad."

—m—

Today I saw seven grave markers, two small ones where a baby or child must lie. How their poor mothers must grieve for them. A baby is the most precious thing in the world; that's the thing you know when you hold your newborn baby in your arms for the first time; when you look down into its face and the two of you stare into each other's eyes, trying to figure out who invented who.

It's important at that moment that you don't look away, before the knowledge has time to set—the knowledge, as you stare into that tiny face, that you're its mother, no matter what, for the rest of your life. That a baby's not just like some egg that you carry around for a week to teach you how shocking responsibility is.

I made the mistake of telling Thaddeus about the grave markers. Wouldn't it be awful to lose one of your little ones? I said.

He told me my thoughts were blasphemous. That a baby is something God sends, and everything that happens to it is his will. And if you lose a child or two along the way, you shouldn't knock yourself out wondering why.

I daren't tell Thaddeus what a crock I think that is. He'd probably strike me down faster than God would.

Speaking of gravestones, he didn't look too good today. His voice was thinner than usual, his whole body seemed a little limp, his face wasn't its usual shade of vermilion.

"Wife," he called to me after supper, "could you fix me an elixir?" The

fire had gone out; the baby was fretting at my breast; I still had all the dishes to wash. And I was still mad about the gravestone conversation. "Fix it yourself," I muttered.

"I don't feel quite up to snuff," he said.

"Maybe God has plans for you," I said in a voice too low for him to hear.

That day at recess, I went to stand near where Jane Brown was standing, by the monkey bars.

"How's your diary going?" I asked her. For a split second, I thought I saw the flicker of an expression—as if she were going to tell me something. Then it was gone.

"Fine," she said.

"There were other things about the Donners," I said. Jane Brown looked at me. "Besides that they ate each other." I'd made Mom take me to the real library and checked out some books. "They had an interesting story." Not that I cared that much about the Donners, because I didn't—it just bothered me, I guess, that everyone's imaginations, Ms. Taylor's included, were so defective. Jane Brown didn't say anything.

"Well, I don't know," I said, and I guess Jane Brown thought that meant "Good-bye." She looked at me one more time and then walked away.

The next day, I went up to Jane Brown before school started. She was taking off her coat at her locker. "I like your outfit," I said. Her eyes moved back and forth, but her mouth stayed in a straight line.

"Thank you," she said.

The day after that, I tried again. "That was a good report on dolphin intelligence," I told her. She gave me the exact same look as the day before.

"Thank you," she said.

The next day, I decided to ask something you couldn't answer with "Thank you," "Yes," or "No," so I sat down next to her at lunch and said, "Where do you live?" She stopped chewing and looked at me with no expression.

"Three Fifty-seven Hillside Road," she said, then she looked down as if she had to get back to her lunch. Then I wished I hadn't unpacked my whole lunch, because I had to sit there and eat it next to Jane Brown, and neither of us said anything else the whole time. When she was done with her sandwich, Jane Brown stood up and walked to the garbage can, threw away her garbage, and went out the lunchroom door.

I decided I wouldn't try to talk to her anymore after that, but it was weird—the very next day, when I got near her in the hallway on the way to recess, I couldn't keep myself from saying, "Hi."

"Hi," she said, and she turned and got in the drinking fountain line. I got in behind her.

"Do you have any brothers and sisters?" I asked her, though her back was to me.

"Yes," she said before she bent down and took a drink. But she never said how many, and I never found out, because it turned out those were the last words Jane Brown and I ever said to each other.

Maybe we wouldn't have become friends anyway. But every once in a while it makes me sad thinking we might have—that after I had said fifty or a hundred things to Jane Brown, she might finally have decided to have a conversation with me, maybe even one that lasted all day and all night, like Mom and Marie had had the first time they met. But because of what happened, there was no chance we'd ever have that conversation, or any other one, either.

It was actually the worst thing that ever happened, at any school I ever went to.

The popular girls had a lot of idiotic games and activities. One thing they liked to do, for example, was write out lists of the people invited to their sleepover parties and tape them to their desks where everyone could see. Then, all week long, they'd cross out names and add names of anyone who had made them mad or gotten mysteriously popular or unpopular overnight.

Another thing they loved to do was march around the playground with their arms around each other, forming a big chain that would plow you over if you didn't get out of the way, chanting ridiculous sayings like *"Hey! Hey! Get out of our way! We just got back from the U.S.A.!"* which obviously made no sense; and their favorite one—"I re*ceived* a procla*ma*tion from the *board* of edu*ca*tion to per*form* an op-

er*a*tion on a *girl*!" The rest of that particular saying had made-up
words in it—the most despicable was "dinkeration"—because that was
the only way to get it to rhyme and make so-called sense and come out
nasty. The most ridiculous and pathetic thing of all was that the boys
had made up the chant, but they were too scared to say it out loud, so
it was the girls who marched around yelling it and squealing with
laughter.

Another of their favorite pastimes was dress-ups. Which wasn't
the thing you did when you were little and a friend came over and you
pretended to be *ladies* in your mom's clothes and jewelry and makeup,
but meant going around the playground in a big herd to someone who
was wearing a dress and pretending you wanted to sweetly say something to them; then, when you got close enough, yelling, *"Dress-ups!"*
and yanking up their dress in front of everyone so their underwear
showed. Only, the day the really bad thing happened, Lauren had the
very creative idea of walking up behind Jane Brown, who was standing
next to me in the four-square line, and yelling, *"Dress-downs!"* and
pulling down on the stretchy elastic waist of Jane Brown's skirt.

The horrible thing was, her underwear came down, too. Lauren
giggled for one second, and then she stopped—you could tell everyone knew there wasn't anything funny about what had just happened.
Also, the moment didn't disappear like normal time, which was freaky.
It stayed there, not moving, for a second too long, like a picture on a
movie screen just before the film burns up, and you knew you would
have it in your brain forever: the picture of Jane Brown standing
there, with an expression on her face, finally—one that nobody had
ever seen before. Her face was red, and inside her body, you could tell,
all her cells were shaking, though the outside of her was completely
still. And lighted up by the playground light was the poor, bare, white
Y of her legs, looking somehow like the loneliest thing in the world,
something that wished it didn't exist, before she reached down in fast
motion, pulled up her skirt, and walked into the building.

After that, I didn't even try to talk to Jane Brown anymore. And it
wasn't because I thought she was a loser like everyone else did. I
hoped she understood, though I doubted there was much chance of
that—I just had no idea how you acted with someone after something

like that had happened, or if they'd even want to have a friend anymore. There was no one I could ask, either. When I came home from school that day, Mom actually noticed something was wrong.

"Did something bad happen at school today?" she asked, but I said, "No," and she just said, "Hmm," and nodded her head like she believed me, though I wished she wouldn't.

—⁓—

Yesterday we passed Chimney Rock; today we can see Scotts Bluff in the distance. That means we have come about half of the way. I told the children they must not ask me again, "How soon until we get to California?" Then I told them they must stop singing "Nine Hundred Ninety-nine Thousand Nine Hundred and Ninety-nine Bottles of Sarsaparilla on the Wall."

We ought to be coming to Fort Laramie soon. Good thing, because we need supplies again. The only thing we have enough of is onions. Today I made scrambled onions for breakfast, onion-and-biscuit sandwiches for lunch, and onion stew for dinner. We are all getting mighty sick of onions. We have seen huge herds of buffalo, and I have heard buffalo meat is quite tasty, but ever since the rabbit incident, Thaddeus sleeps with the gun at his side and won't let me touch it, even though he is too weak to lift it himself.

—⁓—

This morning I awoke to the sound of moans and groans. Annabelle was shaking my shoulder.

"Mama," she said, "I think Amethyst's dying."

"Not again," I said, stretching.

But Annabelle looked frightened. "Come quick," she said.

When I got to the wagon, there was blood everywhere. Soaked through the blanket, smeared on the canvas walls, soaked through Amethyst's nightgown. There was even blood on her hair.

"What happened?!" I exclaimed.

"Oh, it hurts," moaned Amethyst, clutching her stomach. Then it dawned on me.

"Would you wake your brother and go down to the stream and fetch some water?" I said to Annabelle. No use her having to see such a thing yet.

"Is it the monthlies?" I whispered when Annabelle had gone.

"How should I know?" she snapped at me. "You're the grown woman."

"Is it your first time?" I asked. But she wouldn't answer. She gave me the weirdest look—almost as if she were mocking me. But why?

This problem is very mysterious. I suspect the monthlies, but she won't tell me, won't let me look.

"Don't be frightened," I said, not very convincingly.

"I'm not afraid!" she snapped at me. "That's ridiculous!" and she went back to moaning.

"Do you . . . have anything for it?"

"For it?" she echoed.

"You know. Is it the first time?" I asked again.

"First time?"

"Shall I get you a . . . ?" I didn't know. Someday, surely they'll invent something to take care of this mess. "A rag? A pile of leaves? A bucket?" I wasn't sure how much more she was going to bleed.

I was glad she didn't ask me why I didn't know. Because I had never told anyone—not even my mother: I had never gotten it. The doctor said it was quite strange and remarkable, the only such case he'd ever seen. We ought to send you for a special examination at the Massachusetts Hospital for Women, he told me, but I said, No, thank you very much. If I never get it, that's quite all right with me.

The landscape has gotten kind of weird. It's not so green anymore, and everything is so humongous and empty—the endless plains, with nothing in them but grass; the huge, blank, blue sky. It's the first thing you remember every day when you open your eyes: how small you are; how you could just disappear in the huge, wide-open world.

LAKE OF THE SHADOW VALLEY

I had started to not like coming home from school as much as I hated going to school, and I could get a pretty weird feeling sometimes, walking home from the bus, thinking there was no place I wanted to be.

Every morning when Mom kissed us good-bye she'd say, "I might not be here when you come home today. I'll probably be out either job hunting or looking at apartments." Every afternoon, though, there she'd be. Sometimes she would be doing a cleaning project that no one in the world had ever thought of before, like dusting all the electrical cords or mopping the stones of the walk that led up to the house. Sometimes she would be working on her résumé—at least that's what she called it when Marie would say again, "You know, Colleen, I'd really like to help you get that résumé updated," and Mom would say, "Oh, thanks for reminding me," and get on the computer and change the font again. I had actually shown her that computer skill, and then I wished I hadn't, because I didn't like when she'd come down from the computer room with her résumé written in teeny tiny cursive, or Shakespearean letters, or bamboo, and say, "Look! Isn't this cool?"

Or she might be working on the kind of project I liked the least, actually: something mysterious. One day when we came home from school, she was sitting on the living room floor leaning over a big sheet of thick, speckled paper with torn edges, smiling and humming and drawing on it with Rona's fruit-scented markers.

"Hi, sweetheart, how was school?" Mom asked, glancing up for a second from the bright pink shape she was drawing and then back down. When I didn't answer, she didn't say anything, which was good. I didn't feel like telling her what had happened that day.

In the library, when I was going past the boys' table to sit down with my book, the tip of my sneaker had caught on the carpet for no reason and I tripped.

"*Wha-ha-ha-ha!*" went all the boys. "J-u-u-u-st-i-i-i-n-e!" they started chanting in spazzing voices.

"Children!" called Ms. Stott, the librarian, which made everyone giggle. "No loud voices!"

So the boys started whispering my name instead: "J-u-u-u-st-i-i-i-n-e!"

Tripping was only a small deal, I knew, so I was surprised when my eyes filled with tears. They had been doing that a lot lately, and I hated it. Usually I didn't cry—I threw up instead—and I guess crying was better than throwing up, especially at school, but I hated the feeling of the tears building up in my eyes, things falling out of me that I couldn't control. It made me want to stab my fingers into my eyes, push the tears back in. I sat down and looked at my feet, and suddenly I was mad at them. They looked so big and clumsy. My shoes looked like clown shoes. No wonder I had tripped, in my huge, stupid shoes.

Another thing that had happened that day was that when I'd walked past Lauren's desk, she'd looked up, right at my chest, and giggled and said, "Girl, you need a *bra!*" So Kara, who sat next to her, had looked, too, and so had about five other people in their row. I went back to my desk and sat down and folded my arms over my chest, and I hid my feet behind my desk legs and tried not to move for the rest of the day.

"How was school?" Mom asked again. She'd forgotten she'd already said it. Then she said, "Don't you love this paper? I bought it at the stationery store in Amherst."

Rona came in the room. "Who's using my markers?" she said, sniffing the air. She saw Mom's drawing. "What is it?" she asked.

Maybe it was an application for a freelance graphic designer job. Mom looked at her paper, trying to decide where to put the next line.

"What color would you use for a river?" she said. I saw Mom had a big book next to her. It was an atlas, and it was open to the map of Madagascar.

"What are you making?" I asked.

"Nothing," Mom said. But then she moved out of the way for us to see her drawing better, and she smiled like a little kid who wanted someone to be proud of her. "Just a map."

It wasn't a realistic map; it looked more like one you'd see on the inside cover of a certain kind of book, labeled in curlicue writing with the names of kingdoms and towns and valleys and lands; and clumps of miniature trees, drawn in upside-down Vs, for forests; and lakes with little waves on them; and every piece of the landscape would have a name that nothing would ever have in real life, like "Lake of the Shadow Valley" or "Prthyvigrnl Mountains."

"What's it a map of?" asked Rona.

"Hmm," Mom said without looking up. "Maybe somewhere we'll go someday."

"Can I help?" asked Rona.

"Sure," Mom said.

"Help, Justine," Rona told me, and she put a blueberry marker in my hand.

I didn't really want to, but I made a mark on the paper anyway, and then another, and pretty soon all our heads were bent together over the map and the paper was getting more and more wild and colorful. I started on a forest in one corner. Rona made the sun, and a road, and she outlined the road in one color after another, so that it swelled like a bright, fat rope. Then she drew big orange flowers next to the road, and I put two spiky leaves around each one with the green apple marker.

Across from me, Mom had started in on a raspberry border. I started to copy what she was doing on my side, in grape. Then Rona said, "I want to do that!" and she started a border on her edge, too, in passion fruit. I loved the way it felt—our designs creeping closer and closer toward each other, like we were sealing in what we'd made. We should do this more often, I was thinking—huddle together like witches, mixing up combinations of our imaginations. Maybe it would make us better at our life, somehow. I was about to say that to Mom, but I was glad I didn't get a chance to.

Because the whole thing was a trick. Just as Rona's hand and mine bumped into each other in the corner, Mom handed me a thin gold pen and said, "Sign your names, girls, and we'll give it to Danny when we see him."

Rona and I both looked at her. Suddenly I was so mad at myself. Even though more than a month had gone by since Mom had mentioned Danny Martone, I realized how stupid it was of me to have started thinking that maybe the thought of him had disappeared from her brain. Or that she had decided, all on her own, that maybe Danny Martone wasn't the greatest idea she ever had.

"It's the map to his house," Mom said.

"It is not," Rona said indignantly. "It's our drawing. It's Hanley-land."

"It *is*," said Mom, and she took the picture from Rona. "See?" Her voice was gentle, as if she were reading us a bedtime story. She pointed her finger at the pink shape she'd made, with a tiny black dot in its center. I'd thought it was a flower. "This is where we live. And here's Interstate 91." She pointed to the flower's stem. "And here's where Connecticut meets Massachusetts." I got up from the floor and walked to the door.

"What's the matter, Justine?" Mom said.

As if she didn't know. Or maybe she didn't. That was the thing about Mom that made you feel like you were going crazy sometimes, just knowing her: She acted like she didn't know that the things she did weren't normal. Like, if she needed a map to drive to someone's house, why didn't she just go get the kind everyone else used—the folding kind from the gas station—instead of sitting on the floor in the middle of the day, alone, not having a job, inventing imaginary worlds?

"I absolutely do not think it's a good idea," I heard Marie say to Mom later. Marie and Mom were cleaning up after dinner. I was in the living room playing Candy Land with the kids. Cavanaugh was having a do-over every time he landed on something he didn't like, so

Rona was bending the cards on purpose, which was making Cassidy whine that she was going to tell.

"Why?" asked Mom. I moved to the other side of the Candy Land board so I was next to the kitchen door.

"It's just a really full-of-shit plan," said Marie.

Mom was silent, then she said, "I thought you liked Danny. He used to be such a great guy, remember?"

"I liked him fine twenty years ago, but he was never a great guy. He was a spoiled trust fund proto-slacker with a drinking problem, and all he did was use you, if you'll recall. *And,* his music sucked."

"That's not true," Mom gasped.

"Spare me," said Marie. "You always fell for that schlocky tortured sensitive-guy bullshit."

"It wasn't schlocky," said Mom. "He was very punk."

"Sort of like Jello Biafra meets Billy Joel? Give me a break. And you want to get in a car and drive up and down the eastern seaboard trying to *find* this guy? You're pinning your entire destiny on some alcoholic seventies dropout who doesn't even remember you exist?"

"He remembers I exist!" said Mom.

"You've had some actual indication of this?" said Marie. "Did he write to you? Did he call you? Did he send you a *cosmic vibe?*"

Mom didn't answer right away, then she said softly, "I remember *him.*"

She was about to cry, but Marie, of course, had no clue. What was her problem? I could figure it out, and I wasn't even in the same room. Tonight, Marie had already made Mom cry by pointing out that the laundry soap Mom had bought wasn't the environmentally friendly kind. Then she'd put her arm around Mom and said, "Colleen, I'm sorry! I just knew it was something you'd want to know, because you care about the planet."

"You have got to get a plan, woman," Marie said now. "You have seriously got to sit down and figure out how you're going to get your life together."

"And you think I should stay single until I do that," said Mom.

"That's not what I'm saying," said Marie. "Though it probably wouldn't be a bad idea. I know some nice guys. But of course you're positive you wouldn't be interested in any of *them.*"

"Oh, Marie, it's just that . . ."

"It's just that what? That you're only interested in making totally self-destructive choices? That you wouldn't consider going out with a perfectly good man with a real job who doesn't travel around the country in a van making *noise* for a living?"

There was a long silence. Then Mom said, "Well, but I really feel like I need to do this. Danny could turn out to be a really good friend. It's not going to be any big deal. It's not going to turn into anything serious." She was such a liar and not even a very good one. "I'm going to go Saturday," Mom said. "If you don't need me around here."

"In what car?" Marie asked. She and Bill had given us a car they'd bought for cheap from one of their friends.

"Oh," Mom said. "You don't want me to take the car? Well, I guess I could rent one." Then she said, "You know what? Why don't you let me take the kids? We'll have an excursion. We'll go to—what's that place?—Mystic Seaport. We'll have a picnic. It'll be fun. Then we'll just stop and see Danny for a few minutes on the way home, let him know we're in town, and I'll go back and visit him another time."

Marie sighed and didn't say anything for a minute; then a shadow fell across the Candy Land board. She was in the kitchen doorway, getting ready to stomp out, but she turned back and said to Mom, "There's no stopping you, is there?" Then she said, "Would you really take all of them? Because it's not all that helpful to me unless Emerson goes, too."

"Of course Emerson can go!" said Mom.

"Well," said Marie, and she sighed again. "Maybe. What time were you planning to leave?"

—⟗—

We met someone on the trail today. A passing traveler by the name of Alexander Noah Joseph. He rode up from behind us. "Hello!" he said in a weird, slanty tone of voice, startling us.

There was something I really didn't like about him, and after about five minutes I said, "Well, it's been very nice to meet you, Mr. Joseph. I hope you have a pleasant trip to California." Still, he continued to ride alongside us for another hour, blabbing away.

He was completely obsessed with every grotesque thing he could think of that could happen to a pioneer. "Look!" he said, pointing into the distance. "Indians! Hang on to your scalps!" The children were listening with huge eyes. "Just kidding," he laughed. Then he looked around and said, "You don't have a dog? Too bad: if you run out of food, I've heard that dog soup is surprisingly delicious.

"If you die," he said, "you want to make sure they dig your grave really deep or else wolves might dig you up and gnaw on your bones. Just picture it," he said, grinning. "A big old wolf trotting by with your fibia in his teeth."

"Fibula," corrected Annabelle. Then she asked, "Mama, why does he say that?"

Because he's a dipshit, I longed to say, but my mother had taught me to be polite.

"Where did he go?" Annabelle asked, and I saw that Mr. Joseph had dropped behind us and was peering inside the back of the wagon. He rode back a minute later with a weird smile on his face. "Is that your hot lover *in there?" he said.*

"That is my husband," I said.

"Looks like he's about to croak," he said.

Amethyst poked her head through the canvas. " 'Hot lover?' " she said. "What?"

"Whoa, mama!" said Mr. Joseph.

"Mama, why is he saying that?" Annabelle asked again.

"Maybe he's talking to his horse," I told her, eyeing him. I pulled the team to a stop. "Mr. Joseph," I said, "it's been so exceedingly enchanting to meet you. But I'm afraid we have to part company now."

He eyed me back. "It's been a pleasure meeting you, ma'am," he finally said; then he tipped his hat and rode away.

"Why did you make him leave?" Amethyst grumbled. "You always ruin all the fun, Zebulina." Then she dropped the flap and disappeared behind the canvas again.

"I didn't like him," Annabelle said.

"Well, luckily, we won't have to see him again," I told her, and I was glad about that.

THE WORLD'S SMALLEST HORSE

One thing I don't get is how wrong Mom can be. Sometimes she reminds me of something I heard once, about those missiles they shoot toward space: if everything's not exactly perfect—if one of the scientists made a tiny math mistake, and the aim's one jillimeter off at the very beginning—by the time it gets where it's going, it can be really, really in the wrong place.

That's what I was thinking about, sitting in the car on the way home from visiting Danny: if Mom had been one of those missiles, not only did she not hit the target, on purpose or even accidentally, but we had come down on the completely wrong side of the earth, though, amazingly, she seemed not to have noticed at all.

"Enfield, Connecticut," said a passing sign. On the right, a shopping center was going by. I could see a Pizza Hut, a Burger King, and a Friendly's, all closed and dark. It was one in the morning. The whole car smelled like throw-up.

"Well, that was fun," Mom said for about the eighth time. "Wasn't it?"

Everything about the day had been totally putrid.

"Justine," Mom had said about eleven o'clock that morning, "get everyone in the minivan." Marie was lending us the minivan since her children were going, because it was safer.

"Okay," I answered, but I didn't move. We'd been getting ready to leave for Connecticut since eight-thirty, and I knew it would be a while longer till Mom actually got out the door. She'd probably change her clothes again, for one thing. The last time she'd come down from her room, Marie had looked at her and said, "Why, it's Elly Mae Clampett." For another thing, we needed a lot of things to take to Danny's, and Mom had to sneak them past Marie, since for some reason Marie actually still believed we were going to Mystic Seaport. When Marie went to the bathroom, Mom came out of the house carrying the vacuum cleaner. She had the hose draped around her neck like a scarf, and in her other hand, she was carrying her cleaning lady bucket full of Formula 409, Windex, Comet, Soft Scrub, Spic and Span, Pine-Sol, Pledge, Vanish, paper towels, and Playtex gloves.

"Remember!" said Marie, sticking her head in the minivan window when we were finally ready to go. "No sweets, wheat, or dairy!"

"Okay," Mom answered, and smiled right at her, as if we weren't going to stop a half mile down the road at the Store 24 for soda, chocolate milk, powdered sugar doughnuts, M&M's, Skittles, some beer and cigarettes for a present for Danny, and a box of real Huggies to put on Emerson instead of the special diapers Marie bought from Green Planet that turned into, as Mom said, "pee, poop, and cotton soup" the minute Emerson got them on.

Three hours later, we drove into Hartford. I was in the backseat, trying to keep myself from worrying about getting thrown up on. Cavanaugh had gotten to sit in the front because the back made him carsick. And I was the only one who knew what that meant: that it was going to be one of the other kids, in the back with me, who would throw up. At least I was next to the window, so I knew it would only be coming from one direction.

The reason it had taken us so long to get to Hartford was that not only did we stop at the Store 24; the gas station; the Amherst deli for cheese, bread, liver pâté, and biscotti; and Bread and Circus for fruit that was beautiful—we also had to go to two Caldors and a Kmart so that Mom could get flip-flops. Hers had broken the day we loaded the truck in California, and she had suddenly decided she needed new ones before she could see Danny. In fact, it sort of seemed like the flip-flops and Danny had somehow combined in Mom's brain into the one thing she'd decided she needed for her life, finally, to make perfect sense. But finding flip-flops in Massachusetts in September was an impossible task, like something you needed to send a Greek god or a fairy-tale prince out to do.

The lady in the first Caldor pretended not to know what Mom was talking about, even after Mom described them in perfect detail. She just kept saying, "Flip-flawpps. Flip-flawpps. I don't think so." In the second store, the woman said, "That is a seasonal item. We only carry them in the spring." Finally, at the Kmart, Mom found something that looked sort of like Japanese bedroom slippers. They were made out of some kind of bamboo or straw and puffy black cloth. They looked like something a crazy person would wear.

"I kind of like them," Mom said, looking down at her feet. "They're different." She changed back to her regular shoes and tucked the weird slippers under her arm, and we headed for the checkout. "I wonder if I need anything else in here," she said, and as soon as she said it, she saw exactly what she needed—a chrysanthemum in a purple foil-wrapped pot. "People can always use a plant," she said to no one, cheerily.

Cassidy threw up as we were getting off at the Hartford exit. Mom didn't even stop the minivan—she just looked in the rearview mirror and said, "Oh, dear. Do you have everything under control, Justine?" I did, if I could just keep hold of Rona, who was on the other side of Cassidy, trying to open her door and jump out.

"Yuh," I said sarcastically.

I was hoping Mom would look in the mirror and see the expression in my eyes, the way I always noticed hers, but all she said was, "Oh, good, thank you. You're a champ."

A little while later, after we'd gotten off the freeway and driven past a lot of big metal buildings with no windows, we slowed down in a neighborhood that didn't look like anyone lived in it and stopped in front of a dirty white shack. Mom looked at the piece of paper she'd written Danny's address down on.

"We're here!" she said, peering out the window. "I think."

"This isn't Mystic Seaport," Cavanaugh said.

The house had one small, dirty window with a curtain drawn

across it. The path to the door was all cracked and broken, and the yard was made of dirt. Everything about the house told you not to go toward it.

"*Okay!*" Mom said, but she didn't move for a minute. Then—it was the kind of moment when I really wished I knew what happened inside her brain—she smiled, as if we were in front of a little picket-fence house with grass and flowers and a wishing well. "Let's go!" she said, and she opened her door. She went to the back and got out the bags of food and the beer and the magazines and the cigarettes and the chrysanthemum, then she started for the door, as if she'd come there all by herself.

"Mom, come back," Rona said in a miserable, grief-stricken voice.

"Why don't you help me with Emerson?" I said to distract her. Emerson was still sleeping in her car seat. Ordinarily Rona loved babies, but Emerson made her nervous, probably because every time she went near her Marie said, "What are you doing?" or, "Don't even *think* of touching the baby with those filthy hands," or, "Don't tease the baby!"

"She's sleeping," said Rona.

"Just leave her in the seat," I told Rona.

We unstrapped the whole seat, and I picked it up, but it was heavy, and I had to set it down on the ground kind of quickly. I wouldn't say I dropped it. But I think I gave her one of those dreams where you feel like you're falling, because her eyes popped open and she started to scream.

"Give her a treat," I said to Rona. I dragged the seat along by its seat belt as Rona followed, pouring chocolate milk onto Emerson's screaming face.

"You're stupid," Cavanaugh said from behind us, kicking pebbles into our heels. "I'm telling."

"Give me some Skittles," Cassidy whined to Cavanaugh. Cavanaugh yanked the bag away, and Cassidy flew at him, trying to grab it. So that's what Danny saw when he opened the door—Mom standing there with three bags of groceries and a plant, smiling, as if she had nothing to do with the commotion behind her; me dragging the screaming baby up the walk, Rona spattering chocolate milk everywhere, and Cassidy and Cavanaugh clawing at each other's faces.

"Danny!" Mom cried.

Danny just stood there. He looked like he'd just woken up. Finally he said, "Uh."

"Danny!" Mom said again. It was a new low point, I knew, as I listened to the word float up into the air above the front stoop and hang there for a minute before it started to fall, like something that thought it could fly, discovering, Oops. It was a moment that made Dale punching me move up a notch.

"Oh no," she said, "you didn't get my message. It's Colleen! And company," she added, smiling and sweeping her hand through the air like someone in a musical.

"Colleen," he repeated.

"Hanley," she said. His face stayed blank. It looked to me like Mom's face was starting to contort a little under the surface, but then suddenly it brightened up again. "MacNeil!" she cried, as if she'd just made the brilliant discovery of her own name. "Oh, right! It was MacNeil back then! In Santa Cruz! Colleen MacNeil! Colleen MacNeil!"

Danny kept staring. "Huh," he finally said. "You were friends with Marie Phipps, right?"

"Yes!" Mom cried. "Exactly! As a matter of fact, these are her children. Well"—she laughed—"two are mine."

Rona's hand shot up in the air. "I am!" she said. "I'm hers."

"I'm sorry you didn't get my message!" Mom said. "We can leave if this is inconvenient. We should leave." Then she set down the bags and the plant, stepped toward Danny, and gave him a big hug. He looked at me from the middle of Mom's hug and sort of shrugged with his eyebrows.

"It is *so* good to see you," Mom said. "It's been such a long time."

"Well," he finally said. "You want to come in?"

"Oh!" Mom said. "Are you sure? We wouldn't want to impose! We could really just . . . go to the beach or something."

Danny shrugged again. "Whatever. I have to go to work in a while, anyway."

"Oh!" said Mom. "Where do you work?"

"Sliders," said Danny.

"Oh!" Mom said.

"It's a sports bar," he said. "I tend there."

"You're a *bartender*?" Mom said. "That must be so *interesting*!"

Danny shrugged. Shrugging was his big move, you could tell. "I guess, if you think drunk people are interesting." He was trying to edge backwards into his house.

"Well, maybe since we're here, we'll just come in for a little while," Mom said, following him inside. "If you're sure." It was dark behind Danny, even though it was the middle of the afternoon. All the window shades were down, and the walls were made of dark brown fake wood.

Rona went in right after Mom. "It smells weird in here," she said, which was a polite way of putting it.

"Rona!" Mom said. "Say you're sorry!" Then she said to Danny, "I'm sorry."

"Oh, Trent probably has a corpse rotting in some corner," said Danny. "I share this house with a psycho. I live downstairs." He started down into the dark, smelly hole of the basement.

"Oh!" Mom said when we got to the bottom of the stairs, and I saw that it was hard, even for her, to muster up a lie right then. She just stood there looking around, then finally she said, "You have a really great place here!" Danny's apartment was all one room—a tiny kitchen on one side, a bed on the other, two filthy gold stuffed chairs in the middle, and some guitars on stands in the corner. There were dirty clothes everywhere. Mom turned to me and said, "This is what's called a *studio*," then she fluttered her eyes at Danny. "All great artists need one!"

We all just stood there then, not knowing what to do. Silence was never safe around Mom, though. "You know what?" she said. "We have a present for you. We figured you'd be busy, so the girls and I are going to clean your house while you work, or practice, or what*ever* you have to do."

"I think not," Rona said. Danny laughed. For one second, I thought maybe I would like him, after all.

"Rona, that was very rude," Mom said.

"Do you have cable?" Rona asked Danny.

"Rona!" Mom said, as if Rona had asked Danny if he'd changed his underwear that day, which from the looks of everything I bet he hadn't.

"Satellite," nodded Danny. "I get something like six hundred channels."

"Cool," said Cavanaugh.

"Here," said Danny, and he went over to the bed and picked up the remote and gave it to Cavanaugh. The kids all climbed onto Danny's dirty-looking rumpled sheets.

"Well," said Mom. "I don't care if anyone helps me." She started unloading her cleaning lady bucket. "Justine, would *you* like to help?" Danny looked at me and shrugged, then he went over and sat down on the bed, too.

"No thanks," I said to Mom. She tried to look shocked and betrayed, but I watched her with a blank expression on my face. Danny looked at me again, then he patted the tiny corner of bed left next to him. I stood where I was.

Mom was at the other end of Danny's apartment now, rooting around on the floor. She was touching his dirty laundry. "Do you have a washing machine, Danny?" she asked.

"Nope," he said without looking at her.

"Oh. Well, I could go to the Laundromat," Mom said. She bent over and uncrumpled something—a big long-sleeved T-shirt—and held it up to herself. "May I use this, Daniel?" she asked. It didn't matter that he wasn't listening, because she didn't wait for an answer—she stretched the shirt out by its arms and tied them around her waist for an apron. She stepped into the bathroom, then she hung her head back out the door and said, "Are you sure you don't want to help, Justine? It'll be fun."

"Justine," said Danny. He patted the bed next to him again.

Even though there was no way I was going to help Mom, I walked across the apartment to where she was, then I wished I hadn't. I felt my heart cringe when I looked around the door and saw Mom kneeling on the floor in her yellow rubber gloves, smiling and looking like somehow she belonged there—as if that disgusting hair farm was the place she'd been searching to find all her life.

"Justine," Danny called. "Come tell me about your favorite bands. You must like music." Mom stuck her head out the door.

"What do you think?" she called. "With me for a mother?"

"You like those teeny-bopper bands?" he asked me.

"Thank God, no," Mom called. Then she said, "Remember that wild punk band that used to come through Santa Cruz—the one with the lead singer who used to wear all those safety pins in his face—what were they called? I think you and I were together at one of their gigs, at the Catalyst, remember?"

But Danny didn't answer her. Mom stuck her head out again and gave him a weird look. But he was back to looking at the TV and didn't see it, so Mom turned the look toward me instead, as if I had done something wrong.

—⁓—

Where in the hell is Fort Laramie??! The animal food is almost gone, and we are down to our last ten onions. I used up quite a few last night, making a poultice for the baby's tiny chest, and one for Thaddeus, too. We are in dire need of supplies.

The children cried tonight when they saw that supper was onion-and-pigweed casserole.

"Mama," asked Ezekiel, "if God loves us, why doesn't he send us something else to eat?"

"Yes, and why doesn't he make Papa and the baby better?" asked Annabelle.

They watched me, waiting for my answer. I tried to remember all the things Reverend Mallethammer, and our Sunday school teacher, Miss Blibber, and Thaddeus, of course, and even my mother, in her own gentle way, had told me: how God is the reason for everything, the one who makes all the decisions, though when things go wrong, you aren't supposed to blame him. His ways might seem mysterious to you, but you mustn't wonder or ask questions or be discontented. And if you have a problem, pray. If you don't get an answer, pray some more.

But it just doesn't make sense to me. Because if that's true, why bother making a plan at all? Why go to California? Why worry about the money and the food and the weather? Why chop all those freakin onions for poultices, if God's decided he wants someone?

"Why did he give us the baby if she's just going to die?" asked Annabelle.

"The baby's not going to die!" I said, and I put a look on my face like I

was gathering up the answer to their questions. I knew I couldn't tell them
what I'd started to suspect was the real answer. You know how children like
to think somebody's in charge.

Danny and the kids watched three Nickelodeon shows, twenty or
thirty MTV videos, a couple of fake wrestling matches, and an info-
mercial while Mom cleaned. I changed Emerson's diaper, she fell
asleep and woke up, and I changed her diaper again. Cassidy and Cavanaugh had three fights. Rona just lay on Danny's bed the whole
time, staring at the TV. I did finally sit down beside Danny, in the little square spot next to him on the edge of the bed, to be polite. Danny
didn't seem so bad, really. It wasn't his fault that a woman he hadn't
even remembered existed invited herself over to his house with five
kids and wouldn't leave. As soon as I sat down, though, I wished I hadn't.
The spot was too small, and Danny kept trying to talk to me, but his
face was too close, so I could see things I didn't want to see—reddish,
sprouting whiskers coming out of his chin, a weird skin bump on his
lip, a little red vein in his eye.

"What's your favorite subject at school?" Danny asked me.

"I don't have one yet," I said. "School's ridiculous, and my
teacher's an idiot."

"Hmm," he said. "Sounds bad." I shrugged.

"Do you like MTV?" he asked me. He turned to glance at Mom
again. She was in the kitchen, talking to the refrigerator: "Well, you
won't be hard to clean!" she was saying. "You're practically empty!"

Danny turned around again, and I could feel him looking at me. I
pretended to be interested in what was on TV—two guys in tight
underwear trying to stomp on each other's heads.

"How about sports?" Danny said. "Do you play any? Are you on
the track team?" Then I felt his eyes moving. "You have long legs,"
he said.

"I'm in sixth grade," I told him. I kept staring at the TV so I didn't
have to look at him. He switched back to Nickelodeon. *Little Rascals*
was coming on, and even though I never really liked *Little Rascals*, I
felt weirdly happy to see it. "We don't have a track team."

"Too bad," he said. "You've got the legs for it." He kept looking at
my legs, which were starting to itch. "I ran track," he said. He looked

down at his stomach and patted it. "Hard to believe, huh?" He made a muscle with his arm. "I used to be all pumped up." I turned around and looked for Mom. Now she was kneeling with her head in the oven, examining the inside of it as if she were looking at cave paintings.

"That was when I was on my health kick," Danny said. "A long, long time ago." He laughed. Then he said, "But seriously," and he got back to looking at me. "Check out track. It's a great sport. And you've definitely got the build."

I jumped up.

"What?" said Mom when I came near her. "Would you like to finish cleaning the refrigerator while I do the oven? Or you could collect the laundry.

"Oh!" she interrupted herself. She pulled something out of her pocket. "Danny! I found an earring in the bathroom." Then she made her voice all slidy and weird. "I hope you can remember who it belongs to. If it were mine, I'd be really upset about losing it. It looks like it might be valuable."

Danny slumped back against the wall and switched the channel.

"Is anyone hungry?" Mom asked. "Well, why don't I fix something?" she said as if someone had answered her. "We brought chips and salsa. And avocado. Nachos! Does everyone like nachos? We have almost everything for nachos!" She was peeling off her gloves and walking toward her purse. "We just need a few things—cheese, beans, sour cream, chilis, cilantro. Is there somewhere around here I can go for those?

"I'm sure I can find a convenience store," Mom answered herself. She picked up her purse. "Justine, you can watch everyone till I get back, right?"

"Mom!" Rona screamed. She jumped off the bed and ran to Mom's leg.

"Honey!" Mom said. "What's wrong?"

"I want to come!" said Rona.

"Oh, no," said Mom, and she pried Rona off. "I'll be two minutes. You stay with Justine." Rona started to whimper. "Go watch TV some more," Mom told her. Then she pointed at Danny and said, "Nachos. Ten minutes. Be there.

"Preheat the oven, Justine," she said to me, and she took her purse and keys and went up the stairs. Rona started to sob, so Emerson started crying, too. Cassidy got a look on her face like she didn't want to be left out. Danny looked at me, like, Do something.

There's something weird that happens when a baby starts to cry. Even if you don't particularly like the baby, your body sort of points in its direction and makes you go over to it. I went over and picked Emerson up out of her seat and held her against me while she screamed. I took a walk around the room and bounced her up and down. Rona followed me, holding on to the back of my shirt and blubbering.

"Shut up, you stupid idiots," Cavanaugh said, and he leaned over and turned up the volume on the TV. He only sat down for one second, though, then he got up and came over to me. "Where's your mom?" he asked, trying to sound like he didn't care.

"She went out for some stuff," I told him.

"She's an idiot," Cavanaugh said.

Rona ran at him and punched him on the head. "Make him go in time-out!" she wailed. "Justine! Make him go in time-out!"

"Fucker-face!" yelled Cavanaugh. He pushed Rona, and she fell backwards onto the floor.

"You're an ass-hold!" she screeched, scrambling up, then she ran over to me and crumpled into a little heap at my feet and started to sob even harder.

Danny was watching us like we were some weird channel he'd discovered pushing the buttons of his remote. Two minutes were up and Mom hadn't come back. Of course, she had lied—I knew it might be two more minutes, or two hours, depending on what Mom might suddenly decide she just *had* to have to make this day with Danny even more fabulous than it already was.

"Maybe we should have a snack," I said doubtfully. I went over to the kitchen and looked at the beer and cigarettes; the chips, which Mom was going to use for the nachos; the beautiful fruit that Mom would kill me if I gave to the kids.

"Do you have some peanut butter or something?" I asked Danny.

"Peanut butter?" he said, as if I'd asked him for hummingbird meat.

"Yeah, peanut butter?" I said. "Ground peanuts? It comes in a jar?" That made him smile.

"Gotcha," Danny said. "I might."

"Well, could you look?"

"Oh, uh," he said. He got up off the bed and came over and started opening the cupboards, peering into them curiously, as if he didn't remember which ones he kept his food in. "Aha," he said finally, and he handed me a jar of Jif. It was light, almost empty. He turned and went back to the bed.

"Bread?" I asked.

"I really doubt it," he said, shaking his head. "You want me to look?"

"Yes, please," I said, instead of, "Duh." A weird thing happened when Danny passed by us to look for the bread: Emerson, who was still whimpering and had snot running out of her nostrils, leaned toward him and stretched out her arms.

"Here," I said. I stepped toward him and put Emerson in his arms. He looked totally shocked. Emerson stopped crying and looked at me rudely, like she was so happy to be saved.

"Me!" Rona said the minute I let go of Emerson. She stretched her arms up and started to hop up and down in front of me. Suddenly I got the weirdest feeling, not one I particularly liked, as I watched Danny standing there holding Emerson and felt Rona tugging at my shirt. It was as if, without noticing it, I had morphed into some strange life form whose body was a ladder for crying kids to climb up and whose arm ended in a jar of peanut butter instead of a hand.

The thing I *really* didn't like, though, was the way I'd felt when Emerson leaned out toward Danny and I'd loosened my grip on her so that he didn't have any choice but to take her—that moment when she was still connected to me but also connected to him, a tiny little piece of time that seemed to weigh as much as a falling cartoon piano. I wished so bad Mom would walk in the door right then, even though I was furious at her. She was the one who had gotten me into this, whose fault it was that I was standing there feeling the same way I did, sometimes, when I woke up in the middle of the night, in the pitch dark, terrified because I couldn't remember where I was or *who* I was, or tell where I stopped and the darkness started, or whether I even *had* a body anymore. She should be the one standing here having the awful feeling. Though to her, of course, it wouldn't be an awful feeling—

standing next to Danny in the kitchen, passing him a baby as if she were his wife.

The door upstairs opened, and the relief that rushed into me was weird. Even though I had just been holding Emerson, and Rona was whining my name, I suddenly felt like a baby myself. I was starving suddenly, and cranky, and ready to cry. My legs felt all elasticky, too, like the bones had gone soft, and I hoped Mom would get down the stairs and grab me before they folded up under me and I fell down.

"Mom!" Rona cried when she heard the door open. She ran to the stairs and looked up expectantly, then she turned with a shocked look on her face and raced back to me. She leapt through the air, so that I didn't have any choice but to catch her. The person clomping down the stairs wasn't Mom. It was a man in a pair of boxer underpants, carrying an electric guitar.

"Who-o-o-a," he said when he saw us. "Bro," he said to Danny. "What happened here?" Then he said, "Dude, you gotta hear this lick." He headed over to the amp, but when he got near me, he slowed down.

"*Whoa, mama,*" he said, nodding his head weirdly.

"No!" said Rona, throwing her head against my chest and tightening her arms around my neck.

Danny nose-laughed. "You're sick, dude," he said, shaking his head.

"No, really," said the guy, still looking at me. "What are you into down here?" Then he said, "Ha, ha. Just kidding," and he came close to me and held out his hand. Even if I hadn't been holding Rona up with all my strength, I wouldn't have shaken it. I had the feeling he was trying to play a joke on me. "I'm Trent," he said.

"You're stupid," Rona said into my neck.

"Ha," said Trent. "Good one. I like your shorts," he said to me.

"Leave her alone, dickbrain," said Danny.

"Dickbrain," repeated Cavanaugh from across the room, without looking away from the TV.

"*What?*" said Trent. "I was just telling her I liked her shorts."

"I bet you do, you sick fuck," said Danny.

I tried to look down, over Rona, at my shorts. They were just plain khaki-colored ones, nothing so great about them. I knew the right thing to say back wasn't, "Thanks—I got them at Old Navy." What I really wanted to say—what actually felt like the exact right, very important thing to say—was, "Just leave me alone," and get out of Danny's apartment. But I didn't know how I could do that. I couldn't leave the kids, and I didn't think I could get them all out by myself. And even if I did, I didn't know where we would go. Also, I knew it wouldn't be all right with Mom to be rude to her good friend Danny, or probably even to his grody roommate, and I didn't know which rule was more important: to be polite, like she always told me, or to do the other thing she'd always told me ever since I was old enough to remember: "If anyone, especially a man, *ever* gives you an uncomfortable feeling for any reason—even if you can't explain it—just get away immediately, go looking for help, *run*."

I guess Trent saw something in my face, because he came over and elbowed me in the arm and said, "Aw, you know I'm just kidding. Don't go getting all unfriendly, now." Then he plugged in his guitar and started playing some yowling notes at high volume. All the little kids jumped at once. Emerson started to scream in Danny's arms, Rona smashed her face into my chest again, and Cassidy jumped off the bed and came to stand near me.

"Cool," said Cavanaugh, looking like he was going to cry.

When it was over, Rona lifted her head from my chest and said to Trent, "You're not very good." Danny laughed.

"Ouch," Trent said, putting his hand over his heart. Then he looked at me and said, "What about you? What do you think?" He played a loud, blasting note—*wa-aw-wa-aw-wa-aw-waaaaa*. "Do you think I'm good?" he asked, gripping the guitar around the neck and shaking it like it was me and he was trying to shake out the answer. It was weird—even though I thought Trent was a jerk, and as a matter of fact, I had never really liked electric guitar players in general, there was something I had always liked about the kinds of sounds he was making. Even if some idiot was playing them, the notes always sounded to me like someone yelling the saddest, most dire story in the world straight into your bone marrow, something you could understand perfectly, even though if anyone asked what the story was, you wouldn't be able to explain one word of it.

"Do ya think I'm goo-hoo-hoo-hoo-hoood?" Trent sang, and he leaned forward so he was singing it in my face. Suddenly I wondered if he was one of those weirdos who liked to chop kids up into a hundred little pieces for fun. I looked over at Danny. I wondered if he was the type to save us.

When I heard the door upstairs open again, and Mom's voice chirping down, "Hello-o-o! Hope you're hungry!" my brain gave out completely and my stomach took over. A big wave of feeling rushed through me that I guess was relief, except that it didn't feel good at all—it was like the whole day had been a bottle of poison I'd been forced to drink, and suddenly my whole insides were turning to liquid. I set Rona down and walked fast to the bathroom and barely got my pants down in time.

When I came out, Trent was gone and Mom was at the stove. Smoke was pouring out of all four burners. "I'm not sure what's wrong here, Danny," Mom was saying. "Does it always do this when you turn on the oven?"

"I don't know," he said, "I never use it."

"You've never even turned it on?" she asked.

"I can't remember," Danny said.

"Oh," said Mom. "That's so funny." But she didn't even fake laugh. "Justine, how should we do this?"

"Do what?"

"Make nachos without an oven. Hey!" She turned to Danny. "You don't happen to have a butane torch, do you? I'm serious. We could brûlée them." She started pouring tortilla chips into a frying pan. "You wouldn't happen to have a skillet with a handle, Danny, would you?" she said.

How could Mom be so clueless? I was wondering. You could tell Danny was just waiting for us to leave. The kids were all about to lose it completely. A horrible smell was coming out of the bathroom and filling up the whole room.

"Justine, will you please chop the cilantro? Maybe try to get some of the rust off that knife first."

"Uh," said Danny. "I have to go to work pretty soon." Mom pretended not to hear him. She was searching through the kitchen drawers, calling, "Can opener! Can opener!"

"But you guys can stay, I guess," he said to me. "Stay as long as you like. I guess."

"Can opener!" said Mom, and she pulled one out. "Hmm. It's

rusty, too. The Rusty Utensils. What do you think, Danny? Name for a bachelor band?" Danny went in the bathroom and closed the door.

"Where'd he go?" said Mom, when she turned around a minute later. "How's that cilantro coming, honey?"

"He has to go to work," I said. She heard me, but it was like she didn't understand.

"Oh," she said. "I wonder for how long. Ow!" She was trying to shake the frying pan with no handle, like it was Jiffy Pop, but there were no hot pads. "Ow! Ow! We could go to the park. Ow! Or we could—ow!—drive to the beach—it's not all that far. I'd really love to see the beach."

"It's going to be dark soon," I told her.

After a long time, Danny came out of the bathroom.

"Don't you look handsome!" said Mom. He was dressed in a white shirt and a bow tie. His slicked-back hair looked like a beaver pelt.

"Uh," he said uncomfortably. "Thanks." Mom beamed as if he had just told her he loved her. I was running out of energy. I was so tired, I was starting to hallucinate. Watching Mom bustling around the kitchen, chattering lovingly at Danny as Danny got ready to make his escape, I couldn't stop thinking about the the World's Smallest Horse.

We saw it at the fair once when we were on a road trip, when I was about eight. We hadn't planned to stop at the fair. We didn't even know about it. But we saw a billboard when we were driving, and one of the things painted on it was, "See the World's Smallest Horse!"

"Oh!" Mom said, and she hit the brakes. "The World's Smallest Horse! Wouldn't you love to see that?"

We had to pay one dollar each and then stand in line for half an hour to get inside the tent. While we stood there, Mom and I wondered things like How big was it really going to be? Where did they find it? and How in the world could a horse as small as the World's Smallest Horse happen? "Fits in the Palm of Your Hand!" said a sign on the side of the tent. "Amazing! Stupendous!" etc. The man in front of us was saying to his wife, "No way! It's going to be a pony or something."

"Then why are we even standing here?" the wife said.

The husband said, "Nothing better to do. I want to see it, what the hell."

"It's probably as big as a dog," the wife said. Mom raised her eyes at me and Rona like it was so sad about those people, who had no imaginations.

"As a dog?" Rona asked Mom. She was in her late twos or maybe three.

" 'Fits in the Palm of Your Hand!' " Mom said to her. "That doesn't sound like a dog to me. You wait." The woman turned and looked at Mom and smiled. "They love us suckers, don't they?" she said, but Mom just smiled back politely.

When we finally saw it, we couldn't believe it. Well, Rona and I couldn't.

"Where the small horse is?" Rona said, looking around the tent. She was so little that she could barely even say the words; she was so gullible, she still believed in Santa and all that stuff, but even she knew there was no way we were looking at the World's Smallest Horse.

In the pen in front of us was something bigger than a dog and smaller than a pony, with a fat, deformed body and short, knobby, crooked legs. It looked about a hundred years old. The people before us were already on their way out. The woman had taken one look and laughed and said, "Well, I guess we deserved that." The man was ranting: "Fits in the palm of *whose* hand, I want to know! It's not even the world's smallest *pony*! They should give us our money back!"

"Where it is?" Rona kept asking. "The small horse?"

"Oh," said Mom, and she looked at me. "It's sick. The World's Smallest Horse is sick and had to stay home in bed for the day. This is its friend, filling in for it."

"Sick?" said Rona, worried.

"Nothing serious!" Mom said. "Just a little cold."

It was an okay kind of lie to tell a little kid, I decided. It wasn't so important that Rona know the truth—that the thing we'd just spent half an hour imagining didn't exist, and it was our own fault that we were disappointed.

At first, when I saw the horse, I'd felt like the man in front of us— gypped and mad—but then I just felt sad. I'm not sure why. I felt sorry for the deformed pony, who had to stand there all day letting everyone down, when it wasn't even his fault. He was just an ancient, twisted pony who probably couldn't get any other jobs. But also, I felt sort of sorry for all of us human beings, who for some reason had wanted so bad to believe in something that couldn't possibly be true that we'd stood in line and paid money to be disappointed. It wasn't a serious bad feeling, though—it was already starting to evaporate as we made our way out of the tent.

But as soon as we were outside, Mom looked at me and said, "Well, that was quite amazing, wasn't it?"

"What was?" I asked.

"That horse!" she said. "It was so small! It was so great that we got to see it!" and it gave me a creeped-out feeling, because it didn't seem quite like she was telling the lie just for Rona anymore.

"It wasn't really all that small," I said to her, hoping she'd wink at me or something. But she didn't. She looked at me like I was some-body she didn't recognize and said, "Well, the size of the World's Smallest Horse is in the eye of the beholder, I guess," and for a minute, I remember, I'd felt scared, wondering how we could have seen two different things there, inside the tent.

"Well, uh, I gotta go," Danny finally said.

"Oh, really?" said Mom, in a disappointed voice.

"Stay as long as you like," he added, but anyone could see he didn't mean it. "Just shut the door when you leave."

"Okay," said Mom, and she went over to the bottom of the stairs where he was standing. "If we don't see you . . . ," she said. "Well, we'll see you. We'll see you sometime. Sometime *soon*, I hope. It was so great seeing you! *So, so* great!" Then she stepped closer to Danny and gave him a hug. I watched his hands touch her back, and I couldn't tell if he had put them there or if they'd just gone there because of the way she was squeezing him, the way you can make a grasshopper's leg kick even after it's dead. She didn't notice that he wasn't saying how great it was to see her, too. Then right in the middle of the hug, he turned her sideways, so it looked like they were dancing, and for one second I was surprised, thinking: Whatever it was that Mom had been doing all day had worked—in one big, rushing, mushy moment, all the horrible events of the day had turned into exactly what she wanted. Maybe she wasn't crazy after all. Maybe all the things she did that made her seem that way were just part of a big, clever, womanly plan.

Danny didn't bend her backwards in a big kiss, though. He'd turned their bodies sideways so that he could get onto the stairs. As soon as he did, he backed away from Mom. His back touched the stairway wall. "Well, uh," he said, "bye, I guess," and he turned and went up the stairs in giant steps.

"Well, that was fun," Mom said, for the ninth time, as we drove.

"Danny didn't like us," I said. It just popped out. The shopping center was back in the distance, and the landscape had turned back into black hills against a dark blue sky—two shapes that fit together like a puzzle even a baby could do.

"Of course he did!" Mom said. "You shouldn't *say* that." Then, "Why do you say that?"

If Mom would just stop talking for one second, maybe I could stare into the blackness and sort of hypnotize myself, pretend that our life was peaceful and quiet and normal, and tell myself there was nothing to worry about and that my mom wasn't really a complete, total nut bar—that there was some other explanation for how a day like this could happen. "Danny did too like us," Mom said again. "He liked us. He did! Why do you think he didn't like us?"

It was so late, and I was so tired.

"If Danny had a dog," Mom said, "what kind do you think it would be? You know how people seem to choose dogs that are a lot like them? A Lab? They're so loyal and friendly. And handsome, too. Or a golden retriever? They have such sweet personalities, and they're good with children. That's what he'd be, don't you think?" I didn't remind her that the one golden retriever we'd known had been so dumb, he'd ground his teeth to stubs fetching rocks.

"Do you want me to tell you about when I first knew Danny?" she said.

It seemed like the night was getting darker as we drove. The hills and sky were starting to melt into each other.

"There was this one time," Mom said, "I wonder if he remembers. God, we hardly knew each other . . . I don't even know if I should tell you this."

"Then don't tell me," I said.

"We were at this party," she said in a dreamy voice, "an outdoor party, at this fantastic, rocky beach. We'd met before, once or twice, but that night, he actually came up to talk to me, and he was just so . . . it was just so . . ."

The sky was so dark. The last little bit of deep, deep blue was about to disappear from it.

"God," she said. "There is *just* something about him!"

Or maybe it wasn't, I suddenly thought; maybe the sky was getting lighter. Maybe the moon was rising somewhere. I leaned my head as close as I could to the window, but I couldn't see it anywhere.

"That night at the beach," Mom said, "he came up to me and he said—"

"Mom," I interrupted. It suddenly seemed really important to me to be able to tell which was happening—whether the night was thickening, adding molecules of darkness, or losing them; whether the blue underneath the black was trying to appear or disappear.

"Hmm?" she said dreamily.

But she wouldn't know what I was talking about, I knew.

"Nothing," I said as I tried to see through the darkness dancing around my eyes.

—m—

We have finally reached Fort Laramie. I bought flour, oxen food, horse food, cornmeal, beans, rice, and a small amount of dried beef. I was hoping to buy sugar, but the price was shocking. I spent every cent from Thaddeus's money box—the one he told me never to look in. He doesn't know it yet, as he is lying in the back of the wagon, delirious. I have a little money left that he doesn't know about, that my mother gave me, in the small calico bag in the corner of my oak chest. The next supply post is 375 miles from here. If we eat sparingly and make good time, maybe we will be all right.

Also, I took the baby to see a doctor. It cost two whole dollars, but the doctor could tell me nothing. He examined her, frowning and tilting his head this way and that, listening to her heart, tapping her all over; then he looked up at me finally and said, "She's a mysterious little thing."

"That's all?" I said.

"I have no idea what's wrong with her," he said.

"But you're a doctor," I told him stupidly.

"Try poultices," he shrugged. "Nettle tea. Keep an eye on her.

"Where did you get this baby, anyway?" he asked. What an odd question. As if he suspected I wasn't her real mother. Or as if he somehow could tell something nobody knew: I'd wondered the same thing once or twice, looking down into her strange little face, myself.

Marie met us at the door with her hands on her hips and her face twisted. "Where in the *fucking hell* have you been?" she said. Bill stepped forward from behind her and put his hands on her shoulders. She jerked out of them angrily. "Where's the baby?" she hissed at Mom. Cavanaugh and Cassidy were coming up the walk like zombies, rubbing their eyes.

"She's in the back, asleep," said Mom. "Let me put this stuff down and I'll go get her."

"Don't bother!" said Marie. "I can do it! Go get Emerson!" she said to Bill.

"I called," Mom said meekly.

"Yes, that's right," said Marie. "You did call. You called five hours ago to say you were leaving. I've been on the phone to both the Connecticut and the Massachusetts Highway Patrols."

"Oh," said Mom. "I'm sorry. I am *so* sorry. I am *so, so*—"

"Spare me," Marie said, and she stomped off up the stairs after Cavanaugh and Cassidy. Bill came in with Emerson.

"Bill, I'm sorry. I am *so* sorry. I am *so, so* sorry. I am *so, so, so* sorry." Bill didn't get Apologizing Mom, I knew. He would probably stand there all night, till she was sorry to the thousandth power.

"Mom," I said.

"She was just worried," Bill said to Mom doubtfully. "You know. It'll all . . . she'll . . . it's . . . well . . ." He gave a shrug and added, "Well, good night," then he headed up the stairs with Emerson.

Mom stood there looking at me like I was supposed to say something.

"I'm going to bed," I said, and I went up the stairs, too.

———m———

Something wonderful has happened: Today we met a party on the trail.

"Mama, look!" Ezekiel shouted late in the afternoon. He was riding up ahead on Jake. I peered where he pointed; there, in the far distance, rose a dust plume, and at the center of it was a little white spot of wagon.

"Do you think we can catch up to them?" Ezekiel cried.

"We mustn't overwork the oxen," I said. But I was already urging them on.

"What's going on?" Thaddeus moaned from the back. "Zebulina, you're speeding."

"We're just going down a hill," I called. We watched the dust cloud gradually grow bigger until suddenly the children and I realized at the same moment: The wagon wasn't moving away from us at all, but approaching. When it finally drew near, I saw that the driver was a woman about the same age as me, and my heart leapt up in my chest. Maybe she felt the same way, because she was halfway out of her seat, looking as if she might jump down and run ahead of her horses. "Hello!" she called. "I'm Lucretia Jane Brown!"

"I'm Zebulina Walker!" I replied. I listened to the way my name floated over the landscape like a lonely bird.

"Are you all alone?" I asked. I stopped the oxen and jumped down.

"Yes," she said. "Well, no. Not really." She nodded her head toward her wagon. "There's Silas, my husband, in the back. He took sick at Fort Bridger. That's why we turned around."

"You're kidding!" I exclaimed, and I nodded behind me. "My husband's sick, too! Can you stop for a while? Would you like some tea?"

"What's going on?" Thaddeus called. "Why are we stopping?"

"Go back and tell him we've met someone," I told Annabelle. "Tell him I'm helping her mend a horseshoe."

"What does she know about horseshoes?" came his loud grumble a moment later.

"We're praying to God, dear, and it's going great!" I called back to him.

*Then I turned back to Lucretia Jane Brown. "Where have you come from?"
I asked her.*

*"Well," she said, but before she could answer, out hobbled Amethyst,
rubbing her eyes. This morning she'd woken up smiling; then one hour later
she'd complained that she thought she was dying. Now she was smiling
again.*

*"Hello!" she said to Lucretia Jane. Just like I did, she asked, "Are you
alone?"*

*"No," Lucretia Jane said. "Well, yes. Well, I mean, it's just me and my
husband, half-dead in the back."*

*"Husband?" Amethyst said. You could see the color coming back into her
cheeks.*

"He's very ill," said Lucretia Jane.

*"Oh," said Amethyst, casting her head down for just a second. "How
lamentable. Actually, do you mind if I wander back and have a look?"*

*Lucretia Jane Brown and I talked all afternoon. When the sun began to
fall in the sky, we decided to set up camp; and later, when we had finally
gotten the supper dishes washed and the animals watered and fed and tied
up for the night; and I'd put the children to bed; and Silas and Thaddeus
had finally worn themselves out calling for us and fallen asleep; and it was
quiet at last, we talked some more. Amethyst had gone to bed, too. She'd
stood at the opening to Lucretia Jane's wagon, chattering to Silas long after
he'd fallen asleep: "What an interesting fact that you're from Hartford,
Connecticut! I always wanted to visit that very historical place! What a
wonderful, useful job you have! If we didn't have candlestick makers, there'd
be no place for people to stick their candles! Then the world would be dark!"*

*Lucretia Jane and I stayed up talking the whole night. In the morning
we decided to spend another day here.*

*"Thaddeus'll tweak," I told Lucretia Jane. "He has a whole
mathematical equation worked out for our trip—the weight of the
provisions; multiplied by our wagon speed, which increases the more of the
provisions we eat; divided by the number of miles to California. He has a
chart of which days we're supposed to pass which landmarks."*

*"I know," said Lucretia Jane. "We really shouldn't stop, either. Maybe
if I hurried I could get Silas to a doctor in time." The kettle she'd put on the
fire had started to boil, and we poured ourselves more tea.*

* * *

We spent a lovely day. We did our chores together: first mine, then hers. We went for a walk. We talked about every single thing we could think of. We sat in the grass and wove flowers into crowns while we talked. The children played. We walked to the river and went swimming and washed our hair and lay baking in the sun a long time. We brewed tea out of flowers, and it turned out blue, and we laughed as we drank it. We baked a small spice cake and had it with more tea in the afternoon; and that night, after all the work was done, we sat down by the flickering fire and talked some more.

—m—

It was so wonderful, having a friend for two days.

Neither one of us wanted to say good-bye. We stood there a long time, thinking of one last thing after another we'd forgotten to tell each other. In the background, we could hear Thaddeus and Silas having conniptions. Finally I said, "Well . . ." and Lucretia Jane said, "Well . . ." and we clasped each other in a hug. When her face was close to mine, Lucretia Jane checked to see no one could hear. "I have to tell you something," she said into my ear. "It's important."

"What?" I whispered.

"Don't take the cutoff, whatever you do."

"The cutoff?"

"The so-called shortcut to California. There are men at Fort Bridger telling everyone to go that way. But don't do it. Just stick to the real trail."

"Thaddeus loves cutoffs," I said.

"I know," said Lucretia Jane. "So does Silas. But there were bad reports coming from people who tried it."

"Lucretia!" piped Silas.

"Zebulina!" bleated Thaddeus.

"There's one more thing," Lucretia Jane whispered.

"What is it?"

"There's a cache."

"What's a cache?"

"Something buried," she said. "If someone's wagon breaks, or they have

something too heavy to carry, sometimes they bury it and then make themselves a map so that they can go back and dig it up one day."

That sounded like a really terrible idea to me.

"It's in the desert," said Lucretia Jane. "I'm not sure which one. I met a woman. She was on horseback, and she was completely alone. It was odd. I asked her where her party was, but she didn't answer me. All she said was that she'd had some trouble and had had to abandon her things. 'They're back there somewhere,' she said, and she waved toward the west. 'Buried in a patch of orangish sand, seven paces south of a small sagebrush. All my most precious possessions. Feel free to dig them up if you want.' "

"She's not going to go back for them?" I asked.

"I asked her that," Lucretia Jane said. "But she just shrugged her shoulders and said, 'Who knows?' "

"Strange," I said.

"Very," said Lucretia Jane. We both got silent then, suddenly, like a goose had walked across our grave. That story really bothered both of us, you could tell, though I wasn't sure exactly why.

OWNER OF ALL THE SADNESS

When I woke up the next morning, I didn't know where I was. It was raining outside. The rain in Massachusetts sounded different from California rain—it sounded like someone taking a long shower, someone too sad and tired to reach up and turn the water off and get out. I felt tireder than when I had gone to bed. As I lay there trying to swim my way out of the gray, woolly darkness, I felt yesterday coming back to me and wished it weren't.

I got out of bed and went down the hall to Mom and Rona's room. Rona was in Mom's bed, and they were both still sleeping. I could hear a sound like the ocean, and I went to the window to see if somehow the yard outside had turned into a soft, gleaming beach, though I knew, of course, that it hadn't. Outside, everything was gray and black and brown and wet. When I turned away from the window, I realized where the ocean sound was coming from: the tiny TV Mom had bought for ten bucks at the Salvation Army and smuggled in was turned on without the sound. I hadn't seen it at first, propped on a box by the foot of the bed. The TV's screen was about half as big as a sheet of paper, and it only got three channels, in black and white, and even on the best one, all you could see, mostly, were gray, nubbly shapes. But it was sort of nice anyway, sometimes, to sit there together on the bed, huddled in front of the bluish white glow.

I crept over to the side of the bed next to Mom, lifted the covers, and slipped in. "Mmmp," Mom said, but she didn't wake up. She was on her side, facing me. Her hands were wrapped around each other like she was hiding something in them or pleading with someone, and I let them touch my shoulder, but I didn't snuggle close. I wasn't exactly mad at her, even though she had been the one responsible for our Incredibly Putrid Day, but I wasn't not mad, either. I didn't know what I was.

I wondered if there was even a word for the way I felt. All day yesterday my anger and bad feelings at how many things Mom could do wrong had built up till I thought I couldn't stand it anymore; and I was about to tell her, too, how hideous she was making our life, but then I would catch a glimpse of something. An expression on her face that I didn't get, sort of like a combination of scared and sad, but, like, however sad a normal person could get, twenty times sadder than that, even though she was standing there smiling at Danny like a goony idiot. And for one second, I would feel so sorry for her, except that at the very same time, I could feel the anger trying to push the sorriness out of the way, like boys shoving each other in the drinking fountain line, and if you could give a name to that feeling, that's what I had.

As I lay there trying to figure it out, I could feel the memory of the day at Danny's starting to break apart, all the different pieces of it draining from my brain down my spine into a puddle on the bed. I knew I couldn't be falling asleep, because I'd just woken up.

In my dream I was the one who was sad; I mean, I was *sad*, in a way nobody else in the world knew about. Sadness and I were the same thing. I was the owner of all the sadness everywhere, and the meaning of it, too. If anyone wanted to know anything about *sad*, or if they wanted any for themselves, they'd have to come to me. Also—you know how dreams are—I wasn't exactly *me*. I wasn't even a person, actually—I was something soft and cloudy and expanding, like steam filling a room.

When I opened my eyes, it was still as dark as before, and Mom and Rona were still sleeping. Across the room, I could see something— a person, someone old, with gray hair, in a gray dress, sitting and rocking, watching me. Grandma? A wave of such a nice feeling washed over me, it must have pulled me back to sleep again, because the next time I opened my eyes, Rona was leaning over Mom's body with her hands on my face, saying, "Are you awake, Justine? Are you awake?

Are you awake?" and across the room, where the old person had been, was the flickering TV.

"Mmnn," murmured Mom. I watched her eyes open slowly, then start to move back and forth. I wondered if she was remembering yesterday. Because for a second, I thought I saw something: a little spot of clearness, maybe, in her eyes—a little tunnel that might lead, deep down inside her, to a small patch of reality. That maybe, if she thought hard before she opened her mouth, might expand into a place big enough for the truth to edge into, for an honest answer to begin to form.

"Well, that was an interesting day we had yesterday, wasn't it?" Mom said.

I watched the little patch in Mom's eye. Stay, I thought. She put her hands to her eyes and pressed, as if maybe she were slowly remembering the truth, trying to hold the tears in. But when she pulled her hands away, I could see that the little opening had started to close.

"Wasn't it a nice day?" she said.

"It was a *stupid* day," said Rona.

But Mom had gotten a little smile on her face. "No, it wasn't. It was nice. In fact," she said, pushing herself up on her elbows, "it was *quite* nice. Don't you think, Justine? Isn't Danny great?"

"Danny's a *dick-scab*," said Rona, and she took off under the covers.

"Stop it!" Mom said. Then she said, "It's going to be *great* to get to spend some time with Danny again, after all these years. Gosh, I wonder if he's doing anything for Thanksgiving."

I got out of the bed when she said that.

"Where are you going, Justine?" said Rona as I headed for the door. On my way back to my room, I heard Marie and Bill through their bedroom door.

"Well," Bill was saying, in the voice he used to try to calm Marie down, "I don't know . . ."

"I've had it," Marie was saying. "Yesterday was just too much. And you know, it wouldn't bother me so much if she would just *do something!*"

"Well," said Bill.

"Anything!" said Marie. "Write a résumé. Get a job interview. Go to a therapist. Get on antidepressants. Change out of her pajamas before two in the afternoon."

"Well," said Bill.

"Take an office skills class," Marie went on. "Or any class—weave fucking pot holders, for Christ's sake—anything! I mean, have you ever seen anyone with such a highly evolved ability to do *nothing* all day?"

"She works pretty hard, doesn't she?" Bill said. "Around the house?"

"But it's all invented stuff," said Marie. "We don't *need* the patio bricks scrubbed. We don't *need* a year's supply of preserved grapefruit peels. I didn't bring Colleen out here to be a domestic servant."

"Well," said Bill again.

"I want her to leave," Marie said.

My heart clenched up when I heard her say that, not that I didn't want us to leave, too. I wanted to stay and listen some more, but I suddenly felt like I was in a big hurry. I rushed down the hallway to my room. But when I got there, I couldn't think of anything to do besides sit on my bed. That felt terrible, so I went and got the phone and brought it into my room and dialed a collect call to Grandma. But as soon as she said, "Hello, sweetheart!" I knew I wasn't going to be able to figure out what to say.

"How's everything?" Grandma asked.

"Everything's okay," I said. Maybe I could tell her in code. "It's about the same as the last time I talked to you." That had been over a month ago. Now I wished I hadn't lied the last time I'd talked to her.

"Oh," she said. "Well, good. Everyone's still getting along okay? Your mom and her friend, and you and the kids? School's still good?"

"Yeah," I said. "More or less." I tried to make the "less" sound underlined, but she didn't notice.

"So tell me about school," Grandma said.

I just about started to cry, trying to think of how to answer her—I could feel all the things inside me elbowing each other around, trying to be the first to push their way out as soon as I opened my mouth. But it was so weird, the moment I did, I felt everything twist itself together into a big knot. How did that happen? Is that what happened to Mom, I wondered—all the little shreds of truth somehow ended up in a big, unmovable glob inside, while the other stuff—the fake, happy stuff that was easy to say—popped out like party streamers? But why?

"School's okay," I told Grandma. "There are some kids who aren't all that nice."

"Oh?" said Grandma.

"Some boys," I said. I tried to unravel a strand of truth from the knot to give to Grandma, so maybe she could pull on it. "They're kind of jerks."

"Really?" said Grandma. "How so?"

But I couldn't. "I don't know," I said. "It's no big deal."

"Well, as long as you're making some friends," Grandma said. "That's what's important, right?"

"I guess," I said.

"And your mother?" asked Grandma. "How's she?"

"Grandma," I said, "how do you get an apartment?"

"What do you mean, honey?"

"I mean, how does someone find an apartment? What do they need to do?"

"Why are you asking me this?" Grandma said suspiciously.

"No reason," I said. "Well, for school we have an assignment. We have to find a pretend job and a pretend apartment, and write the steps we took to get them."

"Hmm," Grandma said. "That sounds like an odd assignment."

"It's not, really," I told her. "It's life skills. You know, like the thing where you carry an egg around for a month. The sixth-graders at my old school had to do that."

"What on earth for?" asked Grandma.

"Like it's a baby?" I said.

"Oh, for heaven's sake."

"It's so you don't get pregnant," I said.

"In the sixth grade?"

"Or something," I said. "Maybe it's supposed to tell you whether or not you're cut out to have children."

"Of course you are," said Grandma, which I thought was a little weird. How could she know that? I wondered if she just said that to everyone, like "God bless you" after a sneeze. I wondered if she'd said it to Mom.

"What about the apartment?" I asked Grandma. "Are you going to tell me?"

"Well," she said. "All right, I suppose the first thing you do is get the want ads from the newspaper. And they're classified into categories, usually—House for Rent or Apartment for Rent, for example. So you choose which category you want, then you consider the features, like how many bedrooms it has, whether or not it's on the bus line, if it allows pets, if you're required to sign a lease. And how much it costs, of course."

"How much does it cost to get an apartment?"

"It varies. Depending on the neighborhood and how big it is. Does your teacher want you to work out the costs, too?"

"Yes," I said.

"Well," said Grandma, "the cost it says in the ad will be the monthly rent. But when you move in, you usually have to pay three times that, for last month's rent and security deposit."

"So how much would it be?" I asked.

"It's different for each one," said Grandma.

"Just make one up," I told her.

"Okay," she said. "Say for a two-bedroom apartment, eight hundred dollars a month. Times three would be twenty-four. You'd need that much to start out."

"Twenty-four?" I said.

"Hundred dollars."

"A hundred dollars?" I was confused.

"Twenty-four hundred dollars," she said.

"Oh." I got it. "Two thousand four hundred."

"Right," said Grandma.

"Well, then," I said, trying to sound calm. "How do you find a job? Also from the little ads, right?"

"Well, sometimes it's a bit more complicated than that," Grandma said. "There are a number of ways one might go about finding a job. Did your teacher tell you to use the classified ads?"

"Yes," I told her.

"All right," she said. "Well, what do you want to do?"

"What is there?"

"You can see for yourself when you look at the paper," Grandma said. "Are you just supposed to pick something randomly? Or are you supposed to try to find a job having something to do with your interests? Whatever they might be, in the sixth grade," she added sarcastically.

"Um," I said. "Interests."

"Well," she said. "What are they?"

"Oh. Say, like, freelance graphic designer. Or caterer."

There was silence for a minute. Then Grandma said, "Justine, what's going on?"

"Grandma, I've got to go," I said.

"Wait a minute," said Grandma. "Can I talk to your mother?"

"She's not here," I said. That's what I told Grandma every time she called. "Okay, bye, Grandma," I said. "I love you," and I pretended I didn't hear her voice calling, "Wait! Justine! Wait!" as I hung up the phone.

I put the phone back in the hallway, then I went back in my room and got dressed. On my way downstairs, I stopped at the door of Mom's room and looked in. Mom was still in bed. Rona was playing on the floor, dancing a tiny doll around and singing.

"What should we do today?" Mom was saying. I guess she was talking to Rona, even though Rona wasn't looking at her or listening. "I know: We could take a trip to the nursery. Maybe Marie would let me put in some bulbs. Or we could go to one of those places where they make maple syrup." She was staring at the ceiling, as if that's where she was getting her excellent ideas. "We could make soup—I saw a recipe for African groundnut stew. We could put some in the freezer to take to Danny."

"You could look for a job," I said.

Mom looked over, surprised to see me. "Excuse me?" she said.

"Why don't you look for a job today?"

Mom looked at me as if I'd asked whether she wanted to die by firing squad or the electric chair. Then she looked away from me and up at the ceiling again, which didn't seem to be telling her anything anymore. "You're right," she said. "I am a worthless, shiftless human being."

I was having the strangest feeling, as if the room was ejecting me. As if some big, gray force I couldn't see was pushing me away from the door.

"Where are you going?" Mom asked.

"Are you going to get dressed today?" I said.

"Oh," she said, sounding as if her energy was leaving her again.

"Just get dressed, okay?" I said.

She looked at me strangely. I let the gray cloud push me down the hallway and down the stairs and out the back door, and I felt Rona follow.

It was only drizzling now, but the sky was still gray. The trees in the distance, sticking up on the ridges, reminded me of the spine bones of a fish.

"Where are we going?" said Rona.

"Nowhere," I said, and I hated how it sounded: true. Dull and heavy, like a lid thudding shut.

"I don't want to," said Rona.

That's the only place there was to go, though. Marie and Bill's house was on the side of a busy road, and there was no sidewalk, and we weren't allowed to walk up the road or down it or cross it. When you went for a walk at Marie and Bill's, which Marie liked to force everyone to do sometimes, for exercise after dinner, you went to the end of the backyard, walked through the fence behind the garage, and then stepped onto a muddy road made out of tractor marks that went in a big circle around a field of corn, a barn, the neighbors' farmhouse, and then back to where you'd started.

"All right," I said. It felt like the grayness had seeped into my brain cells, like everything was slowed down: my movements, my heartbeat, my thinking. I felt like a frog, getting ready to slip under the mud of a wintery pond. "We're going . . . down the troll path. *If* they feel like letting us past today. They live in the barn. We have to find treasures along the way so we can pay them." I leaned down and picked up a twig. "This is a jewel twig. It's worth twenty dollars in troll money."

"It is not," Rona said, taking the twig from me and throwing it on the ground. "This isn't a troll path. There are no stupid trolls."

It surprised me so much, I couldn't think of anything to say. Finally I said, "You don't believe in trolls anymore?"

Rona looked at me as if I were an idiot. "Of *course* I believe in trolls!" she said. "There just aren't any *here*." She looked around as if she found the landscape about as inspiring as I did. A second later, though, she turned back into familiar Rona.

"This is a poo path," she said. "See?!" She kicked at a pile of soggy horse manure. A piece of it stuck to the tip of her sneaker for a second and then flipped up into the air in front of us. "Yuck!" she screamed, and she ran off down the path to look for more.

Most of the cornstalks in the field were gone—shaved down to dead, hollow nubs, or bent like broken elbows. At the edge of the tractor tracks was a barbed-wire fence and, beyond that, woods. They weren't the kind of woods, though, that made you want to go into them, like the ones in California. They were dark, and wet, and full of black mud and puddles and mosquitoes, Rona and I had found out one day when we'd slipped through the fence and gone to explore. "Remind me never to do *that* again," I'd said after we'd run out, screaming and slapping ourselves all over, and Rona had said, "Yeah, remind me never to do *that* again!"

Walking along, watching Rona run ahead of me, I was having a feeling I'd never had before: There wasn't one thing around me that I could stand to see. The sky; the dead, broken corn; the dark, wet woods; the dead brown grass and the mud everywhere; the leaves, which had started to fall off the trees and lay in wet piles. I hadn't known till we moved to Massachusetts: There's nothing in the world more depressing to look at than a pile of dead, wet leaves.

"Rona!" I called. "I want to go back!"

She didn't answer.

"I'm going back!" I called. "Bye!" and I turned and started walking. She would probably be okay by herself, I thought. The path wasn't very long—you could practically see Marie and Bill's house from everywhere on it, and Rona had walked the whole way before.

So I don't know why I got a panicky feeling all of a sudden, when I turned to see if she was following me and she was gone. I stopped and called for her again. She didn't call back. I started to run. I ran till I saw her, skipping along, kicking at things in the path. I was just going to have to follow her, even though I didn't want to. I felt like crying. I was thinking about how in fairy tales, people sometimes wept different things: frogs and spiders, diamonds and rubies and emeralds. I tried to picture, if I were in a fairy tale, what sorts of weird, interesting stuff would come flying uncontrollably out of my eyes. But tiny balls of hot, salty water was all I kept picturing, and it was just like the day: totally, depressingly real. All I could imagine was just what I could see, ugly and true, going around and around in a brown, muddy circle.

—m—

Thaddeus is gone. Passed on. Pegged out. Deceased. Dearly departed. It happened fast. One minute he was mumbling in a fever dream: "Zebulina, if I've told you once, I've told you a thousand times—I like my biscuits round, not square." And when I went back to check on him a little while later, he was blue and cold.

We had a little funeral. The children sang a hymn they remembered from Sunday school, and we sprinkled a few flowers on him.

"Can we get another papa someday?" asked Ezekiel before we'd even thrown the last handful of dirt onto Thaddeus.

"He was a good papa," said Annabelle, a little unconvincingly. "But maybe it's better he's gone. Maybe in heaven he won't be so crabby."

"Is there yelling in heaven?" asked Ezekiel.

I don't think the baby's going to miss him. He never really gave her the time of day. Once, before he was so sick, I gave her to him to hold for a minute, and when he got tired of it, he laid her down on the ground, too near the fire. "What's wrong with her?" he asked irritably when she started screaming. "Can't you make her be quiet?" he said as I snatched her up, patting at her little smoking booties.

As for myself, I don't think I will, either. I searched for some sadness inside myself as we stood beside the grave. I blinked my eyes, but they remained dry. I tried to remember some good feelings from when I first met him, and thought he was handsome, and liked to watch him playing in the town fiddling band, but I think all his yelling erased them permanently.

Amethyst was the one, actually, who seemed the saddest. Her "oo-hoo-

hoo"-ing drowned out the children's singing as we stood at the graveside. For crying out loud! I almost told her. Put a clamp on it! Then I felt bad. Maybe it's true that she has a delicate, sensitive soul, like Mrs. Jepperson tried to tell me, and I just can't see it. Maybe she feels things differently from the rest of us. Maybe that's why she's so broken up about Thaddeus. Maybe she has a special sense of what makes a man wonderful, but I doubt it.

When we got back, Mom was sitting at the kitchen table, and Marie was standing over her with a bunch of papers in her hand.

"I hope you don't mind," Marie was saying, sounding like she didn't care one bit if Mom minded, "but I took the liberty of circling a few things that looked interesting." She laid the classified ad section from the newspaper on the table in front of Mom. "Also, I called my friend Monique at Amherst College. She says human resources has a board where they list all the available jobs on campus. They open at eight on weekdays.

"And I called my friend Martin, who's the general manager of the Peabody House Inn. He said he'd be happy to talk to you any time you want to call or drop by. They have a few openings—hostess, I think he said, and prep cook. Probably those are both shitty, demeaning, low-paying positions, but the Peabody House Inn has one of the best dining rooms around, and I know they give benefits to their employees, so if you really are interested in a career in food service, it could be a decent opportunity. Martin also gave me a list of the names of some local caterers. He said with the holidays coming up, they're sure to need help. Which I think sounds like a good idea: it'd be a way to pick up some quick money, and it would get you out of the house."

"Get me out of the house?" Mom said, sounding hurt.

"For God's sake," Marie said. "I didn't mean it that way."

"I'm sorry, Marie," Mom said. "I'm so sorry we've been here for so—"

"Jesus, Colleen," Marie said, "it's not that. It's just that . . ." Then she said, "Oh, forget it. Listen, I wrote down Martin's number and also a list of a few places you might try just walking in and filling out an application." She put a piece of paper in front of Mom. "Also," she said, handing Mom another sheet of paper, "I did a little work on your résumé." Then she said, "So maybe you could get started on some of this stuff tomorrow morning. If you want to borrow any clothes, you know, just feel free to go look in my closet. I have some nice, conservative stuff in there, from my nine-to-five days."

The next morning, when I came down from getting ready for school, the minivan was gone from the driveway and the house was quiet. Mom was in the kitchen, and I was surprised to see that she was dressed. She was wearing her sudo-boho social worker onsomb, as Marie called it, whatever the freak that meant. To me, she looked sort of like a genie in the filmy, almost see-through shirt and pants and the red sash with fringes and little mirrors attached. She'd bought the sash and shirt and pants a couple of weeks ago, at One World, the store next to Green Planet in Amherst.

"Ta-da!" she'd said when she came down the stairs in the outfit the day she'd bought it. She'd held her hands out to the side and posed. That's when Marie had made the comment.

"Oh," Mom had said, her smile fading a little. Then she'd said, "Is that what you call this look? I thought this outfit was kind of interesting looking. You know, people out here just *look* different than in California."

"And where were you planning to wear that?" Marie asked.

"Oh," said Mom. "I don't know. Gallery openings? A party? I'm bound to get invited somewhere, sometime." Her face fell, though, thinking about it.

"You'll freeze your ass off," said Marie. "Gauze isn't really a practical look for New England in the winter."

"You're probably right," Mom said. Then she said, "I could wear it to job interviews."

"Mm-hmm," Marie said. "When the local harem advertises, it'll be just the thing."

Mom looked up when I came in the kitchen door. "Listen to this," she said. She was holding the résumé Marie had given her the day before. " 'CEO, Hanley Celebrations. Coordinated, planned, prepared, and served wedding banquets, corporate functions, and private special-event parties for upscale clientele.'

"This Colleen Hanley sounds like one on-the-ball person," she said in a weird, flat voice. " 'Consulting chef, Phipps-Jensen House. Worked as personal household menu consultant to family of five.' I have to say, *I'd* hire her in a heartbeat.

"Actually," she said, "she did a good job with this. Who knows, maybe some poor sucker'll buy it.

"Just kidding," she said. "I am a lovable, capable human being, and I accomplish what I set out to do." That had been her daily affirmation for a while in California—Grandma Bobbie had seen the little card with suction cups on the back of it in a bookstore and bought it for Mom to stick on the bathroom mirror.

Then she said, "It's food service, for God's sake. Things you can train a monkey to do. *If* you can get it to wash its hands after going to the bathroom." She laughed, but in an unenergetic way. I couldn't tell what her mood was, and I didn't like that. Rona and I had to leave for school in a few minutes.

"Rona, come on!" I called, watching Mom's face. "We've got to go," I told Mom.

"Okay," she said.

"Well, good luck, I guess," I said. Then I said, "So, are you going to go to those places today?"

"Hmm," she said. "Maybe. I might. Yes. I will." First, though, she looked like she was going to sit in that spot for a long time.

—◉◉◉—

The landscape has changed again. Sometimes we climb steep bluffs; sometimes we descend into dry creekbeds. The ground is very sandy in places, which makes it hard going for the oxen. They suffer much from the heat, and their hooves are wearing down, too—they're all about two inches shorter than when we started. Sometimes there is no grass or firewood or water at all; and sometimes the water we do find is salty and bad smelling.

I got out Thaddeus's gun today. We are running out of the meat I bought at Fort Laramie already, so I am going to try to shoot something. I think a buffalo would be the easiest thing to hit, though I haven't seen any buffalo for a while.

I took a bunch of practice shots this evening, at a target I made from a flour sack draped over a clump of sagebrush. I didn't hit it, but the wind from one of my shots came close enough to ripple the edge of the sack.

Mr. Joseph appeared again today, out of nowhere. We had stopped for lunch, and I had just finished feeding the baby—or, I should say, trying to feed the baby. She refuses to eat a thing. The children were off scampering about in the weeds, and I was buttoning up the top of my dress when I heard someone say, "Hubba hubba." I whipped around and saw him perched upon his horse, looking down at me in a very creepy way.

"Mr. Joseph!" I exclaimed, more politely than he deserved. When I see my dear mother again, I'll have to remember to ask her why she taught me that manners are so important. And if they always are.

"Please call me Alexander Noah," he said.

"What did you say to me?" I asked.

"I said, 'Hello, hello.' "

"I thought you were hurrying to cross the mountains."

"Oh," he said. I do not like his smile. "I had a little free time. I was worried about you, with your man sick. I thought I'd come back and check."

"Thank you," I said. "That was very thoughtful. But we will not be requiring your assistance."

"What's your name?" he said. I don't know how I knew, so surely, it would be a terrible idea to tell him. I just had a feeling in my bones.

"Julietta Elizabetta Arabella Lillywhite," I told him.

"Jeeu-l-e-e-e-etta," he said. I had been so right. I picked the prettiest name I could think of, and he made it sound like it had fallen in with mud. He smiled at me, a big, ugly smile. If only Amethyst hadn't poked her head out of the back of the wagon right then.

"Oh! Hello!" she said to Mr. Joseph. Then she said, "Why did you tell him that, Zebulina?" She hauled herself out. "Her name's not Julietta Whoozabetta Whatever. It's Zebulina. I'm Amethyst."

He looked at me almost evilly. "Zebu-l-i-i-i-na," he said. "Zebyoo-L-I-I-I-na."

Give it back, I wanted to say to him. As if I were a child, and he'd taken my favorite doll.

"Mr. Joseph," I said, "please don't slow yourself down on our account." He just kept grinning. "You must leave," I said.

His grin broadened sickeningly. "Maybe I will," he said. Then he tipped his hat. "But you will definitely be seeing me again. Zeb-u-l-i-i-i-na. ZEB-yoo-L-I-I-I-na!"

I could hear his voice long after he was gone, stretching my name out over the landscape between us, and it hurt me as if it were my skin itself stretching thinner and thinner, getting ready to tear off my body.

1-800-HELP

School was getting worse every day. It was the worst thing that had ever happened to me in my life. Which meant, basically, that every day was the worst day of my life, except for Saturday and Sunday, which, depending on what Mom or Marie had dreamed up, could also be pretty bad.

"Justine," said Ms. Taylor on Monday, about four minutes after the bell rang. She was looking in her roll book. "Did you forget to turn in your math on Friday? I don't think I have it." She picked up a pile of papers from her desk and started looking through them.

"Um," I said.

She raised her head. "Did you?"

"Did I what?"

"Did you forget to turn it in?"

"No," I answered. Which was true.

"You gave it to me?" She started going through the papers again.

"No," I said.

Ms. Taylor cocked her head at me. "Did you do the assignment?"

"Yes," I said.

"But you didn't turn it in?"

"Right."

Ms. Taylor pursed her lips and put the palms of her hands together like she was going to pray. "Why not?" she asked.

There was no way I was going to tell her. And I wasn't going to cry, either, I hoped. I had had enough of that feeling: the hot wateriness swelling up inside my head, everybody watching me, as if that moment when the film on my eyes broke and tears started dribbling out of my face were so entertaining. It made me want to punch myself in the head when it happened.

The first time I opened my locker and saw the note there—a little folded piece of paper lying on top of my sweater that said, when I opened it, "BUST-ine Hanley I love you, Love, Your Hot Lover"— the heat had gushed through me like someone had emptied a teakettle into my head. I heard giggles and turned and saw Alex and Joey P. and Noah looking at me. I crumpled the note and slammed my locker shut and walked away, but before I got far I had to wipe my eyes with the knuckles of one hand, then the other, and I knew they saw me, because they started laughing even harder.

The second time, they were nowhere in sight. "CHESTine You Sex Goddess, I love you, Will you go out with me?" the note said. But I still felt the hot, ashamed feeling, the tears filling my head. The third time was a little different: *Oh*, my brain understood, not exactly in words, as soon as I saw the note on the bottom of my locker. *This is the way my life is going to be, now.* I still felt like crying, but the tears didn't form. Which was actually an even worse feeling.

What was I going to tell Ms. Taylor, though? She was still looking at me. Not the truth, which was that I hadn't turned in my math because I'd put it in my locker yesterday by mistake, and except for when I absolutely had to, I tried never to open my locker anymore.

Ms. Taylor sighed. "You have the math, but you didn't give it to me." I nodded. "All right," she said. "I'm not sure what's going on here, but we don't have the time to pursue it at the moment. I would like you to go get the math and turn it in. If you really do have it, I won't mark your grade down. Then I'd like you to come see me after school."

I stood at my locker a long time before I opened it. Finally I did the combination and lifted the latch. There was a ripped piece of paper, folded up and fallen to the bottom.

"Juicy Justine," said the note this time. "My heart throbs for you. I heard you are a good french kisser."

It wasn't such a big deal, I said to myself as I stood in the hall by my locker. It was a piece of paper with some words on it. You could just crumple it up and throw it away. Which I did. Then I stood there some more, wondering why I felt so horrible, as if someone had just come up to me and told me that I was really, really in trouble—such bad trouble that I couldn't even imagine what was going to happen to me—for some terrible thing I had done without even knowing it.

There is nothing, as far as the eye can see. A lone tree, on top of a bluff—I give it a name: Hardship Bluff. If the baby dies, that's where I will bury her. I'm not really sure exactly what a bluff is, but the word has a lonely sound: it sounds the way a word would sound if you said it and there was no one around to hear it, no solid object to echo it back.

Thaddeus has been dead two and a half weeks. We are about two hundred miles from Fort Bridger, I think.

Mom's car was gone from the driveway when we got home.

"Where's Mom?" said Rona as soon as we walked in the door.

"She's out looking for a job, remember?" I said.

"When's she coming back?" asked Rona.

"I don't know," I told her. "She had a lot of places to go. Let's get a snack and go watch TV."

I went in the kitchen and got the whole box of organic teddy bear cookies Marie didn't like us to eat and the poison milk Mom bought for us, even though every time Marie saw it, she said, "You know, Colleen, cow's milk is a terrible food. The only reason it's not completely banned for human consumption is that it's *white*," and we took them up the stairs to Mom and Rona's room.

I got the TV out of its hiding place and set it up and turned on the fuzzy shapes of *General Hospital*. There was a piece of paper on the floor by the garbage can, I noticed. I picked it up.

"Justine, I can't hear it," said Rona. I uncrumpled the paper.

"Cucina Milano," it said, "120 So. Main St. Prep/Line cook.

"Peabody House Inn—Martin Shea, Mgr., 555-1260.

"Hearth and Home Kitchenware, 78 So. Main—Owner: Mandy Caron (husband is friend of Bill's)."

"Justine," said Rona, "turn up the sound." Someone was on their deathbed, it looked like, just about to tell the other character the key to life, but the sound was just going, "Shh-shh-shh-shh-shh."

"Amherst College Human Resources, Converse Hall—bulletin board in foyer, give résumé to Monique Prager."

It was Mom's job list. She'd forgotten it. Except why was it crumpled? Maybe she'd memorized everything on it.

"Justine, fix the TV!" Rona yelled.

"Shut up!" I yelled back at her, and I swatted her on the head, kind of meanly. "It's a box of shit! It doesn't fix!"

At the sound of her screech, I was instantly sorry, because suddenly I understood. It was the exact same noise she used to make when she was a baby, too little to do anything but bounce up and down behind the bars of her crib when she was mad or scared or unhappy and no one seemed to be coming to get her out. And in some weird way—because I didn't, exactly, remember the feeling from when *I* was a baby—I understood, about the little seed of doubt starting to grow inside you, as you waited and waited and waited to catch sight of *someone* coming through the door. The only difference between us, I realized, was that I was old enough to do something, if only I could figure out what it was.

"I'm sorry," I told Rona, and I rubbed her on the head where I'd swatted her. "I'm sorry, I'm sorry." I got on the bed with her and put my arm around her. I wasn't even sure what had just happened to me.

She tried to fake cry for a minute, then she looked up at me and smiled and said, "You said shit."

"Yeah," I said. "I know. Shit. Shit, shit, shit, shit, shit."

"Shit, shit, shit, shit, shit, shit, shit," Rona said, and she scooted up as close to me as she could and leaned her head on me; and we sat there for a long time, watching the snowy TV.

Every once in a while I try to talk to Amethyst. It's lonely out here. I love my children, but they're children. "Mama, look at the grasshopper I caught!" they cry. "Mama, how far are we from California? Mama, pretend we're Indians, okay?"

Most of the time, she lies in the back like a human gelatin blob, neither asleep nor awake, moaning or staring. "Ouch!" she says if I hit a bump too hard, then nothing else for a hundred miles. Except every once in a while, when I don't expect it, she'll jump up like a piece of paper catching fire. Then she comes to sit beside me and starts chattering away.

"This has to be the most beautiful spot in the world!" she'll say then. There doesn't even have to be anything there: she could be looking out at a dry, brown, empty plain. "Why don't we just stop here? We could clear a spot and build a house! We could start a town! We could have puppies and kittens and pigs and cows and chickens and goats! And, after a while," she says slyly, "husbands."

"Husbands?"

"Surely someone will come by. We'll build our house right next to the wagon tracks."

There's something about her—she's so infuriating sometimes, but she can be so something else, too. Full of life, maybe you would call it. But, like, too full. It's like if you had a recipe for a human being, and whatever the ingredient is that makes a person alive—that makes sparks seem to crackle off their surface when they're in a great mood—your hand slipped and you poured in nine extra cupfuls. Which isn't a good thing. Which can create sort of an emergency feeling, as you sit and watch the energy build and build and build until you know something has to either burst or collapse. And then it does, and you watch the life drain away through some secret hole inside of her, some black whirlpool that sucks down every last speck of energy.

"What's wrong with her?" Annabelle asks whenever it happens, and I answer, "I don't know." Which I want to be true. I want to believe there's some other answer besides "She's just kind of a nut job, sweetheart."

Sometimes, when she doesn't know anyone's watching her—when she's just staring out at the horizon, settled deep into herself, thinking who knows what, she looks like someone you could talk to. Someone who might listen if you said, "Does it ever scare you, to look up at the stars?" Who might say something back, something quiet and thoughtful and true. Sometimes it looks to me as if she's hiding someone—a whole other person, who might have some interesting things to say—inside.

But at those times, when I say softly, "Hey," she just says, "Huh?"—the sound of a shoe slapping on dirt, an oxen plop falling on the road, and the thing I thought I saw vanishes.

* * *

It was practically dark when Mom came in. The clock said 5:12. Rona had fallen asleep leaning against me, and I was just sitting there, staring at the TV.

"Hey, you two!" Mom said, standing in the bedroom doorway. Rona opened her eyes and burst into tears.

"What's the matter?" exclaimed Mom. Then she started to laugh. "Don't be afraid!" she said. "It's only me." Mom had different hair. It was bluish black and curly. "It's my new look," she said. She came over and sat down next to us. Rona scrambled into my lap, crying.

"Don't cry, sweetheart," she told Rona. "What about you, Justine?" she said. "Do you like it?"

"No," I said. "Not particularly. Did you go to the job places today?"

"We're *talking* about my hair," she tried to joke.

"Did you?"

"Jeez," Mom said, "you two certainly are a couple of party poopers." Then she reached up and peeled off her hair. Rona let out a bloodcurdling scream and threw herself against my body. "It's a wig!" Mom laughed. "Isn't that nutty? They were on sale at Image, and I just thought it'd be fun. Look," she said, and she held up her hand. "I got a manicure, too. See the tiny little stripes she painted on?"

"Did you go to Amherst College?" I asked. "Did you go to Hearth and Home Kitchenware?"

Mom looked at me a minute. "No," she said. Then she said, "But I'm going to! I just decided I needed a psych day. Have you ever heard that expression? I was just . . . doing a few special things to make myself feel ready," she said. "I was *feeding my soul.*"

"Marie's going to go ballistic," I said.

Mom got an interesting look on her face then. *"God!"* she said. "Marie is not my fucking mother! I'm an adult, and I don't have to ask Marie's permission for everything I do!" and for a second I thought maybe it was Teenage Mom, the one who had told Grandpa Victor to fuck himself. Stay, I thought. I wanted to see more of her.

But a second later, she was gone. I watched as Mom's good mood drained out of her. Then after a minute she started to pull off her shoes as if they weighed a hundred pounds each. "You'll have to make macaroni tonight," she said in a dead voice, and she crawled under the covers. "Maybe do it now, before Marie gets home." Marie hated it when we made macaroni and cheese in her kitchen. "Tell her I don't feel well. Or, wait. Tell her . . ."

I waited, but she didn't say anything else.

———ᗰ———

Mr. Joseph snuck up on us again yesterday. We were stopped for the night, and I was down at the stream, fetching water.

"Zeb-u-l-i-i-na," he called. I jumped.

"Allow me to carry your water for you," he said as he got off his horse.

I was mightily sick of him, but the water buckets were heavy. "All right," I said.

"I wouldn't want you to strain your broiling bosoms," he said. But when he knelt to pick up the buckets, he stumbled. Except, it was the queerest thing, I could have sworn he did it on purpose.

"Are you all right?" I asked, not that I cared. He seemed to be having an extraordinarily difficult time getting up.

Suddenly, I had a most unpleasant realization as I watched him rolling around in the dirt at my feet: He wasn't struggling to get up at all. His neck was twisted, and he was trying to look up my skirt.

"Good-bye, Mr. Joseph," I said, grabbing the buckets, "I hope you have a very nice life in California," and I plowed up the stream bank and left him lying on his back, chuckling, in the dirt.

I couldn't stop thinking about it all night, though, and I thought about it all today, too, as I watched the brown hills rising and falling around me, the jagged cliffs coming in and out of view. We could have been on Mars, the landscape was so different from anything I'd ever seen before. Why had he been trying to look up my skirt? I must have wondered that a thousand times today, but I couldn't come up with an answer. What was it that he imagined might be so interesting to see there?

If only I could talk to my wise mother now.

The next morning, Mom stayed in bed till after we left for school. When I was on my way out the door, Marie said, "Hey!" I jumped. "What's with the no-coat, Justine?"

"I'm not cold," I said.

"That's ridiculous," she said. "It's forty degrees outside. You have to wear a coat."

"You're not the boss of her," Rona said, then she ran out the door.

I looked at Marie. I knew she was right. It wasn't the kind of thing Mom would've noticed—Mom didn't even know I had a coat. It was on the list of things we needed to buy for our new life, but we hadn't gotten around to getting it. Mom didn't know that Marie had come home one day with a coat for me that she'd happened to see on sale at Caldor. She'd given Rona a coat, too, surprisingly—an old one of Cavanaugh's.

"Maybe I'll wear a sweater," I said.

"Coat," Marie said, and even though I knew we were about to have a big problem, I liked the way she'd said it. Like she could tell me something true and simple with just one word—something there was just one choice about, and that choice was already made for me. I still didn't go to the closet, though.

"Justine!" Rona called from the yard. For a millisecond, I thought about telling Marie the truth: how, if I wore the coat, which was big and puffy and made of down, I would have to open my locker. You weren't allowed to wear coats in class. I could tell her, too, about how my backpack weighed about ninety pounds now, because I carried everything I needed in it all the time. Also, how every time I thought about opening my locker, my life felt like a bad dream I couldn't wake up from.

Instead, I just stood there thinking about it. What if I did tell her? If I said, "Some kids at school are bothering me," or, "Some boys are putting sexy notes in my locker and calling me names and making fun of me"? I had no idea what would happen. Maybe she would call their parents and yell at them over the phone. Maybe she would go to school and pick the boys up by their shirt collars and call them little motherfuckers. Maybe she would tell Mom what a terrible mother she was for not having one clue about what was going on.

She was still waiting, so I got my coat from the closet, said, "Bye," and headed out the door. On the way across the yard, I took off the coat and went to hide it in the bushes till the end of the day. The back door opened before I even had one arm out.

"Just *put the fucking coat on your body* and leave it on until you get to school," Marie bellowed, and she stood there watching until the bus came, so I had no choice.

At first when I opened my locker I didn't see anything, and the blaring of my stomachache went down a notch. But when I was shoving aside the sweater I'd left in there, to make room for my coat, a piece of paper fell out of its folds.

"Justine, I love your big juicy boobs, love your boyfriend," it said.

I stood there holding the note in my hand. Juicy boobs made me think of when Rona was a baby, the sound she used to make when she ate. She was always in a hurry, and she would get so mad if she couldn't find the nipple fast enough—we used to laugh at the way her head would jerk around, the frantic look she'd get on her face. Then she'd quiet down, and there would just be that noise, and Mom would say, "Justine, can you get me a glass of water?" which I could do, even though I was only five. After I brought it, I would snuggle in on the other side of Mom and feel her breathe and listen to Rona eat. There was another part of the memory, too, though—not as nice—and I tried not to let it into my picture. But, standing there with the note in my hands, I could feel it breaking in.

It was about Dale. He liked to come around when Mom was feeding Rona. "*Wuh-huh-huh!*" he'd say when he'd walk into the room and catch sight of Mom with her shirt open.

"Oh, stop," she'd say, then he'd say something like "When's my turn?" or "Save some of that for me," or "How come *she's* so lucky?" And he'd come up close to Mom and try to nuzzle his head down there, too, so Mom would have to push him off, and Rona would come unattached and start jerking her head around and getting ready to cry, and Mom would say, "Aaah!" as milk dribbled everywhere.

It had given me a bad feeling back then—I hated our nice, quiet moment getting ruined—but nothing like the bad feeling I had now, standing in the hallway with the note in my hands.

Because suddenly the feelings of the memory were all different. Suddenly the look on Dale's face, that I could remember so clearly, wasn't just annoying and stupid—I could see that it was totally sick and perverted. It gave me the feeling that my whole life was a totally rotten thing that needed to be thrown away. I could *see*, suddenly, the way he was looking at Mom's chest as he leaned closer: like it was a place that belonged to him, and everything it ever meant before he came around—the time when it was just a nice part of Mom; the place, though I couldn't remember, where I'd eaten breakfast, lunch, and dinner every day for a little while—was over, ruined.

But I didn't get it. How did it work? I stood there holding the note, trying to figure out how something happening in the present could change a memory from the past; how a few simple, stupid words—*I love your juicy* frickin *boobs*—could make me feel like I did right then—like I wanted to throw up, but with my whole body. I didn't even have a stomachache. I just wanted everything inside of me out, every thought and feeling and part. I wanted to start over—exchange my eyes and ears and organs for new, fresh, blank ones; change my skin; replace my blood. I wondered if I should go to the school nurse. There was no way I was going in the classroom. But then I realized, if I went to the nurse, she would call Mom, and if Mom wasn't there, I would have to lie in the office till the end of the day.

I wondered if Ms. Taylor had started to call the roll yet. I wondered if anyone from my class had seen me. But it was weird: at the exact same time I was racking my brain trying to think of what to do, I was already doing it. I walked down the hall toward the door. I wondered if any other kid in the history of my school had just walked out of the building during the school day and not come back.

I had no idea how far it was home. Maybe two miles, maybe five, maybe ten; I didn't care.

When I got home, I had huge blisters on my heels. There were no cars in the driveway, which was good. I went to my room and got all the money I had—about eighteen bucks. I ran down the stairs and out the door and started down the road. I walked near the trees, in case Mom or Marie drove by and I had to hide. I hoped I could find what I needed at the Store 24, because if I didn't, I would have to walk to the mall, and even though I felt strong, the blisters on my heels had actually been bleeding when I got home, and I could feel that the Band-Aids I'd put on them had already bunched up and gotten lost in my socks. And later I was going to have to walk back to school to get Rona, because even though she knew by now how to take the bus home, she would probably just stand waiting at the first-grade cubbies, where I always met her, until nighttime if I didn't come.

I was lucky at the Store 24; since it was so close to Halloween, they had exactly what I wanted. When I got home, I went straight upstairs with my bag. On my way through the hallway I noticed the answering machine light was flashing and I pushed the button, just in case it was my school. It was. I erased the message. Then I went in the bathroom and locked the door.

I tried to follow the instructions on the package at first, but it was too hard, combing the dye into every single hair. Finally, I just squeezed the whole bottle on my head and rubbed it in and sat there trying not to pass out from the smell. There was a number on the box to call if you had questions, and I went out to the hallway and got the phone, but then I just sat there trying to think of what I really wanted to ask. I had called those kinds of numbers before a few times with Cassie Cannon, my friend in California, when we were bored, and it was actually kind of a fun thing to do. Usually you got a woman, and she was usually nice, even if your question was stupid, like when Cassie and I called Nabisco and asked, "Why are all of your products *round*?"

"Well, actually," the Nabisco lady had said politely, as if she didn't know she was talking to a couple of ten-year-olds, or didn't care, "we make quite a number of products in a variety of different shapes. For example, Triscuits are square. As are Lorna Doones and all the Newtons. Our Honey Maid Grahams are rectangular. Then there are Barnum's Animals, of course. And have you ever seen Sociables?"

I sat there racking my brain, trying to think of what it was I wanted to ask the 1-800 lady, something besides "Is your scalp supposed to feel like red ants are biting it?" Something, maybe, like "Am I going to feel like a different person with suddenly purple hair?"

Finally, though, I couldn't stand the burning anymore. I put down the phone and got back in the shower and rinsed my head. Seeing myself in the mirror, when I finally got the steam off the glass, was beyond weird. It was almost wonderful. It was like if you took wonderful and terrible and combined them into one idea. It felt like one of the important moments of my life.

My head was totally purple. And my hair was hacked. I didn't think I'd cut so much off with the tiny scissors I'd found in the medicine chest—I only wanted to give myself sort of a little spike on top. It didn't look too good, really. Which might not be a bad thing: I looked like someone no one could possibly secretly admire, not even for a joke. Mostly, though, you couldn't look at me and not think, Wow, she really did something! and I liked that idea, even though I wasn't completely sure what it was that I'd done.

I went to get Rona in a hat.

"Why is that hat?" she said when she saw me. Maybe just like me, she didn't know the right question to ask.

"My head was cold," I said.

"No," she said. Then she said, "Why are your ears purple?"

"Come on," I told her, "we'll miss the bus." Also, I wanted to get out of there, just in case Ms. Taylor walked by and saw me.

"No hat," she said. She wouldn't move. "Hat no." She put her thumb in her mouth. "Off hat take." She was turning into a baby in front of my eyes.

"Stop it," I said.

"Errrrn," she creaked. "Baby Rona no stop." She started twirling her hair.

"Stop talking baby talk and I'll take off my hat," I said.

"Okay," she said, taking her thumb out of her mouth. So I had to do it. She stared up at my head for a long moment. If we missed the bus, we'd just have to walk, I guessed. I could take off my shoes if my blisters hurt too bad. I couldn't tell what she was thinking, but she looked completely the opposite of the baby Rona who had just disappeared. Finally she said, "Cool purple hair, Justine." Then she took my hand and we walked together to the bus.

Mom still wasn't home when we got there. The answering machine was flashing again, so I pushed the button. "Could someone please call the principal's office at Oak Grove Elementary right away. We've got a situation we need to clear up immediately," said a woman's voice. I erased it.

We were sitting in the kitchen eating yogurt when Marie came in with Cassidy, Cavanaugh, and Emerson. The second she walked in the phone rang. She picked it up.

"Hello?" she said. "No, this is Marie Phipps-Jensen." Her eyebrows started to move as she listened. "Yes, Justine is here. . . . No, I don't know anything about it." She was looking at me. I was still wearing my hat, pulled all the way down over my ears. "Listen," she said into the phone, "why don't I talk to her and find out what's going on and then I'll get back to you."

She hung up the phone and looked at me like she was waiting for me to say something.

"I skipped a little bit of school today," I told her.

"Well," she said, "would you like to tell me about it?"

"No," I answered truthfully.

She slitted her eyes at me, and I was glad to hear Mom's car outside, even though I knew things were about to get worse. Marie glared at me and went out the back door. I went to the window to watch. As soon as Mom opened the car door, I could see Marie's mouth start to move like an angry puppet's.

Mom came in the door and looked at me, not like she wanted to know what had happened, but like she wanted me to save her from Marie.

"What's going on?" Mom asked.

"Not much," I said. "What's going on with you?"

"Colleen," Marie said in a warning voice.

"Did you get a job today?" I asked Mom.

"You know, they were about to get the police involved," Marie said to Mom. "You can't just treat this like it's nothing."

"What happened?" Mom asked me again.

"Did you get a job?" I asked her again.

"That's not what we're talking about, young lady," said Marie. I could have told her she was wrong, but it would've been kind of hard to explain.

"Justine, tell me what happened," Mom said.

"I didn't feel like staying at school," I told her.

"That's unacceptable," said Marie.

"It's true, though," I said.

"Why?" Mom asked.

"I had a bad hair day," I said. Rona started to giggle, and I couldn't help it—I did, too.

"Nothing is funny!" Marie said. I took off my hat. "Oh, my fucking God in heaven!" said Marie. Mom's eyes got wide. I waited for the tears to start falling out of them. But instead she started to smile.

"Justine!" she said, taking me by the shoulders and looking at my head. "I never knew you had it in you!" She turned to Marie. "I've raised a punk!" she said. "A little purple-haired punk!"

Marie looked at her with disgust. "You are pretty unfuckingbelievable," she said. "This is not . . . Just because . . ."

Mom looked at me like everything was all right. I looked back at her. I was glad I wasn't in trouble. But things weren't like she thought they were, I knew. She probably thought our life was just like a heartwarming TV show, and we had just gotten past the hard part.

That night, Mom came into my room when I was almost asleep and sat down on my bed. "Don't worry about Marie," she said. "I mean, she's the original pink-haired punk. She'll remember what it feels like, one of these days, to be young."

"I really do like it," she added, ruffling my hair again.

"It's only hair," I said. I didn't want to talk about it. When I'd looked in the mirror that afternoon, it had felt like I'd done something so important. But in the shower that night, I'd looked down and seen rivers of purple flowing over my feet. And the towel I used to dry my hair had come away completely purple, too. In the mirror, I could see that the color on my head was already three notches less bright. The spike was still there, though, and in a few days, I knew, I would just look like a purple-tinged idiot. I knew what the kids at school were going to say. And, also, that if there had been any small chance left of having a friend this year, it would be gone now. But the worst thing was, I couldn't even remember why, exactly, my purple hair had felt like such a brilliant solution.

"We should get you some cool earrings to go with it," Mom said. "Maybe a couple of colorful silk scarves to tie around it."

Marie had told Mom she needed to get me some psychological counseling. She'd said it right in front of me. "It's not normal," she'd said. "For a twelve-year-old to leave school without telling anyone, wander around alone all day, then come home and massacre her head. Maybe she's acting out the stress that your life produces in her."

"My life doesn't produce stress in her," Mom said.

"I can find you some names, if you'll let me," Marie said. Mom had made her face perfectly blank.

"We really should start going to more concerts," Mom said now as she sat there in the dark, her hand roaming over my bristly head. "I mean, we haven't been to hear any music since before we got here. That's practically criminal. What do you think? We could leave Rona with Marie and Bill and the kids, and stay out late."

"Maybe," I said, but I didn't mean it. I was trying to imagine the moment when I broke the news to Mom: I didn't even like concerts. I had never liked them. My favorite song was "Down by the Bay," by Raffi. If Exene Cervenka, the Minutemen, and Sonic Youth all fell off a cliff, it wouldn't even make me sad.

"Maybe Marie's right," Mom was saying. "Maybe our life is too stressful. Maybe we need to have more *fun*."

"I know what we need," she said. "We need a boyfriend! Then *he* could take us to concerts. Picture it—you and me, out on the town with something tall, dark, and handsome on our arm." She giggled and gave me a little punch on the shoulder. "Or maybe something short, squeaky voiced, and wearing braces? What do you say?"

"I'm tired," I told her.

"Oh," she said as if her feelings were hurt. "Okay." Maybe she wanted me to stay up all night talking with her, just like Marie had when they'd first met.

"Well, sweet dreams, I guess," she said at the door; and she couldn't see that my eyes were wide-open in the dark.

—⚎—

I hit a target today. It was only a plate—Thaddeus's, actually, that we don't need anymore—propped against a rock, but still, it means that I am making progress. Maybe tomorrow I will try for his cup.

THE NOVEMBER FAIRY

Fall in Massachusetts was completely different from anything that had ever happened to us before. Everyone said it was going to be so beautiful, with the leaves changing colors; and it was, for three days, till they all fell off the trees. Then, no matter which direction you looked, everything you could see was ugly. Everything was either black, brown, gray, or white, including the sky. When the sun did come out, the sunlight was different from normal sunlight: it was like something that had been made in an artificial sunlight factory somewhere and stored in a giant refrigerator and then taken out and sprayed over the state of Massachusetts. Inside the house, there were deep blue shadows everywhere—cold spots that followed you around and settled on you if you sat down somewhere to read or do homework, spreading iciness invisibly over your body. Also, it gave you kind of a weird feeling to see, as soon as you got out of bed in the morning, that the day was already starting to end. It made you feel always sort of on the brink of sad.

It took me a little while to notice that fall was like poison to Mom. At first I just noticed she was talking kind of slow. Then she stopped finishing her sentences. "Justine, if you could . . . ," she'd say. "I just . . ." and she'd turn into a statue. Then she started not getting out of bed sometimes. "Oh . . . ," she'd say from under her covers when I came to the door to wake up Rona in the morning, which Mom had stopped doing, and she might move a body part or two, as if she were thinking about getting up. But when we came back later to say good-bye, she'd be curled in a ball, asleep again, or staring at nothing.

*   *   *

One morning when Mom didn't come down for breakfast, Marie went up to Mom's room and stood in the doorway with her hands on her hips and said, "Colleen, I'm just going to stand here till you get out of bed. And actually, why don't you get dressed while you're at it. Wear that white blouse and the blue dress pants, and I'll loan you a blazer and some jewelry for your interview." Marie had called Martin and told him Mom would come to the Peabody House Inn at ten A.M. on that day.

"Oh," said Mom, "God. Interview. I don't—"

"You know, Colleen," Marie said, "if I have to drive you to the interview myself and drag you in there, I will; that is, unless you'd like me to drop you at the adult day care facility in Holyoke, because someone has to do something here, and even though I know you think I'm being a hard-ass, I also know that one day you'll see, I'm acting as your friend."

"Adult day care center," said Rona, like that was so hilarious, but I could see that it scared her, just like it did me. I didn't even want to know what it was. The pictures you got just from someone saying it weren't good.

Mom got a total of three interviews, and she missed every single one. When we got home from school the day of the Peabody House interview, she was in her room, lying on her bed in her coat. When I asked, "How was your interview?" she mumbled, "It was great." But about half an hour later the phone rang, and when I got to the hallway a man's voice on the answering machine was saying, "Hello, I hope I have the right number—I'm calling for Colleen Hanley. Colleen, I thought we had an interview for ten o'clock today. I hope we didn't get our signals crossed. Please give me a call."

The second interview was at an ice-cream store in Amherst, Sweet Dreams.

"You actually wrote a job letter to an *ice-cream store*?" Marie said when she found out.

I knew Mom hadn't gone to that interview, either, because in the morning, before we'd left for school, I'd gone out and arranged a few pinecones, a graham cracker, and a grape behind the car tires, and they were all still there, unmoved and uncrushed, when we got home.

The third interview was for a receptionist job at a magazine. Mom actually left the house that day—I did the graham cracker, pinecone, and grape thing every day now. But when I asked her when I got home from school, "Did you get the job?" she just said, "Well." She was sitting at the kitchen table with a cup of tea. Marie bought this weird tea at Green Planet that came in a little paper bag marked "Womanly Wisdom," as if you could somehow find that growing somewhere and pick it and dry it out, and then people who weren't born with any naturally could just get it by drinking the tea.

"Well what?" I asked.

"Oh, Justine," said Mom, setting down her cup. "You've gotten so much like Marie. Why does it matter so much to you what I do every minute?"

Mom liked simple, honest answers the least; they were the kind most likely to hurt her feelings or make her cry. "Because someone needs to get a job, and you're the only grown-up," was one that came into my mind. "Because Marie's getting really sick of us and we need to move," was another. I tried to think about how to say either one of them in a nice way.

"Who made you the police, anyway?" she said.

It was like her words knocked into the truth button inside me. Or maybe it was the anger button. "Because you're the mother, that's why," I said.

Mom looked at me like I had just given her the worst insult in the world. "I can't believe you said that," she said. Then she said, "You know, I'm struggling a little bit, in case you hadn't noticed. I mean, it's not exactly easy, being a single mother; moving all the way across the country to a strange place; not having any home or job or money or friends. And I'm sorry you're unhappy. Because everything I do is to make you and your sister happy, and to try to give you a nice life."

Every once in a while on *General Hospital* one of the crazy characters tried to drive one of the good characters out of their mind, and this is exactly how they did it. The crazy character tried to make the normal character think that everything coming out of the normal character's mouth made no sense, while everything the crazy character said was totally sane. It's hard to explain, but you *got* it when you saw it; and it was always a great part of the story when that happened, probably for the exact same reason it felt like such a nightmare when it was happening to you in real life.

Then she said, "You know, sometimes I think Marie's right. Maybe I should open my mind to more possibilities. Be more confident, try something I've always wanted to try." She unfolded a piece of the newspaper that was sitting by her elbow; it was the job section, I saw, and I tried to read, upside down, the things she'd circled. "Apprentice Cabinetmaker," I saw. She saw me looking.

"I circled the ones that sounded the most interesting," she said. "What a great skill to have, to know how to make a cabinet." I tried to picture Mom as a cabinetmaker's apprentice, but all I could see was the cabinetmaker, who was, of course, a guy, and Mom staring at him lovingly while he tried to show her how to hold a screwdriver.

She picked up the newspaper. "How about this: 'Image Consultant. Perform color analysis, wardrobing, skin care evaluation, etc., for male and female clients. Will train.' Getting paid to tell people what to wear! Doesn't that sound fun?" I wondered which I wanted less—a cabinetmaker or a guy who didn't know how to pick his clothes—for our next boyfriend.

"Listen to this one!" Mom said: " 'Seasonal marketing position at small kaleidoscope factory.' Gosh, kaleidoscope factory! *That* would certainly expand your vision!"

Out the kitchen window, I could see the sun was getting ready to drop silently behind the trees. The pale orange sky was actually kind of pretty, but in a wintry way, everything always about to fall over the edge into sadness, giving in to the darkness without a fight.

"I'm going to go outside," I told Mom. She wasn't really listening to me, though. "Maybe you could still go to the receptionist interview," I said. She looked at her watch.

"Maybe," she said, staring into her tea.

I got my coat and stepped out the door and turned toward the last of the light. But I'd only taken a few steps when I wondered, Why do people always head toward the light? Off into the sunset, as they say. I turned and looked the other way, toward the hills to the east. It had a whole different feel that way: of something over, a place already in the past. That didn't sound so bad to me for some reason, so I went that way.

I made excellent progress in my shooting today. I hit Thaddeus's spoon, hung from the limb of a tree, from thirty feet.

The next morning, Saturday, the first thing Mom said to me when I went into her room was, "Do you ever just feel like you have to *do something*? But you don't know quite what?" I didn't tell her that I felt like that all the time now.

"Maybe it's get a job," I said. She looked at me as if I'd spoken in Lithuanian. "The thing you feel like you have to do," I explained.

"No," Mom said, sounding annoyed. "I told you: I don't *know* what it is. That's the whole thing about the feeling. Forget it. You don't understand." Then she said, "Get dressed, and get your sister dressed, too, please—we're going into town."

"Why are we here?" I asked suspiciously a little while later when Mom parked the car in front of Kinko's.

"I have to make some copies of my résumé," she said.

"Here," she said as soon as we got inside, and she fished some money out of her purse. "Why don't you take your sister next door for a cup of hot chocolate?"

"That's not your résumé," I said, looking over her shoulder at the piece of paper she'd pulled out of her tan folder.

"Sure it is." Actually, it was, sort of. It was her résumé, cut into pieces and rearranged, like magnetic poetry. "Experience Free life," she'd taped in a diagonal across the page, "guard wedding cakes with lance. Create high-end reliable joy."

"What is it?" I asked.

"What do you mean?"

"I mean, *what is it?* Why are you doing it?"

"*God*, Marie junior," she said. Then she said, "Does there always have to be a reason?"

"Excuse me?" she said sarcastically when I muttered my answer.

"Nothing."

"No. I'd like to hear what you said."

"I said, 'Sometimes.' Yes, sometimes, it would be nice if you had a reason. And, like, why are you doing that? There's no reason."

I was wrong, though: There was a reason, and I was mad at myself a minute later for not guessing it. From the end of the counter, where she was kneeling on a stool and going through Mom's folder, Rona exclaimed, "Oh! I love this stuff! Can I play with this, Mom?" She was holding up a plastic sheet of press-on type. It was the kind Mom used to use for graphic design. I felt a little ray of hope flicker inside me.

"Oh," said Mom. "It's so expensive. . . ."

"Please, Mom," said Rona.

"Oh, go ahead," Mom said. "Why not? Just make sure to save me some of the a's and n's and y's. Oh, and the capital Ds."

I shot a buffalo today! It was running, even! Well, it was walking pretty fast, anyway.

"Look, Mama!" cried Ezekiel sometime in the middle of the afternoon. He was sitting beside me on the wagon. The sun was baking my brain through my bonnet. The whole world was brown. I felt like I had swallowed a hundred pounds of dust, like my guts and organs were covered with dust, too.

I looked where Ezekiel was pointing. I stopped the wagon and watched the magnificent animal for a minute.

"Stay here," I told the children. "No one move." I went to the back and got Thaddeus's gun.

I just rode right up to that poor sucker and shot him. He looked at me with his big brown eyes, and I aimed right between them. I didn't feel great about doing it, but we need the meat.

Today Annabelle refused to eat.

"I know you're tired of onions and beans and buffalo meat," I said. I

looked closely into her eyes. "Is that what it is? That you're tired of the food?" She didn't answer; she just lowered her chin to her chest and stared at the toes of her boots. I put my hand on her forehead; she had no fever. But I was suddenly frightened. I couldn't bear it if something happened to her.

"Does something hurt you?" I asked. Still she said nothing. "What is it?"

Just then, Amethyst, who was sitting across the fire eating her breakfast, jiggled her eyebrows at Annabelle. "Hubba hubba," she whispered behind her hand.

"What?!" I said.

"Nothing!" Annabelle murmured. Then she wrapped her arms around her knees and buried her head and curled into a little ball. She looked like a potato bug trying to make itself invisible.

"Annabelle's got a boyfriend!" Amethyst burst out, then she fell into a fit of excited giggles. Beside me, I could feel the small, brown ball of Annabelle tighten.

"What on earth are you talking about?" I demanded.

"Tell her!" said Amethyst.

"Tell me what?"

"Mr. Joseph!" crowed Amethyst. "Though I think he really likes me better. He told me I was one scorching pioneer babe."

"What about Mr. Joseph?" I said. He hadn't been around in over a week, and I'd started to think maybe he'd decided to leave us alone.

"Oh, nothing," Amethyst teased. I wanted to rip those dancing eyebrows right off her face.

"I think he's following us," said Ezekiel.

"What do you mean?" I asked him carefully.

"He likes the girls," said Ezekiel. Amethyst beamed. "He tells them so."

How in the world could this be? I was around all the time. How was it possible I wouldn't notice something like that?

"He told Annabelle she had . . ." But he couldn't say the words. Amethyst hid her mouth behind her hand as she was overtaken by another spasm of giggles. In my arms the baby shifted her almost lifeless body. I reached to gather poor Annabelle in my other arm, but her back was hard and rigid under my hand.

It's not fair! I thought in anguish. He's wrecking my life, and there's nothing I can do. But it was so weird—at the exact same time, deep down, a plan was already forming.

Because sometimes you just had to do something. You couldn't just sit there and watch your daughter turn into a potato bug in front of your eyes. You had to make it stop.

The next Tuesday, when I was crawling around on the floor of Mom's room, trying to find some socks for Rona to wear to school, Marie came to Mom's bedroom door and stood there. She had something in her hand—an envelope, and I could see that it had Mom's writing on it.

"Justine, can you go somewhere else right now?" Marie said.

I left the room and went a few steps outside the door.

"This was returned for insufficient postage," Marie said in an icy voice. Mom didn't answer.

"My God, Colleen," Marie said. "This is what you're doing all day, instead of looking for a job? Carrying on an imaginary correspondence with Danny Martone?"

"It's not imaginary," Mom said.

"Oh, come on, Colleen," Marie said. "Tell me the truth: Have you heard anything from Danny since the *wonderful, fantastic* day the two of you shared last month? Any calls? Letters? Postcards? Hang-up calls? Extrasensory communications? Any breath of an indication, *at all*, that Danny Martone is interested in pursuing a relationship with you?" There was silence.

"Really, Colleen," Marie said. "I'm serious. *Have you?* Why can't you answer me?" There was more silence, then Marie said, "I'm going to just lay it on the line. You have to get a job."

"I know," said Mom. "I'm trying."

"No," said Marie. "Like, really: You have to get a job or you can't live here anymore."

"You have been so kind and so generous," Mom said. "I know it's such an imposition for you to have us living—"

"No," Marie said again. "It's not an imposition. It's an adjustment. But we have the room, and you know we think of you and the girls as family. However, Bill and I have talked about it, and we just think we're not doing you any favors by—"

"You're doing me a huge favor—," Mom started.

But Marie interrupted again: "We're not doing you any favors by allowing you to become paralyzed here."

There was silence.

"I know you're scared and depressed right now," Marie said.

"I'm not scared and depressed," said Mom.

"But here's the deal," said Marie. "You get a job—something, anything—by the end of the next two weeks. I'm certain you can do it. I'll help you write letters and make calls to every fucking business establishment in the state, if you want. I'll even pay to send you to a professional career counselor. After you get a job, you can start looking for a place. We can help you out with first and last months' rent and security, if you need, and you know, there's no hurry. Stay till after Christmas if you like."

There was silence again. "So, how does that sound?" said Marie.

"Don't just sit there and not say anything, Colleen," she said. "Don't villainize me."

I felt something unfamiliar then—not exactly sorry for Marie, or like I suddenly liked her, but like I was *on her side*. I was actually sorry when she said the next thing and I couldn't be on her side anymore, even though I thought I knew exactly how she felt: "Oh, *fuck you*, Colleen—this is so unfair. You're being completely manipulative. I am so sick of your passive victim routine I could scream."

—◆◆◆—

Well, Mr. Joseph will be bothering us no more. Don't ask me how I know. Let's just say it was just another sad, unfortunate episode in the history of the Wild West.

Annabelle is on the mend, sitting up by the fire drinking a cup of peppermint tea. "Mama," she said a minute ago. "What happened to me? Was I sick? I don't remember," and I am so grateful for that. The memory seems to be completely erased; and now she can go back to being the little girl she was a week ago.

Mom stopped talking for three days. Each day she left the house before we were up and came home after dark, went straight to her room, and stayed there. The first afternoon, she handed me a bag with a package of cheese, a loaf of bread, two cans of soup, and four apples in it as she passed through the kitchen on her way to the stairs.

When Rona and I went in her room, she would pretend to be asleep. Even when Rona stood there saying, "Mom, Mom, *Mom!*" and shaking her shoulder, she'd act like her eyes wouldn't open.

"Oh," she'd say. "Hi, sweetheart. Please let me sleep, okay?"

On the fourth day, though, in the afternoon, she came in the door smiling. It was a weird smile, though, as if she'd lost her real one and maybe found another one lying on the ground somewhere. Rona and I were sitting at the kitchen table.

"Hey!" Mom said as if she hadn't been missing for the last three days. Rona burst into tears. I had been trying to act like everything was normal—"Mom's out looking for a job," I'd told Rona when she stuck out her bottom lip and said, "I want my mom," or I'd say, "Mom's really tired from looking for a job all day," when Mom walked past us on her way to her room and closed the door. I let Rona sleep in my bed, and gave her a bath every night, and got her ready for school in the morning, and made the bread and cheese and soup for our dinners, and exhausted my brain trying to think of stories to tell her every time it seemed like she was about to get upset. By the fourth day, I was furious at Mom and pretty mad at Rona, too—she refused to change the socks she'd been wearing for three days; she'd woken me up in the middle of the night two nights in a row to ask for water; and after school that day, she'd looked at the snack I put in front of her and said, "No more stupid *cheese!*"

When Rona burst into tears, though, and didn't even go running to Mom but just *thunk*ed her forehead down on the kitchen table and started sobbing, I saw something I hadn't seen before, and I felt terrible for having been mad at her: She had actually been being really good. She was only five and a half years old, and for three days she had been carrying around a broken heart like a heavy stone and hadn't asked anyone to take it for her. As far as she knew, Mom was going to be like this forever. Even I didn't know, actually, if Mom was ever going to go back to normal. It made me want to go put my arms around Rona and say, "I'm sorry," for not having been patient with her.

But Mom was doing it. Mom went over and knelt down and said, "Hey, hey, hey! What's the matter, honey? What's the matter?" and I was maybe madder than I'd ever been right then. I wanted to tell her,

"Cut the shit! You're the one who did it. She's just a little kid, and you act like she doesn't even need a mother."

"Oh," said Marie when she came downstairs from working and saw Mom. "Have you *rejoined* us?"

Mom looked surprised. "Rejoined you?" Marie glared at her.

"I just needed some time to think," Mom said.

"You *needed*," said Marie. Then she said, "Whatever."

"I got a job," Mom said.

Marie's look got a few degrees less mad. "You did?" she said.

"Mm-hmm," said Mom.

"Congratulations. Where?"

"At the Store 24."

Marie looked at her as if she'd said, "Cleaning outhouses." "Say you're kidding," she said.

"Why?" asked Mom.

"You *know* why. You could do a lot better than a *convenience store* and you know it."

"There's nothing wrong with working in a convenience store. I might like it," Mom said. "It's close by. And it has some benefits."

"Like what, discounts on microwave sandwiches? I mean, come on, Colleen. Don't take it. You can find something better."

"But that's the thing," Mom said pleasantly. "I can't. When you're totally unskilled, one choice really isn't that different from another."

"You're not totally unskilled," Marie said. "I know you've said it so incessantly to yourself that you believe it, but you're not. And you know, this is important: The knowledge of that is the only thing that's ever going to save you. The thing is, you have a whole well of experiences inside you, but you just—"

"*Save* me?" Mom said. "Is that how you think of me? As some helpless thing who needs someone to save her?"

"I didn't say helpless," said Marie. "Definitely not helpless. And you'll note that I didn't say you need someone *else* to save you. How about saving yourself?"

"Save myself?" Mom said, trying to sound totally sarcastic, which was something she was bad at.

"Yeah," Marie said, nodding. "Save yourself. That would be an efficient way to do it." I listened carefully. What did she mean? Like, was she going to give some instructions?

"Well," Mom said, "I don't know what you're talking about. I have this job, and I'm going to go to it, and maybe that will *save* me. And if not, *oh well*."

There was silence then, as Marie and Mom glared at each other. Only, Mom smiled as she glared, which had a weird effect.

That "oh well" really bothered me. What had she meant by it? A terrible thought came to me as I sat there listening to the chirpy sound of the words hanging in the air: What if those were your last words? If you just said them, and smiled, and closed your eyes and gave up? Or if you didn't mean them as last words, but they turned out to be? Either way, I couldn't really think of worse ones.

We have come to South Pass. All day, the oxen's nostrils flared wide with every breath as they climbed. I walked all day to save the oxen's strength. Zack has developed a limp. The children took turns riding on Jake. I carried the baby. She looked at me reproachfully all day long, as if she wants to know why I am doing this to her.

Amethyst showed her face sometime in the late afternoon.

"Rrnnmp," she said, emerging, squinting and stretching, when we stopped to water the horses. "Where are we?"

"We've crossed the Continental Divide," I told her. No thanks to you, I didn't add: Didn't you notice the poor oxen huffing and puffing and straining, hauling you uphill while you slept? Amethyst's ability not to notice what's going on around her is quite awesome, actually.

"Something seems different," she said.

"Something is different," I told her. "Would you like to hear an interesting fact about the Continental Divide?" I was about to tell her what I was thinking, that in a certain way, we'd really left the past—all the rivers, from now on, flowed toward our new life like water from a big toilet.

But she just answered, "Not particularly," and turned to crawl back through the canvas.

"Fine," I muttered. "Go lie down. I don't care." Except I did, just for a

second. It kills me to admit it, but Amethyst has a strange power, sometimes, to trick me into forgetting that I am doing all of this absolutely alone.

Mom worked at the Store 24 from five A.M. to two P.M. four days a week. She was gone when we woke up, and by the time we got home from school, she was in bed, taking a nap that usually lasted till our bedtime.

"Colleen," Marie told her at the end of the first week. "It's ridiculous. You're knocking yourself out for a thirty-hour-a-week, menial, minimum-wage job. You have to find something else."

"Marie," Mom said, "you told me to get a job, and I went out and got a job. Now you're telling me to quit it?"

"I see," said Marie. "This is my punishment."

"Punishment?" said Mom, totally unconvincingly. "What are you talking about?"

"Well, it's not worth it," Marie said. "You should just quit. But then of course you'd have to find a new way to *stick it to me*, wouldn't you?"

"Look, Mama!" said Annabelle this morning as we were driving. She pointed to a shrub near the trail. Propped in its branches was a piece of paper. My first thought was that it was from Mr. Joseph, and my stomach dropped, till I remembered it wasn't possible: I'd seen him with my own eyes, lying on the ground with his tongue lolling out and a hole through his heart. Annabelle jumped down from the wagon and ran over to the shrub. She handed me the note, and I unfolded it. Amethyst's head popped from the opening in the canvas. "Is it for me?" she asked eagerly.

"No," I said.

"Who's it from?" she asked suspiciously. "What does it say?"

"Keep up your pace," said the note. "Try to make fifteen miles a day. Don't tarry in this place, though you may be tempted to when the sky is blue and the days are long. Let your oxen get as fat as they can before crossing the mountains, and if you see an antelope, or a prairie dog, or one of those rabbits with horns, shoot it." The note wasn't addressed to anyone, and it wasn't signed.

"*Read it!*" *said Amethyst.*

"*No.*" *I shook my head and folded the piece of paper.*

"*Zebulina!*" *she whined.* "*How do you even know it's for you and not for me?*"

"*Hush,*" *I said. I didn't know. But it made me feel better to pretend it was, so that's what I did.*

On Tuesday, Mom wasn't in her bed when we got home from school. I got us a snack and we did our homework and she still didn't come back. When Marie came down from working, she said, "Where's your mother?"

"I don't know," I said, then I changed my voice when I saw the look on Rona's face. "Probably out doing errands. I think we needed Q-tips." Then I took Rona to Mom's room and we got in her bed under the covers and I turned on the TV. There wasn't anything on but fuzz, though.

"Do you want me to read you a book?" I asked Rona.

"No!" she said. "Story!"

"Oh," I said slowly. It was getting harder and harder for me to think of stories. "Okay. This is a story about a little girl. Named Nora. And she's lost all alone on a desert isle."

"No!" said Rona. "What's a dezzerdile?"

"It's like an island," I said. "A deserted island in the middle of the ocean. And she—"

"No!" Rona said. "No island. Don't have her there."

"But it's going to be a happy story," I told her, though I kind of thought it ruined the whole thing to say it. "It's going to turn out all right in the end."

"No," she said. "Justine, don't tell it to me anymore." Then she stuck her thumb in her mouth and leaned her head on my shoulder, and we just sat there for a long time, staring at the snowy TV. Which was all right with me, because I'd actually had no idea how I was going to make that story come out okay in the end.

Mom walked in in the middle of dinner. She went to the sink and washed her hands, then she sat down at the kitchen table.

"Gee, thanks for letting us know where you were," Marie said.

"Oh!" said Mom. "I didn't think anyone would care!"

"I think your children cared," said Marie.

"I'm sorry!" Mom said. "You weren't worried, were you?" she said, looking at me and Rona. Then she said to Marie, "Well, I quit my job!"

"You did?" Marie said.

"Well, actually, I got transferred."

"Transferred?"

"To a different Store 24," Mom said. "I'll have better hours."

Marie sighed. "Where's there another Store 24?" she asked.

"I'm going to be working at one near Hartford," said Mom.

"*Hartford?!*" Marie said.

"Mm-hmm," said Mom.

"That's insane!" Marie sputtered. "You can't commute two hours a day to a six-dollar-an-hour job! Colleen, I'm serious, I think you need to get some serious professional mental help, because you appear to be completely out of your fucking tree!"

"I wouldn't be commuting," Mom said.

"What does that mean?" asked Marie.

"Actually, I'm thinking of moving down there."

"No!" shouted Rona, and she started to cry.

"Oh, honey!" Mom said, and she reached over and stroked her hair. "Not without you! That's not what I meant! We'll all move. It might be a really good thing for us."

"You can't do that!" Marie said again, and I wished so, so badly that that were true. Because Mom *could* do anything, and might. "Colleen!" Marie said. "You have children to think about. You can't just move to a different state every time you have a problem you want to run away from."

"I'm not running away from anything," Mom said.

"But what about Justine and Rona?" said Marie. "How could it possibly be a good idea for them to change schools again right now?"

"Kids adjust," Mom said. "They're good at adjusting. Besides," she said, "Justine hates her new school. Don't you?" she asked, turning to me. "What do *you* think, Justine? Don't you think moving to

Hartford might be kind of fun? Continuing our adventure just a little farther? Finding a place that's really our own?"

"I won't go," I said. I was actually as surprised as Mom was that I'd said it. Mom stared at me.

"What do you mean?" she said.

I told her the truth as it came to me, from I didn't know where: "I mean, I won't go with you. I won't do it."

"No!" wailed Rona, and she got out of her chair and ran to me. She squeezed my arm with both hands. "Go!" she said. Then she looked at Mom, and I could see there was fear in her eyes. "Don't go!" she wailed to Mom.

"For God's sake, Colleen," said Marie. "I mean, look at this."

"You have to go," Mom said to me.

"No, I don't."

"I'm your mother," Mom said. "And until you're eighteen, you have to do what I tell you to."

"Well, I won't," I said. It might be true, about me not being eighteen, but there were other things just as true: It was a terrible, terrible idea to go to Hartford, one that I just couldn't let happen. Something in me knew that, the way Grandma's kitten Mickey knew, the time we tried to give him a bath once to get rid of his fleas. You could see it in Mickey's eyes: If he had to kill you getting out of that tub, oh well. And I'm pretty sure Mickey didn't have a plan when he felt his paw tips touch the water, just like I had no plan now, just a very important feeling, and the memory of Grandma sitting there soaked, with bleeding claw marks up and down her arms and a long tear in her blouse, shaking her head and looking at the wet paw prints heading away from the bathroom and saying, "Pretty amazing what a two-pound cat can do when he's got his mind made up, isn't it?"

———— ᘇᘇᘇ ————

We came to the Parting of the Ways today. It was a little anticlimactic, actually—just a fork in the road with a small wooden sign listing the two choices: right for the shortcut to Soda Springs, left for Fort Bridger. As I looked at the sign, my stomach hurt, and I wasn't sure why. Both ways looked exactly the same, as far as you could see. Maybe it was the way the sign made it seem like there was a choice. But as soon as you turned either way you realized there wasn't one. The choice was to keep going, that was all. I swallowed my stomachache and smiled at the children.

We stayed there a minute. I pretended to be adjusting the reins, but really, I suddenly felt afraid to go on. I knew which way to take—it wasn't that. But I had that feeling like I was forgetting something. Like I might be about to leave something forever, even though there was nothing around me but the windswept hills, nobody behind me for days. I stood up in the seat and leaned to look at the road behind me one last time. I wished there were someone to wave good-bye to, at least.

The next morning when we woke up, Mom was gone. Marie set bowls of oatmeal in front of us, which gave me a creepy feeling, because it was something she usually didn't do. Then she got out the phone book and called a number. "Is Colleen Hanley working today?" she asked. She listened to the answer, then she pursed her lips and hung up.

"Is she?" I asked, but Marie didn't say anything. Tears started to fall down Rona's face into her oatmeal.

There was one good thing about it: At school that day, I could tell by the way Alex and Joey looked at me when I came in the classroom that there was another note in my locker, but I didn't care. The feeling of caring was like something in the landscape that had seemed huge when I passed it, but was just small in the distance now. I had so much more important things to worry about. Like taking care of Rona, eating, sleeping, and getting out of bed the next morning so I could do it all over again.

———ww———

I have found three more notes. One said, "You are about a month from the mountains. Important to cross by the end of September." Another said, "If you come to a stinky swamp covered with white powder, don't let the animals drink, for the water will make them sick. However, the powder used as baking soda will make excellent bread." The last said, "Recipe for Nettle Soup: Boil nettles 3X in water, taste for salt and pepper, serve."

It's weird about the notes: they never say my name or anything about me. We have seen no parties for weeks—no one knows we're out here. I have no reason at all to think they are meant for me. So I can't explain why I feel more and more certain that they are.

Mom wasn't there when we got home that day. Neither was anyone else. The house was quiet and dark and cold. After our snack— one hard, old, whole-wheat fake Fig Newton split in half and the crumbs from the bottom of a package of rice cakes—we went up to Mom's room, got in her bed, and turned on the TV. When it was almost totally dark, the phone rang. I ran to the hall, but the phone wasn't there, and by the time I found it, there was a message on the machine.

"Hi, all," said Mom's voice. "I just wanted to let you know I'm in Hartford. I'm not sure when I'll be back—I might be meeting Danny for dinner. I'm looking at apartments, and . . . Well, I'll call back later to let you know what's going on." The beep of the message ending made me want to sweep the machine onto the floor. I went to the refrigerator and looked inside, then I checked the cabinets. Then I went back upstairs and got all the money I had: nine dollars.

"I have to leave you here alone for a little while," I told Rona.

"No!" she screamed.

"Well, do you want to walk to the Store 24 with me?" I said. "It's half a mile there and half a mile back. That equals a whole mile."

"No!" she said.

"Well, do you want to have Marie-dinner tonight?" I asked. "It might be leftover cabbage soup."

"No!" she shouted.

"You have to choose one of those three things," I said. "Because we can't just sit here and starve."

"No!" she said again. But at the same time, she got out of bed; and she didn't say anything else—she just followed me down the stairs, through the kitchen, to the back hall. When she got there, she sat down and started putting on her boots.

Rona was okay for about twenty feet. Then she said, "I'm tired, Justine."

"It's just a little way," I lied. "Do you want to sing a song?"

"No," she said crankily. "I want to go home."

"Count to three hundred," I told her. "Then we'll be almost there."

She got to six, then she said, "Justine, my boots hurt."

"I'll buy you some M&M's," I said.

"I hate M&M's," she said. At the end of the block, she sat down on the side of the road. We weren't even out of sight of the house yet.

"You can't sit down," I told her.

"I'm doing it," she said matter-of-factly.

"Come on," I said, tugging at her hand. "If you get up, I'll tell you a story." But my poor brain wanted to cry, it was so tired of making up stories.

"No thanks," she said.

"Please?" I pleaded.

"Nopie dopey," she said.

"Just try," I said.

"Nope," she said. "And anyway, Justine," she said, "I need to go poop. Right now. I really, really do."

When we got back to the house, no one was home yet. Outside there was still some thin, cold, whitish blue light left in the sky, but inside it was dark. The shadows had gathered, the way they did every day, like clusters of tired, silent people hunched in the corners. I took off Rona's boots and went around turning on every light. I turned the heat up to seventy-five, which Marie would kill me for if she found out.

I took Rona up to Mom's room and told her to get in the bed, then I brought her a pile of books and wrapped a quilt around her and said, "I'll be back in a few minutes." She started to struggle out of the quilt.

"Where are you going?" she said.

"I'm going to go downstairs and put the dishes in the dishwasher so Marie won't have a screaming shit-fit when she gets home." Rona giggled. "And then I'm going to take out the recycling, and I'm going to go to the garage and see if I can find a cardboard box for a diorama for school. And then I'm going to put some birdseed in the bird feeder, and then I'm going to come back in and make some hot chocolate and bring it upstairs for us.

"And," I said, "this is the deal: You have to stay right in this bed the whole time and not move."

"Why?"

"It's a magic thing," I told her. "It's hard to explain, exactly. It's like a spell. A spell by the November fairy, who just likes to bug people for the fun of it. If you don't get out of bed, then I can do all those things and get the hot chocolate made and get back. But every time you get out of bed, I have to start over again."

"The November fairy?" she said like she didn't believe me. "Really, Justine?"

"Yup," I said, and she said, "Oh." She believed me, I could tell; I felt a stab of love and sadness, and something bigger, too, something in a whole other category of feelings, though I couldn't tell what it was.

"Got it?" I said.

"Yep," she said.

"It might take me a little while, but don't get out of bed, whatever you do. Then, I promise, I'll be back with the hot chocolate."

I ran all the way to the Store 24 and all the way back, which was something I hadn't known I could do. I bought a box of macaroni and cheese and some milk. When I got home, I burst into the house and ran up the stairs with a terrible feeling. But there, right where I'd left her, was Rona.

"I stayed," she said in a tiny voice. She looked like she was about to cry. Then she asked, "Where's the hot chocolate?" She craned her head around, I guess to see if I'd set it down somewhere.

"Oh!" I said. I'd forgotten completely. And it was weird—I started to laugh, but tears started coming out, too, and I didn't know why. I didn't know why it felt like such a terrible thing that Rona had just been sitting there, waiting patiently for the hot chocolate that she was so sure I was going to bring because I'd said I would.

I woke up on the wrong side of the bedroll today, for no reason I could figure out. I lay in my tent a long time, not wanting to get up and start the porridge. Then Ezekiel called, "Mama! My feet itch," and a thought

tromped through my brain: It's boring taking care of other people all the time. I tried to chase it away, but the thought just stood there sneering at me, as if to say, What sort of mother thinks such a thing?

It's boring being on a journey that seems like it's going to go on forever; doing the same endless chores every day, working so hard to keep everyone safe and happy and alive. It's lonely, living your life with someone always lying down in the back.

"Mama," called Ezekiel again. Beside me, the baby stirred in her cradle. Wearily I dragged myself up. It sure would be nice to just lie there and let a huge crying fit wash over me for about fifteen hours. I took off my nightgown and got into my dress. Sometimes I wish I weren't such a strong woman.

At eight the phone rang. I beat Marie to it.

"Hi, sweetheart!" Mom said as if everything were normal.

"Is that your mother?" Marie asked, bending her neck over me like a cartoon vulture. "I want to talk to her when you're done." I walked into the other room with the phone.

"How are you?" Mom said.

"Fine," I said, and I hated the way the word had automatically come out of my mouth, just like a grown-up. I changed my answer. "Actually, *not* fine."

"Why?" Mom said. "What's wrong? Did something happen?"

"Where *are* you?" I asked.

"Hartford!" she said, like, Stupid question. "I left you a message earlier. Didn't you get it?"

"That's not what I mean," I said.

"Well, what *do* you mean?" she asked.

"I mean what are you *doing*?"

"I've been looking at apartments!" she said. "I think I found one you're going to love. It's tiny but cute, in a really interesting, funky neighborhood, and the rent's cheap—"

"When are you coming home?" I asked.

"Well," she said, "I'm not exactly sure, yet. Are you guys doing fine? Because I was thinking of stopping by Danny's work. And if he's there, maybe we'll go out for dinner. So it might be kind of late when

I get home. And actually, it might make more sense for me to just stay, since I have to work tomorrow morning anyway."

I wanted to cry, and I knew I shouldn't. Not because it would upset Mom, but because if I started to cry, things might get mushy and blurry inside of me, and my eyes might not be able to focus on the things I needed to see, not that I knew what they were.

"What do you want me to make for our lunches tomorrow?" I said.

"Are you mad at me?" she asked.

"Just tell me what you want me to give Rona for lunch!" I said.

"Because I don't know why that would be fair, exactly," said Mom. "I mean, I *am* out here kind of busting my butt trying to make things nice for all of us. I'm just trying to make everybody happy, so please—"

"Lunch," I said.

"I don't know!" she said. "I don't even know what there is! Can't you just look in the refrigerator and find something?"

"There isn't anything," I said.

"Well, then, take school lunch," she said.

Rona wouldn't eat school lunch. I was going to have to go out to the store again. I hadn't stopped to think, in the store, What if Mom doesn't come home at all tonight? I was furious at myself now for being so stupid.

"Did you leave money?" I asked her.

"Get some from Marie," she said. "Tell her I'll pay her back."

"Here," I said, walking back to the kitchen. "Tell her yourself."

"No!" Mom said. "Justine—"

"See you whenever," I said.

"Wait!" she called, her voice suddenly tiny and far away, as I handed the phone through the air to Marie. I had seven dollars and no idea when Mom was coming back. My blisters hurt so much, I couldn't get my shoes past my heels. Marie was already bitching into the phone when I slipped out the door. I was trying to talk myself into staying calm. There were worse things than having to walk to the store in the dark, in November, in your socks, I knew. I really hoped I didn't have to find out what they were.

*We reached Fort Bridger today. It is the 29th of July. I traded
Thaddeus's fiddle, his buckskin coat, his Sunday suit, and his boots for flour,
beans, dried beef, lard, molasses, onions, rice, and cornmeal. Also, I paid a
few coins to a man who called himself a veterinarian to look at Zack's foot.
The so-called vet couldn't tell me anything. He rubbed some liniment on
Zack's hoof and said, "Good luck."*

*Oh, and I got a map. To be honest, I should say I stole it. I saw it in the
supply post and knew I shouldn't spend the last of my money on it, but I was
overtaken by a dire feeling that I had to have it, so I slipped it into the sleeve
of my dress.*

Everybody at Fort Bridger was talking about the cutoff.

*"You go around the Great Salt Lake to the south," they said, "then hook
up to the main trail again at the Humboldt River. It'll save you three
hundred and fifty miles. It's a good road, too—smooth and flat, lots of grass
and water for the cattle."*

*"Are we going to take it?" asked Amethyst as we drove away from Fort
Bridger.*

"Take what?" I asked.

"The cutoff."

"Nope," I told her.

"Why not?" she whined. "It's supposed to be a better way."

"Why do you care?" I asked. Then I saw the shifty look in her eyes.

"I don't," she said. Lying.

"Tell me," I demanded.

"No reason," she said. Then she said, "I met someone."

"Where? When?"

*"At Fort Bridger," she said. "A gentleman." She smiled to herself. Then
she said, "Oh, by the way—he's taking the cutoff. He said he'd be our guide
if we wanted."*

"No way," I said.

"He says the scenery's much nicer," she said.

"Bad reason," I said.

"Please??!"

"Not happening."

"Oh, Zebulina!" cried Amethyst. "Zebulina! Oh please, oh please, oh

please?" She fell on her knees to a praying position, then tipped over and started rolling around on the ground.

"Get a grip," I told her. "Get up. Get in the wagon. We're not taking any cutoffs. Period, the end."

She moaned and cried all day and half the night, but except for not getting any sleep, I didn't care. Sometimes, actually, it feels good being the one in charge. When you can see what the exact right decision is and there's nothing to stop you from making it.

—⁓—

Disaster has struck.

This morning, when I told Annabelle to take Amethyst her breakfast, she came running back a minute later with wide eyes, holding a slip of paper. "Took the cutoff with Mr. Samuel Solomon," I read. "See you in California."

"Who the freak is Mr. Samuel Solomon?!" I swore, then I realized he must be the gentleman she'd met at Fort Bridger. I pounded the side of the wagon with my fist a few times, but it didn't really feel all that good, so I stopped.

"Now what?" asked Annabelle, worried.

"Good ribbance!" said Ezekiel. He had never quite gotten that expression.

"Let's go," I told them.

"Go where?" said Annabelle, looking worried.

"Hush," I said. "Don't worry." Totally faking it. "I'll take care of everything." I had a decision to make, and I made it right then and there. We weren't going after her. She'd made her choice; she was Mr. Samuel Solomon's problem now. It felt good in some terrible way to have the answer to such an impossible problem march right into my brain.

So I can't explain why I did what I did next. Why I started up the oxen and headed the direction that every cell and nerve and brain wave was telling me not to go.

DECISION MAKING
AND PERSONAL RESPONSIBILITY

At school the next day, I was in such a bad mood it was actually kind of scary. I was 99.9 percent sure that none of the terrible things I felt like were about to happen to my body—my brain exploding, my eyeballs bursting, my teeth crumbling into little bits—could really happen, but I had to keep reminding myself of that. By ten o'clock, I was exhausted from sitting there with everything clenched tight, trying to keep myself in one piece.

At two o'clock, just when I thought the day might end without anything stupid happening, Ms. Taylor said, "Class, we have some special visitors." It was two ladies we'd never seen before, and—I couldn't believe it—they had cartons of eggs.

The ladies smiled slyly at us, then one of them said, "I bet you have no idea what's going on! I bet you think we're just a couple of crazy ladies. You probably think we're from the Egg Council!"

"But we're not!" said the other one. "We're here to do a special unit on Healthy Minds and Bodies: Decision Making and Personal Responsibility!"

I felt my hand go up.

"Yes?" said one of the ladies. I wished I weren't about to say the words I could feel headed out of my mouth.

"Can't we do something else? Maybe something halfway educational, like science? Or geography? We haven't done one iota of geography this year."

The class went into a mass conniption. "J-u-u-s-t—i-n-e! J-u-u-s-t—

i-n-e!" went the boys. Luckily, Ms. Taylor was out of the room. The ladies kept smiling, though.

"So you don't think learning about decision making and personal responsibility is educational? Well, guess what? I bet you're not alone! Class, how many of you think: 'Decision making and personal responsibility. Those are two big words I don't have to worry about. I'm only in the sixth grade'?"

The ladies went on for another half hour, telling us the rules of the assignment: You had to take the egg with you everywhere you went, and if you didn't want to, you had to pay someone to baby-sit it; and it was cheating to just leave it sitting in your backpack if you had basketball practice or something. Then one of them started passing out the eggs. When she got to me, I said, "No thank you."

"You don't want one?" she said.

"Not really."

"Why not?" she asked.

"I already know the point of the assignment," I said. I wasn't exactly trying to be rude, but I could hear my voice getting louder. "I'm not going to have a teen pregnancy, and I don't want a freakin egg!"

"Well," said the lady, "you certainly seem to have a strong opinion. Which is not a bad thing. But I'll tell you what. How about if I give you one anyway?" She took an egg out of the carton and set it in my pencil groove. "You can do whatever you want with it, but remember, either way, it's still a decision you're making."

We have traveled three days down the cutoff. No sign of Amethyst.

When I turned the corner at the bottom of the stairs at the end of the day, Rona was shuffling out of her classroom behind some other kids, and I could see she was in as bad a mood as I was. Her eyebrows were pointed in a V on her face, and when the girl in front of her stopped for a second to scratch her knee, Rona pushed her.

"Hey!" said the girl. "I'm telling!"

"Tell, stupid freak—I don't care!" Rona said. As soon as she saw me, she burst into tears.

"What's the matter?" I asked.

"Nothing!" she blubbered, and she hit my arm.

"Ouch!" I said. "Why'd you do that?"

"Because!"

"Did something bad happen?"

"No!" she said. Then she raised her lunchbox in the air and threw it as hard as she could. When it hit the ground it opened up and her lunch went flying everywhere.

"Why didn't you eat your lunch?" I asked her as I picked up the parts of it.

"I hate that lunch!" She was practically screaming. "It was yucky!"

"But it's what you always have," I said.

But it wasn't. Rona usually got bologna and cheese on white bread, all of which made Marie turn over in her grave whenever she saw them. I'd stood in the Store 24 a long time the night before, looking at the choices. All they had was this weird bologna with green and red spots all over it. Which maybe Rona wouldn't have noticed if the outside of the sandwich had looked normal. But the bread she liked— the bright, white, fluffy kind—only came in a huge loaf about four feet long, and if I bought it, I wouldn't be able to afford the cheese. Hamburger buns were cheaper, and they tasted just like white bread, but I should've known that when she saw the hamburger bun, she'd open up the sandwich and inspect it.

I could see the line at our bus getting shorter. "Let's go," I said.

"But I'm hungry!" Rona sobbed, not moving.

"Well, let's go home and get something to eat," I said.

"But I'm so hungry!" she wailed. If we missed the bus, I didn't know what we were going to do. I could walk, but Rona wouldn't be able to make it the whole way, and there was no way I could carry her. And Mom was in Hartford, so she couldn't come get us. Maybe I could call a cab, except I didn't have any money. Then I thought of something.

"Rona," I whispered like I had a secret. "Stop crying. I have something for you." I took the egg out of my coat pocket. "Here it is." I put it in her hand. "Be careful."

She stopped crying for a second and looked down at her hand, then she screamed, *"I don't want a stupid egg!"* Her head started shaking and the strings in her neck tightened and I saw the tips of her fingers turn white as she squeezed the egg with all her might. But it didn't break. *"Aaah!"* she screamed. She was getting ready to throw it, but I held her arm.

"It's not an ordinary egg," I told her. "Don't you want to hear about what kind of an egg it is?"

"Buh-huh-huh," she cried.

"It's a responsibility egg. All the sixth-graders got one. But you're the only first-grader. Do you know what a responsibility egg is?"

She shook her head, still crying.

"It's like a pretend baby." That made her stop crying for a second. "It needs someone to take care of it. It can't get left alone for one single minute."

"Why-hy-hy?" she cried.

"So it doesn't get broken," I said.

"O-o-o-h, no-o-o-o!!" Rona wailed, and she collapsed back down onto the ground. But she held the egg in the air. "Don't get broken!"

"No, but . . ." I could see I'd made a big mistake. "Forget it," I said, and I tried to take the egg from her hand. "It's just an ordinary egg." But her fingers stayed clenched tight.

"No!" she screamed. "Don't take it! It's mine!"

Still no sign of Amethyst. The road is rough going—not many wagons have traveled down it. It is rocky, and steep, and so narrow in places that the wagon can hardly pass. I don't know where those reports the men at Fort Bridger gave were coming from.

"What an adventure we're having," I say to the children when the lurching of the wagon and the scratching of the tree branches against the canvas frightens them. I hate the sound of my voice when I say it. "This definitely feels like the fast way to California!"

As soon as we got inside, Rona said, "I'm hungry."

"Go upstairs and I'll bring you something in a minute," I told her.

After she had gone, I got the telephone. I stood looking out the window as I dialed Grandma Bobbie's number.

"Hello, sweetheart!" she said when she heard it was me. "How *are* you?"

"Good," I said. "Great."

"Really?" she said. When I didn't answer, she said, "Justine?" I was getting ready to tell her the truth, I really was. Which was: Grandma, we need help.

But what would I answer when she asked why?

Because Mom's off the deep end? She moved to Hartford and left us here without any food or money?

Somehow those words just seemed wrong to me. They didn't sound like they could be true. Like, there must be some part of the story I'd missed, something I just didn't understand right.

"Everything's okay," I said. "Everything's great. School's great; Rona's great. Mom got a job."

"She did?"

"At a store," I said. I left off the "24" part. Then I said, "Grandma, I know it's rude to ask, but do you think you could send me some money?"

"It's not rude, sweetheart. I don't mind giving you money. What's it for?"

"Shoes?" I said.

"Goodness. Doesn't your mother have money to buy you shoes?"

"They're extra shoes," I said. "There's this girl at school?"

"Oh?" said Grandma, sounding hopeful.

"Yeah, she's sort of my best friend."

"Oh, how nice! What's her name?" Sometimes lying actually made people happy, and then it didn't seem like such a bad thing to do.

"Jane," I said. "She's really nice. We went to the mall on Saturday and we saw these shoes. They're high-top sneakers in crazy colors, and we wanted to get them and be twins."

"How much do they cost?" Grandma asked, and I knew she would say yes.

"I'm not sure," I told her. "I forgot. But, kind of a lot."

"Well," she said. "How about if I send you seventy-five dollars? You can get the shoes and something for Rona with the leftover."

* * *

Besides getting the food money from Grandma Bobbie, the rest of my plan wasn't all that great: Wait for Mom to come back to her senses. I hadn't gotten to the part yet about what if she didn't. Trying to think those two ideas at once felt like trying to see a different thing out of each of my eyes.

After I finished talking to Grandma, I looked in all the cupboards and the refrigerator, then I made Rona the best thing I could out of what I could find: a grainy, all-natural-peanut-butter sandwich on the brown crackers Marie bought that tasted like goat food. I took it upstairs.

Rona was sitting in the middle of Mom's messed-up bed. Her face was blotchy, but she wasn't crying anymore. She'd made a little nest out of balled-up socks and crumpled clothes on Mom's pillow, and in the middle of it, surrounded by a coiled pair of panty hose, was the egg.

"Here you go," I said, holding out the plate to her, and I sat down on the bed.

"Don't sit there!" Rona screeched. "You're tipping it!"

"Okay!" I got up. "But anyway, that's not a very good place for that egg. You can't keep it there."

"I can!" she shrieked, and she hunched over the egg and shielded it with her body. "This is my egg, and it's staying here!" She sounded like she was going to cry again. "It's staying here forever if I say it is. It's my responsibility egg, and I say what happens to it!

"What is that?" she said, peering over the edge of the plate in my hand.

"A peanut-butter sandwich. Sort of." She picked up the cracker sandwich and took a bite, then she stopped chewing and looked at me like I had just done something awful to her. "I don't like this kind," she said, her mouth turning downward.

"That's all there is," I told her. I took the cracker sandwich from her and took a little bite, too. She was right, it was pretty putrid. "I'm sorry," I said as her eyes filled with tears. Nothing was my fault, but I felt terrible anyway. I watched as she chewed and swallowed with tears running down her face.

"It's all right," she said in a mucusy, peanut-buttery-mouth voice.

"It's all right, everything's going to be all right." But she wasn't looking at me; she was leaning over her little fortress, talking to her egg.

We have found Amethyst. Late this afternoon we came upon her, huddled under a scrubby oak by the side of the trail, crying, no Mr. Samuel Solomon in sight. I've been so angry at her for the past five days, but the sight of her sitting there with her fists to her face, crying her eyes out, did something to my heart.

I didn't even yell at her. "Come on," I said. I walked over to her, and I took her under the armpits and hoisted her up. She was limp as a rag doll.

"He said we were going to get married!" Amethyst wailed, then she grabbed me around the neck and sobbed, "Zeb-u-l-ina!" My heart jumped sideways. "But I woke up and he was gone! Maybe wolves got him. Maybe he stumbled into the stream trying to fetch water. Maybe he got up in the night to answer the call of nature and got lost trying to—"

"Hush," I said. "Hush, hush."

"But—"

"You don't need him," I said.

"I do!" she said.

"You're better off without him," I said. "You have us to take care of you." She didn't look like she thought too much of that, though. "Come on," I told her, but she didn't budge, so I ended up half walking, half dragging, half dancing her to the wagon. That adds up to one and a half, actually.

"But we don't know the way without him," she wailed. I saw worry flash in Annabelle's eyes.

"You be quiet now!" I told Amethyst. "We will be just fine."

But I couldn't sleep at all tonight. I got up to write this. It is the fifth of August. Even though the days are long and scorching still, I can feel the way the sun picks up its pace on its way toward the horizon at the end of the day, like something anxious to get away from us. And last night, we slept under blankets. All I can do is hope that the so-called road we are on hooks up soon to the main trail. We've wasted too much time to retrace our steps to Fort Bridger.

* * *

"Justine," said Ms. Taylor at lunchtime on the fourth day Mom was gone, "aren't you going to the cafeteria?" Everybody else had left for lunch, and I was sitting quietly, pretending to read in our boring social studies book, hoping Ms. Taylor would leave, too.

"No," I told her.

She watched me for a minute, then she asked, "Did you bring a lunch today?"

"No," I said. I did have one, actually, in my backpack, but I'd only made it because Marie had forced me to. Every morning now she watched me as I made Rona's lunch, and when I finished, she'd say, "What about yours?"

I was discovering something, though. I didn't really have to eat as much as I always thought I did. Two days in a row, I'd unwrapped my grainy-peanut-butter-and-goat-food-cracker sandwich at lunchtime, and even though at eleven o'clock I'd been starving, something interesting had happened: The food on the table in front of me suddenly didn't even look like food anymore. And when I looked at it, I didn't even feel like a human being—we were just two unrelated things that didn't need each other, which was perfect.

Even though all I'd had since lunch yesterday was four bites of vegetable curry at dinner and a half bite of Marie's Famous Lead Cornbread for breakfast, instead of feeling weak from hunger, it was weird—I felt great. I felt like I was turning weightless, like my body might float out of my chair. My stomach rumbled, and I imagined icebergs breaking apart in there, melting and turning to vapor.

"Do you need money, Justine?" Ms. Taylor asked. "You know, I have lunch money in my desk, for when people forget theirs."

Then why haven't you ever told us that before, you big fat liar? I thought. But all I said was, "No, thank you," then I gave Ms. Taylor a smile and went to find a place where she wouldn't bother me anymore.

Later that day, I discovered something else I liked about starving.

During the break between language arts and reading circle, Noah walked by and dropped a note on my desk. I'd already decided I didn't care about the notes and I wasn't going to read them anymore. Except that Kirsten saw him do it. "Ooh, Justine," she said. "Aren't you going to read it?" So I had no choice. If I put the note in my pocket with no expression on my face, everybody would think it was a private love letter from Noah, and they'd tease me about it for the rest of my life. If I crumpled it up and threw it in the garbage can, someone would get it out for sure. If Kirsten didn't shut up, Ms. Taylor would hear and probably come over and ask for the note and read it aloud to the class. I opened the note.

"What's it say?" Kirsten asked.

"It says, 'Justine, tell Kirsten Alex has the hots for her,'" I pretended to read.

"No!" she shrieked. "Oh, gross! It does not! Let me see!"

What the note really said was: "Justine, You are looking *hot* today in your new *over the sholder bolder holder*, Love Your Hot Sexy Lover."

The boys really only knew about one female body part, but they had lots of words for it: boobs, tits, titties, bazoombas, knockers, hooters, the usual, plus any other sound that happened to come out of their mouths when they decided to make fun of you: tee-tee, ta-ta, boom-boom, hoobadoobie—which made them sound like big, weird, perverted babies. Usually when they watched me, and giggled, and whispered those words to each other, my chest would feel like it was lighted up in a spotlight, hot and glowing, and I would shrink inside my shirt, turn my back, or slump down in my chair so that my neck was even with the edge of my desk.

Today, though, as I read their pathetic misspelled message about my new nonexistent bra, it didn't even seem like it had anything to do with me. I was so light and airy and full of nothing that I didn't even have a body, it felt like, let alone a chest. The middle of me felt like someone had scooped it out with a melon baller. I felt like just a brain and a pair of feet, which seemed like a perfect combination.

—m—

The way is exceedingly rough. Sometimes we have to stop while I saw branches out of the way, or chop down small trees with the ax, or pry boulders out of the path. It's kind of weird, but sometimes, as I hack and dig and sweat and pry, I have a déjà vu feeling, almost as if I have a memory of this, thin as an old veil.

Maybe building roads is one of the things I remember how to do—something I have always known, deep inside me. But why?

When we got home from school, Mom's car was in the driveway. When I opened the back door, there she was, sitting at the kitchen table as if she had never left.

"Sweetheart," she said, and I could tell from the look on her face and the sound in her voice that nothing good had happened in Hartford.

"What," I said, making my voice as flat and expressionless as hers. She just sat there breathing, as if that's all she could do.

"Where's your sister?" she finally said.

"She's outside."

Rona was outside looking for a four-leaf clover, which was something she did sometimes, because once, when she was four, we'd been walking in the park and she'd said, "I wish I could find a four-leaf clover," then she'd just bent down and picked one. And she had never really gotten over that view of life. She couldn't understand why she never found another one, and it made me sad to watch her try. Today I'd said, "It's November—you're not going to find one." But she'd looked at me stubbornly and said, "But I might."

"So is Danny Martone your new boyfriend now?" I asked Mom. She looked at me weirdly, but she didn't answer.

"Are you moving to Hartford?" I asked.

"No," she said after a long silence. "I'm not moving to Hartford."

"Justine," came Rona's voice before we could see her, "I couldn't find one. I looked every damn place."

She took a step inside and stopped. I guess she hadn't noticed Mom's car in the driveway. She looked at Mom, and I braced myself for a crying fit like the last time Mom came home from deserting us.

"Sweetie," Mom said in the same expressionless voice, and she scooted out her chair a little, making room for Rona in her lap. Rona took a few steps over to where I was. "Oh," Mom said, sounding like her feelings were hurt. Then she said, "What's in the bag?"

That morning, Rona had tried to take her egg to school, stuffed inside a pink ankle sock.

"You can't take that," I'd said, but when I saw the look on her face, I changed my mind. I'd gone and found a miniature shopping bag in the recycling pile, then I'd helped her wrap the egg in two more socks and some washcloths, and I'd said, "But you can't take it out once the entire day, okay?" and she had said, "Okay! Okay, I promise! Oh, thank you, Justine, thank you, thank you."

Now Rona drew the miniature shopping bag close to her chest.

"Are you not talking to me?" Mom asked. "What's in there?"

"Nothing," Rona answered. "Not really," she whispered behind her hand down at the bag.

"Nothing?" said Mom.

"It's mine," Rona said as if that explained everything. "And don't look at it, either."

—⅏—

The road is so faint you can barely see it in places. Yesterday I stopped the wagon and told the children to stay in it while I climbed a small rise to try and get a view of where we were. But even though I climbed all the way to the top, the brush was just as thick and tangled there, and I could see nothing. Maybe I was hallucinating, because on the way back I started imagining that the branches and boughs were tangled veins, the big boulder I walked past near the top was a beating heart. It was like being inside someone else's body. Searching through the thickets for a view was like trying to peer through the wrong sides of someone's eyes. At first I thought it was an interesting feeling; then suddenly I didn't like it at all—I felt panicky and claustrophobic, and I hurried back to the wagon.

There have been no more notes. Whoever was leaving them didn't come this way, I guess. Or maybe they got sick of looking out for me.

MISSED CONNECTIONS

Something about Mom was different after her Hartford adventure, and I couldn't tell exactly what it was. The day after she got back, she'd gone to Marie's friend Martin, and he'd given her a job at the Peabody House Inn. She worked lunch and dinner prep, and five days in a row, she'd gotten out of bed at seven in the morning, taken a shower, put on her clothes, and left. And in the afternoon when she came home at four-thirty, she didn't get right into bed anymore; she did work around the house—carried laundry up and down the stairs; scrubbed the kitchen counters; got out the ironing board and stood there like an ironing zombie, her arm going back and forth, back and forth, while she stared.

She wasn't crying as much anymore, either. But the weird thing was, even though I'd always hated Crying Mom so much, there was something I didn't like even more about the way Mom was acting now.

She walked around like a hollow plastic Mom-doll. She answered questions in a flat voice and stared a lot, and you couldn't even tell if she was thinking anything. And she had a new smile. It looked like the light of a burned-out star to me—something flickering through from a million years ago.

Also, she had a new pastime, and it kind of gave me the creeps. Every day she would bring a newspaper home, and when she got done with the cleaning, she'd sit down at the kitchen table if Marie wasn't around, or up in her room if she was, and open it up to the ads. At first, I thought maybe we were going to start looking for apartments again. But she wasn't looking at apartment ads.

"Listen to this," she said. " 'Tall, beautiful, literature lover. Saw you in Java Joe's reading *Tess of the D'Urbervilles*. I'm a *Return of the Native* guy, myself. Interested in forming a very small book group?'

"Isn't that interesting?" she asked me.

"Listen to this one," she said. " 'Bread and Circus, November tenth. You: blond, green eyes, dancer's body. Me: ponytailed guy. You helped me pick a pineapple. Need help with mango, coconut, cantaloupe. Share fruit salad?'

"That's kind of clever, don't you think?" she said.

"Here's one," she said. " 'Tall guy in glasses and navy blue knit cap on the number twelve bus—you picked up my mitten. Too shy to tell you: I admired your chivalry.' " She looked at me and said, "Chivalry—wow. Don't you think they're fascinating?"

"I don't know," I said. "I guess."

———⚬⚬⚬———

The road is gone. I have no idea where we are.

I have been sitting by the fire tonight, trying to recall every bit of advice my dear, wise mother ever gave to me: Think before you open your mouth; do unto others as you would have them do unto you; dry the baby's bottom thoroughly before putting on the powder; don't salt the bean water; never plant tomatoes before the middle of May.

I miss her so much. She is the wisest, most sensible person I know, in addition to being a perfect mother. Of course, we had an argument here and there—sometimes she disapproved of my manners or criticized my hairdo—but we always ended up laughing.

What if I never see her again?

I've been thinking tonight of my earliest memory of her (besides being born, which everyone says I don't remember, but I do). I was standing in the middle of our living room rug. I was so little, I had just learned to stand up. The rug was braided, in big circles of red and blue, and I was in my favorite spot at the very center, inside the smallest ring. It was a red one. I remember the grown-ups' shoes were huge around me, and each pair led to the bottom of a smiling grown-up's chin. I was clutching Poppy, my beloved doll. It must have been Christmas, because I remember candles, and peppermint, and gingerbread, the smell of a tree, and the sound of people talking and laughing and clinking glasses. I heard my mother say my name: "Zebulina!" Her shiny skirt rustled up to my face, and she knelt down and put her face to mine and said, "You are my precious," and folded me in a silky hug. And it was the best feeling in the world. To be small and loved and in the exact middle of everything. And even when she jumped up and left me, I was still happy—I was happy to stay right where I was, inside the red ring, where I knew she could always find me; I knew she would always look.

I have the rug now, in the back of the wagon. Tonight I had the strongest urge to drag it out and unroll it—just to look at it and maybe feel that feeling again. It is very heavy, though, and my arms ache from all the chopping I did today, and I knew I must save my strength for tomorrow, so I didn't.

When I got to school on Tuesday, Ms. Taylor said, "Justine, can you come here, please?

"Do you have anything for me?" she asked when I got up to her desk. I stood there trying to look stupid, like maybe I thought she meant an apple or a little basket of bath beads.

"Your diary?" she said. Then she said, "You know, if you're having trouble getting your assignments done for some reason—like maybe something's going on at home, for example—we can work together on that. We can make an appointment for after school and sit down and make a plan. You had a very good start here," she said, holding up my old story of Hecate Lorelei, which embarrassed me just to look at.

"But you owe me . . . let's see, one, two, three, four, five, six— My! You owe me ten entries," she said. "I don't want you to get any further behind. I want you to hand in something—anything—by Thursday," she said as the bell rang. "I really mean it," she said. "This is not optional, Justine."

There is nothing to do but keep going. Head west and build the road as I go.

I chopped all day today. My shoulders are on fire, my palms red with blisters.

"You'll have to entertain yourselves," I told the children in the morning. They sang a few songs halfway through and pretended to play a few games, but mostly they watched quietly. I can tell they are frightened. Amethyst finally poked her head out late in the afternoon.

"I'm hungry," she said. I ignored her. She could see I didn't have time to cook anything. There was buffalo jerky; there were nuts and berries that the children had collected in the bottom of a bucket.

"What are you doing, Zebulina?" she asked me.

"I'm trying to build us a road," I said.

"It'll never work," she said airily. She was surprised when I turned on her in fury.

"Do you have a better idea?" I barked.

"No," she said meekly.

"Then just. Shut. Up," *I said.*

At the end of the day, I moved the wagon fifty feet.

The newspaper ads had a name—"Missed Connections"—and after a few days, I really hated them. Because even though it was weird in the first place, it started to get weirder.

"I don't know," Mom said one day. She was talking about Dark-Haired Brooding Beauty and Shy Bearded Mensch. "I wish this ad were a little more *forceful*—I mean, he says, 'Hope you'll call'—what if she thinks that's too wimpy? Maybe I should just call him myself and ask if he's thought about changing it."

Then she said, "And Laid-back Vegan Surfer Stuck on the Wrong Coast—his ad's been in here for over two weeks. I don't think Yellow Braids with a Smile Like the Sun is ever going to answer it. I almost think maybe Freaky Girl with Chocolate Lab would be more his type. I wonder if he's thought of that. Do you think it would be really, really weird if I called and suggested it?"

At least she was smart enough to hide the paper whenever Marie came in. Marie would go ballistic about "Missed Connections," I knew. Marie wanted Mom to go out with a guy named Ron Wesler. She hadn't actually commanded her to—she just hinted about it every day: "I have this friend named Ron," she started out saying. "Ron has his own renewable-energy consulting firm." "Ron lives in a great house in the hills, and he's building a geodesic dome in his backyard!" "Ron's great with the kids; they always love it when he comes over."

"Oh," Mom would say, and, "Really," but it didn't sound like she was really listening, which was weird—usually Mom's ears pricked up automatically, like a dog when it hears the sound of a can opener, at anything having to do with a guy.

You could see Marie gradually starting to tweak out about it. "I really think you and Ron would like each other," she said next. "I think you two have a lot in common." And, "Ron told me he wanted to meet you."

Then she graduated to, "You know, Ron loves the outdoors—I bet he'd love to take you biking or hiking sometime. I really think you should call him"; "My friend Jordan has a pair of extra tickets to the Greg Brown concert. I know Ron loves Greg Brown—maybe you two could go together"; "I'm thinking of having poker night soon and inviting Ron, if that would be okay with you."

But Mom's answer was always pretty much the same: "Oh. Hmm. Yeah. Maybe."

Finally Marie said, "What *is* it with you, anyway? Why is it that you'll fall all over yourself for basically anything with chest hair, except when it comes to one of *my* friends? Is it just that he isn't enough of a *loser* for you, Colleen? Is that what it is? Huh?"

"You know what?" Marie said one day. Mom was heading for the door to go to work, and Marie had asked again about poker night. "I don't even care anymore. I don't care if you go out with Ron Wesler or Joe Loser or that guy who rides around town on his bicycle wearing a wig and pants with a big rip in the ass and no underwear: I am through caring." Obviously she wasn't, though, because eight hours later, when Mom came in the door from work, Marie said, "I invited Ron to Thanksgiving dinner. I hope you'll be civil to him, at least, and, not that you're going to, but if you'd open your mind to it, you could probably have a really nice time."

I've lost track of how many days I've been building this road. Maybe eleven or twelve. That means it is almost the middle of August. We are very late.

* * *

The next morning at school, Ms. Taylor cornered me as usual. "How are you this morning, Justine?" she asked.

"Fine, thank you," I said.

She studied me as if she were looking for messages written on my skin. "Do you have your journal pages for me?" she asked.

I pulled the folder out of my backpack and handed it to her. When she opened it up, she looked surprised.

"My," she said. "I guess you've done quite a bit of work on this." She raised questioning eyebrows at me.

"Yeah," I said.

"Wonderful," she said, not sounding completely sure. "I look forward to reading it."

———≋———

Two days ago, as I was chopping out my road, I thought I noticed that the woods were starting to thin. Then yesterday, around the middle of the afternoon, I definitely saw light beyond the trees. I took the children with me, hiking through the brush, to scout.

After stumbling and pushing our way through the willows for a short time, we found ourselves in a clearing at the top of a mountain, overlooking a huge valley. The children gasped when they saw the shimmering blue water, flat as a sheet of glass, laid across the valley to the west. Behind us there was a great rustling, then Amethyst popped through the trees, too. "The ocean!" she cried. She looked ready to run for it.

"It is not the ocean," I said.

"It is!" she cried. She tried to wrench away from me, but I held on to the tattered sash of her dress.

"I believe it's the Great Salt Lake," I told her.

"We're saved!" said Amethyst.

I didn't say anything. I was glad to see Salt Lake City, but I also knew it wasn't that simple. We have hardly any money left for provisions. We are so frightfully behind schedule, we can't even stop to rest a day. And according to the map, we have two deserts to cross before we even get to the mountains.

"I might stay," announced Amethyst.

"Excuse me?" I said.

"I might stay in Salt Lake City. Depending."

"On?"

She jiggled her eyebrows to make it look like she had some secret answer, but I could tell she didn't.

A reason, I wanted to demand. Just one small one. Come on.

It took us two days to struggle down the hillside and across the valley. We finally reached Salt Lake City late this afternoon.

"Go peek in the back and tell me what Amethyst is doing," I whispered to Annabelle as we neared the edge of town.

"She's sleeping," Annabelle said.

Just as I'd hoped. For the past two days, Amethyst had been saying what a wonderful place Salt Lake City looked like; and how interested she had always been in the Mormon religion; and who needed an ocean when you had a lake like that. She thought I didn't notice her packing her knapsack. So at lunch today I slipped some of the sleeping potion Mother gave me for sick headache into her tea.

We drove straight through Salt Lake City without stopping, except for ten minutes at a supply post, where I spent almost all the rest of the money on a small bit of bacon, some flour, and a little cornmeal. Amethyst wore a little silver ring on her left pinkie, and I slipped it off her limp finger and traded it for gunpowder. I have about a dollar fifty left in my calico bag to start our new life in California.

Now we are camped west of town, in a barren spot near the shore of the lake. The lake is beautiful in a weird, lonely way, but I just don't like it. It is too big and too flat; too bright in the daytime and in the night it is just a big, black smell. They say you bob like a cork if you try to float, and I don't like the sound of that—how can you trust a lake that doesn't act like a lake?

Amethyst is going to be furious when she wakes up. But at least there's nothing she can do here, nowhere she can disappear to: the sand is flat and empty and stretches for miles and miles to the edges of the distant mountains. If she jumps out and starts to run like a crazy woman, we'll just follow and pick her up when she falls from exhaustion.

Supposedly there are springs half a day's drive from here where we can fill our water kegs for the drive across the desert. I hope that is right.

* * *

"Colleen!" Marie said when Mom walked in the kitchen door at five forty-five on Friday night. "Some people are coming for poker tonight! Do you think maybe you could whip up some guacamole? I got a bunch of ripe avocados."

"Oh," said Mom, not particularly enthusiastically. "Poker tonight? Sure, I guess I could make some guacamole." Then she said, "I don't know if I'll play, though."

"Why not?" demanded Marie, her good mood, or fake good mood, on the way out.

"I don't know," Mom said. "I had a hard day. I'm not feeling very social."

"What does that *mean*?" said Marie. " 'Not feeling very social'?"

"Like I don't feel like being around people?" Mom said.

"*Great*, Colleen."

"I'll make the guacamole, though," Mom said. "Where are the avocados?"

"Forget it," said Marie. "I'll call everyone and cancel."

"Oh, Marie," said Mom. Her voice sounded like it was coming through a tunnel. "Don't do that."

"I'm going to," said Marie, sounding just like Rona.

"Fine," said Mom, also sounding just like Rona. "You win." She made her mouth a hard, straight line, which wasn't a look you saw on Mom too often. "I will attend the poker party."

Marie let a little time go by before she said, "Good. It'll be good for you. You'll have a good time, you'll see."

It was a pretty pathetic poker party. Ron Wesler and Marie's baby-sitter, Cinnamon, were the only people who showed up.

Ron got there first, and when Marie saw him, she cried, "Ron! I want you to meet my friend Colleen Hanley! I told you about her: Colleen just moved here from California. Colleen and I have known each other since forever. We're more like family than friends, actually. Wouldn't you say, Colleen? Colleen, this is Ron. Ron runs his own environmental consulting firm, saving the world!"

Cinnamon showed up while Marie still had the door open. Marie looked down at her and frowned slightly.

"Where's Michael?" Marie asked.

"Oh," said Cinnamon. She tilted her head and smiled. "Michael. Michael, Michael, Michael. What can I say about Michael?

"Hi!" she said to Ron, and stuck out her hand. "I'm Cinnamon." Then she explained to Ron, as if he'd asked, "Michael's my boyfriend. My *sometime* boyfriend. My can't-quite-ever-get-it-together-to-decide-what-he-wants boyfriend."

Mom stood behind Marie like a life-size doll.

"Michael's not coming?" Marie asked in a voice like bullets.

"He might show up," said Cinnamon. "I gave him the message." She laughed. "He's a shitty poker player, anyway." Then she said, "Ron, I hope you don't think this is too weird, but, like, can I ask you: Do you believe in reincarnation? Because I think I know what you might have been in another life."

"Colleen," Marie kept saying, "did Ron tell you his consulting business got an award for most environmentally conscious landscaping last year?" "Ron, did Colleen tell you she's a gourmet cook?" "Ron and Colleen—do you two realize you grew up less than a hundred miles away from each other?" She kept asking Cinnamon things, too, like "Could you go in the kitchen and get us some more chips?" And "You know, I promised the kids you'd play a game of Animal Lotto with them—do you think you could do that soon?" And "Did you ever make up those incompletes and actually *graduate*, or are you still technically a Hampshire student?"

Mom just wouldn't do what Marie wanted her to, though, and it was weird. I had never, ever seen her quiet around a guy. She didn't ask Ron a single question—not about his job, or his family, or his favorite foods or books or movies or dog breeds, or what bands he liked, or anything.

I didn't like it when Mom flirted, but I didn't like this more. First of all, I wanted someone to shut Cinnamon up. I didn't want her to flirt with the guy Mom was supposed to be flirting with. I didn't know why it made me so nervous, but it did.

Second, surprisingly, Ron Wesler didn't seem like a bad guy. He had a nice voice, and when Marie introduced them he'd given Mom a nice smile and said, "So you're Colleen, and you moved here from

California three months ago?" and he'd put his hands in his pockets and sort of lifted his shoulders and looked at Mom in an interesting way.

But Mom had just said, "Yes," and smiled a thin, conversation-repelling smile back.

They never even played poker. Cinnamon wasn't smart enough. Marie would shuffle and deal out the cards, then Cinnamon would ask, "What are the rules of this one again?" and giggle. Then she'd look at her cards and say something like "Wait, are three twos higher than two kings?" until finally Marie just tossed the cards into the middle of the table and said, "I give up."

They sat in the living room, talking and drinking beer instead. I sat at the dining room table where I could see them and pretended to read a magazine while I listened. Cinnamon did most of the talking, telling Ron about the really, really awesome movies she'd seen lately; and about the awesome trip she'd taken to Europe and how much it had broadened her mind to see the totally awesome paintings and buildings and eat the totally awesome food; and about her senior project for college—a video diary that was basically like a ten-hour movie about her—and what an awesome experience it had been to make it.

Ron listened politely and smiled, then he turned to Mom.

"Colleen," he said, "I hear you're a foodie."

"Excuse me?" said Mom.

"You're a chef?"

"Oh, no," she said.

"She *could* be, if she wanted," Marie said. "Colleen's a fabulous cook."

"What's your job?" he asked.

"Oh," said Mom. "You know, just general kitchen help."

"It has a name," said Marie. "Doesn't it, Colleen?"

"Gruntwork?" said Mom. Ron laughed, but Marie lowered her eyebrows.

"No," Marie said. "A French word. You know . . . oh, what is it, what is it? For putting together the cold food at a restaurant?"

"Le work gruntay?" said Mom. "I clean shrimp," she said to Ron.

"Peel garlic, pit olives, take the skin off chicken parts—that sort of thing."

"Hey," said Ron. "Someone's gotta do it. So, do you have plans to own your own restaurant someday?"

Mom looked at him like he'd said "fly to Saturn" or "become the queen of Tobango."

"Oh, no," she answered. "No, no, no."

"Well, what, then?" he asked. "Join the circus? Be the head of a major corporation? Invent time travel? What do you want to be when you grow up?"

Cinnamon giggled like *she* got it, when I could see she didn't get it at all. She thought Ron was making fun of Mom. But he wasn't—he really wanted to know, I could tell. Maybe not the answers to his goofy questions, but something about Mom was interesting to him. And she was acting so weird—like even though her body was right there, everything inside of her had turned and was running in the opposite direction.

"You know what?" Mom said. "I know this is going to sound terribly rude, but I have to go in to work really, really early tomorrow morning. We're doing a wedding for three hundred people at one o'clock. So if no one minds, I'm going to go to bed. It was nice meeting you, Ron. Nice seeing you again, Cinnamon."

Marie looked at her with pure hatred.

"Good night!" said Cinnamon sweetly.

"Was it me?" Ron said to Marie and Bill when Mom left the room, and you could tell, even though he tried to make it sound funny, he was kind of disappointed.

I stayed up late. I pretended to read another magazine while I listened to Marie ask Ron about his work, and his life, and his house. He had a real house, and not just some cruddy apartment, and he had built a deck and put a hot tub in the backyard.

"Woo-hoo," said Cinnamon when he said "hot tub," and the silence that followed seemed like it lasted ten years.

When I went upstairs, it was twelve o'clock. I walked quietly down the hallway. When I passed Mom and Rona's room, I saw the light was on. I pushed the door open slowly. Mom was sitting on her bed, still in her clothes.

"What are you doing?" I asked.

"Nothing," she answered, but I could see. She was reading "Missed Connections," and she had a pen in her hand. I really didn't like the pen.

"Did you like Ron?" I asked.

She looked up from the paper and studied me for a minute. Then she said, "He was okay."

"I liked him," I said. She didn't say anything. "I thought he was nice." She still didn't say anything. Finally I said, "What was wrong with him?"

Mom gave me a fake puzzled look. "Nothing's wrong with him," she said. "Why do you say that?"

"You just didn't act like you liked him very much," I said.

"Oh," she said. "I think maybe I just want to take a break from that kind of thing for a while, maybe."

"What kind of thing?"

But she was looking back down at the newspaper. "Listen to this one," she said.

—⁂—

There is nothing, as far as the eye can see. Just white salt and blue sky and the low shadows of mountains in the far-off distance. If the baby dies here, there's not even a tree to bury her under.

Amethyst isn't speaking to me. Once a day or so, she pokes her head out from under the shady canvas and says, "I'm hot," and takes a long drink of water from the precious supply. Then she disappears for twelve or fifteen hours while we drive and drive and drive.

I was surprised when Ron called a few days later. I wondered how he had missed the part about Mom not being interested in him at all. Maybe he just thought she was shy.

"Is this Justine?" he asked when I answered the phone, and when I told him yes, he said, "I really enjoyed meeting you the other night. And your sister. And your mother," he added.

"Oh," I said. "Yeah."

"Is she feeling a little better, I hope?" he said. I guess he thought Mom was acting weird the night of the poker party because she was sick.

"Uh," I said. "Yeah, I guess."

"May I speak to her?" he asked, and when I told him she wasn't there, he gave me his number and said, "Well, will you ask her to call me? When she gets time?" Then he gave me his number again.

Every day for three days, I asked Mom, "Did you call Ron Wesler?"

The first two times she said, "Not yet," with a little singsong sound in her voice that was supposed to trick me into thinking she was going to. The third time, though, she said, "Justine, you have got to get off my back about Ron Wesler."

I didn't even know why I cared so much if she called him back—I had only seen him that one night, and it was always a disaster when Mom had a boyfriend anyway.

The second time he called, I didn't know what to say. "Mom's been working a lot lately," I told him. "Sometimes she's too tired at night to talk on the phone."

"Oh," he said. "It's okay. So how's it going for you?"

"For me?"

"You know, school and stuff?" he asked.

"Well, school sucks, actually," I said. "I pretty much hate everyone there, and I sort of hate Massachusetts, too. Not to be negative."

"Oh, yeah," he said. "School can really suck. Massachusetts isn't all that bad in the spring, you know. Unfortunately, that only lasts one day.

"Well, listen," he said. "Tell your mother I called. Also, you could mention I'm really not such a bad guy. Let me give you my number again."

—m—

The desert was supposed to be thirty-five miles. Well, that was obviously a crock. We have been traveling across it for four days. The containers I filled at the springs are almost empty. There is no grass anywhere, and we are awfully low on oxen food. The animals are half-crazed and suffering.

Poor Zack can hardly stand up. The children and I walk in the blazing sun. I carry the baby, but she's hardly a burden—she is only a wisp of a thing now, like the shadow of someone leaving the room.

I'm trying to figure out what to do. Somehow, though, it seems harder to come up with ideas in the desert. My brain feels as flat and dry and white and empty as the landscape.

Last night I suddenly remembered: That lady supposedly buried her things in the desert. I tried to remember what Lucretia Jane had told me, something about some orangish sand and a sagebrush and six paces, or was it seven? Who knows—maybe she buried a keg of water.

After everyone had gone to bed, I started digging. I dug all night— twenty-five or thirty holes. I even started talking to that woman, on about hole number seventeen—that's how lonely I am. "No offense or anything," I said, "but you could've left a map."

THANKSGIVING

Usually Mom loved holidays, but she didn't seem very excited about Thanksgiving this year. She hadn't said a word about it yet; and when we passed the stuff in the store—the cranberries and piles of nuts and sweet potatoes and turkeys and baking supplies—she just looked at it all like she was from a foreign country and had no idea what it was there for. Which wasn't all right with Marie. She got madder at Mom every day.

"Look, Colleen!" she said, the day Cassidy and Cavanaugh brought home the retarded handprint-turkey plaster tiles they'd made at their wonderful, expensive school. "Aren't these wonderful?" Mom was staring into space. "Colleen!" Marie said. "The Thanksgiving decorations the kids made! Aren't they wonderful?" Then she said, "You know, you could at least fake a little enthusiasm."

A few days later, she tried to get Mom to plan a menu with her. "What do you think about a squash soup to start? And, sweet potatoes or mashed potatoes or both? Should we do the turkey the traditional way or try something new, like maybe smoking it?"

"I don't know," said Mom.

"Well, surely you must have *some* preferences," said Marie.

"I really don't," said Mom.

"You are so completely maddening, do you know that?" Marie said.

"Why? Because I don't care how you cook your turkey?"

"*My* turkey?!" Marie practically screamed. "*My* turkey?! This is a *family* holiday, you know. I would appreciate a little participation from you."

"All right," said Mom. "I'd like to have creamed onions."

"Creamed onions!" Marie scoffed. "Forget it. We might as well cancel Thanksgiving this year."

Every couple of days, though, Marie's holiday spirit would revive itself.

"Who should we have for Thanksgiving this year?" she said a few nights after the creamed onion fight. "Well, my family, of course. Anyone have any ideas?"

"Cinnamon!" yelled Cassidy, but Marie just looked at her, like, Wrong.

"How about Randy and Laura?" said Bill. "We haven't seen them in a long time."

"Oh," said Marie, "I don't think so. Laura always takes over making all the desserts, and you know, she only uses refined white sugar and flour. Colleen?"

"Hmm?" asked Mom.

"Who do *you* think we should have to Thanksgiving?"

"I don't know," Mom said.

"How about Ron?" said Marie.

—m—

"Oh, Mama," whispered Annabelle this morning.

The children beg for water, and I don't even have any good lies to tell them. "I know you are thirsty," I say. "I know. I know." The baby is scarcely breathing. Amethyst finished all the water from the last container sometime during the night.

"I was thirsty!" she said when I stood there looking at her in disbelief. Also, I noticed crumbs on her mouth.

"What have you been eating?" I demanded.

"Nothing," she said. It looked like cornmeal.

"Those provisions have to last all of us till California," I said.

"I don't even know what you're talking about" was all she said.

Late today we found a few small puddles filled with salty, stinky water. The animals drank it and started gagging; even so, I filled a container and made the children have some, too. You should have seen the way the baby looked at me when I squeezed some drops of it from a handkerchief into her mouth.

* * *

Every day, Marie had something new to add to Mom's list of Thanksgiving jobs: "Colleen, I was thinking—maybe you could make the centerpiece out of gingerbread. Like, a big, three-dimensional gingerbread turkey. What do you think?"; "How about if I put you in charge of all the vegetables? I think I'd like to have two different yam dishes this year—sweet *and* savory, since I can't decide"; "Do you think you could research some oyster stuffing recipes?"

"This is going to be fun," Marie kept saying. "I just love having family and friends all together, I really do." So she was pretty bummed out when first her sister Eve, then her sister Carolyn, and then her brother Teddy called to say they were really, really sorry that they weren't going to be able to make it after all.

"Why?!" Marie demanded into the phone when Eve called. "Well, that sucks. . . . No, I *don't* understand. I *don't* understand." Mom and I were sitting at the kitchen table, pretending to read recipes. Marie walked out of the room still talking, so she could be alone, but the whole neighborhood probably heard her scream, *"What kind of a lame fucking excuse is* that?" a few seconds later, before she stormed back into the kitchen and slammed the phone into its cradle.

When Carolyn called, it was basically an instant replay, though Marie added, "All you guys have always hated me. Don't think I don't know it." By the time Teddy called, she was all yelled out. "I know what you're going to tell me, you gutless little creep," she said, "and if you think I give a shit, I don't. Have a frozen dinner in front of the TV for all I care," and she hung up on him, too.

"So now I guess it's just going to be you and me and Bill and the kids, and Ron," Marie said, looking skeptically at Mom.

"We could just do something low-key," said Mom. "We could go out. I could take us all out to a restaurant."

"I will not be eating Thanksgiving dinner in a restaurant this year, thank you very much," said Marie. "Not that you could afford it anyway."

"We could skip it," Mom said. "We could act like Thanksgiving was just a normal day."

"We're not going to skip it," Marie said with hatred in her voice, "and you know, I really would appreciate it if you could at least *pretend* to care about the things that are important to me."

How much longer can this desert be? We're still on earth, aren't we? I've seen the map. It's not supposed to go on forever.

My shoes have worn off my feet from walking.

If we don't find water in the next day or two, we will probably die. I can't really think of anything else to write today.

Marie woke everybody up at six o'clock on Thanksgiving morning, banging pots and pans in the kitchen. At six-thirty, Rona came in my room and said, "I'm hungry, Justine," and when I asked, "Can't you wait?" she said, "No."

"Happy Thanksgiving!" Marie said when she saw us. "Justine, would you mind making breakfast for everyone?

"Oh, not Wheatena," she said when she saw me getting out the box. "I like a big, festive breakfast on holiday mornings. How about some whole-grain waffles? I think there's a recipe in my file over there."

By the time Mom came down, I felt like I had walked twenty miles, chopped a pile of wood, and dug a ditch, and it was only eight o'clock.

"It's about time," said Marie when she saw Mom. "Happy Thanksgiving!"

"Sorry," Mom said in a gray cardboard voice. "What do you want me to do?"

"What don't I want you to do?" said Marie. "Put together a base for turkey broth? Iron the table linens? Start on the pies? How about the centerpiece you said you were going to make? Wait, let me guess: We're not having a centerpiece."

"Oh," said Mom. "No—we'll have a centerpiece. And I'll do those other things, too. Let me unload the dishwasher first, though."

"I won't argue with you," Marie said. "Oh, and I told Ron to come over early, at about twelve o'clock. He's going to make something, a mushroom strudel, I think, over here. I told him you'd help him."

I was up in my room getting dressed a little while later when Mom came in.

"We're going to the store," she said. "Wear warm clothes."

"Why?"

"It's cold out. Can you get your sister dressed? Dress her warm, too." Then she left.

When we got downstairs, Marie was saying to Mom, "I don't really think you need to go out."

"We need cream, though," Mom said. "I didn't know the sweet potatoes called for so much, and it's awful to run out of whipped cream in the middle of the pumpkin pie. Also, I need some extra nuts for the centerpiece." Saying it that way made it sound like she'd actually started the centerpiece.

"All right," Marie said. "And when you get back, you'll start the pies?"

Half an hour later, I asked Mom, "What store are we going to?" We had driven past the Store 24. Stop & Shop was in the other direction. And it didn't take this long to get to Bread and Circus.

"Oh, I don't know," Mom said. "Whichever one we see next. I'm not in a hurry to get back, are you?"

"No," I agreed. But when the landscape started changing, I started to get suspicious. Also, we had somehow gotten on the Massachusetts Turnpike. "There aren't any grocery stores on this road," I pointed out.

Mom squinted at a sign in the distance. "Palmer," she said. "There's probably a grocery store there." But she didn't even slow down at the exit.

"Where are we going?" I said.

"How about the beach?" Mom said.

"Yay, the beach!" Rona said.

"It's November," I said. Mom nodded.

"Marie'll be furious," I said.

"Yeah, she will," Mom agreed.

It had been a long time since I'd thought about the beach; and, I had to admit, a small, good feeling had flashed through me when Mom said the words, even though I knew it was a terrible idea to go.

In California, the days we went to the beach were always good days, even if they started out with Mom and Dale having a big fight and we ended up following Mom out the door with only one shoe on, trying to get in the car and lock the doors and peel out before Dale made it out to the driveway.

Mom loved the ocean more than anything in the world—even though, if you asked her, she'd probably say that what she loved more than anything in the world was me and Rona. But the ocean was the only thing that always made her happy, every time she was near it. I liked the moment when we would turn the corner of West Mar and Alameda and catch sight of the glimmer of the ocean, far, far away, beyond the roads and malls and billboards and rich people's houses; and a slow, dreamy smile would start to creep onto Mom's face, and you could see the unhappiness start to melt into a flat, glistening puddle and ooze away.

When we got to the beach, we'd settle our blankets on the sand, and sometimes Mom would sit there propped on her elbows for a whole hour, not saying a word, just staring out at the water with a look on her face like she had just woken from a really good nap, smiling and going, "Mmm," if Rona or I said something.

All day long we'd ask her, "Do you want to go in yet? Do you want to go in?"

"Mmm," she'd say, "in a minute."

Finally, at the end of the day, when the sun was almost down to the water, and Rona and I had swum so much we were too tired to do anything but sit on the blanket, wrapped in towels, propped up against each other, she would stand up and stretch, twist her hair into a bun, and say, "I'm going in."

I loved to watch her swim. She was a good swimmer, from being on the West Mar swim team in high school, and I loved the way her arms looked—shiny, and brown, and strong, and glistening—as she pulled herself through the waves. And even though in real life, sometimes, she would get tired and sad just from sitting on the couch watching a TV show, and say, "God, I don't know how long I can keep doing this," in the water she could go and go and go. Every time a wave came at her, she'd just crash her body right into it, like it didn't scare her at all.

The beach in Massachusetts wasn't going to be anything like the beach in California, though, I could tell, way before we even got near the water. The sky was gray and unfriendly in every direction; and there was no special light in the distance, inviting you toward it. You just drove past some low, ugly shopping centers, then past some brown fields and leafless trees and big houses that looked like nobody lived in them, then turned a corner and there it was: a huge, paved parking lot with a lot of garbage blowing around it, and beyond that, the flat, dark ocean, lying there looking at you as if to say "What are you doing here, anyway? No one wants you here." Even Mom, when she saw it, just said, "Oh."

"I want to go home," Rona said. She more sort of breathed it than said it, actually, and I wondered if she was talking about California and not Hadley. Mom was driving about one mile per hour through the parking lot, and I knew we were all doing the same thing: looking for some tiny spot of something pretty—a patch of light, a sparkle on the water, a soft, round sand dune, or anything—to attach a good feeling to. There wasn't anything, though, and finally Mom just stopped the car in the middle of the parking lot, opened her door, put her feet on the pavement, and said in the voice of a three-hundred-year-old woman, "Here we are."

"I'm staying in the car," I said.

"Me too," said Rona.

"We could still get home for Thanksgiving dinner," I said. Which was stupid—we all knew that no matter when we got home, the day was going to end in disaster, so there was no reason to hurry back.

"Well," said Mom, and then she just got out of the car, stood up, and started walking toward the edge of the parking lot. She didn't even close her door. She didn't even take a towel, or a blanket, or—it was a good thing I noticed—the keys.

"Mom," said Rona, then, "Where's she going?" Mom had reached the sand, and she was bending down to take off her shoes.

I'm not sure why I did the next thing I did. A lot of the things I was doing lately didn't make sense, exactly—they just felt like instructions from somewhere deep inside myself—the place, maybe, that, if you were an animal, told you to fly south for the winter or walk across the desert till you hit the one tiny water hole you didn't even know was there.

I climbed over Rona, sat there for a second behind the steering wheel, then I turned the key. Rona looked at me with wide eyes and struggled to sit up in her seat.

"*Justine!*" she said. "Do you know how to *drive?*"

Maybe I did. Dale had let me sit on his lap once, in the driveway, and steer. I'd spent a lot of time sitting next to Mom in the car, watching her drive. I knew the brake was the most important thing. If I pointed my toes, I could reach it. "Put on your seat belt," I told Rona. I pressed down on the brake; then I put the shift thing in D and let up my foot, and we lurched forward and rolled. I pressed my foot on the brake and we stopped, fast.

We rolled and lurched and stopped, rolled and lurched and stopped, across the parking lot. Rona was sitting up on her knees, with her egg in its mini–shopping bag clutched to her chest.

"Turn, Justine!" she shouted. I was paying so much attention to the brakes, I'd forgotten to steer. I turned the wheel, the wrong way at first, then I figured it out and pointed the car toward the corner of the parking lot, the direction where Mom was. We were like some massive, lurching blue baby duck, following our tiny little mom.

When I got close to the edge of the parking lot, though, I made a mistake. I stepped on the wrong pedal.

"Aiee!" Rona screeched as the car zoomed forward. I didn't even have time to make a noise; I was way back in the seat, and my foot couldn't find the brake. We were going to crash, I realized as I struggled back up in the seat and saw the end of the parking lot coming; but at the same time, my toe found the brake pedal, and I didn't slam it down, I pushed slowly, and we came to a stop right at the curb. And it was the strangest thing: In that moment, right between the disaster about to happen and my saving us, I *got* it. Or, it was like I *remembered*. Of course, there were some details I'd have to learn, like what to do on a real road with other cars around. But something about driving—

the feeling of going forward, terrified, faster than you wanted to, not quite knowing if you liked it or hated it—felt familiar, almost like it was something I'd always known but forgotten, something maybe I was born knowing how to do.

I turned the car off and put the shift thing in P.

"Good job, Justine," said Rona, in a shaky voice.

"Come on," I said, and I took the keys and got the blanket out of the trunk and locked the doors, and we went after Mom. After a few minutes, we were close enough to call to her, but neither one of us did. She was headed toward the water, walking the way people do through sand—like she was struggling to get somewhere, even though the ground was flat and there was nothing in her way. She hadn't even looked back once. I wondered if sometimes she just completely forgot that she had kids.

"I'm freezing," Rona said. "I have sand in my shoes."

"Me too," I said.

"How long do we have to stay here?" she asked.

"I don't know," I told her.

"Are we going to Thanksgiving?"

"I don't think so," I told her. "Come on."

I unfolded the blanket and arranged it around our backs, wrapping us tight, and we sat down and huddled together, looking across the garbagy sand to the cold, dark water. Mom was standing at the edge of the ocean now, just looking out; and suddenly I was thinking about something that I hadn't thought about in a long time: I was remembering the last time we saw Kim.

We were at the beach that day, too. It was a day that had started in the usual way, with crying and yelling and, actually, the kitchen door getting broken. But when we stepped onto the sand, Mom had smiled dreamily and said, "Isn't it just the perfect day?" And it had turned out to be.

As usual, late in the afternoon—that kind of nice, kind of sad time of day when even though the sun is still toasting your skin, you can feel it getting ready to leave—Mom decided she was going to swim. Rona was leaning against me on the blanket, sucking her thumb, and Mom was standing beside us, bending over twisting her hair into a bun, when I turned my head and saw Kim walking toward us, shading her eyes with her hand. I couldn't believe it. I didn't say anything, because I saw what was going to happen: when Mom finished her bun and flipped her head up, Kim was standing right in front of her. Mom gasped, and both their faces lit up.

"Colleen!" Kim said, and she hugged Mom, and their voices, saying, "It's so great to see you! It's so great to see you!" blended into the sound I remembered from so long ago. And they looked the same as they had back then, too—just like two people who had always been friends, who hadn't had anything bad happen between them. Then Kim came over to me and I jumped up and she hugged and kissed me; and she leaned down to kiss Rona, who had no idea who she was; and she said all the usual grown-up stuff—how much I'd grown and how Rona was just a baby when she'd seen her last, but I forgave her, because I knew if we'd been alone, we would have talked about more interesting things.

She didn't even ask Mom any questions, though. All she said was, "Are you going in?" and, "Come on!" and then they were running toward the water, and just for a minute, they looked like two very big kids, scampering down the sand, pulling at their swimsuit bottoms. When they got to the water, they kept running, and then Mom, and a half second later Kim, dove in and headed away from the shore, doing the Australian crawl, side by side.

"Where are they going?" Rona asked. They were headed straight out toward the ocean, it looked like.

"Nowhere," I said. I knew Kim had been on the West Mar swim team, too. They were both good swimmers; I wasn't worried.

"Are they coming back?" she asked, her voice wavering a little, and I suddenly felt so sorry for her that I hugged her. She was so little, and had to depend on someone else to tell her everything, even whether or not to be scared.

"Yeah," I said, "they will, pretty soon."

We watched as they changed directions and switched to the butterfly. The butterfly was my favorite—I loved how ferocious Mom looked, slamming into the water over and over again. There was so much splashing out there now that you couldn't see anything but water flying and arms whirling.

"Are you sure?" Rona asked.

"Yup," I said, and after a little while, they did; and that was a good feeling—I liked it when the world worked that way.

I was trying to hold the picture in my head now: of Mom's and Kim's bright blond heads bobbing together as they swam back toward us, of the bright sun and the shine of their brown skin and Mom's green bathing suit and Kim's red one as they rose, laughing and chattering, out of the water. But it was hard to do—everything was so different. Nothing was bright, or shiny, or warm, and Mom was alone. She wasn't running down to the water, bouncing and smiling—she was walking slowly, with her arms around herself, moving as if something were pulling her, as if she didn't want to go.

I wondered if Kim had ever been to Massachusetts, if she could even picture such a gray, cold place. I wondered if she remembered us.

"What's she doing?" said Rona, squeezing my arm. I had forgotten to watch Mom for a minute.

"I don't know," I said, to cover up the horrible feeling I got when I saw that Mom's sweater was lying on the ground by her feet and she was unbuttoning her pants.

"*Justine,*" Rona moaned, covering her eyes with her hands.

I turned to look around, to see if anyone was watching, but even though there'd been three cars in the parking lot, we were the only ones on the beach. When I turned back, Mom's pants were off, and she was pulling off her shirt. She was too far away to see goose bumps, but it hurt my skin just to look at her. She was standing there in her bra and underpants, sort of caved-in, hugging herself, and I wondered if she was going to take those off, too. I wondered why I had ever liked the story Aunt Bridget told me, of Mom driving to the beach naked, running down the sand without any clothes on, because it was really terrible to look at her now.

"What's she doing?" Rona said.

"I don't know," I answered, then I said, "Stay here."

"No!" she said.

"I'll be right back. Stay," I said, and I got up and went running down the beach toward Mom. When I turned to look, though, Rona was trying to follow. She was still wrapped in the blanket, stumbling like a little mummy.

"What are you doing?" I asked Mom when I reached her.

"Going for a swim," she said. Then, as if she were reaching far down inside of herself, to the very bottom of the well where the last of her cheery lies had fallen, she said, "I have never *once* in my *life* come to the beach and not gone swimming!"

"But it's November," I said.

She nodded. "That it is. It is November. November twenty-fifth, 1997. Thanksgiving Day."

"Don't go swimming," I said.

From behind us, Rona wailed, "Mom!" I turned and saw Rona step on the edge of the blanket and tip over like a defective Weeble. Her arms didn't even go out—she just fell in one piece and lay there sobbing.

"Please," I said to Mom. I put my hand on her arm, but she slid away.

"No!" Rona was wailing from the ground. "Oh, no! No!"

"Just for a few minutes," Mom said, and she walked to the edge of the water.

Rona was screaming now, still tangled in the blanket. I went back to her and helped her out. "Oh, Mom! Mom! Mom!" she cried, reaching out her arms and opening and shutting her hands like little crab claws.

"It's okay," I told her, making myself sound as convincing as I could. "She's just going swimming." But Rona wasn't stupid. She knew it wasn't normal. "Come on," I said. "Let's wrap up again."

You could tell how cold the water was by the way Mom's body flinched when she took a step in. She didn't stop, though. She just trudged forward, her body slowly disappearing in the water.

"Mom, oh, Mom," Rona moaned, hugging Mom's sweater.

She swam a far way. She swam so far, I thought I was going to throw up. We watched her till she was just a small, splashing spot in the grayness, like a tiny storm making its way out to sea. I sat there on the blanket trying to stay calm for Rona, but it was impossible, and after a minute I jumped up and looked up and down the beach. There wasn't anyone in sight. Where were the people who'd parked their cars in the parking lot?

"Justine," Rona kept saying. "Justine?" and I kept saying, "It's okay. It's okay. It's okay," like a lying machine.

"She has to turn around," I said to myself out loud.

"Is she?" said Rona. "Is she turning around? Is she?"

Suddenly I said, "Come on."

"Why?!" Rona said.

"Shh!" I snapped, and grabbed her by the arm and started running for the car, pulling her behind me.

"What?" she was crying. "What? What are we doing?"

I was having the weirdest feeling, kind of the opposite of when I floated up into a corner to look down on my life. It was more like something was inside of me—or someone: a person I didn't know, someone strong enough to lean down and snatch Rona up and run, carrying her, up the beach; someone who had no plan and didn't need one; someone who could drive. I didn't know where I'd go. To a house. To the highway. I'd just drive till I saw someone, then I'd stop the car and get out and jump up and down until they helped me.

"Justine!" Rona was screaming now. "Justine! Justine!"

I kept on running. Running in sand is like a nightmare of running— your legs do the motion, but you don't get anywhere. I put Rona down and kept running, dragging her by the arm.

"But Justine!" Rona yelled. "But look! But wait! But look!"

"Come *on*!" I yelled at her, then I saw that she was looking at the water, and I looked, too. Mom had turned around. She was coming in, getting closer and closer. She was tired, I could see. She wasn't doing the crawl anymore, or the butterfly; she was doing the breaststroke— the one I'd always hated, the one where you disappeared and then came back, like a mean trick, over and over again.

—m—

There was a note today. My heart jumped when I saw it—a piece of brown paper, just like the others, blowing about on the ground. My hands shook as I opened it.

"What's wrong, Mama?" Annabelle asked, watching my face.

It was blank inside. "Oh," I said, trying to swallow my disappointment, which was like trying to swallow a feather pillow, or a dog.

"What does it say?" Annabelle asked. She was searching my face as if the answer mattered very much.

"Um," I said, swallowing. I held up the blank piece of paper to my face and stared at it with watery eyes. "It says . . . 'Do not despair. You are almost at the end of the desert.' " I just made that up, of course. But I didn't expect the next words that came out of my mouth. " 'If you travel at night, your feet won't get so hot and the oxen will have an easier time of it.' "

"Oh," I said, a little surprised. "That sounds like a very good idea."

———————

Miracle: we have found a spring. We were (most of us) walking today, when the animals all raised their heads at once, as if they heard something we couldn't hear. Then they took off, running crazily, the oxen pulling the wagon behind them. From inside the wagon, Amethyst screamed. I watched in despair—there was nothing I could do but hope that they would stop running eventually, somewhere we could find them, and that the wagon didn't lose a wheel or tip over and smash apart. If not, we were doomed.

The children and I walked and walked, watching the wagon get smaller and farther away. Soon, it was just a speck, and then it disappeared into some low hills and was lost to our view completely. We walked for two hours, my despair deepening with every step. As we got nearer to the hills, though, I began to notice something: The trees around the bottom of them looked big and green. Hope began to grow in my heart, but I wasn't going to say anything till I was sure—maybe it wasn't a sound that had startled the animals. Maybe they had smelled water.

"There it is!" Ezekiel suddenly cried at the same moment I saw it, too: the wagon, tilted behind the trees, sitting in the middle of a small stream. The oxen were still attached to it, and they had their heads down, drinking. There was Amethyst, too. She'd taken my mother's rocking chair out of the wagon and was sitting right in the middle of the stream, soaking her feet, smiling and waving at us. "It took you long enough!" she called.

We spent a comfortable night. We drank and bathed and washed our clothes and drank some more. The children made a little dam and splashed in the pool it made. Even the baby almost smiled when I trailed her little toes in the water.

"This is the most wonderful spot in the world," Amethyst declared. "I could live right here forever." I reminded her she had said that about a few places now.

"Well, it's true," she said. "The world is full of beautiful, fantastic places."

The next morning, Marie went into Mom's room and said, "I'm giving you two weeks to leave."

"What?" Mom said.

"Two weeks," said Marie. "I'll lend you money for rent and a security deposit if you need it."

"But why?" asked Mom. As if she didn't know. "Because I won't go out with Ron?"

But Marie said, "It's everything, Colleen. Just everything. I can't take it anymore. It's better if you leave."

That was the whole discussion. I heard Marie tromping back down the hallway, and when I went to Mom's room a little while later, she didn't say anything except, "I need you to watch Rona today," as if I didn't do that every day automatically; and a little while later she left, and nine hours after that, in the middle of dinner, which Marie forced Rona and me to eat with her and Bill and the kids, she came into the kitchen with a glass smile on her face and said, "Well, I found us a place to live. We're moving on Wednesday."

Another miracle has occurred: We have come to the end of the desert and found the main trail again.

"Hurray!" the children cried when we saw it. "We're almost to California!"

I let them feel happy; what good would it do to tell them what I know: There's another desert coming up. It is the second week of September. Autumn is coming on. You can see it in your shadow in the evening if you turn to look—the thin, stretched shape dragging itself after you like a sorrowful, starving person.

I, too, rejoiced to see the Fort Hall trail, but at the same time, I suddenly felt so lonely. I mean, it's not like I expected to see anyone strolling down it, but I couldn't keep from wondering: Has everyone else made it to California already? Are we the last ones out here? Sometimes I get a feeling like the world is pushing against me, trying to squeeze me out.

We are traveling along the Humboldt River. Amethyst, of course, wants to stay and live here, but we're leaving as soon as the light dawns, maybe earlier.

The animals are suffering greatly. They haven't had any good grass in a long time, and poor Zack is so lame that he can hardly walk. I had to lighten the wagon again. Tonight after everybody was asleep I dragged out my rug, which wasn't easy to do, and unrolled it on the rocky ground. I just had to see it one last time. I guess I was hoping to get the same good feeling I once had, so long ago. I went to the middle of the rug and put my feet inside the red ring, and I tried as hard as I could to imagine being a child again, but nothing happened. The only feeling I could get, as I stood there looking at my big fat toes pouring over the edges of the red ring, was big.

REARRANGER OF THE SKY

We didn't have enough money to rent a truck again, so Mom said we would move what we could for now and get the rest later. Our stuff made a pretty pathetic pile, sitting on the sidewalk waiting to get loaded into Marie's minivan. All we were taking were some clothes and pillows and blankets in garbage bags, a few boxes, and Rona's and my mattresses. Everything else we had brought from California—our couch and tables and chairs and dressers, our dishwasher and washer and dryer—was in Marie's garage, and Mom's mattress wouldn't fit in the minivan, so we were going to come back for it later. It was like you could see our life getting smaller and flatter and emptier, right in front of your eyes.

Still, it was sort of hard not to be at least a tiny bit excited about moving. It seemed like there was a little seed of hope just built into the idea—it always *could* turn out to be good. Even though it probably wasn't going to be *very* good—we were still going to be poor, and go to the same stupid school, and every day was getting even darker and colder and shorter than the one before. But there might be *something* about our new place that would be good: I might have a good bedroom, or there might be a nice spot to curl up and read, where the sun came in, or there might be a nice neighbor kid my age, or a good candy store nearby.

My tiny feeling of hope followed me up to the front door of our new house. When we stepped inside the small, dark, dirty living room, it vanished like a match blowing out.

"What do you think," Mom said, but it didn't really sound like a question. It sounded like all the energy had rushed out of her suddenly. She put the box she was carrying on the floor and sat down on it.

"It needs a little TLC," she'd said when she'd come home Friday from finding it. "But that's the reason it's so cheap. Basically, we're getting a whole house for the price of a one-bedroom apartment in exchange for me fixing it up."

"What do you have to do to it?" Bill had asked, sounding a little worried.

"It needs painting," she'd said. "The plaster needs patching. It needs a new bathroom floor and a little bit of plumbing, and maybe a few new pipes under the kitchen sink, and he said something about *flashing* on the roof. Oh, and he said I could finish the floors if I wanted, and put up a freestanding wall to make another bedroom."

"Do you know how to do any of those things?" Marie asked.

"I'm sure I can find out," said Mom.

"And the landlord's going to pay for the improvements?" Marie said. Mom didn't answer.

"Sure he is," said Bill, then he looked closer at Mom. "Isn't he?"

"Well, he's not going to pay *me*," Mom said. "That's the arrangement."

"But he'll pay for materials?" Marie said.

"Oh," said Mom. "Yeah. Sure. I think so."

Rona was wandering around in the dark, going, "Is this our new house? Mom, where's our new house? Where's my room?"

"I thought those could be your rooms," Mom said, pointing at two doors. I went to look. The rooms were dark and tiny, with dirty walls.

Rona still didn't get it—she was going around to all four rooms of the house, saying, "Where's my bedroom? Mom, where's my room?" and every time she got to one of the bedrooms she just glanced in and then out again, as if she'd looked into the broom closet by accident.

"Where's your room?" I asked Mom.

"This is it," she said. Meaning the one we were in.

"Where's the living room?" I asked.

"You know what?" she said. "I don't really need a bedroom."

"Well, where will you sleep?" I asked.

"In the living room," she said, and she smiled like that was a joke.

"But Mom!" Rona said from the doorway of her bedroom. "How is my bed going to fit in here?"

"Oh," said Mom, and she leaned her back against the wall. "We'll figure it out. We'll figure it out in a few minutes. Justine, could you just unpack a few boxes? Find, you know, the kitchen stuff and the towels and soap and things. I'll be out to help in a minute."

But when I came back from the car, she wasn't sitting on the box anymore, she was lying on the floor curled in a ball with her coat under her head for a pillow, and when I said, "What's the matter?" she just said, "Nothing! Nothing's the matter. I'm just going to lie here for two seconds."

I dreamt about her last night. The woman who buried her things. I must have. Why else would I have woken up thinking about her?

I woke up feeling sad. I lay there imagining her, riding through the wilderness with one or two things strapped to her back. A blanket, maybe, a gun, a little food and water. Everything else—her grandfather clock, her party dresses and fancy shoes, her photograph albums, her favorite books, her little box of keepsakes—lies packed in a hole in the dirt behind her, getting farther and farther away. She's so sure she's going to remember where— that she'll just ride back one day, easy as pie, and dig up her precious possessions—that maybe she hasn't realized yet: There are so many things that can go wrong. Indians might find the cache. Or animals might dig it up, or a big rainstorm might wash it away.

Or what about this: What if she forgot to look behind her as she left? What if she was only looking ahead? Then, if she ever does make it back, everything might look totally unfamiliar to her; she might not recognize the landmarks, seeing them from a different angle. She might get convinced she's lost, even if she's standing in her very own backwards footprints.

Thinking that gave me a stomachache for some reason. Near me, the children were stirring. I got up from my bedroll and went to start the fire. "Good morning!" I smiled at them when they made their way over. I pretended not to be sad. I pretended not to be frightened. I pretended to forget about that woman and what she had buried.

I let Rona pick the room she wanted, and I went into the other one. I tried the light switch, but nothing happened. There was one small window with a torn, dirty window shade over it, and when I went over and pulled the shade to raise it, the whole thing crashed down on my head. I stood there with the torn shade dangling from my hand for a minute, then I sat down on the floor and stared at the cracked wall across from me, at the gray smudges and smears and places where the paint was peeling off the woodwork.

I could hear Rona going back and forth in the other room. "This is a stupid house!" she was saying. "Mom! I can't even fit my bed in my bedroom! I can't fit my stuffed animals or anything! The light doesn't work! I don't want to live here!" After a little while she came in my room and sat down by me. "I'm hungry," she said.

"Is Mom awake?" I asked.

"Her eyes are open," Rona said. Then she said, "This house is too cold."

"Well, let's go turn on the heat," I said, and I got up and pulled Rona up by the hand. I found the thermostat and turned the heat to eighty. In Marie's house, when you did that you would hear a thump and a hum, but here, nothing happened. "It'll get warm in a minute," I told Rona.

"Can we have something to eat?" Rona said, and she ran into the kitchen. I followed her. I knew we didn't have any food yet, though. Rona flipped the light switch on the wall, and a dull, yellowy glow flickered on from the ceiling, shining a sick color, like a poison ray. She snapped it off. She opened the refrigerator door.

"It's broken," she said. "It isn't even cold inside."

I went back to the living room. "Mom," I said. She was facing the wall. I leaned over her. "Mom."

"What," she finally answered.

"We need to get something to eat."

"Oh," she said. "How about if I take you to Taco Bell?"

"Okay," I said. "When?"

"I don't know," she said in a voice like she was dying. "Soon."

I went back to the kitchen. "Come on," I said to Rona. It might be a minute before Mom got up or it might be an hour. Hopefully it wouldn't be two days. "Let's finish unloading the car. Then it'll be time to go get dinner."

It was freezing outside, and dark.

"Justine, where's the Big Dipper?" Rona asked.

The Big Dipper was the one constellation Rona knew. She didn't exactly get it, about stars. "Are the stars coming tonight?" she'd ask if it was a cloudy night—I guess she thought they either showed up or they didn't, depending on what they felt like. If you explained to her that the stars were always there, you just couldn't see them sometimes because they were behind the clouds, she'd say, "What clouds?"

Tonight she said, "Are there stars in Massachusetts?"

I was glad you couldn't see them, truthfully. One abnormal thing about me is that I don't love stars the way everybody else does. Some of my worst memories, actually, are of looking at stars. I especially used to hate it when Mom would make us stay at the beach till it was totally dark and have a *star party*. She'd dig us special chairs in the sand—tilted, so we were practically lying on our backs—and we'd look at the sky while she named the constellations. Except she didn't know so many. So after she'd said "Orion," and "Cassiopeia," and "Cygnus," or whoever else she could see, she'd sit there a minute, then she'd say, "Why don't we just make up our own? What do you see, Justine? Oh, look, an anteater! Look, a bunch of bananas! A jester holding a cake with birthday candles!"

She thought it was such a fun game, but I hated it. Because I could never see anything, and it gave me an awful, scared feeling to try. I would look up at the huge night sky, and I would think about the stories Mom had told me, the things I'd seen in books and remembered from the planetarium—the pictures of gods and goddesses, kings and queens, animals and warriors—and I would start to get nervous, thinking: How was I supposed to rearrange it all? It was too hard. If you changed a constellation, you'd have stars left over—what were you supposed to do with them? Would they just float there alone, without a story to belong to? If you tried to make them into a new picture, by borrowing stars from the next constellation over, you'd just have the same problem, but in a different place. It was like a big puzzle too hard for me to do, and I couldn't tell Mom, because it was such a fun, fascinating game for her: I didn't *want* to be the rearranger of the sky.

When we'd brought in everything from the minivan except the mattresses, which I couldn't budge, I went and stood over Mom again. "Mom," I said.

"Mmm," she answered.

"We need some food."

"Aaah," she said. "Can't we just get some takeout?"

I reminded her that the phone didn't work yet. "Nooo," she moaned, then she said, "Okay. In a minute."

"Are we going to bring in our beds?" I asked her.

"In a minute," she said, then she closed her eyes again.

I went to where I'd piled the garbage bags with the pillows and blankets in them and started dragging them into my bedroom. On the way past Mom, I threw down a pillow and a blanket.

"Let's make a big nest," I said to Rona, trying to make my voice sound like it was going to be so much fun, sleeping without beds.

"I'm hungry," she said.

"Here, you make us a bed," I told her, "I'll be right back." I went to the minivan again, and when I came back I had everything edible I could find in it: four organic teddy bear cookies and a flattened peppermint pattie I'd found in the crack in the backseat; six pieces of fuzzy popcorn from the floor; and a whole, wrapped-up granola bar and half a pack of gum that were in the glove compartment.

In my room, Rona had piled all the blankets together and plugged in the tiny TV. She was staring at it, sucking her thumb. "No channels," she said as I got in the blanket pile next to her, but we sat there anyway, watching the flickering particles and eating the car food.

"I'm still hungry," she said as soon as we'd finished, but all I could say was "I know." There was nothing else in the house except her egg, which I wasn't going to mention. There was nothing to promise her. Not even that tomorrow would be better.

—⟋⟍—

We are nearing the Humboldt Desert. "Gather all the firewood you can," I told the children after supper tonight. "And anything edible: nuts, berries, nettles, wild turnips, anything you see." I have filled all the water kegs, which weigh a ton. I emptied the wagon of everything except for the water, the provisions, the tools, and my carved wooden chest, which I am saving in case we need it for firewood. I strapped the cradle and the gun to my back and a water jug to my side, and I loaded down poor Jake with all that he could carry.

"You have to get out and walk," I told Amethyst. "Please." Finally, I got into the wagon myself, got down on my hands and knees, and rolled her out onto the ground. She screamed, then she cried. Now she drags herself along as if she is dying, falling farther and farther behind. We would actually make better time if she rode. But it might kill poor Zack to put her back in, and we'd make even worse time with a dead ox. Amethyst makes my life feel like a handful of bad choices sometimes.

When Rona woke up the next morning and saw where we were, she started to cry.

"Don't cry," I told her, though I couldn't really give her a good reason not to. Our breath made clouds in front of our faces. "Stay here," I said. I got out from under the blankets and went into the other room. The floor was so cold, it made my feet sting.

"Mom," I said, "wake up."

"Oh," Mom said, and she opened her eyes and looked around. "Oh, my. I slept all the way through."

"We need breakfast."

"Breakfast," she said. "Well, what is there? What should we have?"

"We need to go to the store," I said. "And we need to get the heat fixed."

"Heat fixed?"

"It doesn't work," I said. "We need to call someone." She gave me a blank look. "The person who fixes the heat. Plus we need the phone turned on. And it's a school day. In case you forgot."

"Oh," she said. It looked like she was thinking in slow motion. "Heat, food, school, phone. Let me just get in the shower first, then we'll go find a grocery store."

She went in the bathroom, and I heard the shower make a big banging noise, and then there was a gurgling sound and the rush of water. After a minute it stopped and Mom came back out, looking shocked. "There's no hot water," she said.

—m—

This desert seems almost worse than the last. The sand is very deep, and so hot it burns my feet to walk in it. There are no plants, no trees, just the bare, greenish yellow mountains that loom in the distance. We found some water today, but it was hot! Boiling water bubbling out of the ground. The oxen burned their tongues trying to drink it.

We never made it to school that day. By the time we pulled up outside the school building, after we'd gone to the grocery store, and the IHOP, and to a pay phone for Mom to call the landlord, and the phone company, and work, to tell them she was so sorry she was going to be five hours late, it was one o'clock. As Rona and I were getting out of the car, though, I asked Mom, "How are we getting home today?" She looked at me as if I'd spoken in Dutch.

"Are you going to pick us up?" I asked.

"Oh," she said. "I'm going to be at work. I might not be able to. Can you take the school bus?"

"Does it even go by our house?" I said.

"I don't know," she said. "I wonder if it does."

"Should you go in and find out?"

"Mm," she said. "I'm so late for work as it is—could we just do it tomorrow?"

"So, what do you want to do?" I asked Rona after Mom dropped us off at home. Which wasn't a fair question, really—I already knew what I wanted to do. We were still in our coats—Mom had called the landlord, and he'd told her the problem wasn't that the heater was broken, but that she'd forgotten to order oil for the oil tank like he'd told her to; and the oil company said the truck wouldn't come till the afternoon—and it was too cold to do anything inside like play a game or read a book; and I didn't feel like huddling under blankets all day.

I wanted to find out where we were. I was pretty sure we were still in Hadley, but I wanted to know a few other things, like where the nearest food store was, and which was the road to school, and whether we could walk to town or the mall from our house. And also whether we could walk to Marie's—my best idea about how to get money, if we ran out completely, besides the mall fountain, was Marie's poker fund, and I knew where the key to Marie and Bill's back door was hidden.

It was getting too hard to trick Rona anymore, so I just said, "We're going on a walk so we don't freeze to death in this house."

"Okay," she said, surprising me.

"Put on your scarf and hat and mittens and boots," I told her.

"Okay," she said.

"And I don't want you to complain," I said, since she was saying okay to everything.

"But what if I have to?" she said.

We stood outside the house while I tried to figure out which way we should go. I couldn't see any traffic lights or signs or stores, or hear any traffic noise from any big roads. Our new address was 112 Ida Lane. If I could get a map, maybe I could find our street on it. But of course we didn't have a map. There was a map store in Amherst, but I didn't know which way Amherst was. There was probably a name for that kind of problem, but I didn't know what it was.

"Which way do you want to go?" I asked Rona.

"No way," she said.

"Come on," I said. I walked to the end of the walk and took a right, because when I was little, the first time I walked around the block alone, that's what Mom had told me to do. I'd begged and begged her to let me walk around the block alone, and finally she'd told me, "Okay. Do you know how to walk around the block?"

"Yes," I said, though I didn't.

"You know which is your right, right? Your right hand and your right foot?"

I showed her. She told me to go to the end of the block and take a right, then go to the end of the next block and take a right, and not to cross any streets—just to keep taking rights till I was in front of our house again. I can still remember the feeling, too, when I ran in the front door to tell Mom, "I did it!" It makes me smile to think about it now: how grown-up I thought I was. I was already thinking about the places I was going to walk next: nursery school, my friend Lisa's house, Disneyland. But when I ran inside, Mom wasn't there, and I suddenly didn't feel that grown-up anymore.

She walked in the back door a minute later, just when I was about to start crying; and it wasn't until she told me, about three years later, that I found out I hadn't actually walked around the block by myself that day. She'd followed me. And it was funny—remembering it now gave me a strong urge to look behind me, which I didn't, because—it was ridiculous—I didn't want to get a disappointed feeling when I saw that she wasn't anywhere in sight.

—᠁—

We have reached the Truckee River. The clear, swift-flowing water was a beautiful sight. There is plentiful deep grass here, and big trees, and shade. Ezekiel and Annabelle even caught a fish, which we ate for dinner. It was a most welcome change from beans and onions. This morning a goose came waddling around, and I nailed it. We will stay here a day for the oxen to eat and rest. I wish we could stay longer. In fact, for once I'm with Amethyst—I wish we could stay forever. She wishes it because she's a nutball, though. I wish it because I am afraid.

We walked until our faces were numb. We walked until the light started to leave the sky. First we went one direction for about half an hour. We went in a straight line so I wouldn't forget the way back. Then we came back and went in the opposite direction. Then we did it one more time, in a third direction. Each time it was the same: trees, trees, houses, houses, trees. There were no stores, unless you counted this little boarded-up wooden shack that had "Berries Tomatoes Corn" painted on it; and we didn't see any pay phones, either.

"Just one more way," I said when we got back the third time.

"Justine, no," Rona said in a despairing voice, and I didn't blame her. She hadn't complained at all, amazingly—she'd just held my hand through our mittens and trudged along, every few minutes looking down at her egg in its sock wrapping and saying, "Are you warm enough? Please stay warm enough. Justine, can eggs freeze?"

"All right," I said. "Let's just go in." I wasn't sure how I was going to warm the house up, though. Maybe turn on the oven and open it, though I thought I remembered there was a reason that was a bad idea. I had made Mom buy ten boxes of macaroni and cheese at the store that morning, and I would make one soon if she didn't come home.

As we were heading up the walk, a car slowed down and honked at us.

"Is it a pervert?" Rona said, squinting.

"No," I said, but I took her arm and sped up a little. She twisted around to look.

"He's still there," she said. I turned to look and got a surprise: it was Ron Wesler, peering out at us, waving. He parked the car and got out.

"Hey!" he said. "Justine, hi! And who's this?" he said, looking down at Rona. Rona had come into the kitchen the night of the poker party, taken one look at the grown-ups, and then gone to watch the baby manatees with Cassidy.

"Do I know you?" Ron said now. "You look familiar. Have I ever met you? Did you tell me your name? Wait—let me guess. I'm really good at guessing people's names. They call me . . . the Amazing Name Guesser."

If you were a guy, Rona either loved you or hated you, and you knew which it was going to be in about five seconds. She looked up at him, and her smile spread and she giggled. "Guess the first letter! Guess what the first letter is!" she said.

"Oh, wait, oh, yes, it's coming to me. . . . The first letter is . . . is . . . is . . ."

"R!"

"Yes!" cried Ron in a whisper. "Exactly! And your name is . . . Roba?" he said. "Roda? Ropa? Rola?" By the time he said "Rona," you could tell Rona was in love.

Ron was looking at our house. "So this is it?" he said, and I thought I could tell that he sort of hoped the answer would be no. "Marie gave me your new address. I didn't even know you moved. Speaking of people who like to avoid me, is your mom around?"

"She's at work," I told him.

"Oh," he said, sounding disappointed. "Will she be home soon?"

"She usually comes home around four-thirty or five," I said.

"Well," he said, "do you know if you have dinner plans?"

"Who?" I asked.

"All of you. You. Your mom, your sister."

I thought about how to answer that. Our dinner plans were probably for me to make macaroni and cheese for Rona and me and for Mom to climb into her pile of blankets and lie there for fifteen hours.

"No," I said. "We don't have any dinner plans."

"Because I was thinking maybe I could take you out for dinner," he said.

"Can we go to Chuck E. Cheese?!" said Rona.

"Oh," he said, shaking his head sadly, "I'm afraid last time I went to Chuck E. Cheese I had too much fun and sort of lost control of myself. They told me I could never go back again."

"What did you do?" asked Rona, fascinated. "Did you do something to Chuck E. Cheese?"

"Mom's usually pretty tired when she gets off work," I said. "She has to stand on her feet all day. She might not want to go out."

"Oh," he said. "Well, then, what about if I made you dinner? Do you think she'd be too tired to come over to my house for dinner? I'd let her sit down in a chair." Then he said, "No, wait, I know: What about if I made you dinner here? Then she wouldn't even have to leave the house."

"Well," I said.

"What do you like?" he asked Rona. "Squid? Liverwurst casserole? Zucchini pie?" She squealed and laughed.

I was going to be in so much trouble. "We like spaghetti a lot," I said.

"Chicken!" said Rona. Or maybe I wouldn't be in trouble. No man had ever made us dinner before, unless you counted Jiffy Pop and burnt grilled-cheese sandwiches, Dale's specialties. Maybe Mom would like someone making dinner for her. That would be normal, to like something like that.

"How about steak?" said Ron.

"Yeah, steak!" Rona said.

"Okay, steak it is," said Ron. "How about if I go get some food and come back and get it started. Do you think that would be okay?"

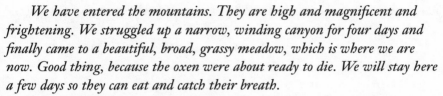

We have entered the mountains. They are high and magnificent and frightening. We struggled up a narrow, winding canyon for four days and finally came to a beautiful, broad, grassy meadow, which is where we are now. Good thing, because the oxen were about ready to die. We will stay here a few days so they can eat and catch their breath.

The children love it here at Truckee Meadow. They frolic and play in the long grass. Every once in a while they run up and say, "I'm hungry," then I force myself to smile gaily and say: "How about a delicious dried wild turnip root? A nice, juicy onion slice? Some delightful goose jerky?"

"I just want to get you to try new things," I tell them when they make a face.

Last night I let the children sit out late with me, and we looked at the stars.

I didn't tell them: The night sky frightens me now. It never used to.

Thaddeus used to love to tell me the story of the sky, when we were courting. We'd sit outside in the backyard at night, and he'd point out warriors, kings and queens, heroes, animals, monsters—things I could never see. I mean, Perseus, the son of Zeus, holding Medusa's head in a bag? Come on.

"There's Hercules," he'd say. "There's Pegasus, Taurus, Orion." He especially liked Cepheus and Cassiopeia. "The only married couple in the sky," he liked to say, wink, wink, and squeeze my hand.

He'd go around the whole sky, telling me what was what, till every single star was used up, even the smallest, faintest one, way out in the corner of the universe, that I was hoping he'd miss; and I remember wishing sometimes that a star could just be what it was—a glimmer of ancient light—instead of the sword tip of a warrior or the eye of a ram or the point of a god's crown.

I liked the way if you got rid of all the pictures, the sky and your brain sort of melted together into one huge, black, endless place, completely empty and, at the same time, completely full—of anything you wanted to imagine, any story you wanted to tell.

Well, it's my sky now, and I don't have any story for it, nothing to tell the children.

"Tell me about the lion again," said Ezekiel. Leo is his zodiac sign, so naturally he loves the lion best. I didn't tell him: I can't even find the dippers anymore.

"Where are the twins?" asked Annabelle. Then, softly, "Mama?"

"Shh," I said. "I'm waiting."

"Waiting for what?" they both asked.

"I'm waiting for the stars to tell me something," I said. Then I closed my eyes and gathered my arms around myself, and I listened for some sound, some story, a word, anything, to whisper up from deep inside my body.

When Ron came back, he was carrying bags of food and a cardboard box with a frying pan, a big wooden pepper grinder, and a bottle of olive oil sticking out of it. A little while after Rona and I had gotten back from our walk, the oil truck had come and a guy in big, dirty boots had tromped down into the basement, and a few minutes later all the radiators had started hissing, and the kitchen was warm now. I stood beside Ron as he unpacked everything he'd brought. He had even brought his own cutting board and his own knife. "Do you like ratatouille?" he asked, pulling out a can of tomatoes.

"I don't know," I lied. Ratatouille, I knew, was like if you took everything left in the disposal after you cleaned up after dinner and cooked it and put it on a plate. It had eggplant in it. "It sounds good," I said. "It sounds like something I'd like."

"I *love* raddatooie," Rona said dreamily, gazing at Ron. "I love it ten times as much as Justine does."

When I heard the car, I said, "I'll be right back," and ran to the door.

"Oh, hi, honey," Mom said lifelessly before I could tell her that Ron was in the kitchen. "My God," she said, setting her purse down like it weighed a thousand pounds. "I am so exhausted. I might just have to lie down for a little while. Do you think you could . . ." She walked past the kitchen door and froze.

"Mom!" cried Rona. She slid off the counter and ran over and hugged Mom around the legs. "Ron's here! We're making you tenderline!"

"I see," said Mom.

"I invited myself," Ron said to Mom. "I wanted to make you guys dinner, but it sounds like maybe it's not a very good time . . ." He was sad and adorable, looking at Mom, like, Please say I can stay? Please say I can stay?

"No!" yelled Rona, and she ran to Ron and grabbed his legs. "Mom!"

"I missed you guys at Thanksgiving," he added.

Maybe Mom remembered her own rule then, of never being rude to anyone. Or maybe she was deciding she might like Ron a little after all, except it didn't sound like it. She spoke in her three-hundred-year-old woman voice.

"Oh," Mom said. "It looks like you went to a lot of trouble. Please stay."

----m----

I have a hard decision to make: Pack up and get going for the pass, or stay here at the meadow a while longer and let the oxen get stronger? They eat and drink all day, barely lifting their heads, and I do have to say, they are looking a little better.

The baby was fretful all day today.

"What?" I kept saying. She probably wouldn't tell me if she could, though. I don't think she likes me, but somehow I don't blame her. She probably wants some guarantees in her life—something besides that I'll carry her and change her diaper and hold her in my arms as she gets weaker and weaker. Maybe that's why she refuses to get better. Maybe she doesn't want to waste her time becoming a child until she can see some good reason to.

All day I worried about what to do, and all day I watched her, and all day I couldn't shake the feeling that she knew something she wasn't telling; and maybe, somewhere deep inside, I knew it, too. In the middle of the night

I woke up and understood. Thick clouds covered the stars. Icy air filled my lungs. Cold needles were falling on my face.

Snow. I heard the word as if someone had said it. I looked at the baby, who was lying next to me with open eyes. Was it possible that she had? But she'd never even said "Mama" yet. I watched her, but her face wouldn't tell me anything. The snowflakes fell in her eyes, and she didn't even blink.

I couldn't understand Mom. All through dinner Ron talked and smiled; he asked us questions and listened to the answers; he got up and got us more glasses of milk and water when we ran out. Mom barely even talked to him at all. We were eating on the living room floor, sitting around a tablecloth he'd brought, since our table was still in Marie's garage. I'd never even heard of a man having his own tablecloth.

"So what did you do at work today?" Ron asked Mom.

"I peeled and deveined five hundred shrimp," she said. "I picked forty pounds of crab. I pulled the strings off a case of snow peas." It sounded like maybe it was supposed to be funny, except Mom didn't smile at all.

"Well, somebody's got to do it," Ron said. "Or all those drunk wedding guests would be choking on their pea strings. I think prep work is a very noble profession," he said, in a kidding voice, but a nice one.

Mom laughed a little. Then she said, "Well, it's not a noble profession. But it's the best I could find."

"If you could be doing anything you wanted, what would it be?" Ron asked, and it was weird—for some reason that made Mom's smile disappear. You could feel the air around her tighten.

"Nothing," she said.

"Nothing?" said Ron, waiting for Mom to explain.

But she just said, "That's right," and her eyes wandered away from him, like, Next topic.

I finally dragged Rona away from Ron at nine-thirty. She started to cry, but Ron knelt down and gave her a big hug and said, "Hey. Don't cry, Scona. If you don't cry, I'll come back soon and play fourteen games of War in a row with you."

After I put Rona to bed, I lay in my room on my mattress on the floor, and I felt like crying myself. I was just so tired. I was tired of try-ing to figure out what we were going to eat every day; I was tired of being cold and bored in our dark, ugly house; I was tired of trying to keep Rona's spirits up all the time. But mostly, I was tired of Mom, I thought, as I lay there listening to Ron's voice—soft and deep and rumbly, like the sound of the heater going on—and Mom's answers, small and weightless, like garbage scattering in the wind. I was tired of trying to make her like Ron through the powers of my brain; I was tired of trying to figure out the big mystery of her.

If I understood the Mystery of Mom, then maybe I would under-stand why, when Ron said, "You know what, Colleen? I'm not really sure why I like you so much, since you obviously don't like me, but I do. You know, I could just be your friend, in a sort of no-strings-attached way. Wouldn't that be okay?" her answer was, "Oh, you know. I just have a lot going on right now. I'm probably not the best person to be friends with." And I would be able to understand why, a few minutes after he said, "Well, I have to warn you, I'm very persis-tent, and I also really liked making dinner for you and your girls, so I'm going to call again, probably too soon," and left, Mom had picked up the phone and dialed, and after a minute had said, "Trent. Hi. This is Colleen Hanley. I don't know if you remember me, but, uh, well, I'm a friend of Danny's, remember? We met on the stairway, in your house? And, uh, I hope you don't think it's too weird, my calling you, but, you know, I enjoyed meeting you and was sort of wondering if you might like to go hear some music sometime or something, and, uh, well, my number is 413—that's Massachusetts—555-7060, and, uh, so, give me a call, thanks, bye."

We left the meadow at daybreak. All day long, thick flakes fell lightly. The children ran alongside the wagon and whooped and played. They caught snowflakes on their tongues, asked me a hundred times if I thought enough would fall for a snowman. By evening it had begun to cover the ground.

I wasn't expecting snow so soon. It is only the fifth of October. According to Thaddeus, we should have a month left, at least.

* * *

Mom dropped us off at school on Friday and told us to get on the number four school bus at the end of the day. "Just tell the driver where you live," she said. But I guess the bus driver didn't really have any idea why I was saying, as we got on the bus, "We live at 112 Ida Lane," because he didn't answer me or say anything to us the whole ride. Finally, at the last stop, after all the other kids had gotten off and Rona and I were still sitting there, he turned around and said, "Last stop." I looked out the windows, but nothing looked familiar. I wasn't sure what to do. I went to the front of the bus, and Rona followed me.

"Do you know where Ida Lane is?" I asked the bus driver.

"No," he said. "Why?" I'm not sure why I didn't tell him the truth: Believe it or not, my little sister's and my life is so ridiculous that we don't know where we are or how to get home.

"No reason," I said. "Thanks. Come on," I said to Rona.

"Where are we?" she asked as the bus drove away. I looked down for a minute, at her big blue eyes staring right into mine. I wondered if she would still believe anything I told her. It would be kind of nice to have someone to tell the truth to, and maybe that's what she wanted as she looked up at me, waiting. I tried to remember how I felt when I was almost six, but I couldn't.

I wondered if I should just tell her: Well, truthfully, we're a little bit lost. Or a lot, I'm not sure which yet. And I'm not sure whether or not it's an emergency.

She kept looking at me, and when I didn't answer, she looked down at her egg. "Don't worry," she told it, patting it with a fluttery hand. "We're just going for a little walk. Justine is taking us. We'll be home soon. Right, Justine?" she added in a different voice—small and a little wavery. And even though I felt a little disappointed, and suddenly lonely, I knew what to do.

"This way," I said, and turned us in the opposite direction of the way we were facing, so that it seemed like I had chosen that direction deliberately, and we started to walk.

———ɯɯ———

The snow fell all night and has begun to cover the trail. I watched the sky all day today, trying to figure out what to do. It's too late to turn back to

Salt Lake City or Fort Hall. The animals are too weak to cross the desert again, and we don't have enough food left, anyway.

The sky looks full of snow. I wonder if it's snowing all the way from here to California.

"When are we going to be home?" Rona asked.

I gave her the same answer I'd already given her about twenty times: "Pretty soon." It was starting to get dark already, and something colder than rain but wetter than snow had started to fall from the sky.

"I wish we were home," she said. "My head's all wet. When are we going to be there? Are we almost there?"

I knew I had to do something. From where we were, I could see five houses, and I tried to figure out which might have someone nice living in it. I chose one with filmy white curtains and a Christmas wreath on the door under a painted wooden sign that said, "Welcome."

"Why are we going here?" Rona asked as we went up the walk.

"Because we need help," I said, then I saw that was a mistake. Rona's forehead wrinkled.

"Why? Why do we need help, Justine? Why do we? Are we lost? Are we still in Massachusetts?"

"We just need to use a phone," I said. "To call Mom."

"Mom'll be worried," she said. "Right?"

I didn't answer that. I rang the doorbell. It took a long time for someone to come to the door, and when it finally opened, there was something I totally didn't expect on the other side, something that, if I'd expected it, I never would've rung the doorbell in the first place—it was a kid. It was a girl who looked maybe a year or two younger than me. She stood and stared.

"Um, is your mother home?" I said. I sounded like a dorky little salesman or something.

"Just a minute," she said, and she ran off. A minute later she came back with her mother. The mother opened the door all the way and stood looking at us.

"Could we please use your phone?" I asked.

"Oh," said the woman, sounding puzzled. "Sure." She opened the door wider, then she looked at us more closely. "Are you in trouble?

Do you need help?" I really wished the girl would leave, or at least stop staring at us like we were weird little freaks, which we were.

"I just need to call my mom," I said. "We were out walking. But it's getting kind of dark."

"Come on in," said the woman. "Gosh, it's getting really nasty out there. Not a very nice day for a walk. Let me get you the phone." The girl just kept on standing there, staring. Her mother came back a second later with the phone.

I dialed our new number, and it rang and rang and rang.

"She's not home?" the woman said when I finally hung up.

"No," I said.

"Oh no," Rona said, and she looked up at me.

"She's probably at work," I said. Then I had to dig through my backpack for her number at the Peabody House Inn, which I didn't have memorized yet. But when I called there, the person who answered just said, "Colleen *who*?" and went to ask somebody else and then came back and said, "No, she left. Okay? Bye," and hung up.

"All right, thanks," I said to the dial tone.

"Do you need a ride somewhere?" the woman asked.

"I have to try one more number," I said. I wished they would leave me alone for a minute, but we were all standing together in the hallway. I dialed Marie's number.

"It's Justine," I said when Marie said, "Hello?"

"Hi, Justine, what's up?" said Marie.

"Rona and I are sort of . . . somewhere, and we need a ride."

"Need a ride?" she said.

I was trying to figure out a way to make it sound like I was talking to my actual mother. "Yeah. We don't have one," I said. I also didn't want the woman and the girl to know about the school bus incident.

"Where are you?" Marie asked.

"I don't know," I said. "Hang on."

"1575 West Durham Road," the woman told me.

"What in hell are you doing all the way out there?" Marie said when I told her. "Where's your mother?" It was just too hard—I couldn't do it.

"Because we didn't get off at the right school bus stop, and Mom

isn't home and I don't know where she is, and she doesn't know where
we are," I said. The girl's eyes widened, like that was the most awful,
strange, scary thing she had ever heard. My list of least favorite moments in my life was getting longer and longer.

"Oh, for fuck's sake," said Marie. "Yes, I can come get you, but is
there a grown-up there, so I can get directions?"

"What do you mean, you didn't get off at the right school bus
stop?" Marie demanded as soon as we were in the car. "Now, tell me
again what happened?" I guess she thought because she was rescuing
us, it was her business, and I didn't actually think she was completely
wrong.

"Your mother told you to ask the *driver* where you lived?" she
said, and even though I said, "Well, not exactly," she just started going, "Unbelievable. *Un*believable. Unbe*lie*vable!" By the time we got
to our house, she was pretty furious. "Which one is it?" she demanded
as she drove slowly down our street, and I remembered she hadn't
seen our new house yet.

"That one," I told her. She looked at it in disbelief, and I decided
not to make the unfunny little joke I thought of: "Just wait till you see
the inside."

"Oh, my fucking Lord," she said when she walked through the
door. "What is this, a crack den? Is there any *heat*?" she said, going for
the thermostat. "Are there any *lights*?"

"Pack up some things for you and your sister," she told me after a
few minutes. "You're going to have to come to my house."

"No!" said Rona. "I'm not."

"I can't spend my whole night here, and your mother is obviously
AWOL, and I'm not going to leave you here alone."

"Mom is not an awol!" said Rona.

"We can stay alone," I told Marie. "We do it all the time."

"Absolutely not," she snapped. "Now get your stuff together."

"Don't worry," Rona was saying into her little shopping bag.
"We're not going. We don't live with you anymore, so you can't boss
us around," she told Marie.

"Come on," I said to Rona.

"FYI," Rona said to Marie as I pulled her around the door of her bedroom. FYI was an expression she'd learned from being around Marie. "I'm not going."

"FYI," called Marie, "you little twerp, believe me—if I could leave you here all by yourself, I would."

Rona looked up at me then, like, to see if that could actually happen, but I just said, "Just *be quiet*, okay?"

By the time Mom walked in the door five minutes later, Marie was in a complete frenzy.

"Marie," said Mom, surprised. "What's going on?" Then she looked around and said, "I wanted to get everything a little more fixed up before you saw it."

"This place is a stinking rathole, Colleen," Marie said, "and I hope your landlord is paying *you* to live in it, but that's not really the important issue here."

"What's wrong?" Mom said.

"*What's wrong?*" mocked Marie. Rona and I were in my room. She was trying to run into the living room, but I was holding her like a wrestler, with my hand over her mouth.

"Why are you so upset?" Mom said. "What's the matter?"

"What's *the matter* is that your children were out wandering in the middle of nowhere, ten miles away from here, in the rain, in the dark, with no idea where they were, because you can't be bothered to perform the very minimal basic parental duties, and I swear to God, I'm thinking about reporting you to the authorities. Either that or asking you to let them live with me until you either get some professional help or miraculously turn into a mother again."

Mom was quiet for so long that I started to wonder if she was even still out there.

"I'm sorry, Colleen," Marie said, "but I just think right now you're not being a very good mother. And I think maybe you should consider letting them come stay with me until you pull it together."

Mom was silent. Rona had stopped struggling, but my hand was still over her mouth, and when Marie said that, I had to clamp it back down.

Finally Mom said something. "Me without my girls?" Then there was another long silence, as if maybe she was trying to picture it. So was I, and I couldn't. I couldn't picture Mom coming home to a cold, dark, empty house at the end of the day, not having anyone to say "Oh, I don't know if I can do this anymore" to; not having someone to sit in the other room while she lay in her bed for fifteen hours feeling like she was going to die; to remind her it was time to go to the grocery store again.

"Oh, God," Mom said. "I can't even think about this." Then she said something really scary. "Maybe I should just send them back to live with Dale for a while." Rona stopped squirming under my hand, and she looked up at me with a terrible look.

"He *is* their father," Mom said. "Well, Rona's."

"You can't do that," Marie said.

"Why not?"

"Didn't you say he was physically abusing Justine?"

"Well," Mom said. "Maybe he could just take Rona for a little while. His mother dotes on her." Poor Rona was looking at me with terror.

"And Justine could stay with me," said Marie.

"Oh God," said Mom again. "Marie, you just have to let me think a little. Just go, and I'll call you tomorrow, I promise."

I didn't need to think, though. I'd already figured out what I needed to know: Whatever I had to do to make what Mom had just said not happen, I would do it. I would work as hard as I could to make it look like our life was perfect. Because I just knew: If Rona went to live with Dale and Grandma Evelyn, I might never see her again. And who knows—if I went to live three miles away at Marie's house, I might never see Mom again, either.

We had a very difficult time today. The snow is up to the oxen's shins, and they slip and stumble with every step. The rags that I've wrapped my feet in quickly get soaked and then freeze solid and are quite uncomfortable to walk in. I am limping almost as much as Zack is.

The children have started to complain of the cold. "Run ahead and see if you can find some sticks!" I tell them, trying to keep my voice gay. "See if you can find any nuts! Tell me if you see any animal tracks!" It is better for them to keep moving.

Amethyst has not been out of the wagon since the snow started. She must come out at night to answer nature's call, but during the day she stays behind the canvas sleeping, or pretending to. I gave up on making her walk—it was too much work shoving her out of the wagon every day.

THE SAD PRINCESS SMILES

On Saturday, Ron drove over and asked Mom for a date. He'd called a couple of times during the week, and Mom hadn't called him back, so I did, on Friday. I knew Mom would kill me if she found out. But I wanted to give him some clues.

"Justine!" he said when he heard my voice. "What's going on?"

"Well," I said, "I wanted to call, just in case Mom didn't call you back. She doesn't really like talking on the telephone—I don't know if she told you that."

"Well," he said, "that's good to know. But are you sure it isn't just me she doesn't like?" Then he said, "Don't answer that! Actually, why don't you tell me a few things she does like."

"She likes music," I said. "She likes going out to hear bands." I left out the part about how she was usually obsessed with somebody in them. I didn't know how to tell him the thing I really wanted to tell him, though. I wanted to tell him the Secret of Mom, so he wouldn't get discouraged—but what was it? If you wanted Mom to like you, you had to be more of a loser? You had to live in a dump and hate kids and not know how to make your own dinner, let alone anyone else's, and most of all, you had to be mean to Mom? Or if not exactly mean, everything you did had to make her look sort of like a sad, pathetic idiot? And you had to not call, because somehow the ones that didn't call were the ones she ended up liking the most; and lately, actually, Mom's favorite guys were the imaginary kind—the ones she'd never met, who didn't know she even existed. But of course, I didn't know how to tell him any of that.

"Justine?" Ron said. "Are you still there?"

"She likes vegetarian food a lot," I said.

When Mom opened the door on Saturday, Ron said, "Hey, Colleen, I was wondering if you wanted to go out tonight. There's this really great band playing down in Springfield, and there's a new Indian restaurant down there that serves all-vegetarian food I've been wanting to try." And he looked at me and winked.

"Maybe we could go to Chuck E. Cheese!" cried Rona, but I said to her, "No, it's just grown-ups."

"*No!*" said Rona. Mom looked at me suspiciously.

"I don't know," she said to Ron.

Then Ron did something I never saw a guy do before—he got down on his knees at Mom's feet and he made praying hands.

"Please," he said, looking up at Mom. "Please, Colleen, just say yes to *one* date. If you don't like it, I'll never ask you again, I promise."

Mom actually laughed. It was like a moment in a fairy tale—the one where the prince finally makes the sad princess smile.

—∿—

It has been snowing for four days and nights. The drifts have reached a depth of four feet or more in places, and it is very hard going. The wagon wheels groan and creak, and the poor oxen look like they're about to give themselves a hernia. I walk alongside them and sink up to my knees at every step. The children ride, since the snow is too deep for them to walk through. They are frightened now and no longer think of playing. Also, it is hard to find firewood, for it is hidden under the snow. So, exhausted as I am at the end of every day, I have to get out the ax and chop down trees.

I started to say a prayer before bed tonight. "Dear God," I said. Then I stopped. If God knows and sees everything, then he really doesn't need me to tell him what I need. So I sat and thought instead. I thought and thought and thought, and I listened to the wind howl, and I thought some more. It felt a little bit like a prayer, anyway.

When I woke up on Sunday morning and went out to go to the bathroom, I saw something that made my heart skip: Mom's blanket, on the living room floor, was a bigger lump than usual, and when I tiptoed closer, I saw that Ron was underneath it, too. So they had probably had sex—Grandma Bobbie was the one who'd told me that's what it meant when someone said two people had slept together. Well, first she told me it meant they were *having relations*, which, she finally admitted after I asked nine or ten times, "But what does that *mean*?" meant "having sex." And Mom and Ron had slept together, definitely. They still were. I watched them for a minute. Then Ron moved, and I scurried back to my room. I lay there in my bed, wondering if, in an hour or whenever Mom and Ron woke up, our life would be changed.

After about ten minutes, I heard Rona's feet pitter-pat out of her room and then stop, and then she squealed, "Ha!" and I heard a loud, "Uhnn!" which meant, I guessed, that she had jumped on Ron, and then Mom's voice going, "What? Oh. Hunh. Nn," and Ron saying, "No, no, no, you can't come under here," and Rona saying, *"Why?"* and Ron saying, "You just can't. I'm not at liberty to reveal why."

So I went out and got Rona, which was the last thing I wanted to do. I was glad Ron and Mom had had a good time on their date, and Ron had stayed, but there was something a little jagged that had cut through my brain when I'd seen their bare shoulders peeking out from under the blankets, and I didn't want to see them again. It was a little like when a dog or cat comes home from the vet with a weird part of them shaved, and you realize how good it is that they have fur there ordinarily.

"Hi, guys," I said, not looking at them.

"Hey, Justine," said Ron. "Good morning. Did you guys have a nice time last night?"

"Yeah," I said, and, "Come on," to Rona. I picked her up, and she started to howl, "No! No! No! I want to stay!" and pound on me with her fists.

By the time we went out again, Mom and Ron were dressed and in the kitchen, drinking coffee.

"My God," Ron was saying, "Colleen, you *have* to get a bed over here. I don't even care if I never spend the night again—you can't sleep on that cold, hard floor." He stretched, then he rubbed his hand down Mom's back. "How about I help you bring it over today?" Mom didn't say yes or no, she just smiled a not-all-there smile. "Because we can't have you suffering now, can we?" he said, and he brushed his hand across Mom's hair. "Oops," he said when he saw me watching, and he pulled his hand away. "All right, I confess," he said, "I like your mother," and then he put his hands over his face like he was embarrassed.

It snowed another foot in the night. Today, as we staggered along, Zack fell on his knees in the deep snow, and I had an awful time getting him back up. I don't think he can go any farther. I'm not even sure we are still on the trail anymore. I've decided we're going to stop and stay here till I decide what to do.

I will try to dig out some grass for the animals tomorrow. We are almost completely out of food. The children grumbled when I gave them watery rice porridge again for breakfast. The baby tightened her lips together and refused it completely. "Eat," I told her softly. I don't know what else to do. "Eat. Please." I have never seen a baby who survives on as little as she does.

Mom was ecstatically happy for almost two whole days. It started building up from Sunday morning: she smiled a few times as she sat drinking her coffee, and when Ron touched her on the back of the neck, she sort of pushed her head against his hand like a cat. And her voice was soft and murmuring, though she didn't say much—just, "Mm-hmm" and "Mmm" and "Hmm." Ron went to the store and came back with food for breakfast; and I watched Mom watch him while he made it, and she stayed quiet, but in a good way, which never happened to Mom around guys.

After breakfast, Ron said to Mom, "I'll clean up," and while Mom was in the shower, he did the dishes and fixed the window over the sink so that it closed all the way, and he stood on a chair and took down the dirty, fly-filled glass thing from the ceiling and emptied it out and washed it and unscrewed the burned-out lightbulb; then he stood on the chair and turned the new bulb and said, "Let there be light," and pretended he was God when it suddenly lit up with his hand still on it.

Then, because it was a long time before Mom got out of the shower, he sat back down with Rona and me at the stack of boxes we'd been using for a kitchen table, and we did the crossword puzzle from the newspaper, though we weren't *really* doing it, because whenever he would read a clue—" 'Explore: eight-letter word beginning with P' "— Rona would yell out something like "Loolaboolapoopoo!" and he'd say, "Oh! Right! Why didn't I think of that? L, o, o, l . . ." etcetera.

After a while I gave up on the puzzle and just sat there, sneaking looks at Ron out of the corners of my eyes. I didn't know if he was handsome or not, but I liked the way he looked. He had dark brown hair and something else I really loved: dark whiskers, which were darker today than they'd been yesterday. Also, I really liked the smell of Ron, and I liked his big, thick hands and his square fingernails.

Mom finally came out of her room dressed in a good, normal outfit—jeans and a thick, soft, light blue woolen turtleneck—and when Ron saw her he said, "Wow, you look very nice." Then he said, "You know what I'd really like to do today? I'd like to help you get your bed from Marie and Bill's, and your table, and stop at home and get my toolbox and then go to the hardware store and get some stuff to fix your faucet leaks, and maybe something for that hole in the tile in the bathroom floor, and I'd like to get some smoke alarms and put locks on all your windows, too. Does that sound okay?"

By Sunday night, we were like an instant sponge family—one you dropped in water that popped up in one day. Ron had brought Mom's bed over, and he had also brought us an extra TV he had, one that was big enough to see from across the room, and a VCR, and a cart for them to roll around on. Mom and Ron were sitting on the bed. He had his arm around her, and she was leaning into him, and Rona and I were on the floor with our backs against the bed, and we were watching *Sleepless in Seattle*. Ron and Mom had cooked spaghetti for dinner, holding big glasses of red wine and smiling at each other as they opened cans of tomatoes and chopped green peppers, and Mom had looked a way I'd never seen her look before. I didn't even know the word for it. It wasn't *happy*—happy seemed like a thin, light word to me, flat and shiny, like balloon skin, with no deep places for important things to go.

But there in the kitchen, smiling in her fuzzy blue sweater, with the big, round, red glass in her hand, her movements weaving in and out and together and apart with Ron's as she went from the sink to the stove to the counter, the steam from the spaghetti water fogging the windows and closing us in in a nice way, she looked different than usual. She looked like she was all, completely there—like she was living in her actual life, right in the moment it was happening, and not already on her way to a different place, like the past, or the future, or la-la land.

—ɱ—

I succeeded in digging out a little grass today, which the animals have already eaten. I melted big pots of snow for water, as we seem to have lost the river. I ground some of the oxen food with a stone and made it into soup, which the children absolutely refused to eat. I have to admit, it was pretty putrid.

The rest of the day, I sat and watched the snow swirl. I thought. I tried to figure out if there were some choices hiding somewhere that I just couldn't see.

On Monday, Mom was home from work right on time. She sat down smiling at the kitchen table and said, "What do you girls want to have for dinner tonight? Roast chicken? Beef Stroganoff?" Then she said, "Didn't we have a nice time this weekend?"

"Yes!" said Rona. "When is Ron-Ron coming over again?"

"Oh," said Mom, "you like him, don't you? Maybe we'll see him tonight."

Ron had stayed over again on Sunday night. In the morning he'd kissed Mom good-bye and said, "I'll call you after work," then he'd driven us to school, and when we were getting out of the car, Rona had said, "Bye-bye, Daddy-Ron."

"Are you and Ron going to get married?" Rona asked Mom.

Mom made a little laughing sound. "You silly! That's not how it works! You have to get to know each other first!"

"And then?" said Rona.

Mom shook her head. "Honey, we just started seeing each other. You never know what's going to happen." But somehow the sound in her voice didn't match the look in her eyes, and she didn't seem exactly the same as she had yesterday. She seemed like someone who wanted to jump out of time and into the next place, and I wished Ron would hurry up and call.

Half an hour later, Mom was still sitting in the same spot. She had a magazine, and she was opening it and shutting it, looking around the kitchen, rearranging the salt and pepper shakers on the table. "So, chicken, I guess," she said, but she kept sitting there, like maybe the chicken was going to walk in the door.

"Well," Mom said a while after that. "I don't know, I don't really feel like going to the store. Justine, do we have anything here that we can have for dinner?"

At six o'clock the phone rang. Even though it was sitting there right in front of her, Mom just looked at it while it rang three and a half times, then she picked it up and said slowly, as if she had just woken up, "Hello?" Then her face relaxed, and she smiled and settled back in her chair, and her voice got low and curvy, like she was talking to someone she had a nice secret with, and I knew it was Ron.

"Yes," Mom was saying, "I had a fine day. A very nice day, actually"—and her voice got lower—"I had a lot of very nice things to think about while I pitted olives and sliced onions and made three hundred lobster raviolis. . . ."

"No, nothing," she said. "Just sitting around mulling over what to have for dinner." I waited for her to invite him. "Oh," she said, acting like whatever he had just said had surprised her, "would you like to . . . ? Sure. . . . We could do that—we haven't started anything yet.

"Whenever. Whenever you'd like to. There's no hurry. We'll just be here."

When she said good-bye to Ron, her voice was like waves of honey pouring out of a jar; it was like a comb with big, wide teeth smoothing over your head. The second she hung up, though, something weird happened—you could see her body sort of contract with relief, like a big breath exhaling for so long that it almost ended in a contortion, a fist twisting and squeezing her heart. I didn't know what I had just seen—why she had sighed that long sigh of relief when nothing bad had even just happened.

"Okay, get dressed, you two," was all she said, though. "Ron's taking us out to dinner."

* * *

We went to the Golden Phoenix for dinner and had a fun time— our drinks had little sticks with fake fruit on the ends sticking out of them, and of course Rona ordered the pu-pu platter because she thought the name was so hilarious, and she and I had mu-shu, and for once my pancake didn't break. Ron told stories that made Mom laugh the whole way through dinner, though maybe you had to be a grownup to get why they were so funny: "I come from the most normal family in the world," was one thing he said, "In fact, it was so normal it really kind of screwed me up," and Mom practically cried with laughter at that.

At the end of it, when we were in the car, Ron said, "Uh-oh, when's your bedtime, guys?"

"Ten million o'clock," said Rona.

"Nine-thirty," I said.

"Yikes," said Ron, and when we got to our house he looked at Mom and said, "Well? I guess I should let you guys get to bed on a school night, huh?"

"Oh," Mom said, "you can come in if you *want* to. I can make coffee or something."

"Actually, I have a few things I need to finish up for an early meeting tomorrow anyway," he said. "I goofed off so much this weekend, I got kind of behind. It'd probably be better for me to just buckle down. But I really, really hope I get to see you tomorrow. And every other day this week, too, actually." He leaned over and kissed Mom on the lips, then he turned to us and said, "Good-bye, ladies." Then he kissed Mom again, on the cheek this time, and said, "Bye," to her, but when we got out of the car, the look on Mom's face was all wrong.

When we got in the house, Mom went to the kitchen table and sat down. So I got Rona ready for bed and read her a story even though it was already past her bedtime, and as I was leaning down to kiss her forehead, Rona said, "Justine?"

"What?"

"I love Ron."

"Yeah, he's nice," I said. But deep in the back of my brain, I wished she hadn't said it.

Mom was still in the kitchen when I left Rona's room. "What are you doing?" I asked.

"Nothing," she said.

"Well, are you just going to sit there all night?" I said.

"No," she said.

"What's wrong?" I asked.

"Nothing," she said. Then she said, "Do you think Ron likes me?"

"*Duh,*" I said, and she smiled a little bit.

"Yeah, it seems like he does. How weird, huh?"

"No," I answered, but that wasn't the complete truth.

"Do you think he had fun tonight?"

I wondered why grown-ups were so weird. Anyone could see that everyone had fun tonight. We went to a restaurant, we ate, we laughed, and we had fun—there wasn't really any other way to look at it.

"He's really a wonderful guy," Mom said. "Do you think? Do you think he could possibly be as great as he seems?"

"I don't know," I said. It was a weird question, and I didn't want to be asked it. "I'm going to bed."

"Okay," she said, then she said, "Good night." Then she said, "Do you *really* think he likes me?"

In the middle of the night, I woke up—either I heard a noise or I had a feeling in my sleep—and I went to Mom's room. Her bed was empty. I looked out the window and the car was gone. I looked around, but there were no notes. I wondered if she had gone to Ron's, and I went and got the phone and stood there with it in my hand for a minute, trying to tell myself it was probably okay to call him; but I knew it wasn't. It was three-thirteen A.M.

I stayed up waiting till she came home. I sat in the corner of her bed, with my arms around my knees and my back against the wall, so I wouldn't fall asleep. I didn't even turn on the TV. I just sat there and stared at the wall on the opposite side of the room, trying to see patterns on it—anything: shapes or shadows or individual molecules of darkness—but I couldn't. The wall was flat, dark, empty. Every once in a while I'd think I could see something—just the start of a shape—

the molecules of darkness massing toward each other in a knot, about to make themselves into something I could make out, something with a meaning, but then I'd blink and realize there was nothing there.

Finally, around four-thirty, Mom walked in the door. She walked over to her bed and stood there, slowly nudging her shoes off with her feet, unbuttoning her coat. She jumped and gasped when she saw me.

"Oh, my God, you scared me!" she whispered. "What are you doing up?"

"Where were you?" I said.

"Nowhere."

"Why did you go out?"

"No reason," she said.

"Well, what were you doing?" I asked.

"Nothing," she said.

"Did you go to Ron's?" I said.

She looked at me weirdly then. "No," she said. "Why do you ask that?"

Then her face got a worried look, and I suddenly saw something: I saw the power she had, to whip up problems out of thin air. I could see it, even though nothing was moving—it was like her brain, going over and over and over a thought, started to stir up problem particles, and around her the air started to thicken in clots, and every clot was a problem getting bigger: Maybe I'm not really Ron's type, and he's too nice to tell me. Maybe there's someone else he's more interested in than me. Maybe he thought he liked me more than it turns out he really does.

Those were some of the things she said, then she'd look at me, like, What did I think of that? "Maybe everything's happening too fast for him," she said. "Maybe he decided he's not all that attracted to me." I lay down on her bed and shut my eyes. "I mean, if he's so wonderful, doesn't there *have* to be someone else in the picture? Like someone he works with? Or an ex-girlfriend somewhere?"

When I opened my eyes again, I was still in Mom's bed. The clock said 9:10. School started at eight-fifteen. Rona was standing at the side of the bed, shaking my knee, saying, "Justine, Justine." Mom was at the end of the bed, in the same place she'd been when I fell asleep, sitting and staring as if she didn't see Rona.

"Can you get dressed by yourself?" I asked Rona, then I got up to make breakfast.

"Mama, help me," she said in baby talk, but Mom didn't move, and surprisingly, Rona just left and went in her room. When she came out she was wearing an orange-and-black Halloween turtleneck, a brown skirt, green corduroy pants underneath the skirt, and a red zip-up sweatshirt.

"Nice outfit," I said.

"Thanks," she said.

After we had eaten breakfast, I said to Mom, "Can you drive us to school now?" She was still dressed from the night before, so she didn't need to do anything to get ready. "And write us a note for being late." It was ten o'clock.

"Mom?" I said.

"What?" she said.

"Will you drive us to school?"

"Oh," she said.

"Don't you have to go to work anyway?" I said.

"Should we take a taxicab to school?" I asked after another little while had gone by.

But then she shook her head slowly. "No," she said. "No, I'll take you. Let me just get ready and I'll take you."

It was one o'clock when we finally left for school. Mom wandered around in her towel for a long time after her shower.

"Can we go soon?" I said.

"Mm-hmm," she said. Then she said, "Can you girls just leave me alone a few secs—I need to . . ." But she didn't say what she needed to do.

After about forty-five more minutes, I peeked out of my room to see if Mom had maybe just forgotten about taking us to school. She was sitting on her bed, still in her towel. She had out her red book, which I hadn't seen in a while and I didn't want to be seeing now; and she was writing something.

"Mom . . . ," I said, but she said, "Just a minute, just a minute. Really, honey. I'll be ready in just a minute."

* * *

We never did make it to school that day. When I peeked in at Mom for the fourth time, around twelve forty-five, she wasn't even doing anything—she was just sitting on her bed with her red book and her pens and paper and X-Acto knife near her, staring.

"Will you take us now?" I asked.

"Okay," she said. "Go out to the car, I'll be out in a second."

"This isn't the way to school," I said about twenty minutes later. We were driving up a winding road through the woods.

"Do you really want to go to school?" she said.

"*Yes!*" I said.

"It's kind of late, though."

"We can't just skip school," I said.

"Okay," she said. Then she said, "I just want to stop one place, though. It's on the way."

"Where are we?" I asked when Mom stopped the car in front of a house. I knew, though.

"Nowhere," said Mom.

"It sure looks like somewhere," Rona said.

"It doesn't look like anyone's there," Mom said.

"Anyone like who?" I asked.

"Where do you think he is?" Mom said.

"Who? Ron? Is it Ron? Is it Ron?" said Rona.

"Could he be . . . let's see . . . possibly . . . at work?" I said totally sarcastically.

"Hmm," said Mom.

"What are we doing here?" I asked.

"Oh," she said. "I just want to drop something off." Then she took a folded piece of paper out of her red book, and a gold pen out of her purse, and she wrote something on the outside of the folded paper that I couldn't read. Then she put the paper into a red-and-gold-flecked envelope she had made herself, got out of the car, and went and put the envelope in the mailbox.

Ron called at six, just like he had the day before. "Hey, Justine!" he said, then his voice got a little weird. "Can I talk to your mother?"

I wondered what she had put inside the red envelope to make him sound that way, but listening to her side of the conversation, I couldn't tell. It was just, "Mm-hmm, no, no, no, nothing like that, it's just, well, I don't know. It's just me being stupid, I guess. I'm sorry. . . . No, no, no, everything's fine. Really. . . . No, no, I guess not. . . . Okay."

Then I heard her say, "Nothing, what are you doing tonight? Would you like to come over for dinner? I'll cook," and I was glad that the look on her face couldn't go over the phone when she said, "Oh! Okay! No, no, no, no, no! That's fine—you do what you need to do; I understand." Then she said, "Tomorrow? Yes, that would be nice," and she smiled a big fake smile, I guess to get her voice to come out right when she said, "Okay, have a good meeting and I'll talk to you tomorrow."

It is still snowing. We will prepare to spend the winter here. I don't know what else to do.

I chopped wood all week and have built us a shelter. It's a little rickety, and snow sifts in through the roof, but it's better than nothing. Also, I built a platform for the fire out of thin logs and branches; otherwise the fire quickly melts the snow beneath it and starts to sink away.

The children and I have moved into the shelter. Amethyst, though, insists on staying in the wagon. I'm afraid she's going to freeze in there, but she refuses to come out.

Tomorrow I will start shoveling a little corral for the animals.

THE LORIS

I felt sorry for Ron before we even opened the door the next night and found him, smiling, on the other side of it, thinking he was just picking up where he'd left off two days ago. So much had happened between him and Mom in the past few days, and he didn't have a clue about any of it.

"Oh," Mom had said when she hung up the phone the night before.

"What's the matter?" I asked.

"Nothing," she answered, looking miserable.

"Well, what did he say?"

"He said there's a city council meeting he has to go to. They're discussing a proposal to buy wind power for the city buildings or something."

"But that's okay, right?" I asked.

"Of course it's all right!" said Mom. "I just met him! I don't *own* him! We're not a couple. He can do what he wants!"

After about fifteen minutes, though, she called Marie, whom she hadn't talked to since the day Rona and I got lost, and after she'd lied about the reason for calling being that she wanted to get the recipe for Marie's putrid whole-wheat cinnamon rolls, she said, "Can I ask you a question about Ron?" and it sounded like Marie was telling her a long story in answer to her question: "Who was his last girlfriend? Do you know her? Does she live around here?"

She had the weirdest look on her face when she hung up—almost like fear.

"I was right," she said. "He does have one. Her name is Christina."

That was another thing poor Ron didn't know, as he stood smiling at our door with his bottle of wine and his bag of groceries, looking like he wanted me and Rona to get out of the way so he could give Mom a kiss hello—Christina had been at our house all day. Not the real Christina. When Rona and I came in from school, Mom was in her sweats, and it didn't look like she had been to work, and the first thing she said to me when I said, "Hi, Mom," was, "Christina's probably petite, don't you think? Marie described her as 'slight'—don't you think that usually means petite? I wonder if he has a preference for petite women. Probably. Most men do, depressingly."

Mom knew a lot about Christina—some things that Marie probably told her, like that her last name was Swenson. "She's probably Swedish," Mom said, "Oh God, she's probably beautiful, and six feet tall."

"But I thought you said she was petite," I pointed out.

"You know what I mean," Mom said in a despairing voice. "But you know what? I'm sure she's really nice.

"She does Feldenkrais bodywork," said Mom. "That must be very appealing to a man—bodywork. I'm sure she's really smart, too."

Some things I doubted Marie had told her. Like Christina's address and what her house looked like. Or the kind of car she drove. "She lives in Pelham," Mom said. "On Moose Ridge Road. It takes a special kind of person to live in a rural, isolated environment, don't you think? Someone with a lot of inner resources. She's probably very creative—her house has a nice, eclectic, funky look to it. And she drives an old Volvo station wagon. That's sort of a down-to-earth car, don't you think?"

One thing I'd noticed about men that was sort of sad but sweet was how they could sometimes just totally not notice things. Or it took them an incredibly long time, like that slow-motion animal in the zoo, the loris, whose cage I always stood in front of for a long time, fascinated, wondering why on earth there would ever be such an animal.

"You know," Mom said to Ron out of the blue about five minutes after he got to our house, "if only I had the inner resources to live out in a remote place, and garden, and have a dog, and just sort of be by myself more often, I think I'd be a better person."

"Huh," said Ron. "Really?" Then he smiled and said, "But what about when you ran out of chocolate ice cream at ten o'clock at night?"

"I really admire people who do bodywork for a living," she said a little while later. Ron was standing behind her in the kitchen, squeezing her shoulders. Ron's chicken piccata was just finishing cooking, and they had glasses of white wine tonight.

"You do? Why?" he asked.

"Oh, I don't know," she said. "It seems *real. Honest.*"

"Maybe," he said.

"You're very good at that, by the way," she said. "Where did you get so good at that?"

"I don't know," he said. "Maybe from tennis? Having strong wrists?"

Later, I heard Mom trying to give him some better clues. Rona and I had gone to bed and they were in the living room, watching basketball with the sound off.

"So, hey," Ron was saying in a voice I liked. "I know you probably can't take a vacation yet, since you just started. But maybe in the spring? Have you ever been to the Caribbean? Do you think you could get a week off and find someone to take care of the girls?"

"Can I ask you something?" Mom said.

"Sure," said Ron.

"What kind of qualities do you like best in a woman?"

"Best?" he said, sounding like he thought it was a weird question. "Uh. I don't know. Your qualities."

"My qualities?" Mom asked.

Ron laughed and said, "Fish much? Your qualities. Well . . . beautiful. Intelligent. Alive. Vulnerable."

"Hmm," Mom said. Then she said, "But I mean qualities like creative. Self-sufficient. Self-confident. Woodsy. Do you like things like that?"

"Woodsy?" Ron said, and he laughed again. "Um, I think I like that in a room freshener better than a woman."

Mom was silent then, and I said a little prayer, to no one, to help Ron understand. I could picture her starting to spiral down inside. You wouldn't see it unless you knew her.

"Well, in terms of physical type," she said in a quieter voice. "What do you like best?"

"Like you," he said. "I like women like you."

"But, do you prefer petite women?"

"Is that what you are?" he asked.

"No," said Mom.

"Well, no, then," said Ron. "I don't prefer petite women."

"Have you ever had a petite girlfriend?"

There was a silence then, and when Ron spoke again, his voice was different somehow. "I don't know, Colleen. Petite? Why are you asking this?"

"No reason," Mom said. "But, yeah, petite. Like, size four or under, if you ever bought her clothing."

"Well, then, yes, I guess I have had petite girlfriends."

"Like, all of them?" Mom said.

"Yeah," he said. "I used to keep them in a little box on the back porch. What's going on, Colleen?"

"Nothing," she said.

"Well, good," he said, trying to get back his other voice. "Then can we drop this line of questioning, because I feel like . . ." Then there was silence, or maybe some kissing sounds.

And then Mom talking again. "So, what were the most admirable qualities in some of your ex-girlfriends?"

"The quality of shutting up when they were being kissed," said Ron, and then there was definitely more kissing, and then Mom said, "But, like, of all of your ex-girlfriends, what was the—"

"Stop it!" said Ron. Mom didn't say anything. "I mean, I'm sorry, but can we please stop talking about my ex-girlfriends?"

"Okay," said Mom in a kind of small, hurt voice. "But can I ask, is there any *reason*?"

—⁓—

I tried to walk a little way today. The snow let up in the afternoon, and I thought I would just try to get to the little rise I could see in the distance, to see if I could see the road.

"You stay here," I told the children, wrapping them in blankets. "Don't

move. You mustn't leave the wagon no matter what, and I'll be back before you know it."

"But Mama," they said, frightened.

Amethyst lay huddled in the corner, completely out of it. "Keep an eye on her," I told Annabelle, and I handed her the baby. I gave them some food—I tried to tell them it was trail mix, but it was really just the last of the cornmeal crumbs, some dried coffee grounds I found in the bottom of the pot, and a few dried apple pieces that I'd been saving for a special occasion like Thanksgiving or Christmas, but who cared about the holidays now?

"You'll be fine," I told them. "I'll be back before you know it."

Which turned out to be the truth. I didn't get far. The tiny spark of hope I set out with quickly died as I sank to my hips in the snow. My feet burned with cold. My wet dress felt like it weighed a thousand pounds. And the little rise in the distance played a game of hide-and-seek with me. The closer I got to it, the flatter it got, until it was gone. Then it began snowing again, and I became worried that if I didn't turn back, the snow would cover my tracks and I wouldn't be able to find my way back to the children.

I turned around and followed my footprints, or I guess I should say bodyprints, back around a patch of trees and was surprised to see the wagon. All that effort and I hadn't even walked half a mile. I was completely exhausted. A tear trickled out of my eye, and I wiped it away and put a smile on my face. It is so hard sometimes, being strong for the children. I don't know how my own mother did it: I never saw her cry, not once. Not for one second, ever.

Tonight as I write this, I am filled with despair. I don't know how I will ever find the strength to go on.

Perhaps tomorrow I will try to fashion myself a pair of snowshoes.

In the morning, Ron was gone and Mom lay in her bed a long time after Rona and I had gotten up, saying, "Oh. Oh, God. Why am I so tired this morning? I'll get up in a minute, I promise," though she never did, so Rona and I missed school again that day.

Mom's work called, and she said, "I am *so, so* sorry—I'm running a little behind today, but I'll be in as soon as I can." Then she lay there another hour, saying, "You know, I don't know why I thought someone like Ron would even like someone like me. I mean, he's so together and self-motivated—of *course* he's going to like a certain kind of woman *not* like me," and, "It always gets so complicated—why is it always, always like that?" and, "Why can't it ever just stay like it is in the beginning?"; and I guess she was talking to me and also sort of not, because she just kept going even if I walked out of the room for a while.

Finally, after a few hours, Mom dragged herself out of bed and got dressed and left for work, except another hour after that, someone from the Peabody House Inn called and said, "Is Colleen there?" and when I said, "No, she's at work," he said, "Is *that right?*" When I said, "May I take a message?" he said, "Yes, will you tell her if she wants to keep her job, she'd better call Martin ASAP with a hell of a good excuse, and *maybe* I'll consider it."

Of course I should've guessed where Mom was. I don't know how she did it—maybe she went to Christina's house and just pretended to be someone strolling by, wanting to ask a question or two about her *amazing* garden; or maybe she followed her to the grocery store and asked her questions in the vegetable aisle; or maybe she called for some Feldenkrais bodywork, pretending to be someone with a pain.

"I met her," she said in a voice of doom when she walked in the door at four o'clock.

"Who?" I asked.

"*Christina*," she said.

"So?" I said, trying to pretend that that wasn't scary.

"She seems really, really wonderful," Mom said despairingly.

"How do you know?" I asked. "And anyway, so what?"

"Yeah, I guess," Mom said, then she said, "Oh! This is just so fucking *hard*. Every time. Why does this kind of thing always happen to me?" and when I said, "But what *happened?*" she gave me that look, like, If you don't understand, I can't explain it to you, and then she said, "I'm going to lie down for a little while."

We are almost completely out of provisions. I have made all the weird things I can think of—flour soup, onion skin tea, salt-and-pepper "pie"—

but I can't trick the children any longer into thinking there's anything left to eat. They cried after supper tonight—acorn-paste balls and fried baking soda.

This afternoon I lugged Thaddeus's gun around for a few hours, in wide circles around our wagon, but saw no animals except for a few crows, who taunted me and flew off when I raised the heavy gun and tried to aim at them. At one point I noticed blood in the snow and my spirits lifted, thinking perhaps there was a wounded animal nearby; then I realized the tracks were my own footprints, the blood was from my poor, numb, frostbitten feet.

Ron called that night, but Mom answered the phone, so I didn't get to talk to him. Not that I knew what I would say. Love was like math—there were some problems you just couldn't solve if you were a sixth-grader, unless you were some weird little genius, and who'd want to be?

Mom's voice had tears in it the whole time she was talking to him. "I just can't talk to you right now, Ron. . . . I don't know. . . . I just don't *know*—nothing's the matter. . . . I don't *know* what's the matter. . . . I don't *know* what I want. Well, I know what *I* want, but . . . Oh, I don't know what I'm saying. Maybe I just need some time to think. Maybe I need to be alone."

"Is Ron coming?" Rona asked as soon as Mom hung up.

"No," Mom said miserably.

Rona stuck out her lip. "Why?" she said.

"I don't know, sweetheart."

"You told him you wanted to be alone," I pointed out to her.

"I didn't," said Mom.

"I heard you."

"Well, that's not exactly what I meant," she said.

"But I want him to come," said Rona.

"I know, sweetheart," said Mom. She put her arm around Rona. "But maybe he just decided it was too complicated. With all of us. You know, most guys want something easy."

"You're crazy," I said. I didn't mean it to come out quite like that. But I just wanted it to stop—all the wrong things that were coming out of her mouth. Poor Rona was probably going to be confused permanently.

It was a bad mistake to say that, I saw too late. Mom's face froze, and then all the bones inside it started to melt. "Maybe," she said as the tears started to run out of her eyes. "Maybe I am. Maybe that's what the problem is. Maybe you're right," and Rona started to cry, too, but when Mom reached out for her she twisted away and yelled, "You're *all* crazy. You're crazy turdface poopbuckets!" and ran into her room and slammed the door.

———∞———

There is no more grass to be found. I am feeding the animals the seeds we brought to plant when we got to California, but those will be gone soon, too. I found a few bean skins in the bottom of a bag today and boiled them for dinner. The children are getting weak. I will have to do something soon.

Ron came to see us on the weekend. He called at twelve o'clock, and when I said, "Mom's not here," he said, "I know—she's working a wedding today, right? Stuffing twelve bushels of dates with goat cheese or something?"

"Yeah," I told him. At least that's where she'd said she was going.

"Well, good," he said. "Not that I don't want to see your mom," he added quickly, "but I was thinking maybe you and me and Rona could do something. Lunch?"

"Okay," I said.

"Do you think it would be okay with your mom?" he asked.

"Yes," I said.

"Do you think we should ask her?" he said.

"No," I said.

"Right," he said slowly, maybe trying to sound like he understood more than he did.

We had a nice time with Ron, though I had kind of a weird feeling the whole time. I felt like I missed him, even though he was sitting right across from me, eating a cheeseburger and making up knock-knock jokes with Rona. His knock-knock jokes were even worse than Rona's: "Knock-knock." "Who's there?" "Phil." "Phil who?" "Phil like another French fry?" he said, and he waved one at her face.

When he dropped us off, he said, "Well, maybe I'll see you guys this week."

"Tomorrow!" said Rona.

"Well, we'll see how—"

"Tuesday!" she said. "Tuesday's my birthday!"

"It is not," I said. "Her birthday's February twelfth."

But Ron said, "So, is it your unbirthday? What a coincidence: Tuesday's my unbirthday, too. Maybe I'll come by on Tuesday and we'll have a party," and Rona said, "Okay!"

—⁓⁓—

Something terrible has happened. I went out to the corral today to find that all the animals except Zack were gone. The snow fence I'd built was trampled down in one spot, and hoof holes led away into the deep snow. I followed the tracks for a while but had to turn back before I got far. They will probably starve to death out there. And if it doesn't stop snowing, I won't even be able to find their bodies.

Ron did come over on Tuesday, with a little cake from the Stop & Shop that said, "Happy Unbirthday, Xyzona." He'd called and left a message, which I watched Mom listen to, but when she answered the door, she acted surprised to see him.

"Ron!" she said with the brightest, phoniest smile, one he had definitely never seen before. "Come on in!"

All night Monday, Mom had spent lying on her bed wondering what Ron was doing and why he wasn't calling. But he *had* called— he'd called on Sunday night to ask Mom if she wanted to have dinner on Monday, and she'd said, "If you *want* to. But you don't sound like you really *want* to. I mean, it's okay if you want to just spend a little time on your own. . . . No—that's *not* what I'm trying to say. . . . No, no—oh, I don't know. But whatever you want, that's what I want. . . . Really, though? Because you really don't sound like you *want* to."

When he walked in with the cake, though, it was like that phone call never happened. He reminded me a little bit of my friend Andrew, from preschool—at the end of every day, Andrew and I would be in a big fight over who had used too many of the train tracks, or whose Hoppity Hop had bounced higher, but every morning, Andrew would squeal when he saw me and run over to me and give me a big hug.

I wanted everything to go back to normal between Mom and Ron, but I just knew, from a certain sound in Mom's voice as soon as she saw Ron, that it wouldn't. Her voice was bright and hard, like colored plastic, and so was her smile.

"How was your day?" she asked Ron.

"Fine," he said.

"And your night last night? Did you have a nice night?"

"Not particularly," Ron said.

"Oh, I'm sorry," Mom said. "Why not? What did you do?" Then she said, "Oh, well, you don't have to answer that."

"Nothing," said Ron. "I didn't do anything. Remember? I needed *time alone*. Not that I have any idea why."

After we ate the cake, Ron said, "Well," and looked at Mom, like, Now what?

"You probably have to go," said Mom. "And work or whatever."

"Well, I do have some work, as usual," he said. "I have clients coming early tomorrow from Boston, and I haven't finished preparing. But I can stay for a while."

"Well, whatever you want," said Mom in her bright voice.

"What do *you* want?" he said, and he stared at her and did some grown-up thing with his eyes that I didn't quite get.

"Whatever you do," said Mom.

"Oh, my *Lord*, Colleen," he said, and he started to sort of fake beat on his head with his hands. "You could drive a reasonable man around the bend, do you know that?" And, I could tell, he was completely surprised when he looked up and saw tears in her eyes.

"I'm sorry," Mom said in a terrible voice. "I'm sorry. I'm sorry. I'm . . ." and I wished so bad he would do what no one ever did with Mom—just put his arms around her and hold her the way Rona needed holding sometimes, like when she was having a massive shit-fit in the Kmart, but he didn't. He smiled a smile that, you could tell, on another guy might be pre-yelling, and he said, "I really can't deal with this." He stood there shaking his head for a minute, before he picked up his coat and headed for the door. "I'll call you tomorrow, okay?" he said to Mom. "Maybe we can straighten things out then." Then he tipped an imaginary hat to me and Rona and went out the door.

—m—

I killed Zack today. He was suffering anyway, I told myself as I looked into his big, sad brown eyes and pulled the trigger, but I still felt awful. So now we will have food for a while, though if we live till the snow melts, we'll have to walk to California.

Tomorrow I will butcher him; I'm going to save his hide, too, to spread over the roof of the shelter to keep the snow from coming in. I'm not exactly sure how to get it off, but I suppose I am about to learn.

Have you ever skinned an ox? Oh my God.

Mom didn't get out of bed till noon the next day.

"I can't," she said when I asked her if she was going to take us to school. "I just can't, Justine."

When Martin, her boss, called, I told him what she'd told me to say: "She's on her way."

"Is she," he said, making it not a question at all.

"Uh-huh," I lied.

"Well, I really hope that's true," Martin said, and he hung up on me.

Mom lay there, limp and lifeless, staring at the ceiling, for about three hours. Then suddenly she jumped out of bed and said, "I can*not* spend my life just lying in bed, mooning over some *guy*!" I liked the way that sounded, of course, and I watched her back as she headed for the shower, imagining that the person who'd said that really lived in our life.

"Are you taking us to school?" I asked after she had gotten out of the shower and was getting dressed.

"Maybe in a little while," she said. "Okay?" and I didn't even bother to say sarcastically, "Oh, okay. How about, like, at four o'clock?"

"Where are you going?" I asked when she headed for the door.

"Are you going to the grocery store?" but she just said, "Nowhere. See you in a bit, okay?"

I am trying to make a pair of snowshoes from bent branches and dried strips of Zack's skin. I'm not exactly sure where I'd walk if I could, but just doing anything seems better than sitting in one spot and starving to death.

The children are happier now that their stomachs are full. Amethyst, though, refuses the meat. "I just really, really don't like oxen meat," she said when I took her a plate.

"That's ridiculous," I told her. "You're starving."

But she just said, "Oh, no," trying to sound light; then she crawled on her hands and knees back to her bedroll and collapsed, pulled the blankets up to her eyes.

When Mom walked in the door at five o'clock, she had someone with her.

"This is my friend Christina!" she said to me and Rona. "Christina, these are my girls!"

"Hi," Christina said to us. She looked a little like she wasn't quite sure why she was here.

"Christina does bodywork!" said Mom. "She's like a magician with your body—she can fix all your creaks and cracks! And she works in a beautiful studio in her house in the woods!"

"She also does fung shway!" Mom said. "Isn't that exciting? She's going to fung shway our house! Christina, can I get you some tea?" It was almost dark in the kitchen, but instead of turning on the lights, Mom said, "Justine, could you find us some candles?

"I just love candlelight," she told Christina. "Well, I noticed you use candles in your bodywork studio; you must feel the same way."

When I had lit the candles, Mom said, "Why don't you girls go find something to do?"

"Are we having dinner tonight?" I said.

"Of course we're having dinner!" she said.

"Well, should I start it or something?"

"In a while," she said. "Now go do kid things"—she smiled at

Christina—"so we can have grown-up talk while we sit and drink our tea."

Mom did most of the talking, though. I listened to them from my room. "I'm so glad I met you!" Mom said. "I haven't made any friends yet, in Massachusetts—you know, I just work all the time, and spend time with my girls. Well, what do you spend your time doing? Do you go out a lot? Do you have a lot of friends?

"So how long exactly *have* you lived in . . . is it Pelham?" Mom asked. "And how did you end up there? Have you *always* lived alone up there?

"Do you date?" asked Mom. Then she said, "I'm sorry, that's probably too personal. But, I don't know, I'm just wondering, what sort of place is this for a single woman? Have you been single long?"

When Ron showed up, it wasn't exactly the best moment of anyone's life. I got to the door first. "He-e-ey, Justine," he said, but there was something missing from his voice. He didn't sound kidlike anymore. He sounded tired and like everything was so complicated, just like a regular grown-up.

"Hi," I said.

"Is your mom around?"

"Um," I said. "Sort of." Which was lame: you could hear her voice from the kitchen.

"I don't know," she was saying, "I just really admire that you've built a whole business all on your own, and that you live out there in that wonderful, really very *spiritual* spot you've created for yourself. And you seem so *strong* and confident. I really admire that."

Christina laughed. "So, you want to start a fan club?"

Ron tilted his head and looked at me with the weirdest expression on his face.

"She has a friend over," I said lamely.

"I don't know how strong I am," Christina said. "I mean, I was a basket case for a year and a half after my boyfriend and I broke up. I did get that whole garden put in, though, and the tilework in the kitchen. And I got my business off the ground. So, let's just say I made the most of a bad situation."

"Bad situation?" said Mom. "Oh, I'm sorry. How long ago was that?" she said. "When you and your boyfriend broke up?"

Ron went to the kitchen door, opened it, and walked in. He stood there looking at Mom and Christina, and I waited for the yelling to start. When he spoke, though, he was quiet.

"What is this?" he said. I could see Mom from where I stood.

"Ron!" said Mom, smiling at him. "This is my new friend—"

"I know Christina," Ron said.

"You're kidding!" said Mom. "You two know each other?" No one said anything. "That is such a huge coincidence, considering you're the only two people I've met in Massachusetts, basically. So, Ron, then you know all about Christina's new business, and her wonderful house, and what a fascinating person she is? I went in for some bodywork, and suddenly I was learning all about the zen of building a stone fence. And Christina's agreed to look at our house and help me do some fung shway on it!"

Ron stood there, kind of shaking his head, then he said, "I'm sorry, but this is just a little bit too weird for me."

"Why?" Mom said, her eyes wide and sort of Shirley Temple–ish.

"Ron's my ex-boyfriend," Christina said. "Didn't Marie tell you?"

"Marie?" said Mom.

"She told me you'd been asking a lot of questions about me." It took Mom a minute to answer that.

"Oh," she said, "well, Marie knows so many people in the whole-living and wellness community, when I found your name in *Many Hands*, I asked if she'd heard of you."

"Mm-hmm," said Christina as if she might not believe that.

"You know what?" Ron said then. "It might be because I'm a guy, and I don't really understand what's happening right now, but I have to tell you: This is freaking me the fuck out. So I'm just going to leave now. Colleen, call me if you want. Christina . . . well, you know, nice to see you, I guess.

"Justine," he said as he turned toward me, but I could tell he didn't have anything special to say to me. He was just saying my name because he liked me. Rona had come running out of her room when she heard the sound of his voice, and he said her name, too, then he smiled and pointed at her and went, "Tch," and he did the same thing to me, and I looked at Rona and wondered if she knew, too, it was his way of saying good-bye.

As soon as Christina left, Mom's big, fake smile came off her face.

"What do you think he meant?" she asked me. " 'Call me if you want'?" There was kind of a desperate sound to her voice. "Justine," she said, "what do you think he meant? 'Call me if you want'? Do you think that means he wants me to? Or that he doesn't care if I do or I don't? Do you think he meant *tonight*, or just sometime in the future?"

Then she said, "You have to make supper for you and your sister tonight, can you do that?" and she just left all the tea stuff on the table and went and curled in a ball on her bed. I went and stood over her a minute.

"What's the matter with you?" I said.

"That woman!" Mom said, and suddenly she started crying. "She just has it all together, and I will *never* have it all together like that!" At the sound of Mom crying, Rona came out of her room, but she didn't say, "Mom, stop crying," like she usually did, or get on the bed and try to pull Mom's face into a smiling shape; she just stood next to me, watching.

"How can someone like Ron *ever* like me when he used to be with someone like that?!" Mom cried.

But I didn't say what I knew I was supposed to: "But Ron likes you! He really likes you a lot!" because even though it was true, I also knew it didn't matter. Because there were other things more true, I could see. It didn't matter if the greatest, smartest, nicest, richest guy in the world was in love with Mom, because the guy wasn't the problem. Mom was the problem. Mom was the whole problem, all by herself. Something nice had started to happen to us, and she had wrecked it, and I didn't have any idea why.

It started snowing again sometime in the night. It snowed all day, and is snowing still, this evening, huge flakes as big as lace doilies. It's snowing too hard to make a fire. The children huddle against me inside the shelter,

wrapped in blankets. The poor baby looks at me like she was so right about everything. I touch her cheek, sing to her, tickle under her chin to try to reassure her, but it doesn't seem to be working. She lies so still, sometimes I can't even tell if her heart is beating.

If she dies here, I won't even be able to dig her a grave—the ground is frozen hard as granite.

SNOW

As soon as I got to school the next day, Ms. Taylor called me to her desk and said, "Do you have an excusal note for yesterday, Tuesday, last Thursday, and last Friday?"

"No," I said. She looked at me, and I looked at her.

"Were you sick?" she asked.

"No," I told her.

"Justine . . . ," she said, and it was like she was trying to stare right into me. "Is there something going on at home that it would help me to know about?"

I wondered how it could possibly help Ms. Taylor to know about the things that went on in our life.

"No," I said.

Later that day, she called me up again. She had my diary on her desk. For a second I thought maybe she was going to tell me how much she liked it, even though I had broken the rules.

"Justine," she said, tilting her head and giving me a strange look. "Are you *sure* everything's all right?"

"Yes," I said.

"Everything's going all right with your adjustment to your new home?" I wondered what she pictured when she said "new home."

"I guess," I said.

"How's your father?"

"My father?"

"There's not anything wrong with him, is there? Health problems, or anything like that?"

"Not that I know of," I said.

"And your mother?"

"She's allergic to shrimp," I said.

Ms. Taylor sighed. "Well, I just ask because . . . there are some very interesting things in here." She looked at me like I was supposed to say something.

"Thank you," I said. Ms. Taylor was a bottomless container of sighs that day.

"I would say some *odd* things, really," she said, and she tilted her head at me.

"It's all true," I said. I don't know why I said it. The words were sort of like a mysterious bird that just flew in and lighted on my shoulder for a second, then flapped away.

"What's true?" Ms. Taylor said.

"The story of Zebulina Walker. She was a real person."

I could tell she didn't believe me. "She was my relative," I said. "She was my great-great-great-grandmother and her parents were from Scotland and she went across the country alone with her children in a wagon and got caught in a snowstorm and they all . . ." I suddenly realized something: If she was my grandmother, they couldn't all die in the mountains. Ms. Taylor was looking at me as if she didn't believe me, and it suddenly made me so mad. Why was she so sure I didn't have an ancestor who did those things?

"So what happened to her?" Ms. Taylor asked.

"That's for me to know and you to find out," is what I said.

—— ⁓⁓ ——

It is getting harder and harder to find firewood. I've chopped down all the trees close by. The children shiver and shake so much I'm afraid they're going to crack their teeth. Yesterday I walked a long way on my bloody feet and chopped down a big tree. It took all morning, and almost all of my strength, and I forgot to think of this: When it fell, it buried itself so deep in the snow that it was impossible to get out. I tried for a while, but it was no use. Finally I dragged myself back to the wagon, emptied everything out of my grandmother's carved oak chest and pulled it out and chopped it into pieces. I threw it on the fire and it made a nice flame all evening. I'm not sure what I'm going to do about firewood tomorrow, though.

I was starting to get pretty worried about Rona. It was like she was turning into a little Mom—she had started to spend a lot of time in her room alone, and if I peeked in to check on her, she usually wouldn't be doing anything—she'd just be sitting there, sucking her thumb and staring, or holding a book, closed, on her lap, or lying on her side in a ball, and sometimes tears would be falling out of her eyes. One day when I went to get her after school, her teacher said, "Can I talk to you?" and told me that Rona had sat in her seat crying silently all day, and did I think I could get my mother to come in so the teacher could talk to her.

That night, when I went in Rona's room to tell her to get ready for bed, she was sitting on her bed with a drawing pad and a pen, and she was making circles on the paper—deep, black, angry ones, over and over on top of each other.

"What's that a drawing of?" I asked.

"Nothing!" she said, and she drew the next circles even harder, so that the pen ripped through the paper.

"What's the matter?" I asked her, but all she would say was, "Nothing." But a little later, when we were watching TV on my bed, suddenly she took her thumb out of her mouth and said, "O-o-h," sadly, and started to cry.

"Justine," she moaned when she could catch a breath, "why doesn't he come back?"

"Well," I said, but I had no way to explain it. "Grown-ups are just weird. He and Mom just didn't really get along, I guess."

"But I got along!" she wailed, and she cried for another half an hour.

The snow has reached a depth of over ten feet. I had to start burning the wood from the shelter for the fire, so now we are moved back into the wagon.

It's the most aggravating thing, though: Amethyst has moved out. She sits outside, wrapped in a blanket and shivering next to the fire all day long, and at night she lies down next to the embers.

We are living on a steady diet of oxen meat, except for the baby, who eats nothing. There's not a drop of milk left in my flat, shriveled breasts, and she clamps her mouth tight when I try to give her prechewed oxen jerky. The only thing she'll let me give her is snow—an icy mouthful from my hand now and then.

On Wednesday, after school, when Rona and I were almost to the bus stop, I realized something. "Where's your egg?" I asked.

"Nowhere," she said.

"You took it to school today," I said.

"I did not," she said.

"You did too. What did you do with it?"

"Nothing," she said. Then she said, "*N-o-t-h-i-n-g—that's what you mean to me*, nothing, *absolutely* nothing!—*boom, boom, boom!*"

It was a cheer that Mom had taught me in California when I'd found her yearbook with the cheerleader pictures in it, and I'd taught it to Rona. Rona had loved that cheer as soon as she heard it—she and her best friend from preschool, Ariel, had gone around saying it to each other all the time, and shrieking with laughter, because to a little kid, I guess, telling somebody else they didn't exist was, like, the worst insult you could give.

"Go get it," I said. Not that I cared about the stupid egg. It was just that, I knew, if she really had left it at school, ten minutes after we got home, she would probably have a shit-fit about it, and if Mom was still home crying, too, I didn't know if I would be able to take it.

"Uh-uh-uh!" she sang. I put my hand in a crab claw around her neck and turned her around and made her walk back toward the building.

"*Ow!*" she screamed. "Justine, stop! You're hurting me! I can't breathe! I can't breathe!" All the little kids were staring at us.

"Where is it?" I said when we were back in her classroom.

"Nowhere," she said.

"Is it in your desk?"

"No, and it's not in the garbage can in the back, either."

We went to the garbage can, and I found the mini–shopping bag and let go of Rona's neck. "Why'd you throw it away?" I asked.

"That's for me to find out," she said.

On the way back out to the bus, she said, "I want it."

"No," I said.

"Oh," she moaned. "Eggy-eggy, please? Justine? I'm sorry, egg. Oh, I want it, please?" When I finally gave it to her, she said, "Oh, thank you," and waited about four seconds. Then she stuck her hand in the bag, took out the egg, and threw it against the ground as hard as she could.

I'd forgotten that I'd switched Rona's egg in secret, a few weeks before, when we were still at Marie's. I didn't know how long eggs lasted, but I'd started to worry that it would go rotten, which would be a disaster. I thought maybe a hard-boiled one would last longer.

Now, she watched the egg as it cracked and rolled and came to rest in some dirt next to the sidewalk—broken, dirty, slightly out of shape, but still an egg. Rona stared like she didn't even know what she was seeing.

"It's not even real," she said in a terrible voice. Then she surprised me. She didn't burst into tears. She didn't go over and stomp on the egg. She didn't sit down on the ground and refuse to move. She just looked at it one more time before she turned her head and walked away, as if she were headed for a different part of her life.

Since we have no oxen, I don't suppose we'll need the wagon after the snow melts. I took the ax and chopped off a little piece of the back of the wagon box for firewood this morning.

I tried to walk a little way on my snowshoes today, but the oxen-skin cords quickly tore away from the wood. I was out of sight of the children, so I sat down in the snow and cried a little. It was strange how quickly that got boring, though. There are things my body seems to know: It would kill for a bowl of strawberries and cream, a hot potato, a glass of milk. It's dying to feed the baby. But it doesn't really want to cry, I guess.

After a few minutes I got up and made my way back to camp.

"How did the snowshoes work?" the children asked eagerly. I hid them behind my back and gave them the best smile I could.

"Stupendously," I said. "Now I just have to make a few improvements." I went to work building up the fire so I could warm my fingers and get to work.

At nine o'clock on Thursday morning, the phone rang. I was in the middle of making eggless French toast with our last piece of bread. We didn't have any syrup, either. Mom hadn't gotten out of bed yet. Maybe we would make it to school that day and maybe not.

I answered the phone, and then I went in Mom's room and said, "Mom, phone." She didn't move. "It's Martin," I told her. "He said if you don't go in today, you're fired." I tried to hand her the phone, but she didn't put her hand out. I laid the phone in front of her mouth and went back into the kitchen.

After a little while, I heard her moving around, and when I peeked in, I could see she was actually dressed. "Oh," she said when she saw me. "I can't do this."

"Mom," I said when she had her hand on the doorknob, "you need to go to the grocery store, too."

"Oh, my God, Justine," she said, "I can't. I just can't."

"But we're out of food," I said. "We need milk and bread and eggs and peanut butter."

"Oh, God," she said, and she let herself out the door.

She came back a pretty short time later. She opened the door and handed me a plastic grocery bag with what looked like her last ounce of strength. Then she covered her face with her hands and stood there, her body rocking slightly.

"Did you get fired?" I asked, but she didn't answer. I looked in the bag. All it had in it was a huge package of chicken legs and a box of rice. "Should I make this?" I said. She didn't answer. "I don't know how to cook chicken," I said.

Mom took her hands away from her face.

"Can you girls just . . . ," she said, but she didn't say what she wanted us to do. Disappear, maybe, I thought. Or maybe grow up. Then she lay down on her bed and said, "I needed a better-paying job, anyway," and she turned over, and after a few minutes it really looked like she was asleep.

Amethyst is sinking. When I came out this morning, I was shocked to see her up to her shoulders in the snow. But when I got close I could see what had happened: The fire had melted the snow beneath it and around it, including the spot where Amethyst sat.

"Climb out," I said.

But she just said, "No."

"Come on," I said.

"You can't make me," she said.

I pondered that a minute. It was probably true.

"Suit yourself," I said. As if I were giving her a choice, one she hadn't already taken.

Amethyst's head has disappeared. The children peer over the edge of the pit and look at her, but she won't talk to any of us anymore.

"What's wrong with her, Mama?" they ask.

"She's deranged from hunger," I told them. Every day I throw her down a little oxen steak or some jerky, but I have no idea whether or not she eats it.

Annabelle noticed yesterday that our pile of oxen meat doesn't look that big anymore. "Mama," she said with an awful look on her face, "the meat's almost gone."

"I know," I said. I didn't have any lies left to tell her. "But don't worry. I'll think of something."

Saturday morning when I woke up, Rona was standing over me.

"FYI," she said, and she pointed toward the window.

I could see from where I lay that thick snow was falling. I'd thought a lot about how exciting it would be when the first fat, white flakes started to swirl through the air. It had been about five years since we saw snow—Rona probably didn't even remember it. But today, as I lay there, I didn't feel anything. It didn't seem like Rona did, either—she just went to the window and stood there without moving for a few minutes, then she turned and walked out of my room. I wondered what was wrong with us. Everybody knows kids love snow.

———m———

The wagon is getting smaller and smaller. I spend all day now trying to keep the children from worrying. Today I made up a story—about a boy and a girl stuck on a desert isle in the middle of the ocean. The hungry waves are eating the island inch by inch.

"But they know what to do!" cried Ezekiel before I could get to the part I had made up, about a ship of good sailors happening upon the isle and rescuing them.

"They get buckets and wheelbarrows, and they go to the middle of the island, where there's plenty of sand, and they fill up the buckets and take the sand to the edges of the island and spread it around till the island's big again."

"But won't they run out of sand?" I asked. "What then?"

"They can't!" said Ezekiel. "The sand goes all the way to the middle of the earth."

Annabelle nodded. "It goes all the way to China," she said.

"If it starts to run out, it'll make itself into more," said Ezekiel.

Children have so much optimism. And for a moment, looking at the little pile of firewood I had chopped that morning, I felt optimistic too. Though there was no reason. There are hardly any trees left in sight, and I can't chop down the whole wagon with winter coming on.

Though I suppose I could try building us an igloo. An igloo might actually be a good idea.

Monday it was still snowing. I shook Mom's shoulder a long time before she rolled over and opened her eyes and groaned. She had never even gotten out of bed the day before.

"Will you take us to school?" I said.

"Sure," she said, then she closed her eyes. When I came back from getting dressed, she was still lying there.

"Mom," I said.

"What?"

"Will you take us to school?"

"Sure," she said. "Why don't you guys go wait in the car."

"But you're not even out of bed," I said. Slowly she sat up and put her feet on the floor.

"I'm up," she said. "I'm up. I'll just throw on some jeans and a coat and meet you in a minute. Go."

Rona and I sat in the car for fifteen minutes waiting for her to come out. The snow had covered all the windows, and I couldn't find a scraper, and it was weird, sitting inside the gray shell of snow. You could be anywhere—under the earth, floating in space; for a second I let myself imagine that I had no idea what was outside—that I had never seen the world or imagined it existed. Maybe this was what it was like waiting to be born.

Or maybe Rona and I were the only two people left in the world, I suddenly imagined; maybe here, inside our thick-shelled snow egg, was the one small, disappearing warm spot left in the world, and everything else had turned to the ice age. I wonder if I gave Rona ESP right then, because she suddenly said, "I want to get out," and shoved open the door, which was frozen shut. "She's never coming," Rona said, and we both knew she was right. She wasn't coming, and she wasn't even looking for us. When we got back in the house, there she was, under the covers, curled toward the wall.

—m—

Every day I go and look down into the hole. "Please come out," I tell Amethyst. She is ten feet down now. "Stand out of the way," I say, and I throw down some meat and a few pieces of firewood. It uses up the firewood faster to have two fires, but I have no choice—I can't let her freeze to death. I had the children dig steps in the side of the hole so she could climb out, but she just sits, staring at her meager fire and muttering to herself: "Remember the gentleman who looked my way at Fort Kearny? Remember Samuel Solomon? I wonder if he is wondering where I am. Zebulina, can't you get me to California any faster than this?"

It snowed for four days, so maybe they were having snow days at school. Maybe that's why no one called. Or maybe they thought we had just moved someplace else. Or maybe they had just forgotten about us—maybe after a few days of not thinking about Justine and Rona Hanley, the idea of us just sort of disappeared from the world.

Outside, snow covered everything. Our car looked like it had a big, white hairdo, a puffy white robe. The world was slowly losing its shape, everything getting softer and rounder and whiter; and the sky wasn't in the right place anymore; it was right outside our windows, pressing in.

On Tuesday, Mom dragged herself out of bed for a shower.

"I guess I better go to work today," she said.

"But aren't you fired?" I asked. Which was a mistake, I guess. She was halfway to the bathroom, but when I said that she stopped and put her hands to her face and stood there, rocking back and forth for a really long time.

Then she said, "Maybe if I explain the situation, he'll understand," and she finished her long, hard journey to the shower. About half an hour later, I heard my name, sounding like it was coming from really far away. When I went to the bathroom door and said, "What?" though, all she said was, "Justine."

"What?" I said again, but she didn't answer. When I opened the door the water was off and she was standing in the tub, naked and shivering and crying.

"What's the matter?" I asked, my heart pounding. Our whole life felt like an emergency now.

"There aren't any towels," she said, and when I got her one, she held it like it weighed a hundred pounds as she wrapped it around herself and crept back to her bed.

Everything went completely white today. We were sitting inside the wagon as usual; I was listening to the baby breathe—such a small sound in the midst of such a big silence.

"Mama, come!" Annabelle called urgently.

"What is it?" I asked. I hurried to the front of the wagon and knelt behind her, peered with her through the canvas flap.

"I don't know," she said, and when I looked out, I understood. There was no sky anymore. The world was coming apart, falling toward us in a gazillion white pieces. Beyond the snowflakes was more whiteness, and even though I knew 99 percent for sure that the world must still exist, it was awfully hard to believe. It looked like everything might end two feet from our faces; or the whiteness might go on forever.

"Go inside," I told Annabelle gently. "I'll be back in a minute."

I wrapped myself up and climbed down from the wagon. I tied one end of a length of rope to the wagon and the other around my waist so that I could find my way back, and I went in the direction of the pit.

I peered over the edge, but I couldn't see a thing. No smoke rose from the fire. I called, but there was no answer. Not that she ever answered me. I crept around the opening, looking for the stairs, and found them after one and a half times around. I climbed down carefully to the bottom and stood there, feeling sick. Amethyst was nowhere to be seen. As my eyes adjusted to the darkness of the pit, though, I noticed a murky shape, and when I stepped toward it I saw that it was a sort of shallow cave that Amethyst must have dug into the wall of snow. My heart flip-flopped when I saw her motionless body curled inside it.

"Amethyst," I whispered. I touched her shoulder.

"What?" she said, as if I were disturbing her.

"You're alive!"

"You came all the way down here to tell me that? I'm freezing. Can you build up my fire?"

"You have to come out," I said.

"I won't."

"You have to."

"I don't," she said.

"But you're going to die down here," I said.

"Oh, well," she said. I peered at her face through the veil of snow falling between us. My nose was practically on her nose, but I still couldn't see her clearly.

"I'm going to have to drag you out, then," I said.

"Try," she said, shrugging.

One curious thing about Amethyst is, for someone so weak, she is incredibly strong. When I put my hands on her shoulders and tried to shove

*her toward the stairs, she wrenched herself away with such force that I fell
backwards on my hindquarters into the snow.*

*I got up and tried again. I crawled halfway into the hole and tried to
grab her around the waist, but she threw me to the ground again. I tried
again, and she threw me to the ground again. Finally I just sat there, the
snow falling on my head. I knew I should get up, but I couldn't move. I was
having a feeling like my insides were made of glass and everything in there
had just broken—and it came from knowing: here was something I just
couldn't do. She was so freakin stubborn, and that made her the winner; and
I didn't know why it mattered so much, but I just hated the way it made me
feel: small and weak and as powerless as a child.*

*Slowly I pushed myself off the ground. I limped my way to the stairs,
climbed up, and followed my rope back to the wagon. "I'm sorry, children," I
said when I got there, and I made them stand up so that I could pull Zack's
hide out from under their bottoms. Then I climbed down and followed my
rope back to the pit again. "Amethyst!" I called. No answer, of course. "I'm
throwing Zack down," I called. "Wrap yourself up so you don't freeze to
death." I threw down a little bundle of jerky, too, and a few pieces of the
wagon, and went back to wait out the storm with the children.*

On Wednesday, Mom actually got all the way dressed.

"Are you taking us to school today?" I asked.

"Sure," she said. "You guys go wait in the car—I just have to do
my hair."

I wasn't falling for that again, though. I went in my room and sat
down on my bed to wait, and when I got up, she wasn't in her room, and
she wasn't in the bathroom—she was in the kitchen, with her coat on
and her body slumped, her cheek resting on the kitchen table, and there
was a look in her eyes, which were open, that made my heart race—they
were flat like cement, and for one second, she looked like she was dead.

"Mom?" I said, and I hurried over to her. All that moved were her
eyes, searching for mine.

"Don't go to school today," she whispered. "Okay?"

"Okay," I said, and my brain didn't even have to think about it—it
was like someone was speaking a language I'd never heard before, but
that I somehow understood, right into my bones.

———ɯɯ———

I fed the children the last mouthfuls of Zack yesterday. I didn't tell them the moment I've been dreading is here.

This morning I went to the hole again. I didn't bother calling. I climbed down the stairs. There was the hide I'd thrown down before—a small piece of it sticking out of a snow-covered mound. I knelt and dug it out. Underneath was Amethyst.

"Listen," I told her. "Now you really have to come out." She just stared at me and didn't answer. Even half-dead, she seems to enjoy aggravating me.

"I'm really sorry to have to do this," I said, "but . . ." I lifted the oxen hide from her. It felt much heavier than it had before; I staggered under its weight. "Come on," I said, heading for the steps. "Please come up. Or else you'll freeze to death." But I didn't look back. I only had enough strength to do the next thing I had to do.

First I had to build a fire. "You'll have to move, darlings," I said to the children as I began to hack away at the wagon with the ax. "Cover your eyes," I told them as the splinters flew. When I was done with that, I put water on to boil in the biggest pot we had.

Then I had to singe all the hair off Zack's hide. If you ever want to smell the worst smell in the world, by the way, singe the hair off an oxen hide. I cut the hide into pieces and put the pieces in the water and boiled them a day and a night and half of another day. By the time it was done, I had used almost half the wagon for firewood and the children were weak from hunger.

If we live, by some miracle, and someone asks me, "What was the low point of your journey?" I hope to be able to tell them: Eating oxen-hide soup, aka glue, with the wind whistling through our half-a-wagon. I really hope it is the low point, anyway. The poor children cried as they bravely choked it down. All I could think, as I forced the thick, foul-tasting mass down my throat, was, I hope I don't die tonight, because what a freakin horrible last meal this would be.

I lay on my bedroll feeling ill for a long time after the children fell asleep. Then slowly I sat up and made my way outside. There was a little moonlight leaking out from behind the clouds, and the fire hadn't died completely. I sat down next to it and started work on a new pair of snowshoes.

On Thursday, Mom finally made it through all the steps of taking a shower, getting dressed, and getting out of the house. She didn't even say anything as she left except, "I have to get out of here," which made Rona burst into tears.

I watched her through the window as she tried to brush the snow, which was about four feet high, off the car. She wasn't even wearing a coat—she just had on a sweater, and her arm looked so thin as she tried to sweep it through the pile of snow on the roof. She looked the opposite of how she did when she swam—she looked tiny, and weak, and exhausted, like it was just her against the snow, all fourteen million tons of it, and I hated seeing that so much.

Finally she gave up trying to clean off the car. She'd made a little spot on the windshield, and two little spots on the front side windows, and she pried the door open and got in and after about twenty tries got the car started. The wheels started spinning, but the car didn't move anywhere, and the faster Mom spun them, the louder they got, till they sounded like someone screaming. She stopped, then she spun them again—over and over again—and she was doing something else, too: she was rocking, forward and back, like her small body was the thing that was going to move the car through all that snow. Even when the wheels stopped spinning and she had turned off the engine, her body still kept on rocking, inside the car, for a long time.

Rona came up behind me while I was looking out the window.

"Where's she going?" Rona said.

"Nowhere, I don't think," I told her.

"I don't care," she said. We watched a little while more. Mom had stopped rocking and was just sitting there now. "Is Ron coming tonight?" Rona asked.

"No," I said. When I looked at her again, there were tears sliding out of her eyes.

"Well, are there any other grown-ups?" she said, and she tried to make it sound like "Oh, by the way, not like I care or anything—I was just wondering . . ." But her voice was shaky.

"What do you mean?" I said, but I knew exactly what she meant, and what the answer was, too.

Looking out at the snow today, I had sort of a hallucination. I imagined the snow was my mother's lace curtains, and for a moment I thought I was in the dark sitting room of our house in Hadley, looking through whiteness into more whiteness beyond.

I'm worried that I am becoming deranged from hunger.

The children ask for stories of when I was a little girl, but I can't think of any—my memories flicker like a dying light.

Where did I get this baby? I thought today, just for a second, when I turned my eyes upon her. Whose children are these, and what am I supposed to do with them? I stared at the gray blue snow, and for a second it looked like the world was closing. Just for a second I imagined I was inside some warm, dark, furry body and the place I was in was getting smaller and smaller, and when it closed completely, I would be gone.

In the morning, I looked down at Mom in her bed, and I didn't even ask if we could go to school. I brought her some cold chicken on a plate, even though I knew she probably wouldn't touch it, and set it on the floor next to her bed. I hadn't seen her eat anything in a while. Sometimes she crept to the kitchen, but all she ever got was tea, and she didn't even drink that, she just sat with her hands around the cup.

Rona wouldn't eat chicken for breakfast, either. It's true, the chicken wasn't that good. Mom had finally told me how to cook it— "Just put it on a pan and stick it in the oven," she'd whispered as if she were saying her dying words, and when I went in later to ask, "For how long?" she was either sleeping or pretending to be asleep, so I left it in for two hours, just to be safe, and it had turned out pretty much like chicken jerky.

"Well, do you want some rice?" I asked Rona.

"I want oatmeal," she said, and she started to cry.

I went to Mom's bed again. "We need a snow shovel," I said. She didn't open her eyes or lift her head. I went to my room and got dressed, then I put on my jacket and boots and a scarf and hat and mittens.

"Where are you going?" asked Rona.

"To find a shovel."

"I want to come," she said, sounding scared.

"You can't," I said. "You have to stay with Mom." We both looked at Mom, and Rona got a scared look on her face.

"No!" she said. "Justine, don't make me!"

"Okay," I told her. "But you have to dress warm *and* eat some chicken."

My Dear Mother,

You will probably never receive this letter—most likely it will be buried here with us in the snow. I will tuck it in the top of my dress, where, if we're found, someone may think to look. A strange thought—my private places gazed upon by strangers.

I just wanted to tell you, in case I never see you again: You were a wise and fine mother to me. I never wished for a different mother, never ever. I love you more than words can say.

The children are asleep now. We will survive this night, but I'm not sure how many more. We are living on oxen-hide glue. Maybe the snow will stop. Maybe someone will come along.

The poor baby. All this time and she still doesn't have a name. Thaddeus and I imagined we would name her after the place we arrived, but if she dies here, I will name her after this place. I will have to name this place, then. I don't have any idea where we are.

The snow was over my boots, and I had to lift my legs high and wide with every step. Poor Rona could barely make her way through it. She had to walk behind me, in my footprints. The snow was still falling, and the world was white, and the sky was close around our heads. It was like walking through endless curtains that opened in front of you and closed behind you every step you took.

At the fourth house I tried, a Grandma-type woman answered the doorbell, and I put on a cute-kid smile and said, "Do you have a shovel we can borrow—we just moved here from California and didn't even know you needed to have one."

The shoveling was a lot harder than I thought it would be. The snow was heavy, like wet sand, and after five minutes my arms and shoulders were aching and I had huge blisters on my hands. Rona had gone inside and was watching me from the window, and I turned my face away so she wouldn't see the tears that had started to leak out of my eyes, though I was trying not to let them. I let them freeze on my face, and I kept shoveling. After about an hour, I'd only done about an eighth of the driveway, though. I didn't think I should keep the shovel, so I headed back down the street, and when no one answered the door at the Grandma-woman's house, I leaned the shovel on the porch railing and left.

When I got home, Rona ran to the door, crying. She had her boots on. "Where did you go?" she said.

Mom was awake and sitting up in her bed. The room was still dark. "Justine," she said, "will you get me the phone?" When I brought it to her she said, "Can you two leave me alone in here for a little bit?"

"Come on," I said to Rona, and I took her in my room. I closed the door, but not all the way, and I turned on the TV, but without the sound; and even though it was *Rugrats*, Rona didn't even care. She just stared at the screen at Chuckie pounding on the closet door for Angelica to let him out.

Maybe Mom was calling Grandma. Maybe she was calling Aunt Bridget or Marie. I hoped she was, even though I wasn't sure what any of them could do. Give Mom instructions that she would actually follow, like You have to get out of bed, eat something, take a shower, and go beg for your job back?

But maybe just talking to one of them would be like spinning a thin thread, connecting her, and us, to the rest of the world again, and maybe if there was one thread, we could somehow spin another, till we were attached again by a strand strong enough to hold us.

But she wasn't talking to Grandma, or Aunt Bridget, or Marie.

She was leaving messages: "Um, hi, Danny, it's been a while since you heard from me, but I just wanted to make sure you knew I haven't forgotten you, and I was hoping we . . . I was hoping . . . well . . ." But she just stopped in the middle and waited a long time, then said quietly, "Okay," and hung up.

Her next call went, "Trent, hi, it's Colleen again, and I was just calling to say hi, to see if you, to see if you . . . well, I don't know, if you wanted to, ah . . . well, please just give me a call. If you want to."

Then I heard paper rustling, and when she spoke she said, "Hi, you don't know me and I don't know you, but you took out an ad"—the paper rustled again—"in December second's 'Missed Connections': 'Studious Blond Goddess drinking a tall latte in the Globe Cafe' . . . , Well, uh . . . I'm not really sure how to do these things, and . . . uh, I'm sure it was some *other* goddess you were talking about—ha—I mean, of course I would never describe myself as—" And then I guess she got cut off. Either that or a little glimpse of reality flashed across the corner of her brain. But I didn't think it was that, because a second later she was dialing again, and she said, "Hello, you don't know me and I don't know you, but I saw your ad in the *Valley Voice*, December second: 'Bread and Circus parking lot—you stole my space *and* my heart with your funny smile . . . ' "

After that one she was quiet for a while, and I lay there thinking I should go check on her soon, and also thinking maybe I wouldn't, because even if I did, there wouldn't be anything for me to do, anyway; and I guess I must have fallen asleep, because the next thing I knew, I was opening my eyes and the house was quiet, and *Rugrats* wasn't on anymore, and Rona was asleep beside me. I had no idea what time it was. I went to the window and stood looking out. The light had left the sky. It was hard to tell what time it was anymore, but it didn't really matter anyway, since we mostly stayed in the house and didn't go to work or school. We were sort of like animals now, sleeping at weird times, and I remembered how I always used to think, when I saw a cat sleeping, that it looked so delicious to just curl up anyplace, anytime, close your eyes and drift away, but really, it didn't feel that good. Maybe it felt a little like dying.

Beside me, Rona opened her eyes, and I could tell by the look on her face she was going to be cranky. She was probably starving, since she'd refused to eat breakfast and I hadn't made anything else. We were going to have chicken and rice again for dinner, and if she didn't want that, I didn't know what I was going to do.

"I have to go pee," Rona said to me in a "we're going to have a fight" voice.

"So go," I told her.

"Don't tell me that!" she said.

"Then don't," I said.

"I hate you, Justine," she said.

"Why?" I said.

But she got up and stomped out of the room. I heard her stop in the living room; then I heard her suck in a big breath, as if she were about to let out a loud wail. But it didn't come out. Instead she whimpered, "Mommy." I jumped up and went to the door.

Mom was on the floor beside her bed. She was on her hands and knees, and it looked like she was trying to go somewhere, but she couldn't figure out what even babies know: It's practically impossible to crawl in a nightgown. She put her knee forward and there was a ripping sound, then she crumpled to the floor.

"Mom, are you all right?" I said, trying not to sound scared. She pulled herself a few inches forward by her fingers, like a worm.

"I want some water," she said.

I ran to the kitchen, and when I came back with the water, she was up on her knees again. "I need to get up anyway," she said. "I need . . ." She crawled a few more inches and then crumpled to the floor again, then she just lay there hugging herself.

Rona was standing next to me, but she started to back away, then suddenly she turned and ran to the front door, yanked it open, and ran out into the snow. Basically I was right in the middle of two people losing it completely. I ran after Rona.

"Wait!" I yelled. She was already to the end of the walk. She didn't have any shoes on. Neither did I, I realized as I ran down the porch steps and through the snow after her. She was running right down the middle of the street now.

"Stop!" I yelled, but she kept going. When I finally did catch up to her, I had to swoop down on her and grab her, and when she tried to twist away, we both fell down in the middle of the snowy road. She was crying—long, low-pitched sobs that seemed too big to be coming from her little body. I squeezed her tight, like I'd seen Mom do when Rona had a tantrum in the Kmart, as we sat there in the middle of the road.

"Come on," I said finally when her crying had stopped a little. I stood up and got Rona to stand up with me.

"My feet are burning," she said.

Her feet were completely bare. I had my socks on, at least. I leaned down and picked her up, though it was practically impossible to carry her anymore—her feet almost touched the ground, and I swayed under her weight. She had her arms around my neck and her head in my neck, but suddenly she raised her head up again, so her face was about two inches from my face. She looked me right in the eyes, and there was nowhere for me to look but right back into hers.

"I don't hate you, Justine," she said.

"I know," I said.

"Justine?" she whispered, and it was scary—I could see from her face that I was the person she thought knew all the answers now. "Is our mom going to die?"

God has forsaken us. There is only me. The thought is round like an egg.

"Mama," Annabelle said today. We were staring out at the snow; you couldn't see the ground or the sky—just swirling white space in front of your eyes.

"What, sweetheart?"

"Are we going to die?"

Oh! I thought. I feel like I know the answer to that! If I could just remember. If I could only remember the answer to that, I would tell her the truth. I wouldn't lie.

ELECTRIC PERSON

That night, after Rona was asleep, I called Grandma. I took the phone outside so Mom wouldn't hear. She was in her bed, asleep or awake— I really couldn't tell anymore.

"Grandma," I said when she answered, but I let a long, long silence go by when she said, "Justine?"

I was sitting on the stoop, looking at the trees and sky. It had snowed on and off all day, and the sky was flat and dark. There were no stars, so I knew it must be cloudy, but you couldn't see clouds. You couldn't see anything—the sky was so dark, it was impossible to tell if it was full or empty, if it went on forever or stopped right above your head.

"Justine?" Grandma said again. "Is that you? Hello?"

"Hi, Grandma," I said.

"Well, hello, sweetheart," she said. "How *are* you?"

"Grandma, is it snowing there?" I said.

"Snowing?" she said. "Of course not. Why?"

"No reason," I said.

"Is it snowing there?" she asked.

"Grandma?" I said again.

"What, sweetheart?"

"What if we wanted to come back?"

"Come back?"

"To California."

"If who wanted to?" she said.

"Me and Rona, I guess," I said. "Or . . . I don't know."

"Well, you could always come back," Grandma said. "Of course you could. Maybe your mother will bring you for a visit this spring. Maybe you could come spend a whole summer with me sometime."

"What about sooner?" I said.

"Why, Justine?" asked Grandma. "Is something wrong?" I didn't answer that.

"How would it work?" I said.

"How would what work?"

"Would you come and get us?" I said.

The next morning when I woke up, someone was pounding at our door. Dale, I thought when I was still half dreaming, and I started to get a stomachache in my sleep. I jumped out of bed and went into the living room. Rona was already there, looking at the door, scared. Mom was in her bed, either sleeping or pretending to be asleep. I knew she wasn't dead, because I saw her feet twitch and her eyelids move.

I went to the door and tiptoed to see out. It was Marie, and I knew why she was there. I had finally told Grandma the truth. "What do you mean, 'so sad she can't walk'?" Grandma had said. "What do you mean, you don't go to school anymore?" Then she'd said, "Listen, are you all right there for tonight?" and when I told her yes, she'd said, "Promise me if you need anything, you'll call Marie Phipps, and I'll call you back in the morning."

I opened the door and Marie stepped inside, carrying a bag of groceries. "I was ringing the bell *forever*, God!" she said, though I don't know why you'd think, looking at our house, that the doorbell would work.

"Colleen!" she said, striding across the room. She went to the window and pulled up the shade, but the room didn't get any lighter. "Colleen!" she said louder, going over to Mom. Then she looked at me and said, "Get yourself and your sister ready for school, and I'll take you." Before we walked out the door, she said to Mom, who hadn't moved, "Colleen, I'm taking these kids to school and I'm coming back, and if you could get dressed, that'd be good, because you have an appointment with my doctor at ten-thirty." When she dropped us off, Marie said to me, "At the end of the day, I want you come to my house. Just get on the bus you used to take," in a voice like, Don't even bother arguing, not that I wanted to, actually.

"So are you taking us home?" I asked Marie at about five o'clock that afternoon. We'd had a snack and done our homework, and we were out of things to do.

"Nope," she said.

"But what about Mom?"

"I'm going over to check on her after dinner, but you're staying here tonight."

"Can't she come over here?" I asked.

"Sure she can," Marie said, "but I can't very well wrestle her to the ground and drag her to the car if she doesn't want to come."

"I want to go home," Rona said.

"Tough," said Marie, and Rona didn't even say anything back— she just stood next to me in the kitchen doorway, holding my hand, and I really didn't like how we seemed right then: like two scared kids, just standing in our life watching the grown-ups do things.

—m—

I don't know how long we have been floating in and out of sleep. We lie together like a litter of kittens. When I open my eyes, I can't tell if I'm dreaming or awake. Sometimes it seems lighter, then it seems darker again, and I try to figure out whether it's day or night, then I remember it doesn't matter and I go back to sleep.

The next day at school, Ms. Taylor said, "Class! I know you're going to hate to see the pioneer unit end, but I'm going to ask you to finish up your diaries now. I'd like you to hand them in at the end of next week."

"*What?!!!*" everyone shouted.

"Yes," she said, smiling at us and nodding like we were kindergartners. "It's time to reach our destinations and go on to a new unit. Everyone must be at *least* to the Columbia River by now, right?" That was another thing I was going to get in trouble for, probably—everyone else had gone to Oregon, because that was the way *Timothy and Tabitha* had gone. "So you're almost there!" she chirruped. "Just finish them up! Have your pioneers get to where they're going, and if you like, tell me a little about what their new lives were like."

Like you could do that.

I was probably just going to have to get a zero on the whole assignment. Which I really didn't care about at all, except for one thing: Ms. Taylor was the only sixth-grade teacher, so if she held me back, I'd get her again, and I'd probably have to spend the rest of my life in the sixth grade, since I would never be able to do her stupid assignment the way she wanted me to.

Marie had told us to come back to her house after school again, and we stood near the buses for so long, while I tried to decide which one to get on, that we almost missed them both. When the last kids were climbing onto the bus that went to Ida Lane, I said, "Come on," to Rona. I might even have changed my mind again, but right then Marie drove up. Maybe it had dawned on her that her prisoners might try to escape, or maybe she really was just passing by on her way from errands.

"Get in," she said. The bus pulled away.

"Will you take us to our house?" I said when we were in the car.

"I can't," said Marie. "We have to pick up Cassie and Cavvie. We're late as it is."

"Afterwards?" I said.

"Actually," she said, "why don't we just wait and give it another day?"

"Give what another day?" I said, but she didn't answer me.

When we got to Marie's, I headed up the stairs.

"Where are you going?" Marie called, but I pretended not to hear. I could feel Rona's shoes right behind my heels. She hadn't been more than two feet away from me, except at school, for the past two days. On our way through the hallway, I got the phone and dialed our number. No one answered, and the machine was off. I let it ring till the answering machine turned on. "Mom," I said when the beep sounded, "are you there? Are you there?" and I hated the picture of my small, lonely voice, floating from room to room in our cold, dark, empty house, looking for someone who wasn't there. But I hated the other picture, that I was trying not to see, even more, of my voice hovering above Mom's curled-up body.

"Come on," I said to Rona before I even hung up the phone, and she knew what I meant without my having to explain to her. She was already at the door. We snuck down the stairs, through the living room, into the front hallway, and out the front door, which no one ever used. We didn't even get our coats. It was gray and cold out, and something thin and razory was falling from the sky—something that you almost couldn't see, but that hurt, slicing into your skin.

Rona didn't even complain. We held hands and walked in the road, and when a car came by, I pulled Rona up into the snowdrifts so we wouldn't get killed, though a few times we got sprayed with freezing gray slush. By the time we got to our house, we were soaked.

When we opened the door, Mom's bed was empty. There was the weirdest light coming from the kitchen—as if maybe God was in there. I felt the creeps coming on.

When we went in the kitchen, though, we got a surprise: There was Mom, sitting at the table. And she was dressed. She was gripping a cup of tea. On the table in front of her was a white metal rectangular box, and out of the box shone a blinding white light. Her face, with the light shining on it, looked like the bright side of the moon.

She looked at us for a minute like we were someone she almost recognized; then, after a very long moment, she said, "Hello, sweethearts," in a voice that sounded like she was calling through a windstorm, from a long way away. She gave a flickering, watery smile. "What are you doing here? I was going to come get you." Then she glanced, in slow motion, at the kitchen door and said, "How did you get here? Is Marie . . . ?" She hadn't seemed to notice that we were soaking wet.

"What is that thing?" I said.

"Oh," said Mom, and she turned her face back toward the light.

"It's my new light. Do you like it?" She closed her eyes and leaned closer to it. "Marie got it for me. It's supposed to put me in a better mood." She shrugged.

"It cost two hundred and fifty dollars," she said in an ancient voice. Then, after a long pause, she said, "She is really a good friend."

"Look," she said, and she gestured in slow motion to a piece of paper on the chair beside her. "She wrote out a whole set of instructions. I'm supposed to sit in front of it three hours a day, to start." She shrugged again. She sounded like the three-hundred-year-old woman's older sister. "Maybe it's working."

Have you ever noticed sometimes that the harder you look, the less you can see? You squint and stare, tilt your face closer; and suddenly you'll realize: whatever it is you're trying to see, it's not going to be coming in through your eyes. And you can't quite figure out: What part of you is it, that needs to understand?

I opened my eyes sometime in the afternoon yesterday, or maybe it was morning. I lifted the flap, and in the whiteness I saw something—a moving, grayish white shape, appearing or dissolving, I couldn't tell. It was a person, I'm almost sure of it. She had white hair, and she was wearing a white apron.

"Hello?" I said to the snow.

The next morning when we woke up, Mom was in the kitchen, sitting in front of the light. She had coffee in her cup, so at least I knew she'd moved since the night before.

"Hey," I said.

"Hey," she said. Then she said something that surprised me: "There's some lunch money in my purse. Get your breakfast and get dressed, and I'll take you guys to school."

When we came home that day, Mom had a new job, gift-wrapping at Astral Glow in Amherst, just until Christmas. Marie had brought

Mom an application and watched her fill it out, then she'd driven her to Astral Glow and spied on her, pretending to be a customer, till she handed it in. Mom told me that story while she sat at the kitchen table in front of her light, with her eyes closed, maybe trying to pretend she was at the beach. Astral Glow was a weird store that sold books and wind chimes and rocks and juice, and I never went in there because I didn't like the weird, hippie smell, but Mom said, "I like it okay. The music is kind of soft and restful. The people who work there seem nice."

Marie had gotten Mom pills, too. "What are those?" I said when I saw her shake one out of the bottle and lay it on the kitchen table next to her tea.

"Happy pills," she said without any expression. "Who knows?" she said.

—m—

Who is that woman in the snow? was the first thing I thought when I opened my eyes again. I had no idea how long I'd slept. The children were still sleeping. Could it have been Amethyst? But the woman was old, gray. Strong. Maybe it was the person who left the notes in the trees and forked sticks and propped on the rocks. Maybe she knew I couldn't get to the others she'd left—the really important ones that told me what to do to get us out of this mess—and she'd come to deliver them herself. Maybe it was someone sent to find us. Could it have been my mother?

Do I have a fever? Please, God, don't let me die before the children. I can't bear the thought of them out here all alone.

I am going to find her.

It was hard work struggling out of the wagon. I started climbing down, but something stopped me—had someone whispered to me? I listened but didn't hear anything else. I turned back and got Thaddeus's gun, and I loaded it with numb, clumsy fingers.

The snow had already covered her tracks.

"Please," I called. I strained to make the shape appear again. There it was—a shoulder, materializing out of the whiteness. Then it was gone and I realized it had never even been there in the first place.

I was pretty sure I was going crazy.

I'll always wonder what made me turn around just then. It wasn't a sound—the crack of a branch or a crow caw—I'm sure of that. The silence filling my ears was as loud as the ocean. Maybe it was my sixth sense. Or maybe it was knowledge, the kind you don't even know you have until suddenly it starts moving around inside of you, like somebody slowly waking up. The thing that, if you pay close enough attention, tells you what you need to do. The thing I used to call God.

I felt the hair on the back of my neck prickle. I turned. And I gasped: There she was. And she was freakin huge. And hairy.

My arms were shaking as I raised the gun.

It hadn't snowed in two whole days, and on the third day, when we walked out of the house in the morning, the sun was actually shining. Mom stopped in her tracks as soon as she came out the door. She closed her eyes and stood with her face stretched up to the sky.

"Oh, my God," she said, *"sun!"* and she didn't move for so long, I thought maybe we weren't going to go to school after all. Then she opened her eyes and remembered what we'd been doing and followed us toward the car.

Mom worked from twelve until four, and every day at four-twenty, she walked in the door and went straight into the kitchen and turned on her light and sat down in front of it as if she were an electric person recharging herself. After about half an hour or so, she might notice us, if we snuck in to make a snack.

"Hey," she would say if she was really tired; or, if she had a little more energy, "How was school today?"

One day, when Rona and I were in there making cinnamon toast, she said, "You know, we have to talk about Christmas." I looked over at Rona. Like all little kids, Rona loved Christmas. Or at least she had up until now. I couldn't tell anything, though, from her face.

"You guys haven't told me what you want for Christmas yet," Mom said.

Like, Duh—we were going to stand over her while she was crawling around the house dying and tell her what we hoped our presents would be.

"What do you hope Santa brings you? Maybe something he can get when he goes shopping at Astral Glow?" she said, and winked at me.

Neither one of us answered, though. I was surprised that Rona didn't. She didn't say anything till that afternoon, on the school bus.

"Justine, is Santa Claus coming this year?" she asked suddenly, and she turned her face up to me. A few of the kids around us turned to look; one of them, I saw, was a mean-looking fifth-grader, and I hoped he'd keep his mouth shut. Not that I knew what I was going to tell her.

Rona answered before I could, though. "He's not," she said. "I know he's not. Right?" She was watching my eyes.

"Right, Justine?" she said. I just couldn't say it, though.

"He's not," she said then, but her voice didn't even sound sad. "Justine," she said gently, and she put her hand on my leg and her face close to mine, and she looked right into my eyes. "He's not coming. But don't worry. You'll still get a present. I'm going to buy you some press-on nails."

—⚍—

The next morning when I opened my eyes, something was different. It took me a minute to figure out what it was: the sun was shining. The flap of canvas that hung over the opening was lighted up white, and a hot blade of sunlight slashed across my face.

I crawled to the opening and caught my breath. It was so incredibly beautiful outside. A thick, soft blanket of glittering, unbroken white lay over everything. The world looked like a delicious cake nobody had cut into yet.

There, lying half-covered in snow where I had shot it, was the bear.

Behind me, one of the children stirred. Ezekiel. "Shh," I said, turning. "Go back to sleep. When you wake up, there'll be breakfast." I took out the knife and got to work.

At school the next Thursday, Ms. Taylor said, "All right, class, the day you've been dreading is here! Time to hand in your diaries!" and she started walking around the room to collect them. When she got to my desk, she said, "Diary, Justine?"

I looked up at her. "I didn't finish it," I said.

"But I told you last week I'd be collecting them."

"Well, mine's not done yet."

"Well, when *is* it going to be done?" she asked.

"I really couldn't tell you," I said.

"What do you mean?" Ms. Taylor said, but I just looked away. She'd never understand, and I wasn't even going to try and explain.

—⟨m⟩—

I skinned and butchered the bear. I made a fire and cooked big steaks for all of us. I threw one down to Amethyst and called, "Breakfast," and I didn't wait to hear how she felt about bear meat.

After we ate, I sat still for a bit, waiting for some of my strength to return, then I went back to work on my snowshoes. I'm trying a new design.

"Just you wait," I said to the baby as I drilled and sawed and braided and waxed. I'm afraid if I stop talking to her, she will die. "Before you know it, we'll be in California, where it's sunny all the time and you can have peaches and oranges and avocados to eat every day." If we had a normal life, she would be starting to walk now—pulling herself up on chubby legs and taking shaky little steps, instead of spending her whole life lying in a pile of freezing blankets. That seemed like the saddest thing, suddenly—that she might die without ever having walked anywhere.

The sun had been out for almost a whole week. The snowdrifts were even starting to shrink—the roads were black and shiny and wet where the melted snow had trickled onto them; and some little bits of dead grass in our yard were peeking through in places.

Marie came over every day. "Knock knock," she'd say, opening the door with the key she'd made for herself and charging in. She'd look all around—I wasn't quite sure what she was trying to see—then she'd go find Mom and start asking her questions: "Does that light box seem to be helping? What about the Zoloft? Has it had any effect yet? Did you go to work today? Are there any bills here that you need to get paid? Have you been to the grocery store?"

* * *

One day when we got home from school, the house smelled like paint, and it was so strange, the feeling that flooded over me when I walked in the door. Paint suddenly seemed like the best smell in the world to me, better than chocolate, or lemons, or roasting chicken, and when I went in the kitchen, there was Mom, standing on a stool, painting the wall.

"Hi, honey," she said. And she smiled.

"Why are you doing that?" I asked.

"No special reason," she said. "The place just needs it, and I got off work early today"; and that seemed like a such a good answer to me, so much better than something like "Trent might visit, and I wanted the place to look nice."

When Grandma called that night, like she'd been doing every night, and said, "Justine, how are things?" I said, "They're good, Grandma."

"*Really?*" she asked.

"Yeah, I think so," I said, and for once I wasn't lying.

"I was thinking," Grandma said. "If it's all right with your mother, maybe I could send you and your sister some tickets to come visit me in the spring. Would you like that?"

"Oh, that would be so great!" I said.

And when she asked, "May I speak to your mother, please?" I said, "Sure, just a minute," and I went and handed Mom the phone.

—⅏—

I am almost finished with the snowshoes. I made them from wood I sawed from the wagon floor, which is much stronger than the branches I used before, and the walking part isn't actually made of cords, which was the problem in the first place—it's made from the wagon floorboards, with triple-thick laces of dried, twisted bear guts coming through the drilled holes to attach them to our feet. I made them square instead of curvy; they look sort of like strong, miniature rafts for our feet. I think it is a very good design. When I am all done I will wax the bottoms with bear fat, so that they will glide easily across the snow.

* * *

We are eating bear steak; I want the children as strong as possible when we try to cross the mountains. I throw one down to Amethyst for every meal and make sure she's moving, invite her to come up by the fire with us. The wagon will be all gone soon. Sometimes I get frightened when I am prying pieces off of it, taking apart the place that's been our home for the past eight months with my very own hands.

MASSACHUSETTS, CALIFORNIA, TIMBUKTU

"Wow," said Mom, looking out the window on Saturday. "It is just a gorgeous day. I feel like going somewhere today. Does anyone feel like going somewhere? I don't have to be at work till four."

"Where should we go?" asked Rona.

"I don't know—downtown? We could do our Christmas shopping."

"I don't have any money," I said.

"Me either," said Rona.

"I do," said Mom.

"Where'd you get it?" I asked, but I knew: Dale had sent a child support check for Rona. He'd sent it to Marie and Bill's, and Marie had brought it over and said to Mom, "That asshole, it's about time. But the question is: Is he ever going to send another one?"

"Nowhere," Mom answered me. Then she said, "Come on, let's get dressed and just go. Who knows when we'll get a nice day again?"

The baby woke exceedingly poorly today. The color of her skin matches the gray of the sky. She lies in my arms and looks at me like she wants to tell me something. I am pretending to be busy writing this. Whatever it is, I don't want to know, and for once I'm glad she can't talk.

Early this morning, I climbed down the snow steps into Amethyst's pit. I had her snowshoes with me.

"Here," I said. "I made these for you." From her pathetic position huddled in her snow cave she managed to make a face up at me, like, How very queer of you. I almost smiled.

"Come up now," I told her as gently as I could. "You have to practice on the snowshoes. When the weather breaks, we need to be ready."

"Let's go get some hot chocolate," Mom said as soon as we had parked the car in Amherst. "We can plan our attack while we drink it."

"Wait!" she said as we were passing the fancy kitchen store, Hearth and Home Kitchenware, on the way to the Globe Cafe. "I know what I want to do!" and she veered into the doorway. Inside, she walked straight to the counter and asked the lady there, "Where are your gingerbread molds?" Beside me, Rona jumped and clapped her hands once, then she just stood, breathing, watching Mom.

Every year that I could remember, one Saturday or Sunday before Christmas, Rona and I would wake up and Mom would already be up, in the kitchen, and she'd have the gingerbread molds out. The mixer would be out, too, and the kitchen counter would be covered with bowls and canisters and measuring cups and spoons, and Mom would be in the middle of making a big batch of gingerbread, or the white icing that turns hard as rocks, and on the kitchen table would be a big grocery bag full of every kind of candy that exists.

We would spend all day making the houses and decorating them, eating all the candy we wanted. Sometimes we wouldn't even get dressed. We would mix and bake and build, saying, "*My* house is going to be a brick house." "Well, *my* house is a wood house!" "Well, *my* house is two hundred years old, and twelve beautiful sisters live in it!" "Oh, wait, I forgot something!" and we'd add another layer of candy to the roof; and Mom always did amazing things that neither Rona or I could do with the thin licorice ropes. And no matter what stories we made up as we built, in the the end it was always the same: a perfect little village, made up of three houses sitting on their icing-covered tinfoil, next to a shiny tinfoil lake—Mom's, all beautiful and perfect; and mine, which always won the prize for most creative; and Rona's, which was the messiest and most likely to fall down any minute, but Mom and I called it "Most Elaborately Decorated" and always let her win grand prize, which would be something like a package of Hostess cupcakes, after all the candy we had eaten.

And the thing about those days was, no matter how crappy the day before had been, or what terrible thing was going on in our life, they were always perfect days. I didn't know how it happened, really, but once a year we would have a day like that, and on those days, too, Mom was a perfect mother.

I hadn't seen the gingerbread molds when I was unpacking the kitchen stuff in our new house, though. I guessed we had left them in California, and I'd felt a little sad, though truthfully I knew there was no way we would have a gingerbread day in Massachusetts. That was before the sun had come out, though, and Mom had gotten out of bed.

—— ɯ ——

Last night, I did something all by myself, after the children had gone to bed. The moon wove in and out of the clouds, and in its changing light, I dug a hole. Maybe I shouldn't have spent the energy. But I have already left so many things lying in the wilderness. At least if you bury them, you can tell yourself you're not saying good-bye forever.

There were only a few things left, anyway. Good-bye for now, I said silently to the framed picture of my mother, and I kissed her face through the glass. You were a perfect mother. There has never been a mother like you in all the world.

I took out the cradle that my father, whom I don't have any memory of, carved for me. I was glad I hadn't used it as firewood. Even though I've always thought there was something maybe not exactly bogus, but off *about the whole story—my mother claimed he had made it and that he liked to look down at me with love as I slept in it, but I'd never quite believed her, not deep down. Maybe he didn't really carve it, or maybe I'd never slept in it—I just really think that if that had happened, somewhere inside of me, I'd remember. But I didn't care anymore. My babies had all slept in it. Perhaps Annabelle will use it for her babies someday.*

Finally, I put in Poppy, my little doll I've had since I was smaller than Ezekiel. Her head is made of china, so she is too heavy to carry over the mountains.

Then, though it was almost too dark to see, I got out a piece of paper and a pencil and I walked all around, drawing a map. I had to draw it mostly by memory, since I couldn't see too much in the dark: the hills to the east and the mountains to the west; the shape that the pine trees made on the hillside in the far-off distance; the field of boulders that had gradually become just big, white, rounded shapes under the snow. I labeled everything in as much detail as I could: "Humongous spruce with little elbow sticking out of top"; "Three tall rocks that look like they're having a conversation"; "Granite cliff in the distance with outcropping shaped like a giant ear."

Then I made an X where my things were buried. I laid down the map and picked up the shovel. But as I began covering them with dirt, the hugest sadness plowed into me. I was remembering standing at the edge of the other hole I'd dug—the one we'd put Thaddeus in. And realizing, this was the same thing. And I'd known it from the moment I'd started digging—it had just taken the truth a while to catch up with me: It was a funeral. We were never coming back.

After we left the kitchen store, Mom said, "Now what?" It was weird, though—even though she didn't say anything, or move any direction particularly, except down the street, I got the feeling she already knew where she wanted to go.

"Hot chocolate?" said Rona.

"You know," said Mom, "why don't we save that till later? Why don't we start our shopping instead?"

"We could go to Humpty-Dumpty," Rona said. Humpty-Dumpty was a toy store.

"Or Kaleidoscope," I said. Kaleidoscope had all sorts of cool things.

"Yeah, Kaleidoscope!" said Rona.

"Okay," agreed Mom. "Or we could start at the Marketplace. There are so many stores in there."

"Kaleidoscope," Rona grumbled.

"All right," said Mom. "We'll go to Kaleidoscope right after we go to the Marketplace.

"Let's go to Soak!" Rona said as soon as we set foot in the Marketplace. Soak was a whole store about bathrooms, and Rona liked to go in there and smell all the different flavors of bath beads.

"Hmm," Mom said. "Why don't you two go in there and I'll come meet you in a little while?"

"Okay!" Rona said, but I said, "No."

"Why?" whined Rona.

I didn't answer her. The reason was, I didn't want to lose track of Mom. "We'll come with you," I said to Mom.

"Well, okay," said Mom. "I just want to go down to that shoe place—what's it called?—for a few minutes."

The name of the shoe store was Walk the Walk, and Mom bought herself a pair of red cowboy boots for two hundred and seventy-five dollars there. I didn't even ask why because of the way that question suddenly felt huge to me, like, Is there really a God? You might hear an answer you didn't really want to know.

I just sat there, sort of in shock, watching her turn her foot this way and that, going, "Oh! Wow! Well, I know I shouldn't. But why shouldn't I? I've had a hard few months, I deserve a little pleasure, don't I?"

"Oh, Mom!" Rona was saying. "I love these boots!" She was down on the ground, gazing at them and stroking them as if they were baby animals.

"I think I'll just wear them out," Mom said to the salesgirl when she'd finally made up her mind and paid for the boots.

"Excuse me," the girl said as we turned to go. "Don't you want these?" She was holding out the boot box with Mom's old shoes in it—her blocky wooden clogs that she'd had forever and wore when she had to stand on her feet all day for work.

"Oh," Mom said, turning to look as the girl tried to hand her the boot box. "I don't know. Those things are so old. I think you can just toss them."

I held out my arms for the box. The girl looked from Mom to me to Mom again, but Mom had already turned and was walking out of the store with Rona. Finally the girl put the box in my arms. "Thanks," I said, and I turned to follow Mom.

"Can we go to Soak now?" Rona said as soon as we were out of the shoe store.

Mom looked at her watch. "Oh, you know?" she said. "It's just about lunchtime. Why don't we have some lunch first?"

"No!" Rona complained. "Soak!"

"We will, we will," Mom said. "We'll spend an hour there if you want. But first let's get something to eat. Where would you like to eat?"

"The Nutmeg Tree!" Rona said. Rona loved the clam chowder and corn muffins at the Nutmeg Tree. We could see the sign for it from where we stood.

"Sure, we can go to the Nutmeg Tree," Mom said. "Or . . . there's this place up the block from here—Lulu's."

"I want clam chowder," said Rona.

"Justine," Mom said. "Where do you want to go?"

"The Nutmeg Tree sounds okay," I said.

"Okay," Mom said, "let's go to the Nutmeg Tree." Rona started skipping down the hallway.

"You know what?" Mom said when we caught up with Rona at the door of the Nutmeg Tree. "I changed my mind. Let's go to Lulu's instead."

Fine and clear this morning. I have finished packing everything I can carry and making up small packs for the children.

Early this morning, before the sun was up, I went out to the pit. I carried a bundle for Amethyst—a knapsack packed with a blanket, some clothes, twenty pounds of frozen bear meat, and a pair of thick socks I sewed from pieces of the edge of my quilt. They look sort of like oven mitts for the feet, but at least they'll work better in the snowshoes than those little cloth slippers. I stood at the edge and called down.

"We're leaving now," I said. I made my voice even and strong. "Are you coming?" I asked, though I knew she wouldn't answer. I don't know what it is that makes me ask anyway, every time.

"I hope you are coming," I said. "I want you to come," I added. I stood there a moment more and listened for a sound—a rustle, a breath, anything. Any sign at all that she knew I existed, the same way I used to listen for God when I prayed.

I threw down the knapsack. I'd chopped the rest of the wagon into firewood early this morning and hauled the pieces to the side of the pit, and now I threw them down, too. "Stand out of the way," I called gently.

"Just in case," I added, too softly for her to hear. It was really more like I was talking to myself. "I don't know what else to do," I whispered. I threw down a pack of matches. Last but not least, I let the map flutter down—the one from Fort Laramie, that showed the way to California. That was hard for me to do—a feeling of terror flooded me as it left my hands.

"Remember the top is north," I said softly. "Make sure you're holding it the right way. Try to find the road again. I colored it red.

"Are you listening?" I said. "Can you hear me?

"Well then," I said. "It was nice knowing you, I guess." That wasn't right at all.

"I hope we see you in California." It was ridiculous. I could stand there all day trying to think of how to say good-bye to Amethyst and never find the right way, because there wasn't one.

Meanwhile, the sun had come over the ridge and the children were asking for breakfast.

Inside Lulu's Mom said, "You two can have your own table if you like." We must have looked at her weird, because she said, "You know—if you want to be like grown-ups and sit by yourselves. That's fun sometimes."

"Okay!" said Rona. Mom was smiling at us sweetly, but my brain had snagged on something in her voice. I felt a shadow move across the sun.

"No thanks," I said.

"All right," Mom said, shrugging. "Can we have that booth, please?" she asked the hostess. On the way to the booth, though, she said, "Oh—actually, that table by the window looks nice." When we got to the table and the hostess had set our menus down, Mom walked to each of the four chairs, trying to decide which one to sit in. Finally, she sat down next to the window. Rona and I sat down across from her.

"Actually," Mom said, "why doesn't one of you come sit by me? Rona, come on."

"I don't want to," Rona said.

"Please?" said Mom.

"Nope."

"Justine?" said Mom.

"*Why?*"

"Please?" Mom said. I got up.

"No!" screeched Rona. "I want to sit by Justine!"

"No, honey," Mom said. "You move over and sit by the window. You'll look nice, with the light coming in on your hair." Rona looked at Mom defiantly and got up and stood next to me.

"*Fine*," Mom said. "Forget it." I sat back down. So did Rona. Mom picked up the vase of flowers and moved it around a few different places in front of us till she seemed happy with where it was.

"What do you want to eat?" she asked, opening the menu.

"Clam chowder," said Rona. Mom looked up and down the menu. "How about black bean bisque?" she said.

We set out just after daybreak. I kept turning around to see if Amethyst had decided to climb out and follow us. But the landscape behind us was perfectly still. Nothing moved at all, and we hadn't gone far before our campsite just looked like all the other trees and rocks and snow, like a place where nothing had happened, where no one had been.

When the waiter came to take our orders, Mom looked at me and Rona and said, "Why don't we wait a little bit?"

"*Why?*" Rona and I both said at the same time.

"We're going to wait a little bit," Mom told the waiter. "Here," she said, and she rummaged in her purse and pulled out a pen and an envelope and handed them to Rona. "Why don't you draw some pictures or something?" Then she straightened up in her chair and started stretching her neck all around, watching the people in the restaurant like she was at a play. I noticed she kept looking toward the door.

"Tic-tac-toe, Justine," said Rona, pushing the envelope and the pen across the table at me. "I'm Xs."

As I was reaching for the pen, Mom said, "Oh!" When I looked up at her, she had the weirdest expression on her face. She looked like a gate inside her somewhere had just opened—like she was *holding* it open, just waiting for the wonderful thing she saw, that no one else could see, to come rushing in.

And I realized something right then—something that made my heart crash inside of me: She had never, ever, ever, ever, ever looked at me that way. Not even the moment I was born. I followed her gaze to see what she was staring at. There, in the doorway of the restaurant, was a tall guy with blond hair and a black leather jacket, who we'd never seen before.

"Brian?" Mom called, and she stood halfway up in her chair and waved and smiled.

"Who's stupid Brian?" said Rona.

"Shush!" said Mom.

"Colleen?" he said, looking confused as he came near us. He looked from her to us to her again, then back to us, as if we were some strange little creatures of a species he'd never seen before.

"It's so great to meet you!" Mom said, and she held out her hand. There were a lot of things I didn't like right then about what was happening, but one, especially, was the way Brian's smile didn't match Mom's smile. It was flat and puzzled.

"These are my girls!" Mom said. He kept on staring. "Justine and Rona?" Mom said, as if she wasn't sure she remembered our names. "I guess I didn't mention that, did I?" Mom laughed.

"Brian," she said, "would you like to sit down?" He didn't look like he was sure he did.

"But . . . ," he said. "Wait a minute. I'm confused."

Welcome to Colleen-World, I wanted to say.

"Justine, what's happening?" Rona leaned forward to ask.

Mom was nodding her head. "I know, I know, I have a terrible confession to make. Rona, scoot your chair over so Brian can sit down." Brian didn't move.

"So the deal is, I'm not Willowy Blond Blue-Jean Baby," Mom said. "But it's all so random anyway, right? I just thought I'd do something brave.

"I have the boots, though!" she added, and she stuck out her foot a little, then she looked up at him and smiled. " 'Closet Line-Dancer,' right? I liked that part. Well, also, the 'Good-looking, goodhearted guy' part!"

"Justine!" whispered Rona. I looked at her, and I just felt so sorry for her. She was still so little. "What's happening? What are we doing here?"

Brian took a small step backward.

"Your imagination is wonderful, Justine," Ms. Taylor had said the last time she'd called me to her desk. She had my diary in front of her. That's what I was thinking about, looking at poor Brian's stupid face. "But you're getting way off the track. You have to try to think in terms of facts more. Try to think in terms of things that could actually happen. It's *history* we're talking about, not *invention*. Do you understand what I mean by—"

"I know what facts are," I'd interrupted. "I made macaroni and cheese three times this week. Last Sunday my mom stared at the wall from four-thirty P.M. to seven-fifteen P.M. It costs three hundred and eighty-five dollars for a new clutch. On December twelfth, Alex Brennan called me a cock-sucking cunt."

I also knew the answer to Rona's question. Looking at Mom, twisted in her seat, her face stretched up to Brian, I knew the answer to Rona's question "What are we doing here?"

We are waiting. We are waiting in this place—it doesn't matter if it's California or Massachusetts or Timbuktu—for Mom to change.

Maybe I'll grow up first.

The thought has no shape, no color; it's like a breath of cold air in the middle of nowhere. Gulped in and breathed out as if everything else in the world was gone. Everything except you, taking that icy breath and not being able to tell if it was your first one or your last one, if you were dying or being born.

"Justine!" said Rona. "Justine, pay attention to me!" and her voice snapped me out of it. "I have an idea, Justine!"

"Well," said Brian, looking like, I gotta go. Mom looked like a week-old balloon somebody was sticking a pin into. I stood up, and so did Rona.

"We'll meet you at home," I said to Mom.

"No, you won't," she said. "What do you mean?"

"I mean, we're leaving."

"You can't leave," said Mom. "How will you get home?"

"Walk, I guess," I said.

"You can't walk!" Mom said.

"FYI?" Rona said to Mom, and she put her fists on her hips. "We *can.* Come on, Justine."

"Justine, wait," said Mom. "Just a second, Brian," she said.

—ɯ—

Today I named the baby. We buried her as best we could, under the snow beneath a rock ledge on the west side of the hill. Perhaps someday we can return to this spot and put up a proper marker.

I buried her in the snowshoes I made for her. Even though in my heart I knew she would never walk a step in them, I was glad I'd made them. It made me smile to see her lying with the strong little boards, small as mousetraps, strapped to her feet, as if she were about to march over the mountains and live to tell the story of how she made it after all.

The sun shone all day today. We hobbled and wobbled along on our new snowshoes. They are awkward and heavy as hell, but we actually got a few laughs watching each other tumble into the snow every now and then, and by the end of the day, everybody's walking had improved. We have food for a month. The weather looks promising. If the sun shines tomorrow and the day after that and the day after that, maybe we will make it to California.

**PLEASE DO NOT REMOVE
DATE DUE CARD FROM POCKET**

By returning material on date due, you will help
us save the cost of postage for overdue notices.
We hope you enjoy the library. Come again and
bring your friends!

FALMOUTH PUBLIC LIBRARY
Falmouth, Mass. 02540-2895
508-457-2555

DEMCO